Hi Manon,

Hope you enjoy

all the best.

Roger.

Jaded Jerusalem

Roger Cottrell

Published in Great Britain by
L.R. Price Publications Ltd, 2022
27 Old Gloucester Street,
London, WC1N 3AX
www.lrpricepublications.com

ISBN:978-1-915330-26-0

Jaded Jerusalem

Roger Cottrell

Prologue – Jack and the Beanstalk

November 1979

May, rather than April, had proved the cruellest of months as the decade of conflict and strife drew bitterly to its close. And here, in Flintshire, in North Wales, far from the summer's waving euphoria in Downing Street, winter had struck like a thief in the night, engulfing the surrounding countryside and woods in a canopy of anonymous yet treacherous snow. Heavy flakes continued to fall almost in slow motion from the opaque vault of a sky and ran in dirty tears down leaded windows while the big house itself stood in grim foreboding, with cold walls of Welsh stone.

The yellow lights at the windows were like rheumy, sightless eyes.

It was a hollow skull of a place, full of misery and treason, despite the sign at the iron gate, as brightly coloured as Thatcher's garish promise of a free-market future. Small wonder, as the same PR firm that projected the government's positive image did likewise for *Font-y-Llewellyn* and the archipelago of other care homes, all the way down to Wrexham, that was privately administered at Social Services' behest. To the outside world, this stone edifice was a place of safety and sanctuary—a shelter from the storm. But a second, even cursory glance, beyond the tall stone walls might suggest that all was not well in this house on the wasted borderland after all.

Rather, as Jack the Giant Killer knew, from his nursery rhymes and crimes and from his bitter experience within these walls, the monsters of childhood nightmares roamed the cheerless dormitories and dark, panelled corridors, reeking of polish and pubescent testosterone. Far from a place of safety, this was the house where the Beast slept and where its damned servants meted out abuse and degradation in its honour, and that of their newly Crowned Queen of the Damned on May 3, 1979. As for the stout walls of solid Welsh stone, as much as those of any prison, they did not serve to keep the outside world out so much as to keep the Care Home's warehoused victims in.

Jack had always known the place was haunted, with ghosts of murdered Druids and boys, built as it was on the ruined Temples of a once Magick Albion, here in this Jaded Jerusalem, this grey and divided land. Its history was long, and it had been a stronghold of Royalist resistance during the revolution. As Jack led the younger boy, Stephen, aged only 11 years old, to the housemaster's study, he could almost feel the painted eyes of dead and treacherous aristocrats that followed him from the walls.

Many were the times he had come here to be administered with the cane that was doled out on an assembly line basis by Llewellyn, the owner and administrator of this private Hell run and financed at the behest of the state. Many were the time he'd come here for much worse or to wait, in dreaded anticipation, for the polished black cars that crunched on the gravel outside, past the statues and fountains, to take him to nearby hotels or else the

Mews in South London, or the guest house in the capital. This, after all, was the ante-room to the archipelago of abuse where the rich and powerful came to pay perverse tribute to The Beast.

And right now, the door was locked.

Jack felt the tightness in his chest, his heart pounding, an unpleasant taste of copper fear like bile in his mouth, and in that haunted moment, it was as if the very walls of the house exhaled in response.

Music filled the corridors accompanied by young voices, sounding strangely angelic in the sinister shadows. In the school gymnasium, John Llewellyn himself would be the master of ceremonies in his tattered black gown in a world where teachers with Bachelor's degrees were still rare. Trying to force the locked door, using a screwdriver to prise against the jamb, Jack imagined the housemaster's glazed and dark-eyed stare, bombed out on Valium and damaged himself in a Japanese prisoner of war camp in Burma decades before.

Hopefully, Llewellyn wouldn't notice the two missing boys, like back teeth in a row, absent from the relentless kicking by the prefects ranked at the back of the hall. If these were the best days of his life, Jack reasoned, with grim gallows; humour, it was downhill all the way after this.

There was a crunch of splintered wood, and the door opened, sagging like a broken jaw. In its place, the shadows beckoned with a reek of leather, mocking him like a Devil in the dark.

3

"Wait here," Jack instructed the younger boy, Stephen, and then stepped into the dark void. "And keep a lookout."

The Giant Killer stepped into the dark void, flicked a switch, and let the weak light fill the room.

It was the colour and texture of urine.

Fee Fi Fo Fum!

The stoic image of John Llewellyn, in his graduation gown, looked down on him like a portrait of hate.

Now Jack worked feverishly at the locked mahogany desk to the muffled sound of singing in the hall. Still, his heart pounded, and his sweat was cold, the oxygen seemingly sucked from his lungs. It could have been a phone box, he thought, to be robbed or else a slot machine, but the stakes were much higher in this particular game.

"For fuck sake Jack," hissed an anxious Stephen, looking like a tough and streetwise Cherub. "Get a move on!"

Jack gritted his teeth and suppressed his frustration.

"I've got to find these bleedin' photos en' I?" he snapped.

Like the door before it, the drawer splintered open with a reassuring crunch.

And inside were the photographs.

Filthy disgusting photos of their shared and dirty secret: evidence of their nursery crime.

It was the television news that had given Jack the idea, beaming like a vision from the bulbous black and white screen. It was archive footage from May, and through the snowstorm of static, Thatcher had been waving triumphantly from the upstairs window at Number 10 with her trusty aid at her side.

The news was showing the night of the election victory on May 3, 1979.

There were flashing camera bulbs and a news anchor, Richard Brunson, practically gloating at the British public.

But it was the face of the smiling man, stooping next to the Iron Bitch herself, waving from the upstairs window that Jack recognised from the civil war pageants, the mock battles, or fumbling and abusing in hotel rooms, in the offices of the PR firm in London, and in the guest house in the capital.

The same leering face that Jack held in the photograph in his hands right now.

Fee Fi Fo Fum!

His heart still racing, Jack all but felt and smelt the sulphurous breath of the Beast upon his neck.

Jack, the Giant Killer, had hit the Jackpot.

"Bingo!" he said, stuffing the profane yet precious photographs into the deep pockets of his overcoat.

Suddenly, Jack became aware of the sound of somebody urinating. Looking up, astonished, he saw young Stephen pissing against the picture of John Llewellyn. Despite a deep and ever distending shadow of dread, Jack had to laugh.

"Nice one, Steve!" Jack said, grabbing the smaller boy's arm. "Come on, mate. We're getting out of here!"

Jack practically dragged the younger boy down the haunted stairwell, once more past the ancient gallery that was stuffed with eyes.

5

They were stopped dead at the door by the pale apparition, like an inexperienced ghost.

Pop eyes and badly nourished, 14-year-old Andrew stood before them.

Apparently, Andrew was bunking off from evensong as well. Now he stared at Jack as if he were some malevolent Pied Piper, dangling the keys to both liberty and death.

Andrew nervously shook his head as if the fear of freedom and uncertainty terrified him. He shrank away.

Stephen tugged at Jack's arm.

"Come on, leave him," he said in accusation. "He's chicken."

Jack unbolted the door and flung it wide, feeling the cold winter air that was sucked into the hall like an unwelcome guest. Flecks of snow dissolved on his face and at his feet as he pulled Stephen through the portal into another realm.

And one was left!

The next thing they knew, like invisible men, they were leaving footprints like bread crumbs in the treacherous snow. Changed in the night, like Alice, and with a cold wind of hate at their back, they ran for an adjacent copse of trees and the forest beyond, its conifer green hidden beneath its heavy canopy of snow.

And then they were gone.

*

Evensong was drawn to its miserable conclusion, and John Lewellyn had returned to his study, like a night creature to its lair. Pale and dark-eyed, and with a face drawn into a permanent grimace, he had longish hair and a nervously frayed lower lip.

Llewellyn stopped dead in his tracks when he saw the door sagging open like a broken jaw. Beyond, his desk was violated, like his victims, and looted of its ransacked contents like the detritus of a looted and broken mind.

But the precious photos were gone.

Colour drained from Llewellyn's face making him resemble a bloated corpse.

"What the..."

Llewellyn's voice trailed off; then came the simple statement of dread.

"Oh, Christ!" he said.

*

Jack dragged Stephen through the woods, weaving a crazy zig-zag path through the bracken and ferns, feeling a sapling whip maliciously against his face. A female fox, astonished, scattered in furtive terror as the boys cursed and lost their footing and scrambled on all fours in the snow.

The distended shadow of the Beast drew closer at their back.

Jack winced at the shooting pain from a twisted ankle and heard his own laboured breaths in the snow-filled void. Ghostly ectoplasm formed from his frozen breath. Jack struggled for oxygen through waves of pain as if the very life force was being sucked from his lungs.

His heart pounded in his head.

And somewhere in Hell, a phone was ringing like the tolling of a manic bell.

PART ONE: JADED JERUSALEM

Chapter One

Deep in the cottage near the Welsh borders, with the Black Mountains forming a frozen wave to the West, a charmless black phone rang like a damned and demanding child in its out of fashion Bakelite crib. A naked light bulb came on like a weak and fickle sun, and Azazel, first of the fallen nine, gripped the receiver in a claw-like hand.

"Yes," he said, in clipped English that belied his private school education, despite the scruffiness of his almost hippie attire. With a beard and long hair and a Barbour raincoat as out of style as the phone and room, few would have recognised the former mystic bodyguard of British Movement leader Colin Jackboot Jordan.

Inducted early into the secret world, following his casting out by heavenly insurrection and revolt, Azazel never used his own name or identified himself on this, his "special" phone.

Down the line, between the wheel of fire and the abyss, the agitated voice of the school housemaster cried panic at the killer in his hovel and lair. A degenerate queer with a weakness for young boys, the author of the foul network that had helped bring the Iron Bitch to power, Azazel despised John Llewellyn and all he stood for. But he had his uses. As Roberto Fiori said in the handbook that was *The Political Soldier*, there were moments on the path to nationalist revolution and the new nobility of blood

10

and soil when they had to serve as shock troops for the bourgeoisie.

Against the reds, the wogs, the queers and the fucking women—the future belonged to those who were prepared to get their hands dirty, and Azazel was born to Empire after all.

As Llewellyn droned his confession of the damned, in lieu of sacrament and absolution, Azazel's eye ran along a bookshelf above the door. There were ancient tomes by Crowley, a dog eared copy of *Mein Kampf* and a newer copy of AK Chesterton's *New Unhappy Lord*. There were also works by Darre, Roberto Fiori's *The Political Soldier* and William Pearse's prophetic novel, *The Turner Diaries*.

On his wailing wall, his game hunting trophies belied his African roots before private school, dishonourable discharge and his first arrest on civvie-street on firearms charges in Yorkshire in the 1960s. There had been Lord Lucan and Airey Neave, both trophy kills, and he'd been on safari ever since. Mountbatten didn't happen on his watch. But most of all, the Fallen Angel's attention was drawn to the painting of the Great Fall inspired by *The Book of Enoch* and Milton's *Paradise Lost*.

Azazel and the rest of the nine transformed from angels of light into serpents of the infernal pit.

It was then that Llewellyn delivered the bombshell down the line.

Azazel's response was cold as ice.

"You expect me to do what?" he asked flatly.

Suddenly, Llewellyn's tone became threatening. But Azazel could still sniff the fear and hear it as a razor's edge of hysteria in the other man's voice.

"Listen," Llewellyn rasped. "I don't give a shit how you feel about this or anything that goes on here. You're part of this, remember? And if we go down, so do you. Just stop those two little bastards and bring back those fucking photos."

Azazel heard the phone slam down on its cradle on the other end of the line.

*

In his violated office, the Housemaster looked up with a face like thunder.

Andrew stood in the doorway, another tough cherub looking like Oliver Twist.

Llewellyn grimaced through frayed lips, and then he bellowed like a Minotaur in its lair.

"What the hell do you want?" he demanded.

Fearfully, Andrew wondered what other colours Llewellyn could do other than road rage red.

*

The snow was thickening, like cold soup.

Sheet lightning flashed in the hollow void beyond the brooding shield of advancing cloud.

There followed a drum roll of thunder as the Mighty Thor threw a tantrum in Valhalla.

Snow turned to sleet, and the cold and dirty water rained like a dirge for all humanity.

Back at the house on the borderland, as Jack knew, the alarm would be raised and staff pressed into service as a posse. There would be sniffer dogs, baying and straining on leashes in the rain and snow.

Through the leaded window and pasty-faced, Andrew would be watching the caravan of flashlights, like fireflies, and knowing how Judas felt in the Garden of Gethsemane.

Huddled now in a ruined wall of overgrown stone and slate, Andrew shivered and shuddered and suffered, and he was turning blue.

Jack nudged him, waking him up. He was sure he could hear dogs in the distance, baying for blood, like damned souls chasing a spectral huntsman across the night sky.

Stephen puffed open his eyes.

"Stephen," Jack whispered, urging him to wake up. "Come on, lad. We got to go."

The younger boy got to his feet, exhausted. Jack took his hand and led him away.

*

The Land Rover, in charmless khaki, tooled towards the border and the Black Mountains beyond.

Croeso i Gymru said the sign: "Welcome to Wales."

To the east, behind heavy clouds, the dawn was breaking in pastel threats of the heavy storm to come; the omens were of hard and terrible rain.

At the wheel of the vehicle, army surplus, Azazel looked grim and determined.

It was open season once again, and the hunting had just begun.

*

As if in a medieval sanctuary, the two boys struggled to the frayed and ruined edges of the sacrificial road.

The darkness had given rise to an approximation of daylight under a low winter sun, but then the damp fog had settled, dissolving the fields and woods.

Still, Jack dragged the younger boy behind him towards the white line in the middle of the road.

"Come on, Steve," Jack pleaded as every muscle in his body screamed. "Don't give up on me now. We're nearly there, lad. Get these photos to the police, and it will all be over."

It was what they had planned when they took their reckless dash for freedom, and right now, he was hanging on to that thought like a crucifix — or a drowning man, clutching at a straw.

Strange that at that very moment, muttering his Hail Marys as if by rote, Jack should stumble and lose his grip on the other younger boy.

Shit!

Jack was still delivering prayers, like junk mail, to an uncaring absentee God when two huge orbs of light emerged through the mist like some metal machine monster from the James Bond movie, *Dr No*.

The vehicle emerged from the dead ground dip in the road, like a bad crayfish omen from the depths and was travelling at speed. And it was travelling straight towards them.

Chapter Two

Every year the Walker family had holidayed in North Wales, using Porthmadog as their base and touring the region in their modest Hillman Hunter as far south as Bala Lake, Betws-y-Coed and Barmouth, where the train line ran by the seafront.

Mr Walker was at the wheel of the car with his daughter in the back.

Terry Wogan was on Radio 2 on the dashboard as they drove.

Not that it was the holiday season, but they had fallen in love with Snowdonia over the years and were now house hunting. According to Mrs Walker, the best time to see a prospective new home in the country was during the winter when it was at its worse.

The two running boys, in the middle of the road, materialised from the opaque mist as if from nowhere.

There was the older boy, ashen, who shielded his face from the full beam headlamps and the rapidly advancing car. He was pop-eyed with terror like a white rabbit caught in the disembodied spotlight like an inexperienced ghost.

Somehow he had managed to push the second boy, the tough-looking cherub, to one side as the bonnet of the car struck the older boy like a skittle in a bowling alley, bouncing his small rag doll body with an ominous thud against the now dented metal shell of the hood, then cracking the windscreen and hurtling over the roof.

Photographs burst from the boy's pocket across the wet tarmac like evil confetti, win, lose or draw.

"Oh my God!" sobbed Mrs Walker as she gripped her husband's arm.

The daughter in the back, clutching her copy of *Just Seventeen*, was speechless – her young face was a mask of horror.

Mr Walker hit the brake, and the Hillman screeched to a halt.

The younger boy, the one who looked like the streetwise Cherubim, looked on in horror as his friend's body bounced, with unpleasantly spasmodic movements, upon the damaged tarmac of the sacrificial road.

Her spell of horror broke – the daughter screamed as Mr Walker emerged from the car.

"Oh, my sweet Christ," Mr Walker said simply, followed by an order, "Stay there!"

Walker ran to where the small boy's lifeless body lay on the road. Still warm, like a member of the Undead, the boy's eyes were glazed and lifeless, and blood had trickled like a small wellspring from his mouth.

At first, Walker didn't hear the sound of the approaching Land Rover engine through the gunny-bag damp of the saturated void nor see the second set of headlamps staring like the eyes of some metal machine beast. Fighting back the tears and with his fist drawn to his mouth in horror, he first saw and realised that the boy was dead before he also saw, with utter revulsion, the content of the dirty photographs scattered in a flush across the road.

"Oh my God," Mr Walker blubbered as if a nightmare had been compounded by a nightmare.

Then he noticed the Land Rover's khaki silhouette as it took form through the swirling mist.

The vehicle drew to a halt, and the next thing that Walker knew, a long-haired man with a red beard and an out of style Barbour jacket had emerged from the vehicle whose engine was running.

Mr Walker was trying to form words. He was still trying to speak when the bearded man in the Barbour jacket calmly produced a Beretta pistol with a silencer that stared at Mr Walker like a cold and sightless eye.

The man in the Barbour jacket barely flinched as he shot Mr Walker through the head, causing sheep to scatter and the small Cherubic boy at the side of the sacrificial road to turn and vanish into the mist and the anonymous moorland beyond.

In the Hillman that was now like a dented metal coffin, the daughter screamed as her father's head burst like a blood gorged melon.

"Daddy, no!"

The killer, who was the fallen angel, Azazel, the first of the nine, walked calmly towards the car whose engine was still running. Two bullets were delivered through the already shattered windscreen, and the screaming ceased. Azazel went back to where the photographs lay scattered on the road and looked down at them with disgust. In truth, he hated queers more even than he did blacks and Jews, and the soulless consumerism of the modern age, the debauched decadence of the ruling class and of the permissive society. To Azazel, homosexuality and paedophilia were one and the same, and if proof were needed, the evidence was in the squalid photos scattered at his booted feet.

A one-time member of the British Movement and a founder member of Column 88, Azazel felt nothing for the family he had murdered nor, in all honesty, for the young boy lying lifeless as a discarded marionette on the ground. He had killed before, usually for the state, such as when he first and casually bludgeoned Lord Lucan's nanny to death and then dispatched the wastrel Lord in person at a ferry port on the coast, leaving a tell-tale bloodied piece of pipe in the borrowed car to send the cops on a wild goose chase.

The military coup plot in Britain had been cancelled, as Callaghan succeeded Wilson and Thatcher waited in the wings. More subtle but also more sinister methods were then deployed to keep the politicians in line. Only Lucan, who had been on the periphery of the coup plot and lucidly saw himself as a British Hitler, couldn't keep his mouth shut.

Then, when Colin Wallace had briefed Airey Neave about the paedophile ring at Kincora, in Northern Ireland, Azazel had dispatched Neave as well, feeding the narrative of Thatcher's tough stance on terrorism in the process. Dominic McGlinchey, who claimed the hit for the INLA, got the details wrong when interviewed on BBC, and the special-forces mercury tilt device was way beyond their technical capabilities in any case.

But what was going on in the care homes disgusted Azazel, in Kincora, here in North Wales and in South Vale in West Norwood, London.

An edifice of political power and abuse built on buggery.

As Azazel slowly gathered together the photos, an idea formed in his head, and while he didn't quite know what he was going to do next, he knew he would think of something.

*

For miles, it seems, Stephen had run and run — the tough and streetwise Cherubim now hunted and hounded by the fallen angel and his brood, at the very behest of Satan himself.

The Beast had stirred.

Stephen hadn't recognised the man with the red beard as one of his regular abusers, either in ridiculous Cavalier attire or in the PR firm or guesthouse in South London. But Stephen had learned to use his wits to survive in this world of cruelty that he didn't quite understand and to recognise in the bearded man a predator to be feared. Here, clearly, like the night-time monster at the window, in and under his bed, down the toilet or in Parliament, was another instrument of the Beast that sometimes slept and lurked beneath the city streets and in the infernal pit.

Trying to blot out the trauma that had come with the killing of Jack, his giant-killing champion and protector, Stephen had run and staggered for miles across open country before spotting what looked like a village or rural community, huddled around shops, a pub and a war memorial, as well as neat small cottages of Welsh stone. The pub was shut, like the village itself, but then Stephen spotted the small rural police station with its tell-tale blue lamp.

Police, it said, and then *Heddlu,* in Welsh, and there were posters about Colorado beetle and rabies at the door. For a moment, Stephen stood feral, like a wolf boy, before the blue doorway of this rural outpost of authority before he entered.

There was no bulletproof glass, not in the country police station, and the front desk seemed abandoned like that of a ship lost with all hands at sea. But every inanimate object in the reception area seemed tall and threatening for all of that. It was with no little trepidation that Stephen, with trembling hands, rang the bell. An eternity later, or so it seemed, a desk sergeant shuffled into view, looking dishevelled and threatening and slightly annoyed to be dragged from the card pool taking place out back.

Like photos scattered on the sacrificial road: win, lose or draw.

"What do you want?" the desk sergeant accused as if anybody under 25 years old was a potential collar to be felt.

Barely coherent, Stephen blurted out his story, the torrent of abuse and Big Jack's death, like an accidental anarchist on the sacrificial road.

"Now come on, lad," the cop continued to accuse. "We don't like young troublemakers round here, telling tall tales. It's a crime to waste police time, do you know that? We could send you to prison."

Memories of home in South East London slowly crowded back into Stephen's memory through the gunny bag fog he had erected to screen out the abuse. Real monsters made myth and the reek of blue serge; as his father was arrested, his mother screamed, and Stephen was taken into care.

It was then that the pass the parcel game of real abuse had begun and, rewarded through drink and drugs, faded fuzzy into a grotesque form of normality. Now, he could see that the cop hated him on sight, the way that everyone in authority seemed full of hate for youth in general and Stephen in particular. The Housemaster, teachers and prefects, all in their pecking order of cunts, the bigger boys set against the smaller ones, all with someone lower down the shit-pile to kick. The sergeant had no doubt heard about the boys in the care home and knew that they were trouble, constantly thieving and on-the-rob and always fighting with the local boys. With their unfamiliar English accents, they were like a lost tribe of Viking Berserkers sent to inflict misery on the ordered lives of the settled Celts.

Stephen played the only card that he had. He laid down a solitary, crumpled and disgusting photograph clutched like roadkill from the tarmac of the sacrificial road like it was the Ace of Spades.

Sergeant Bastard, with his future shocked national service mindset, his hatred of youth and a modern world that had gone to Hell, looked at the photograph and swallowed hard.

"Follow me!" he said and clutched up the photo as he did so, like a raven psychopomp

21

devouring the flesh of dead Jack on the sacrificial road. He opened up a door in the front desk, almost like a Judas gate, and led Stephen like he were a prisoner into the back where cops with rolled-up blue shirts smoked, drank whisky and cheated each other at five-card stud.

There were portraits of the queen and of Margaret Thatcher on the wall — the poster girl of the Police Federation during the 1979 election. A thick cloud of smoke hung like city smog over the card school, and the eyes of the country cops were all upon him with suspicion.

"In there," the sergeant ordered as he indicated a cell.

It stank of piss.

Stephen's mind had focused on this one fact when, with an ominous finality, the cell door shut behind him.

Chapter Three

And so it came to pass, in these end days of Revelation, that the Lamb of Judea broke the Seventh Seal, and the four horsemen of the apocalypse were let slip, to do as they wilt.

Phone calls and Masonic connections, and then John Llewellyn, in person, was driving towards the rural police station, like a white-knuckled pale rider whose Morris Oxford car was named death. And with famine, pestilence and famine on the foggy land, he pulled up in the police station car park where the engine of the parked car ticked like an unexploded bomb.

The Housemaster entered the station like he owned the place, which, given his rank in the local craft, and its society of secrets, he very nearly did.

He rang the bell and conjured up Sergeant Bastard like an elemental demon at a séance.

From the cell that stank of piss, Stephen heard their muffled incantation, as if they were arguing in some arcane and cabalistic language. But he recognised the voice of the Housemaster immediately, and his speaking in tongues struck moral terror in his small heart.

The sound of approaching footfall was now like that of cloven hooves.

There followed the rattle of jailers keys like the chains of Marley's ghost, and then the door to the cell that stank of piss was yanked open.

Sergeant Bastard was framed in the door with a face like thunder.

"Let's be having you," he said, with the stink of whiskey on his breath. "I told you before the police don't like young boys who tell tales."

"No!" Stephen protested as he was dragged without ceremony from the cell. "You're the Police! You're supposed to help me!"

This wasn't the way that Jack Regan or Kojak would have done it on TV.

Now, John Llewellyn towered over him like the false God of hate that he was, with his dark eyes, his permanent grimace and that horribly frayed lower lip. He was Moloch, the fallen confederate of Azazel, who was one of the nine, and whom men knew as the God of Child Sacrifice and War.

"Causing trouble, as usual, are we?" the Housemaster said. "You know that wasting Police time is a criminal offence, Stephen?"

Stephen had never heard of Kafka, but even through the waves of mortal terror, the absurdity of the situation was not lost upon him. He was the victim here, but he was the one being treated like the accused. Don't tell tales. Don't grass on your abuser, but dishing out the abuse, that was alright. Especially if your tormentors and harpies were in a position of authority and you weren't. You were just shit because you were on the tail end of abuse, and you were being abused *because* you were shit.

Victim be damned — you had brought it on yourself.

Probably by being born.

Grabbed by the scruff of the neck, like an animal, Stephen was dragged towards the black

Morris Oxford, sullen as the car of a serial killer on Cannock Chase on Shaw Taylor's *Police Five*. Out back, unbeknown to Stephen, his solitary snapshot of away-day abuse was being barbequed to post-apocalyptic ash.

The leather seats of the car stank nauseous in Stephen's nostrils, like the killing machine of the Yorkshire Ripper or some deranged villain, in a JG Ballard novel that was addicted to traffic accidents and the sexual possibilities of wounds.

Like the cell door, that of the car slammed shut behind him as if he were a prisoner in nearby Portmeirion: number rather than a free boy.

He saw Sergeant Bastard and a more senior cop, whom he would later know was Superintendent Gordon Anglesea staring through the window, like the mirror reflection of a broken mind, as the car engine started up and they drove away. In later life, he would remember, there was classical music on Radio 3 as they followed the sacrificial road without maps back to the House on the Borderland, as if it were a jaded Oz.

Stephen remembered it was called *Dance Macabre*.

When they passed the scene of Jack's tragic accident and of Azazel's murder of the Walker family, all traces had gone as if consumed by The Beast itself. Unbeknown to Stephen, the Hillman car was already being fed into the gorged mouth of a scrap-yard crusher, in a graveyard of cars, cash in a brown envelope and no questions asked.

It had taken Jack and Stephen all night, in the spiteful snow and cold, to cover the woods and sparse fields with their flocks of feral sheep, yet

25

already the foreboding edifice of the care home loomed through the thinning mist like a concentration camp at the end of history and at the end of the road without maps.

The big steel gates opened like the mandibles of The Beast or of some Biblical Leviathan there to consume them. Gravel crunched beneath tyres as the car drew to a halt, and once more, like a suspect device, the engine ticked like an unexploded bomb.

Andrew stood with a prefect gripping his collar as Stephen entered, and the look of contrition and shame on Andrew's face left no doubt as to what he'd done.

"You little bastard," Stephen yelled as he was manhandled towards Llewellyn's study. "You grassed us up!"

"Where's Jack?" Andrew responded, Pinteresque as if their very shared language was now a barrier between them. "What's happened to him?"

And then Jack was gone into the House of Fun: the House of Pain.

Years later, when cleared of charges of paedophilia and having successfully prosecuted a number of local and national media, Superintendent Anglesea would compare himself to a kindly Dixon of Dock Green.

But Stephen wouldn't forget what happened under the real blue lamp, and somehow, someway, he would have his revenge — long after the Sandman came, and all the naughty children were put to sleep.

Good night all!

*

More ritual, more murder, more rites of the dark arts.

On the television, now in poor-resolution colour, the war in the South Atlantic plays on repeat performance, carefully choreographed, amidst the Union Jack bunting and orgy of near fascist patriotism on the screen.

Dressed in blue, the Iron Bitch once more bravely implores the damned youth, like Ahab luring them to their death, and the 1983 election, bought and paid for by the Spirit of the Falklands, had already been in the bag.

Only a year before, the Tories were spat on and vilified wherever they dared to go. A threatened confrontation with the coal miners was cried off so the government could build up its stockpiles for a repeat performance.

Maggie, Maggie, Maggie! Out, Out, Out!

Now, the middle market tabloids announced that, after the Battle for the Falklands, the Battle for Britain had to begin. And much like Azazel, who is her unwelcome errand boy and malevolent poltergeist, Thatcher has read and understood her Machiavelli and knows the importance of committing all her atrocities at once.

And Azazel, he has done his small bit, too, to erase the past and reshape Jaded Jerusalem in a new and grotesque image.

In this grey, divided land, they are all Albion's lost children now.

Earlier this evening on Police Five, now re-branded as Crimewatch, the scene of Azazel's latest handiwork and installation art had been on display in a stone house outside of Shrewsbury with roses in the garden. Blue and white crime scene tape had fluttered like tawdry bunting, and an attractive female BBC reporter

27

with a West Country accent had appealed to the Great British public to do their bit. Hilda Murrell, spinster pensioner and anti-nuclear activist, had been sexually assaulted and discarded like rubbish, to die a shivering death of hypothermia in a field, a short car drive from where her house had been burgled the night before.

It had not been Azazel's mission to murder the elderly woman, the way he'd been instructed to kill both Lord Lucan and Airey Neave. Rather, like the hapless Walkers on the sacrificial road, she was collateral damage – at the wrong place at the wrong time. Because of her tireless campaign against the Hinckley C Reactor, Murrell had already secured the unwelcome attention of the Nuclear Police via ZEUSS investigations in Norwich and their local subcontractors, Sapphire Investigations here in darkest Shropshire.

But Sapphire also did dark work and alchemy for MI5, as well as hiring members of the Far Right for murkier operations after they helped the National Front (of which Azazel had never been a member) compile dossiers on Anti-Nazi League activists nationwide. That was how Azazel got involved, of course, but when he and his team burgled the old woman's house, they weren't looking for anything to do with the anti-nuclear campaign

Rather, it was all to do with the choreographed pageant in the South Atlantic that had kept the Iron Bitch in power.

Murrell's nephew Rob Green had been an officer in Naval Intelligence, and rumour in Whitehall's paranoid corridors of power suggested as by Chinese whisper that damaging information related to the sinking of the Belgrano *had somehow found its way into Hilda Murrell's safe. That and the logs of the Captain of* The Conqueror, *the British Naval submarine that sank the* Belgrano *as it left the Falklands' exclusion zone. Azazel's*

28

brief, and that of his team, had been to burgle Murrell's house and retrieve what incriminating information they could from the lucky dip of a safe.

She was supposed to be out, not bursting in when they were using acid to corrode the lock on the ancient safe.

The sexual abuse, the evidence of Satanic ritual, those had been Azazel's personal touches, the signature of his installation art, but even if the Deep State hadn't ordered the old woman's murder, they were now accomplices who would have to help him cover his tracks.

Azazel had been interviewed by cops after the murder, but Special Branch had intervened in the investigation set up by the West Mercia Police, which does not have a designated full-time murder squad in any case. For a while, they thought about putting Rob Green himself in the frame, but the charges wouldn't stick, and he was vilified as a Walter Mitty fantasist instead. Luckily, Azazel was connected to a man called Norris through the care home abuse network over at the Black Mountains in Wales, and some victims of Sodomy from the warehouse of the damned would eventually be put in the frame.

Meanwhile, Azazel's MI5 handler, far from happy with the situation, wanted him to lay low in a safe house in Fife, Scotland, for a while.

Only Azazel had other ideas – other plans and other mischiefs for idle hands to do.

Amidst the Nazi regalia and mystic symbols, the painting of the Fallen still holds pride of place, as if it were Azazel's personal portrait of Dorian Gray. The nine fallen angels led by Azazel, who had sided with Satan during his heavenly insurrection, were cast out and transformed as he himself had been transformed from Angel of Light into serpent of the infernal pit.

There had been many shedding of skins since he started, yet this lumber-room of his covert memory, like the picture, connected both to his past and apocalyptic vision of the future. The Odal Rune spoke of the paramilitary group, Column 88, that he had created, while the cabalistic and runic lettering, rich in magic and in symbolism and power, spoke of his mystical belief that the ignorant would dismiss as witchcraft and Devil worship.

On TV now, the cavalry charge at the Battle of Orgreave, as the medieval passion play that was the miners' strike, struggled for Albion's lost soul.

And on the table before him, lit by candles in the pattern of a pentagram, there were the photographs that Azazel had scooped up and kept from the sacrificial road in North Wales six years before.

It was time for Azazel to be or not to be.

It was time for Azazel to act or not to act.

And having so acted, it was also time to put all the naughty children to sleep.

Chapter Four

An alluring smell of cooked bacon and sausage woke Terry Vaughan from his slumber, lying prostrate and alone in the marital double bed. It was his day off, and strong sunlight poured through the bedroom window, causing him to shield his eyes as reality came into focus.

The warm indentation at his side indicated that his wife, Eileen, hadn't been up long, and the sounds from the downstairs kitchen, together with the alluring smells, would have told him that breakfast was being prepared even if he wasn't a detective by trade.

Sizzle.

Dressed only in jockey shorts, Terry got to his feet and padded barefoot down the stairs.

The television news was on, with more images of the strike and of the previous year's cavalry charge at the Orgreave coking plant. But repetition had reduced these images to the point of decontextualised and electronic wallpaper, stripped of meaning, beyond the relentless mantra of the government and its media stooges that the unions were holding the country to ransom.

Now King Arthur was on the TV, being grilled by a servile Nicholas Witchell.

Terry's heavily pregnant wife, Eileen, was putting the finishing touches on a breakfast to die for. Sausage and egg, bacon and mushroom, baked beans and hash brown. A feast fit for a king. Terry went up to his wife, put his arm around her and lovingly kissed the nape of her neck.

"You shouldn't, love," he said in an accent that was pure Rhondda Valley. "Not in your condition."

"I'm pregnant, Terry," she smiled. "It's not an illness."

"If you say so, love," he said and blew a raspberry on her neck. A bad rendition of *Come on Eileen* by Dexy's Midnight Runners followed as he headed towards the dining room table, confounding the shibboleth that all Welsh people can sing. The BBC Morning News continued on, ignored with its drip-drip commentary about the strike. Through the window, in the cul-de-sac of semi-detached houses where they lived, kids were going to school.

In the further distance, beyond the huddled cluster of stone houses, often brightly painted, the pit head dominated the town. But its steel wheel was silent now, like a Martian from an HG Wells science fiction novel, what with the strike entering its second bitter year.

Terry's breakfast was placed in front of him, and it tasted as good as it looked. He fondled his wife's rear, accepted a kiss and attacked the plate like a military operation.

In the front room, furnished according to Eileen's taste, photos revealed the recent contradictions of their past life since they started courting in college in nearby Merthyr. Terry had been doing his A levels, supposedly as a prelude to university, until he was lured into joining the job instead when the posh bird from Newport told him to be quiet in the college library. Weeks later and they were going out — his first-ever snog — and from that point onwards, inseparable. Their wedding photo held pride of place in the front room, but there was also a portrait of Terry in his police uniform and of his father, on retirement, still wearing his mining helmet, in front of that iconic pit.

Now Terry was a detective sergeant with a nice house in the suburbs courtesy of Margaret Thatcher's massive pay rise for the Police. As for the Vaughan family, they were all but at war with themselves, like the country itself, or had been until Dad had fallen sick.

Terry ate his breakfast and savoured it. A welcome day of rest beckoned.

And then the phone rang.

"Bugger it," said Terry, his mouth still full and instinctively knowing it was work. "Who the bloody hell's that on my day off?"

*

As the children filed towards their school, following an invisible Pied Piper, they passed rank after rank of police riot vans. All of them had meshed up windows and what was called "Paddy Pushers" on the front. The Northern Ireland conflict had been going on for 17 years now, and the toys of repression were being brought home. As for the cops that formed the government's army of occupation and were described as Police Support Units, few of them were local as the government, like the Romans in Britain, didn't use locals to suppress their own tribe. Britain doesn't have a full-time riot squad like the

French CRS, and the Police Support Units, nominally composed of riot trained regular cops, had been created under Civil Defence legislation introduced in 1974. For the duration of the strike, they were coordinated through the National Reporting Centre at New Scotland Yard.

The local cops had little to do with it, and it showed.

This morning the PSU cops had white shirts, and everybody knew that the cops in white shirts were the worst. They were from the London Metropolitan Police, notoriously the most corrupt Police Force in the UK and either battle-hardened from the race riots that had followed Swamp 82 or else raw recruits signed up for the repression and all the overtime that went with it.

Behind the leering phalanx of cops, the mute walls of the small town were awash with rhetoric like the song about the bells of Rhymney. "Save the Pits," said the red and white livery of the Labour Party *Militant* tendency, mimicking the font and masthead of its publication. A poster from *Socialist Worker*, a little more stylish and professional in its graphics, said, "Coal Not Dole." That of the Revolutionary Workers League, straight from the playbook that was the Transitional Program of 1938, and like a clock that was stopped and sometimes right said: "General Strike now!"

A fat cockney cop with a red neck and bald head licked his lips as a pubescent short skirt strutted past. Her name was Siobahn. She had a very short skirt and long legs, and her parents probably shouldn't have let her go out dressed like that at all.

The cop whistled and then shouted out.

"Schoolgirl pie," he said. "Mmmmm-mmmm! Fancy a bit of truncheon, darling?"

Siobhan looked at him with baleful hostility, hating him and everything he stood for, both as a cop and a filthy disgusting letch, in a country where Sam Fox regularly wore a schoolgirl uniform on Page Three and where pop stars and celebrities had been fucking groupies of all ages and sexes for two decades now. Small wonder Britain was wired up wrong. On the wall behind the dirty cop with his sagging beer gut like a limp and flaccid cock the graffiti showed a pig in a policeman's uniform. A brick was bouncing off its head, and the legend said: "kill pigs now!"

The schoolgirl smiled but kept on walking just the same.

Two lads in slightly scruffy school uniforms, like hand-me-downs and white Paul Weller socks, were following up behind. They saw the altercation between the cop and the schoolgirl and weren't slow in taking up the battle cry of their parents and older brothers and sisters.

"Your Maggie Thatcher's Boot Boys, You're Maggie Thatcher's Boot Boys, La-la-la-la, La-la-la-la!"

Hostile glances from the surly PSU cops indicated that the boys would best cut through the canal on the way to school. It was a dismal stretch of stagnant water where abandoned shopping trolleys and other rubbish and detritus gave the primordial appearance of a dinosaur's graveyard.

Still, the chanting continued, much like the dinosaurs and in the face of historical adversity.

Maggie, Maggie, Maggie, Out, Out, Out!

Perhaps the whole town was a dinosaur's graveyard now.

Only today, there was something else.

Floating among the rest of the rubbish, in the filthy green water, the body of a young girl in her early 20s floated like a discarded and waterlogged quilt. Somehow, despite the squalid nature of the find, the rubbish that had congregated around the water-logged corpse gave the appearance of an angel's wings.

The chanting stopped. In its place, one of the boys said: "Fuck me!"

*

The colour drained from Terry Vaughan's face as his wife looked on, concerned. Already, she knew that their planned day off had been scuppered, ruined, but there was something else that suggested this was bad.

Terry replaced the phone in its cradle.

"Dead girl in the canal," he said. "Looks bad, probably murder."

"What?" Eileen demanded.

"I've got to go," he said

"But it's your day off," she protested.

"Yes," Terry replied as if in apology, but he was already grabbing his coat. "I know. I'm sorry, love."

There was an awkward pause.

"We're short-staffed," he added as an apologetic afterthought. "You can blame Maggie Thatcher and King Arthur for that."

Already, half in jest, Eileen referred to Terry's work as "the other woman."

"Speaking of striking miners," Eileen said, perhaps a little too frostily, "Your brother called."

Terry's response was slightly hostile. He and Johnny had barely been on speaking terms since the strike began.

"What does he want?" Terry asked.

"It's your dad, in the hospital", Eileen replied. "Johnny says he's taken a turn for the worse. He wants you to go and see him."

"Didn't know the old communist bastard was still talking to me," Terry smiled thinly. "I'll phone Johnny later."

Terry kissed his wife's cheek, but the ghost of frostiness and distance was still there — his lovely and slightly posh Eileen almost pouting like a schoolgirl. Mum could say that there was nothing worse than a working-class snob, but he'd already told Mum that where his wife was concerned, she could keep her opinions to herself.

He hated it when there was any kind of barrier between them.

A little sheepishly, Terry left the house and walked to his Ford Sierra car. Above, the sky was heavy and brooding, with a dirty grey colour that already bore the texture of a corpse on a mortuary slab.

Terry hoped it wasn't an omen as he started up the engine.

He turned on BBC Radio 4 as he did so.

"In Shropshire, police announce a new lead in relation to last year's murder of Hilda Murrell," the radio newscaster said. *"In an exclusive in this*

morning's Sun, *journalist Orla O'Regan claims that Willie McRae, the Scottish Nationalist politician found shot dead earlier this week, had been linked to the Scottish National Liberation Army."*

Terry drove away.

Back in the kitchen, in the house, lovely Eileen threw the remains of Terry's lovely breakfast into the bin.

Chapter Five

At the pit head, the pickets swarmed, seeking strength and safety in numbers, pushing against the line of PSUs as another coach of scabs filed through.

Astons of Worcester scab-wagon

And then there were the angry tribal chants, among the pushing and shoving, as the pent up rage of the striking miners formed a hot white fist of fury in their collective minds. They were at war, and they were losing, and they could sniff the fear of the scabs in their wagon like it was carrion.

"The workers, united, will never be defeated! The workers, united, will never be defeated!"

Slowly, the bus inched towards the gate, which closed around it, swallowing it whole like Jonah by Leviathan. There were some arrests, courtesy of the PSU snatch squads, and recreational beatings and violence dished out by the police.

Johnny Vaughan was among the pickets in his stylized pea coat that almost belied his love-hate relationship with his working-class roots. On his lapel was a portrait badge of Leon Trotsky and the slogan: *Coal Not Dole!*

"Scabs," Johnny yelled. "Fucking scab bastards!"

And then he joined in the chant as the gate was forced shut. And as usual, the focus of their anger was on the police.

"Maggie Thatcher's Boot Boys! Maggie Thatcher's Boot Boys. La-la-la-la! La-la-la-la!"

39

The next thing that Johnny knew, he was being carried away, as if at some rock concert turned out wrong, in a sea of bodies and violence, which was how he usually started the day.

The Damned Youth of the Somme: the Damned Youth of the Rhondda.

They were all of them Albion's Lost Children, now.

*

To a crash of police radio static, the dead girl's dripping body was being hauled to shore by frogmen and other cops in a Gemini inflatable as Ted, the pathologist, arrived at the crime scene.

Even from where he stood, on the canal towpath, Ted could see that the dead girl had a plastic bag over her head.

All around him, the blue and white crime scene tape fluttered like tawdry bunting at a fete. SOCO officers, in white coveralls, pulled the body ashore and carefully removed the plastic bag to reveal what remained of her face. Once pretty, perhaps, it had been smashed in with some heavy instrument, almost as in a grotesque parody of a sex act.

The hammer had been the Yorkshire Ripper's weapon of choice, but this looked more like the work of a Leon Trotsky ice pick.

"Oh my word," Ted said.

A young uniformed cop turned to one side and vomited.

*

Now that the last busload of scabs had gone into the pit, the shouting and yelling had diminished. In fact, most of the pickets had now dispersed to the soup kitchens to watch daytime TV. But a handful of dedicated pickets remained at the gate, huddled around a crackling brazier in an old dustbin. There was Johnny, of course, and Bryn Williams and Alun Jones.

Adjacent to the gate, a sign reminded them that the mine was owned by the National Coal Board and was operated on behalf of the British People.

And all of a sudden, 1948 seemed a long time ago.

Across the debris-strewn road that formed a kind of no man's land, there was a similar token presence of police PSUs.

Bryn stared at the cops.

"They were alright to start with," he said almost sorrowfully. "Know what I mean?"

Johnny lit a cigarette and snorted.

"What?" Johnny asked, slightly irritated as his lighter failed to catch. "What are you talking about, Bryn?"

"The coppers," Bryn said, "When they were local lads; before they shipped in these bastards from all over the shop."

Johnny exhaled a cloud of smoke.

"Fuck the lot of them," he disclaimed. "They're all the storm troopers of the Bourgeois state."

"What?" Bryn laughed. "Even your brother?"

Johnny sneered and stared across the road. There was a singularly unpleasant looking cop in a white Metropolitan Police shirt, toad-like and with no neck; a fat fuck who kept staring at him like he wanted some. Johnny didn't know it, but it was the same bastard who'd taunted the schoolgirl earlier.

Now he was waving his wage packet, taunting.

"Keep it up, lads," he said in his alien London accent. "Plenty of overtime for us; you bunch of losers will pay off my mortgage yet."

Johnny's response was angry and to the point.

"Hadn't your whore of a mother heard of abortion?" he yelled.

Bryn motioned for the younger man to be quiet.

"Ssshh, lad," he said. "Don't let them wind you up, son."

Johnny smoked his cigarette to the butt. He threw it into the brazier.

"Bastard coppers!" Johnny said. "I hate the fucking lot of them, including my brother."

*

When Terry and Eileen had been doing their A levels in college in Merthyr, there'd been a program called *Threads* on TV depicting the impact of a nuclear attack on Sheffield. Now, as he drove through his native town, which was no longer his town, with a dead sky that wasn't his sky, and dead and nameless streets that were not his streets, it was as if that nuclear holocaust had already happened.

Protest and survive.

The posters and rhetoric were alien to him, too.

The sky, like a brooding omen, was the colour of gunmetal and the texture of a corpse on a mortuary slab.

When he arrived at the canal crime scene, there was another ghost from his personal past in the form of Clever Trevor O'Carroll, a contemporary of his younger brother at the local comprehensive school. With a leather tie and white socks, looking like a scruffy second generation Mod, the local reporter was chain-smoking in an agitated way as he hovered by the blue and white crime scene tape.

"*If it bleeds, it leads,*" Terry reminded himself as he spotted Trevor reach for his reporter's notebook, stuffed into his pocket.

As Terry got out of his Ford Sierra, the newshound hurried towards him.

"Hello, Terry," Trevor said breezily. "How's Johnny?"

"Probably all the better for steering clear of you," Terry growled as he carried on walking. "Our Johnny always was easily led."

"Well, that's not a very friendly thing to say to an old School mate, is it, Detective Sergeant?"

"We went to school, Trevor," Terry said. "I didn't recall we were ever mates."

"Then I suppose you wouldn't like to comment about this dead girl then?" Trevor continued.

God loves a trier, Terry told himself as he ducked under the blue and white crime scene tape. And Trevor was certainly trying. A uniformed cop stopped the news hack from following Terry to the canal's edge.

"Then you'd suppose right," Terry said.

Trevor swore under his breath. He called after the detective.

"Here, hang on," he yelled. "I might have something for you if you'd just shagging well, listen."

Ted was waiting for Terry next to the dead girl, now on a gurney.

"What have you got for me, Ted?" Terry asked.

"Blooming heck," Ted replied. "They must be short-staffed if they're making a rookie sergeant head of a murder investigation."

"Thanks for the vote of confidence," Terry glowered. "They're short-staffed on account of the revolution."

He looked hard at Ted.

"Anyway, what makes you so sure it's murder?" he asked.

Ted indicated the corpse.

"See for yourself!" Ted said. "Trauma to the face probably caused by an ice pick. She's not been in the water that long so we reckon she was killed last night or early this morning. The PM will confirm that."

Terry grimaced as he looked at the corpse.

"Tell the truth," Ted continued. "If the Ripper wasn't in Broadmoor, I'd reckon this for one of his."

Terry looked up, worried.

"Don't say that, Ted," he said. "This town's at war with itself, same as the rest of the bloody country. The last thing we need is a serial killer on the rampage."

Ted raised his hands in surrender.

"Don't shoot the messenger," Ted said. "I'm just saying it is as I see it."

Ted's attention was then drawn to where Clever Trevor was still arguing with the uniform cop.

"Who's the Paul Weller fan with all the mod cons?" he asked.

Terry sneered.

"Clever Trevor O'Carroll from the local rag," Terry told him. "What passes for a crime reporter in these here parts. Truth is, he was a mate of our Johnny's at school who went to Oxford, fucked up with a third-class degree and came back home with his tail between his arse. I think the editor took pity on him."

"Sounds like you don't like him," Ted ventured.

Perceptive, Terry thought. Ted should be the detective.

"He fucked with my brother's head at school," Terry accused and was shocked at the bitterness in his own voice. "Smoking dope in the senior common room: acid and speed. Probably the same reason he fucked up at Oxford. And he still hangs around with a local drug dealer we know of called Mickey Draper."

Terry looked at Ted.

"Do you have anything for me?" he asked. "On the dead girl, I mean?"

"Well, we know her name," Ted said.

"What?"

Ted produced a student union ID in a plastic bag. It showed a smiling and pretty young girl; in her early 20s.

"Susan Higgins," Ted said. "Swansea University. But I'm sure she's local. The name definitely rings a bell. Besides, you've not seen Exhibit A yet, have you?"

He indicated a nearby bridge.

Chapter Six

The brazier crackled.

Johnny, accompanied by Bryn and Alun Jones, stared across no man's land at the small knot of cops.

Eventually, Alun spoke.

"What I don't understand is Neil Kinnock? Where's Neil Fucking Pillock and the Labour Party in all this?" he demanded. "Not to mention the TUC? I mean, they're supposed to represent us."

"Scared 'ent they," Bryn said.

"It's worse than that," Johnny waded in, shaking his head. "The whole labour bureaucracy owes its position to concessions from the capitalist state. Only now the rules of the game have changed, and the days of beer and sandwiches at Number 10 have definitely gone; only our so-called labour leaders don't get it."

"What's up, Johnny?" Alun laughed. "Been reading books again, have we?"

Johnny continued to stare at the cops.

"As a matter of fact, I have, Lenin and Trotsky, mostly," he said.

"Trotsky?" Bryn rolled his eyes. "Your dad won't like that."

"Yeah, well," said Johnny. "Stalinism's part of the problem, ain't it? It's why capitalism's still here."

There was the sound of a car engine, powerful, and then a flash Triumph Stag appeared and pulled up near the pit headgate.

"What the fuck's this?" Bryn laughed in disbelief.

A man got out of the car wearing an expensive leather jacket and longish permed hair. He had a battered leather case similar to a school satchel.

"Well, he can't be with the *Socialist Workers Party*," Alun said. "He hasn't got a plastic bag."

Johnny smiled ruefully.

"SWP are all students, anyway," he said. "Don't you lot know who he is?"

The man was walking towards him. Suddenly, a grin of realisation registered on Bryn's face.

"Yeah," he said. "It's that Zack Miller off of *Coronation Street* or one of the soaps."

Zack was smiling as he arrived.

"Morning comrades, lovely day for it," Zack said.

Zack produced a batch of tabloid newspapers from his satchel, which bore the hammer and sickle of the Fourth International and the title: *Daily Advance.*

The headline said it all: "General Strike Now!"

"Done your homework, Johnny?" Zack asked.

"Yeah," said Johnny. "*State and Revolution* and *What Is To Be Done?* All ready for the next Party educational, comrade."

"Good lad!" Zack nodded with approval. "I'll get you into of the *Capital* reading groups as well, and then it's off to the Red House in Derbyshire for cadre training."

Alun and Bryn looked at each other. Alun noticed that Zack was smiling, but he also noticed that the smile didn't reach his eyes.

"Oh, yes, comrade!" Zack said. "We've big plans for you; don't you worry about that."

*

To an accompanying crash of police radio static, Susan Higgins' body was loaded into an ambulance.

Terry followed Ted underneath a brick bridge, which resembled a foul-smelling grotto or some grim parody of the tunnel of love. Terry had to crouch as he followed the pathologist through the damp archway of brick that wore graffiti and rhetoric like tattoos. There was a big hammer and sickle and another poster in support of the strike.

Terry grunted.

"Wall to wall politics around here," he said in disapproval. "The whole town's drowning in fucking rhetoric."

"The whole town's drowning full stop," Ted retorted. "Face it, Terry, you joined the job to get away from all this working-class shit."

"I joined the job to make a difference, Ted," Terry corrected him.

"Really," Ted mused. "With a nice posh and pregnant wife all the way from Newport; I mean, you'd really like your sprog to go down the fucking pit, same as your dad, wouldn't you?"

Terry was beginning to look angry.

49

"Just get to the point, Ted," he growled. "What are we doing here?"

They were emerging back into daylight as Ted pointed to a wall.

"Well, for a start," he said. "That wasn't there yesterday, was it?"

Terry squinted as he looked up.

A new fly-post had been placed along a wall over the faded montage in support of the strike. It depicted nine angels, in the process of metamorphosis, being cast from heaven into the infernal pit. A message, in English, at the bottom of the poster was surrounded by strange symbols, like something from a *Led Zeppelin* album cover.

The message said: "Azazel is coming. She is the first."

"Now, it could be a coincidence," Ted continued. "But I'd wager there was a connection between this piece of installation art and our dead girl."

Terry turned to him.

"You mean that the girl was the centre of the installation," Terry tested. "As if the killer thought it was a work of art?"

"Who knows?" Ted shrugged. "Perhaps the body was tethered there but broke loose, or maybe the killer was disturbed. But mark my words, if this bastard is a serial killer, and the organised crime suggests it might be, then he's also about to paint his masterpiece."

"Bloody hell, Ted," Terry said, shaking his head. "What does it mean?"

"I'm a scientist, Terry," Ted said. "No imagination. Maybe you should ask Clever Trevor with his failed degree from Oxford?"

*

In Police Headquarters, adjacent to an open-plan office, Detective Sergeant Dermot Brady was sitting at an office desk like a chain-smoking bear in his cave. Brady had a reputation as a beery faced thug in Special Branch, and the younger officer standing in front of him looked nervous as they listened to a cassette recording of the tapped phone conversation from union headquarters.

The younger cop, to Brady's disapproval, was black, suggesting that standards had gone downhill since the introduction of the Police and Criminal Evidence Act the previous year.

The voice on the phone was that of Zack Miller.

"Don't worry," Zack was saying. "I'll head up there first to make sure there's only a token police presence. Then, just before the TNT shipment comes out, we move our boys in and attack the scab lorries at the entrance."

It was what the strike had come to now, as it dragged into its second year, like some hit and run guerrilla war in some third world pox hole of a country that nobody had ever heard of.

And here was a fucking jungle bunny in Special Branch — whatever next.

Fucking women and shirt-lifters most like.

Brady drew on his cigarette and added to the thick pall of smoke that hung over his desk like city smog.

"That's Zack Miller's voice all right," Brady said, revealing a strong Birmingham accent.

"Yes," said the black cop. "He's a full-time organiser for the Revolutionary Workers League."

Brady snapped back at the smart-arsed black bastard.

"I know who the cunt is!" he retorted. "What I want to know is why he's been massing his troops here when the main coal shipment is over there."

The young cop looked furtive, Brady thought. *Fucking Black Cunt!*

"Perhaps their intelligence isn't as good as we thought?" the younger subordinate ventured with a shrug.

"In more ways than one, the Red Bastards," Brady sneered. "Fucking pit villages. Stupid Welsh names all sound the same to me."

The door to the office was ajar when a uniformed cop turned up with a soft knock.

"Special delivery for Detective Sergeant Brady," he said.

Brady frowned.

"What's this?" he asked. "Fucking Christmas come early or what?"

"Don't know, Skipper," the wooden top said with a shake of the head. "Just some motorcycle dispatch geezer."

Brady grunted, signed for the package and tossed it in the in-tray next to his Imperial typewriter.

"You still here, son?" he asked the uniform, accusing.

The wooden top fucked off, and Brady turned his attention to the spade cop in front of him. If he'd had his way, all of this black scum would have been sent packing on a banana boat after the riots and Swamp 82.

Fucking Scarman!

Brady pointed a meaty finger at the black detective as if in accusation.

"OK," he said. "Move the wooden tops to this place where Zack the Hack is. But if we get this wrong and the Guvnor comes on my case, then I'll blame you, all right?"

The black detective swallowed

"Right, you are skip," he said.

"OK then, fuck off!"

The black cop seemed to breathe a physical sigh of relief as he left.

Brady grabbed the package in the in-tray in his battle-scarred ham of a bruiser's fist.

"Shall I take the money or open the box," he mused.

Brady used a letter opener and slit the packaging cautiously, like a throat, as if half expecting an incendiary bomb inside. He'd worked the Irish circuit, after all, back in the West Midlands and had been a member of the Serious Crime Squad "Heavy Gang" that had fitted up the Birmingham Six on account that they were drunken Fenian Micks on the way to an IRA funeral in Coventry and had to be guilty of something.

Not a bomb, but there was inflammable material in this "Suspect Device" for all that, and it was certainly blowing up in his face.

The first thing to fall from the ruptured brown parcel was a copy of *MAGPIE,* the scurrilous journal of the Paedophile Information Exchange, run by some degenerate of a former civil servant in Egypt called Neville, whose bent arse had been saved by MI6 in the 1970s. But it was the Instamatic photograph of the painting of the nine angels that really caught his attention.

That and the filthy incriminating photographs scraped from the tarmac like roadkill in 1979 that fluttered to his desk like evil confetti.

Brady, his fat red face resembling a bloated corpse, jolted back in his chair as if he'd received an electric shock.

Moments later, he'd slammed the door to his office.

Brady was sweating now, like the proverbial pig, and his ham-like fists were visibly shaking— those very same fists that had beaten countless confessions out of countless collars that needed feeling.

Cautiously, Brady turned over the picture of the nine angels falling from heaven and recognised the handwriting and its gothic flourish immediately.

It said: *Azazel is coming for you!!!*

Brady grabbed the receiver of the Trimphone on his desk.

Azazel, like the ripper, was back from Hell.

Chapter Seven

Clever Trevor was still waiting for Terry when Terry left the crime scene and its unfinished installation art.

Not far from where Susan's dripping body had been placed, on the canal towpath, by the police frogmen in the Gemini inflatable, a filthy black crow with a beady eye had settled as if it were indeed the psychopomp of legend come to claim the revenant soul of the recent dead and carry her to the underworld.

Or bring her back.

Terry felt suddenly unsettled as the crow squawked at him, speaking in tongues, and he thought about a poem by Poe that he'd read in college in Merthyr.

Terry looked towards Clever Trevor and scowled.

"Haven't you a women's guild meeting or something to report?" he grunted. "Interview a miner's family down at the local soup kitchen, maybe?"

"Doesn't sell papers, Terry," Trevor said, as if he were the dirty crow on the canal towpath, gorged on roadkill and the souls of the dead. "Not like murder."

If it bleeds, it leads, right?

"Who said it was murder?" Terry snapped; for all that he knew that the crime scene and factory would already be leaking like a sieve.

Trevor smiled unpleasantly.

"This does," he said, reaching for his pocket. "Arrived for me personally in the office mail this morning; otherwise, that bitch of a news editor would have got her paws on it."

Trevor called his news editor, an embittered spinster who lived with her sick mother, the "Screech Owl", and the overpainted bitch made his life a misery. A product of the dying trade in local news reporting beyond which The Screech Owl would never progress, she hated the new breed of graduate entrants with a vengeance and made Trevor's life hell.

"I made a photocopy," Trevor said as he handed the crumpled envelope to Terry.

The picture of the nine angels cast from heaven was identical to the fly-post at the crime scene. Flipping it over, Terry saw a swastika and a proclamation in an artistic, gothic flourish.

It read: *"Azazel is Coming! For Each Week, the Communist Scum of the NUM Holds Albion to Ransom One of O'Leary's Whores Will Die."*

Hitler was a failed artist, too, Terry told himself.

"Withholding evidence in a murder investigation is a crime, Trevor," the detective growled.

"Bollocks!" responded Trevor in genuine indignation. "I gave it to you, didn't I?"

"Only because you want something," Terry grunted as he bagged and pocketed the evidence.

"Oh, right, and what would that be?"

"A meal ticket to the national tabloids to get you out of this falling circulation crap hole of a town, that's what."

Trevor narrowed his gaze and sneered.

"We've all got our price, Terry," he said. "And we all know what yours was."

Cops, reporters and crooks, all of them class exiles, like streetwise Arthur Seaton's struggling to escape their dying proletarian roots — all of them struggling for the room at the top.

It was at that point that the filthy black crow chose to fly away.

Trevor indicated the crime scene with his head.

"Party member was she?" the reporter asked.

"What do you mean?" Terry responded, genuinely confused.

"The dead girl," Trevor persisted. "Was she in the Revolutionary Workers' League? Only they've been all over the picket lines like a rash, and O'Leary's their fucking guru. Party General Secretary or whatever the fuck they call it."

"Thanks for the tip," Terry nodded. "But I'll need a proper statement from you down at the station."

Terry began to walk away, leaving Trevor indignant.

"Come on, boyo," Trevor pleaded like a truculent child. "You've got to give me more than that!"

Terry stopped and turned.

"Alright then," Terry said. "Being as you're so fucking clever, Trevor, and went to university and fucked up on drugs, so maybe you can tell me what all this Azazel shit is about."

"What?" Trevor laughed as if genuinely surprised. "You mean you don't know?"

Now it was Terry's turn to look angry and indignant.

"According to the *Book of Enoch*," Trevor said. "Which has been removed from official versions of *The Old Testament*, Azazel was chief of the nine angels that aligned with Satan during his insurrection in heaven and were cast out. There's also a reference to it in *Paul to the Corinthians*, but the main popular reference is in Milton's *Paradise Lost*."

Terry hesitated, reluctant to give Trevor any credit at all.

"So what you're telling me is that our murderer is Satan's Right-Hand man," he snorted.

"Or thinks he is," Trevor continued. "Angels are messengers, Terry, good or bad. This cunt's trying to tell us something, mate. Crack what it is, and you crack the case. You get Detective Inspector, and I get a job on the National Tabloids. What about it, partner?"

Terry had to smile in spite of himself.

"You're game Trevor; I'll give you that," he said. "But I'll still need that statement down at the station. As for any developments, you'll have to contact Inspector Pratt. He's the Press Officer at the factory."

Terry got into his Ford Sierra and started the engine. He wound down the side window as Trevor yelled indignantly.

"Aye," shouted Trevor. "Pratt by name and Pratt by fucking nature — the arsehole's never in!"

"I know," Terry said as he drove off. "That's why they made him Press Officer."

Trevor looked after him with a face like thunder.

"Rozzer bastard," Trevor said

*

Flintshire, North Wales, 1979

Jack lies dead on a mortuary slab, cold as the polished steel walls that form his makeshift crypt.

Jack's 20-year-old sister, Roxanne, who is his only surviving relative, stares at the body in tearful silence beyond grief and beyond words. She is skinny and badly nourished but still attractive in a cheap and tarty way, in her short leather skirt and sexually provocative clothing despite the occasion.

Then again, her work clothes are all she possesses.

Another tear, like mercury on glass, runs down her cheek, smearing her black mascara.

In the room with Roxanne is a pathologist in medical greens and an awkward-looking uniform cop. The cop clears his throat and speaks as if embarrassed.

"Miss Parry," the policeman asks furtively. "Can you confirm that this is your brother, Jack?"

Roxanne nods as she sniffs back tears.

"I'm sorry, I didn't get that, Miss Parry," the Policeman says.

"Yes, it's him," she croaks as she flashes him a suspicious glance. "Hit and run, you say?"

"Looks like it," the cop replies. "Frankly, I doubt we'll ever catch the culprits. No witnesses, you see? What we don't know is why he was running away from the care home after all the support they gave him."

Despite her grief and tears, Roxanne utters an incredulous laugh.

"You don't know?" she sniffs.

The Police Officer's expression knits into a frown.

"Miss Parry," he says. *"Given the unfortunate nature of your profession — "*

Roxanne flashes him a hostile glance.

"What? The fact that I'm on the game, you mean?" she declares.

Now it is the cop's turn to look uncomfortable.

"You forget I went to a care home, too," she snaps.

Roxanne kisses her dead brother and crosses herself before leaving with a seductive clicking of killer high heels.

She doesn't notice the Missing poster on the walls that asks about the whereabouts of a Liverpool family called Walker.

Chapter Eight

The convoy of Police Riot vans thundered towards the pit entrance where Johnny, Zack and the handful of pickets were huddled with their placards and papers at the pit gate.

Inside, with their baseball bats and knuckledusters, the PSU cops in full riot gear were singing like a choir of drunks.

"We're Maggie Thatcher's boot boys! We're Maggie Thatcher's boot boys, la-la-la-la, la-la-la-la!"

Like Paul Weller said: *That's Entertainment!*

Zack Miller stood grinning as the convoy arrived, full of adrenalin and hate, and kicked up djinns of dust like advancing dragsters of the apocalypse.

At Zack's side were Alun, Bryn and a handful of others. They watched as the riot cops, like Romans in Britain, disgorged and formed into phalanxes to do battle with a phantom army.

"Lovely day for it, lads," Zack called to the assembled storm-trooping line.

Zack looked at Johnny and winked.

*

Elsewhere in the Rhondda, a real riot was kicking off.

A TNT scab wagon was now circled, at a pit gate, by feral pickets who greatly outnumbered the cops. The truck was completely immobilised within this raging sea of angry humanity and was being shaken from side to side like a rudderless ship in a storm.

The angry pickers circled like dervishes or jackals, sniffing a wounded wildebeest on the veldt.

The cab door was yanked open, revealing a squashed montage of angry eyes. Rough hands grabbed at the driver, whose cold piss ran down his trouser leg, and he was pulled into the sea of humanity just as the windscreen was smashed in with an iron bar. The driver was carried off like a slam dancer at some malevolent *Live Aid* rock concert that had turned out wrong.

More pickets industriously attacked the radiator grill. The driver's idiotic Confederate flag was snatched from the ruptured and violated cab and ripped to shreds along with Sam Fox, getting her creamy tits out for the boys.

Finally, the CB banner was looted that declared, *"you have just eyeballed fireball."* That was ripped to shreds as well.

Lighter fuel was now spilt on the slashed driver's seat like cursed holy water and set alight.

Within minutes the truck was in flames, and the pickets chanted and cheered.

"We are the Reds, we are Reds, we are-we are — we are the Reds!"

That was entertainment, all right.

*

In the pub, Zack the Hack was treating Johnny to a well-earned pint, well away from the NUM club.

In a snug with opaque glass windows, they sat with copies of the *Daily Advance* that proclaimed: "General Strike Now!"

Johnny still had his copies both of *State and Revolution* and *What is to Done,* cheap and mass-produced by Progress in Moscow. There was also a copy of *The Transitional Program,* by LD Trotsky, published by the Party itself.

The paradox here was that, while a striking miner, Johnny had always detested work at the pit and dreamed of escape, much like Arthur Seaton in *Saturday Night and Sunday Morning.* The only reason he became a miner was that he fucked up on drugs at school, and if, like his brother, he'd had the chance to do his A levels at technical college, he'd be fucked if he would squander the chance to go to university and join the filth just so as to marry some posh stuck up bint. Tell the truth, Johnny had been all set to apply for a Foundation Course to get into the university when the strike started, and if he had his way, he'd never go down the pit again.

Only now he had a new ambition, right? To be part of the leadership of the revolution — to be like Zack the Hack.

Bryn had commented that Johnny was even starting to walk and talk like Zack the Hack.

Johnny looked up from his pint and saw Zack looking ruefully at his new protégé as he delivered his best soap opera smile.

He was the cracked actor late of *Coronation Street,* after all.

And as Bryn had also noticed earlier, the smile never once touched Zack's eyes.

63

*

On Dermot Brady's desk, the Trimphone shrilled like a demanding child.

He gripped it in his huge and battle-scarred hand and murdered it in its crib.

"This is Detective Superintendent Ridgeway," said a languid London accent. "I'd like to talk to Detective Sergeant Brady."

"Brady, speaking," the Birmingham accent bellowed. "And we've got a problem.".

Brady stared at the offending package he'd received earlier.

"If it's a calling card from a certain gentleman, then join the club," Ridgeway was saying.

"The bastard's back, Ridgeway", Brady spat. "And he wants something. And I'll bet a pound to a piece of shit it was him who killed that Trotskyist tart you were talking about."

"We don't know that," Ridgway said. "Not yet."

"The fuck we don't!" Brady guffawed. "We got to stop the bastard, Ridgeway, and do it properly this time. And we need to get our hands on you know what."

Anyone hearing a Detective Sergeant talking to his superior like that may have raised an eyebrow but what mattered in this conversation was how the two men were ranked in the society of secrets.

"So, what do you suggest?" Ridgeway asked.

"Who's the leading officer on the murder inquiry?" Brady demanded.

"Young Detective Sergeant on the fast track out of Hendon," Ridgeway replied. "Terry Vaughan. Bright lad; a couple of A levels."

"Is he Craft?" Brady demanded.

"A Mason," Ridgeway retorted. "No. And his father's a bit of a Red: ex-miner dying of silicosis. Only it's his Trot brother we're more worried about."

"Wonderful," said Brady, burying his head in his hands. "You've got to replace him, pal, and find a way of putting me in charge."

"We can't do that, and you know it," Ridgway responded harshly. "However, given that the young girl's a Trot, if you can cook up a political angle, then I can attach you to the murder investigation same as you were attached to the Hilda Murrell case in Shropshire. That way, you can throw Vaughan a few false leads while we conduct our own investigation the old fashioned way."

At that point, Ridgeway's voice developed an edge.

"And there's one more thing," he said.

A knot tightened in Brady's stomach like a hangman's noose.

"What?" he asked.

"When you're on Vaughan's team, you play things by the book, OK?" Ridgeway ordered. "You're not back at Steelyard Lane beating confessions out of the Birmingham Six now. And there's another thing, Sergeant."

Brady swallowed. His lips were starting to draw into a feral; snarl.

"Go on," he said.

"You might outrank me in the craft, but in this station, it's Guv to you," Ridgeway said. "And one other thing, never communicate this kind of business on the phone ever again."

Brady was fuming when Ridgeway hung up.

*

The visions of the aftermath of some nuclear holocaust returned as Terry's Ford Sierra moved like a marauding shark through the dead streets under a brooding sky.

The stone houses that were not his houses: the posters of political rhetoric that were not his rhetoric.

The hungry ghosts that were not his ghosts and the machines poised to take over the world.

On the ugly grey-green hillside, like something from a novel by Dashiel Hammet, the pit head with its big steel wheel still stood like an HG Wells Martian, the way that it had always looked to him as a child — an alien stranger in a strange land.

At Terry's side, the young black woman PC was dressed, on Terry's instruction, in civilian clothes, but it was obvious that they were cops, and a street survivor spat at the car as they passed.

Terry ignored it and drove on.

Then the WPC, eyes wide, saw the graffiti image, amidst the fly-posted political rhetoric, that depicted a pig in a policeman's helmet. Again, a brick bounced off the pig's head, and the graffiti said, *kill pigs now* as if Charles Miller Manson was suddenly at large in the Rhondda.

"It feels like enemy territory," the WPC said.

"It is," Terry replied. "That's why we didn't use a police car."

Dixon of Dock Green was dead, Terry reminded himself, and nobody talked about policing with consent anymore.

Curtains twitched as Terry pulled to a halt outside the Higgins residence, which was a modest terraced miners' cottage in an anonymous, dead street that hardly needed a name. There was a poster in support of the strike, in the window, in the typeface of the Revolutionary Workers League.

General Strike Now!

Terry braced himself: policing with consent might be dead, but intrusion on grief was still the worst part of the job.

Mrs Higgins appeared in the doorway, and Terry was almost furtive with an apology when he produced his police ID.

"Mrs Higgins," he said as gently as he could. "I'm afraid we have some bad news."

Neighbours had appeared on doorsteps and stared as Terry, the wicked messenger, delivered his lethal blow. They saw Mrs Higgins put her hand to her mouth and shake her head in denial. They saw her scream and then break down in tears.

The two police officers gently eased Mrs Higgins inside.

Her face was now a red-raw wound that bled tears instead of blood.

Terry ordered the WPC into the kitchen to make a pot of tea.

Chapter Nine

Mrs Higgins' hands were still trembling as she accepted a strong cup of tea.

Terry looked up at the young woman police officer.

"Thanks, love," he said as he looked over to a copy of the *Daily Advance* on the coffee table near the sofa. Its front page said: *"Exclusive: Interview with Arthur Scargill."*

"Mrs Higgins," Terry said. "We've spoken to the university, and Susan's lecturers said she was very active in support of the strike. Mrs Higgins, is that true?"

Mrs Higgins sobbed as she nodded.

The teacup rattled as Mrs Higgins put it down.

She sniffed.

"Mrs Higgins," Terry continued. "If we're going to catch the bastard who murdered your daughter, I really need to look at her room."

Mrs Higgins, distraught and still in shock, seemed not to hear him.

"Mrs Higgins, is that all right?" Terry persisted.

Mrs Higgins nodded, and Terry got to his feet. He indicated for the black WPC to stay with the distraught mother.

"Where's your husband, Mr Higgins?" the WPC asked.

"Down the Miners' Club collecting our food parcel," Mrs Higgins said.

Terry climbed the stairs and quickly found the dead girl's bedroom. At first glance, it was fairly typical of a young girl her age, but there was also a Polaroid photograph of Susan with a megaphone at a demonstration in support of the miners. At her back, resplendent with a hammer and sickle and a number four, for the Fourth International, was the red banner of the *Revolutionary Workers League Central Committee.*

Terry clocked his own image, in a girlie mirror, like the divided self that he had become and, feeling slightly like a pervert or a dirty old man, he started rummaging through the clean female underwear in the drawer underneath.

Terry's father had been in the Communist Party even after the Hungary Uprising in 1956, and something about this young girl's room unsettled him, the way that his conversation with Clever Trevor had unsettled him earlier. In a way, he knew that they were all class exiles desperate to escape a proletarian community in terminal decline, whether as criminals, cops or journalists, all products of the same crap school that was not their school, in a working-class crap-hole of a town that was not their town. Sillitoe would have got it, and Ken Barstow and Ted Lewis

John Lennon: Working Class Hero.

Dad quoted Antonio Gramsci, the Italian Marxist, about the nobility of manual labour, but deep down, even Dad knew that it was a shower of *shite,* and the last thing he actually wanted was for *either* of his sons to go down the pit that was actually now killing him on his hospital bed. In the end, against all the odds, what with Johnny being the big reader, it was Terry who got the solid A level results and then he'd squandered the chance to get a university place, as his father put it, to become a class traitor and join the Police. They'd tried to put pressure on him to hand in his papers — his family when the strike started — but he was married by then and newly promoted to Detective Sergeant with a mortgage and a nice semi-detached house in the suburbs.

And now his wife was pregnant, and the strike was all but lost in any case bar the bookkeeping.

His family had never really cared for Eileen, whom they thought to be slightly stuck up and with airs and graces.

Mum said there was nothing worse than a working-class snob, and Terry had told her to keep her opinions to herself.

The family could pick the bones out of that, too.

Terry had recently passed his Inspector's exam and was waiting for a vacancy to emerge, hopefully far from this shit hole of a town. As Lennon after Barstow said, there was still room at the top if you smiled as you killed.

If you want to be like the folks on the hill: a working-class hero is something to be.

Terry, the voyeur of grief, had found something in Susan Higgins' underwear drawer.

It was a flyer for a public meeting that announced that Liam O'Leary, General Secretary of the Revolutionary Workers League, was to speak at

70

a local miners' hall, along with the Secretary of the Regional NUM.

The topic was: *The General Strike and the Revolutionary Party.*

Terry sneered. Also, in the underwear drawer, like the sarcophagus of some ancient plundered tomb, he found a Party membership card, complete with photographs and a succession of ticks like school house points that told him her Party subs were up to date.

And then he saw something else, lurking at the bottom of the underwear drawer, like Hope at the bottom of Pandora's Box.

At second glance, it proved to be a pregnancy testing kit, much like the one that his wife had used.

Terry studied it and was astonished, if not slightly shocked.

There was no doubt: Susan Higgins was pregnant.

Terry hesitated, feeling like a thief, and then placed both the flyer and the pregnancy testing kit in his pocket.

As for Liam O'Leary, his own brother's latest hero of the moment, his idol with feet of clay, Terry couldn't wait to see the bastard perform.

A working-class hero is something to be.
If you want to be a hero, well, just follow me.

*

Mr Higgins returned from the miners' club, clutching the family food parcel. It was how the family had survived since the strike started, on handouts and by begging outside the supermarket, as if in the prophecy of some terrible, dystopian future.

When he arrived at the anonymous, stone-grey street on which they lived, the first thing he noticed was an errant sheep wandering down the middle of the road.

Then he saw the unfamiliar Ford Sierra parked outside his door.

Mr Higgins entered his home, already suspicious, and saw the young black woman consoling his wife. Still, his wife's face was red from crying, and her eyes glistened from puffy sockets like diamonds that were as immortal as human misery and dust.

Suspicion turned to alarm on Mr Higgins' face.

"What the..." he began, as his wife rushed with further floods of tears into his arms.

"Oh God, Thomas!" she cried.

When Terry came down the stairs, Mrs Higgins was once more crying a dirge for all of humanity.

*

Za-Za-Na-Satan!

So says *Goetia,* which is *The Dark Book of Solomon,* and a favourite of Crowley to be recited at length in sexual ritual deep in the dank orifice that is the burial chamber of the Great Pyramid of Giza.

Do as Thy Wilt being the whole of The Law.

As for Azazel, like Crowley, he has wandered the wilderness, too, and surrendered to temptation, which accounts for his projected hatred of homosexuals and all degenerates to be bombed in London gay bars.

Except that Azazel's drugged debauchery was far worse, as the walls of the care homes knew, with their secrets and unquiet ghosts. So nowadays, Azazel dwells alone, bereft of his eight fallen companions, in a stone Shropshire cottage near a circle of Celtic standing stones and with the Black Mountains forming a frozen wave of igneous rock to the West.

The sun has set, now, on crime scenes and picket lines and the unquiet graves of murdered Druids and trade unionists; on the Romans in Britain in their police riot vans and burned out trucks in coal depot yards. Local Pagans claim that through the proximity of the nearby megaliths and a domed Celtic burial ground, the cottage is itself built on a lay-line; only the lay-line has turned septic and evil.

Zaz-zaz-na-Satan!

So say the words of The Black Mass, the Dark Pope, and what with three sixes being all lined in a row.

In his potting shed of a darkened room, gloomy as the pit and with distended shadows that are as opaque as the abyss, Azazel performs acts of alchemy, like ritual magic, with trays of hypo solution and photographic cards, which is the nominal excuse for the darkness that his dark soul actually craves. By the dim light of his photographic apparatus, focused on the emulsions in the photographic trays, the montage of Nazi regalia and esoteric references is still gloomily visible on Azazel's Wailing Wall.

Pride of place is still afforded to the nine angels that have been cast out, following the insurrection in heaven, of which Enoch and Milton wrote. And for Azazel, this is nothing less than the depiction of his own rite of passage and painful metamorphosis from Angel of Light into Serpent of the Infernal Pit.

Lucifer is the bearer of light, after all!

Outside, in the Shropshire countryside, the sun has long since set and died behind those dark volcanic mountains, like the tombs of Los, consumed by the Egyptian Goddess of the Nile, a ship sunk with all hands that bear witness to its own valiant death. And as that burning blood-red sun had been swallowed, whether by the ocean itself or by the jaws of Leviathan, so its last rays painted the receding clouds in pastel shades of blood red, pink and grey, like the shields of a receding ancient army on a cursed, Roman sacrificial road, or a flotilla of ships with tattooed sails. And then the sky had faded from gunmetal grey to umber and then into black, as a pale moon and the first stars had faded or shivered into life.

In the developing tray, images take form, as if by magic and the ritual stealing of souls, and Azazel sees again the detective, whose name is Terry Vaughan, at the crime scene art installation where Azazel's first masterpiece had been so rudely disturbed. On the wall, like a mirrored projection of the Fallen Angel's own broken mind, other photographs are surrounded by cabalistic writing and runic incantations of magic, such as Susan

Higgins on a demonstration and Tracey Hepburn, another Red activist, arguing with the geriatric demagogue who is Liam O'Leary, leader of the Revolutionary Workers League.

Rebuild the Fourth International: The Social Revolution in the West and the Political Revolution in the East.

In the photo that Azazel has surreptitiously taken, moving anonymously through the revolutionary ranks like a Maoist fish in peasant waters, Tracey Hepburn argues with the old Irish bastard inside O'Leary's black polished BMW car, permanently parked near the Party headquarters in Beehive Place, a cobbled enclave off of Electric Avenue in Brixton.

But pride of place among Azazels' photographs, in his stealing of souls placed like Tarot cards in Magick formation, goes to the pregnant young woman outside a supermarket in the Rhondda, placing money in the plastic bucket of a begging striking miner's wife. This is Terry Vaughan's wife; Azazel knows, and being pregnant, like Sharon Tate, when she was butchered by Manson and his Family, her death will unleash ever more waves of psychic energy that Azazel needs to regain his rightly place in the Astral Firmament alongside Satan himself.

Azazel grips the appropriate ice pick that he used, like an Egyptian Meshtyw, to claim Susan Higgins's damned soul as his own and sees it still freshly bloodied from his first ritual trophy kill, and then he smashes it into Eileen Vaughan's fuck face image in a Yorkshire Ripper parody of a sexual act.

This is exactly what he is going to do to the policeman's wife, turning hunter into quarry, the moment he believes that his art installation is complete.

PART TWO: THE GOSPEL ACCORDING TO JUDAS

Chapter Ten

The sun had set beyond the mining town, huddled in the valley of the Rhondda, gouged by ice thousands of years before, and the shadows had long reclaimed the dead streets as their own.

Mute rhetoric screamed defiant from the posters that covered every wall and corner and terraced gable end, but those streets knew, as did their ghosts, that the war was already all but lost and that the Romans in Britain had won. As for the silent, brooding pit head that dominated the town, since the birth of the industrial revolution, like a Martian from an HG Wells novel with its steel wheel of an all-seeing eye, it knew this, too, as did The Beast, which still remained buried and sleeping between seams of coal, with the buried ruined temples of Magick Albion, the bones of murdered Druids and miners, and the stench of rotten wood, firedamp and bloody death.

They were, all of them, Albion's Lost Children now.

Outside the supermarket that was visible from the small, open-plan office of the local rag, the miners' wives still rattled their plastic buckets for hand-outs, but even in the miners' villages and communities, the well of generosity was starting to run dry. *Dig Deep for The Miners,* the stickers on the bucket said, but all that was being dug was a mass grave as far as Clever Trevor O'Carroll could see.

Dying in the Ditches for King Arthur's Barmy Army, Same as Wilfred Owen's Damned Youth of the Somme.

Fuck That!

And Fuck this dying fucking town as well.

As Trevor watched the wives huddled at the supermarket entrance with their plastic buckets, a police riot van cruised by with all the silent menace of a marauding Great White Shark. This was the army of occupation, Trevor knew, and the future face of policing without consent — the British Empire, with no place to go, reduced to exploiting, oppressing and fucking over its own.

Trevor was trying to look busy as he sat in front of the ancient Imperial typewriter strategically placed on his wooden desk. There was talk of computers being introduced to the disgruntled grumbling of the sub-editors who lurked upstairs, but Trevor reckoned he could be the hell out of Dodge by then. His desk, as usual, was chaotic and cluttered, with pink duplicates of typed copy impaled on a spike and an overstuffed ashtray, as well as a notebook in scrawled Teeline shorthand that was close by.

Trevor, his leather tie awry, smoked another of the soft pack red Malboros that he had chain-smoked all afternoon and looked to where his moron of an editor, known as *Motor-mouth,* was talking to *Screech Owl,* the ageing and painted bitch of a news editor who made Trevor's life hell. *Motor-mouth* was a farm boy from Banbury in Oxfordshire, thick as the cow shit between his ears and the beer-bellied product of a managerial training course in America, who thought that off diary investigation

79

had no place in the routine of a local newspaper. According to *Motor-mouth*, they were in the information game, lubricated by good and servile relations with local police, chamber of commons, dignitaries and Masonic Lodge, and it was Trevor's duty to un-learn all the nonsense he'd learned at university, so he could spend the rest of his life focused on what the sociologist C. Wright-Mills once called the almighty unimportant fact. *Motor-mouth's* idea of recreation was shagging his secretary in the upstairs office, but he also played rugby and currently sported a shiner of a black eye.

Trevor drew and exhaled the exquisite, baked American tobacco and sat beneath his pall of smoke and scribbled cartoon caricatures in his reporter's notebook as the conversation droned on, willing the pair of them to piss off and hopefully die. Also, on Trevor's desk, on the other side of the typewriter to his notebook, an *Exclusive* in *The News of the World* showed members of a South Wales Ku Klux Klan chapter burning a fiery cross at an undisclosed rural location.

Trevor clocked the bi-line of the story by a reporter named Orla O'Regan.

Trevor was thinking about the name when the editor called out to him.

"Night, Trevor," *Motor-mouth* said. "Don't work too late. You've police calls early with Inspector Pratt tomorrow."

"Aye!" smiled Trevor, falsely, through the thick pall of cigarette smoke.

Pratt by name and Pratt by fucking nature!

At last, the editor and the *Screech Owl* both fucked off, causing Trevor to heave a sigh of relief.

The door slammed shut—goodbye.

Trevor stubbed out the smouldering *Marlboro* cigarette and then reached for the phone on his cluttered desk. Nine for an outside line and then more digits with a London prefix punched into the buttons.

A ring tone sounded, and then the office door opened.

Trevor quickly put the phone receiver back in its cradle as The *Screech Owl* walked in.

"Bloody contact book," she smiled falsely through thickly packed make-up, then headed for her desk and picked it up. "Good night, Trevor," she added frostily and then finally left.

Trevor heaved a sigh of relief.

*

With the relentless rattle of the Undead turning in unquiet graves, the tube train hurtles through the bowels of the ancient city, with its buried rivers and broken pillars of forgotten Temples of which Blake once wrote beneath the cobbled scales of deserted streets where the Beast sleeps.

Derek Hepburn stares through the dirty window of the tube train carriage that surrounds him like a high-speed aluminium coffin hurtling across the River Styx. Every so often, he sees sparks fly in the opaque void as he thinks of Judas and the Garden of Gethsemane, of false idols and betrayal.

Like his native Rhondda Valley, where he had once laboured in the infernal pit, the part of the East End where Trevor dwells is awash with posters and rhetoric, but there is scant evidence of this fact among the commuters, nervous as rabbits, hiding behind their right-wing tabloids in the speeding sarcophagus with him, on the way to suburban Fulham. In fact, they regard him with timid aggression, in his jeans and pea coat that is almost a uniform for the Security Directorate of the Revolutionary Workers' League. With his Leon Trotsky badge and proclamation of Coal Not Dole, he may as well be a leper to this sullen sea of frightened faces who dote on the Iron Bitch's every word.

Elsewhere in the capital, as divided as the whole country, banners furnished by the Greater London Council proclaim public services to be under threat. The graffiti beneath the railway arch, close by the gothic and feral wilderness that is Mile End Cemetery, and the very tower-block where Derek lives, screams out Class War and Reclaim the City, complete with the symbols of the anarchist group. But this is mere bravado and defiance, and Derek knows it, as the dark and sluggish tide of The Thames turns against the working class and Left, in a City transforming from Jekyll to Hyde, from light to dark, and where the Beast is now stirring to consciousness. Already, false temples are being erected to the Beast by the Docklands Development Corporation – all in mocking adversity to the local population who are being cast and squeezed out.

"Gentrification," the sociologists called it, this exorcism of the proletariat. Derek calls it something a bit more blunt and colourful than this. Only yesterday, he'd seen off two well-dressed louts who talked like East End barrow boys and had laughed as they attacked a group of students from the London School of Economics raising money for the miners' strike. A bucket of coins had been kicked across the mouth of the tube station, attended by sadistic laughter, and the next thing Derek knew was a *red mist of rage as he laid into the pair of City Boy acolytes of The Beast.*

His own daughter was a university student, as well as a Party member and a supporter of the strike, and he was a former miner from the Valleys himself.

"Thanks, comrade!" the students had said, not knowing that he was Judas and had blasphemed against the Holy Sacrament of Democratic Centralism and all the Orwellian doublethink intrinsic to the commandments of Liam O'Leary and the Party Line.

But it was the betrayal of his black friend, Americk Fraser, the murdered social worker employed by Lambeth Council, that bothered Derek much more than the false Prophet that was Liam O'Leary, with his army of apparatchiks and feet of clay.

To his shame, it had been Derek who recruited Americk to the Revolutionary Workers League back in 1977, when Derek had peeled away to London and kissed both the valleys and his failed marriage goodbye. The heady smell of revolution was already in the air in these far off days when Derek, like Judas, had sold the paper and built the Party ahead of his induction at the Red House in Derbyshire into the Security Directorate headed by the Brothers Grim. Americk had bought a copy of the Daily Advance, *and then they'd headed back to Americk's pad in Clapham to listen to* Linton Kwese Johnson *and chill.*

Americk had seen recent action against the fascists at the Rock against Racism Carnival in Lewisham and was on the point of joining the recently formed Anti-Nazi League. Derek, then a devout apostle of O'Leary's secular church and of its sacred line, had tried to persuade Americk of the error of his ways and that anti-fascist mobilizations simply train the army and police ahead of an imminent coup. What Derek hadn't realised was that even when he'd recruited Americk to the Party, the young social worker continued to involve himself in the ANL.

It was the second carnival in Victoria Park and Brick Lane that had brought things to a head.

The Clash *had been gigging with* Sham 69, *and Paul Weller had been looking at his watch when the Chinese whispers spoke in tongues to the crowd that the National Front was running riot in Brick Lane. In fact, Americk was among the first to tell a bunch of young punks at his back to follow him and, defying both Paul Holboro and the* Socialist Workers Party *stewards; they'd fucked off to Brick Lane to do Battle with the Fascists.*

This time it wasn't like Lewisham, and they were outnumbered, what with the Police Special Patrol Group openly siding with the Front. The next thing Americk knew, bruised and bloodied, he was in a police station, about to be charged and thrown in a cell with a bunch of boneheaded representatives of the master race.

In genuine fear of his life and of losing his job, Americk had phoned the Party Headquarters in Brixton to try and get someone to arrange his bail. And it was then that his problems really started.

To Derek's own shame, he hadn't been at Carnival 2 or Brick Lane, but he was attendant, like an unwelcome spectre at the feast, when Americk faced down the secular equivalent of the Spanish Inquisition in his own flat in Clapham, where he and Derek had chilled and listened to Inglan is a Bitch.

Never mind that the name of the Anti-Nazi League, and of Paul Holboro in particular, was now mud among the Asian community in the dark and narrow recesses of London's East End or that the Asian Youth Movement was formed shortly afterwards.

Never mind that the ANL was reduced to a passive recruitment conduit for the SWP or that Tony Cliff wound the whole circus up, in any case, after the riots in 1982.

It was the fact that Derek did nothing to defend his friend and comrade, Americk Fraser, from the wrath of the Brothers Grim that made him Judas, and anything he planned to conspire tonight against the corrupt Party of Liam O'Leary was a matter of small consequence in comparison.

Derek had felt sick to the pit of his stomach, and his entrails had seemed turned to lead as he picked up the telephone receiver and heard what he was expected to do to his best friend, in the name of Bolshevik Party discipline and of the revolution. In truth, he'd never liked the Brothers Grim, a pair of surly Asians who had modelled the security directorate on the East German STASI and convinced O'Leary early to support the "excesses" of the Chinese Cultural Revolution like the pair of closet Stalinists that they were. When Derek was inducted into the Security Directorate at the Red House, he thought he was defending the Party against fascists and other forms of attack. Instead, when he wasn't pumping iron in the gym or turning over the engine of O'Leary's BMW, he was slapping Party comrades around to keep them in line.

That said, Derek had been nominally unemployed since he arrived in London's land of gold and poison and the Party, as a total institution, controlled and was his life — true Bolshevik that he was, if the Party leaders said that two plus two equals five then so be it, comrade.

Just like George Orwell said.

But Derek didn't quite know what he'd think as he approached the flat in Clapham.

That flat where he'd shared such good times with the black man who was also his best friend.

When he arrived, the abuse had already begun, and he could hear the smashing of crockery and the beating of flesh inside, as well as the screaming voice of one of the Brothers Grimm. Already sick to the stomach and to the core of his very being, Derek had approached in hesitant trepidation like a small child bearing witness to domestic abuse.

The door was unlocked and sagging like a broken jaw. The yellow light from inside suddenly seemed to be the colour and texture of human urine.

And then that horrible, hectoring voice, once again and now completely audible.

"You were told, ordered to stay away from the Anti-Nazi League and from Carnival 2," one of the Brothers Grimm screamed. "As Liam says, all these ridiculous anti-fascist protests do is train the police in state repression!"

To Derek's utter horror, as he entered the hallway with the torn posters and works of art, he saw his best friend knelt before the screaming Party thug, with blood gushing from a wound to his head that glistened crimson red against his black skin. All around Americk, like the ransacked contents of a broken mind, were the detritus of broken crockery and more of Americk's defiled personal possessions.

The Brother Grimm, who had clearly struck the black social worker in his own crib, stood before him stabbing a meaty finger at Americk's kneeling form, the way that O'Leary did it at political meetings. It was even called "The O'Leary Finger" and was a characteristic mannerism of most of the Party cadres who did more than sell the Daily Appeal.

86

"*The National Front...*" Americk started to blubber

"*The National Front?*" his Asian tormentor echoed. "*When the state comes for our Party, they won't need the National Front.*"

Then Americk looked at Derek, and the Welshman knew how Judas really felt. *The dark eyes that implored him spoke of betrayal more than fear or pain, and when the second Brother Grimm emerged from the kitchen, instinct told Derek to intervene the way he'd done against the two louts at the tube station. But Derek's conditioning, as a Party member, told him that to do so was a counter-revolutionary act and he remained paralysed in confusion and horror instead.*

Again, like George Orwell said: two plus two equals five.

When the second Brother Grimm stepped forward and also struck Americk, Derek flinched. He swallowed and forced back an urge to be sick, but still, he did nothing.

"*You're expelled,*" the second brother spat the words like a curse or hex. "*Plus, you're in arrears of Party subs.*"

The thuggish second brother leaned forward, his face a feral snarl, and whispered so that Derek could barely hear it.

"*As for the other business,*" the Brother Grimm said. "*And you know what I'm talking about. Just keep your mouth shut!*"

Both brothers shoved the kneeling Americk as they left.

They shoved Derek, too.

"*You're late, comrade!*" the one brother snapped so close that Derek could smell his foul breath. "*Now, come with us.*"

Derek looked one last time towards his best friend, kneeling bloodied in the room, and he saw Americk stare back at him in baleful hatred. It struck Derek to the heart and to the very core of his being, but when one of the brothers called him, he came to heel like the obedient dog that he was.

He could still feel Americk's stare as a wind of hate on his back.

He can still feel it now as the tube train pulls into the station – the rattle of the doors and instruction to mind the gap.

Derek never saw his friend again because, two weeks later, Americk was murdered in docklands, where the temples of the Beast were being erected beyond stout mesh gates. Americk had been handcuffed to a supermarket trolley – doused with lighter fluid and then incinerated and cast as a screaming human torch into the dark waters of the Thames.

Officials from Lambeth Council had retrieved sensitive documents from his flat after he was killed, and the Daily Advance *sang his praises as a brave comrade murdered by the fascist Right.*

It was then that Derek started digging, tearing at the veil of lies and tears that formed his personal purgatory.

He had let his best friend down in life.

He will not let him down in death.

Derek leaves the station, like Hamlet *stepping onto a stage and feels the night breeze like ghostly fingers on his face.*

*

Clever Trevor waited until he was sure that neither *Motor-mouth* nor *Screech Owl* was coming back, what with what he was about to do amounting to high treason on a declining local rag in a dying town.

According to the newspaper House Agreement, which even the NUJ branch was signed up to, the editor had to have the first refusal on all stories.

The trouble is that if Trevor offered anything decent to the *Screech Owl*, it got passed on to a more senior reporter, with *their* bi-line on it, and then that Muppet got to sell the story on to the tabloids for six hundred quid a pop.

Plus, all the glory!

And Trevor, yet to pass his NCTJ, still on a junior reporter's pittance of ninety-six quid a week.

Fuck that!

Trevor went to the toilet and snorted a line of speed. He stared at the stranger in the mirror, in the slightly ruffled Mod attire as he savoured the rush.

There was a minor roaring of blood in his ears as the whole world became incredibly slow.

But Trevor's confidence had returned: his self-doubt banished.

Then he went back to his desk and lit another cigarette before placing his call.

Chapter Eleven

Orla O'Regan stared out of her window in the tastefully decorated yet strangely impersonal flat in Fulham that she rented and anxiously thought about her most recent exclusive in the Number One *Sun.*

Orla smoked and had a glass of white wine to hand.

On the television, with the sound turned to mute, in some rural location, Police Support Units in riot vans forced a busload of flying pickets onto a motorway's hard shoulder. The cops then proceeded to smash the bus windows with their truncheons and beat the striking miners to a pulp.

Orla tried to ignore the casual and recreational violence on the screen.

She was waiting for someone: someone important.

Attractive and in her thirties, Orla had started working for News International just as Rupert Murdoch was beginning to exercise his political muscle and really intervene in terms of editorial content on Britain's leading circulation tabloid

When the Australian, who was now a US citizen, bought the then *Daily Herald,* it was a staunchly Labour-supporting paper aimed at a working-class audience, and for a while, Murdoch kept to this script in order to preserve his proletarian audience and circulation figures intact. *The Sun* had supported the 1974 Miners' Strike and the February election of a Labour government under Harold Wilson that followed it. But things changed with the emergence of Thatcher, the so-called winter of discontent that followed Callaghan's punitive IMF-led austerity and the de facto soft coup of May 1979 that delivered the Iron Bitch to power.

In particular, they changed with the Falklands War and *Up Yours Galtieri* and the near fascist orgy of patriotism that followed, in 1982, when *Iron Britannia* was truly born.

Since then, and in return for his loyal support of Thatcher and suppression of all stories detrimental to her premiership, Murdoch had been allowed to purchase both *The Times* (once the UK paper of record but now just another Daily Bullshit) and B Sky B, as the new era of satellite TV dawned. In fact, Murdoch now owned 60 per cent of Britain's media, regularly meeting with the Prime Minister at Number 10 and Chequers, alongside DJ Jimmy Saville and her other favourites, and was anxious to keep it that way.

He had plans for Britain's future beyond Thatcher, too.

There were rumours of a move from Fleet Street to Wapping, and Canary Warf, as the London Docklands Development Corporation built its new temples to Mammon and finance on the rubble of London's once-great docks and in bitter and deliberate adversity to the needs of the local working-class community and Greater London Council that served it.

Gentrification or social cleansing: take your pick!

Meanwhile, Orla's position on the paper, as one of its key investigators but still staunchly socialist, was becoming precarious as she had never completed her formal journalism trading, which was the way that News International liked it. It meant that its staff only knew the Murdoch way of doing things and would have difficulty, without accreditation, getting a job anywhere else. Only recently, Orla had been all but forced to write a story, with her own bi-line, linking the late Scottish National Party politician, Willie McCrea, to Steve Busby's Dublin based Scottish National Liberation Army and a terror plot involving the poison Risin in Birmingham that seemed all but a phantasm of her Special Branch contact's imagination.

McCrea was a drunk and could well have committed suicide by shooting himself with his own revolver at the wheel of his car, which was currently the official narrative on his death. But he'd also been a fierce opponent of NATO and the US nuclear submarine bases in Scotland. In exchange for writing the story, further smearing the already dead McCrea, Orla had also been rewarded with a further exclusive on an alleged Ku Klux Klan chapter in South Wales, and the story had been taken up both by the anti-fascist magazine, *Searchlight* and by Gavin McFadden at the award-winning *World in Action* at Granada TV. The problem here was that neither *Searchlight* nor *World in Action* could find evidence that the Ku Klux Klan unit actually existed, and the more that she looked at it, the more the picture itself seemed stage-managed to Orla.

It was as if she was being played, but she couldn't understand why.

Orla was also concerned about her latest story, which she felt certain her thuggish bully of an editor would be eager to suppress, and this was why her copious notes were not in her office but here in the relative refuge of her flat.

It was also why she'd chosen her modest home to meet her latest, very frightened but angry news contact, who had been a very close personal friend of a senior social worker employed by Lambeth Council.

The senior social worker had been murdered following an *internal* inquiry into child sex abuse at the South Vale Care Home in West Norwood.

The copious notes and files compared the rumours of child sex abuse in an archipelago of care homes in Flintshire and throughout North Wales with the movement of alleged abuse victims in care between South Vale in Lambeth and a home in Islington. All the care homes seemed to be connected to a PR firm in Pimlico and a guest house also in the capital, and there were relentless references to official involvement at the highest of levels.

Some of the files referred to a road traffic accident in 1979 in which a boy from a care home in Flintshire was knocked down and killed while running away.

The boy was called Jack Parry, and it was an alleged hit and run.

There was a family called Walker who went missing on the same day; their car mysteriously vanished into thin air.

There were relentless allegations concerning the Mason-riddled Police in North Wales, their London counterparts and an eight-year-old Asian boy who went missing the day of the Royal Wedding in 1981.

Lambeth Police were particularly on the radar: Eltham and Croydon.

The most recent newspaper clipping referred to the murder of Americk Fraser, the social worker from Lambeth, who just happened to be black. Again, the official narrative, and that of much of the Left, was that Americk was murdered by fascists in a racially motivated killing. He had been active in anti-fascist politics, after all, and on face value, it certainly looked like it, what with the man being sadistically handcuffed to a shopping trolley in docklands, set alight with lighter fuel and then delivered a human torch into the dark and sluggish waters of the Thames. Only Orla's source thought otherwise, and so did Orla, for that matter.

Slowly, she was putting together a jigsaw of evidence, and she didn't much care for what she saw.

Orla smoked and thought about her contact, yet to appear, like Romeo in the streetlight, when her phone rang.

*

After the glowing obituary in the Daily Appeal, *it was Liam O'Leary in person who hijacked the family's grief at the memorial service at Stratford Methodist Hall.*

Derek, like Judas, sat in the front row alongside Americk's nine brothers and sisters. Nieces and nephews sobbed as O'Leary, in his late seventies, hectored the congregation in a Tipperary accent with spittle on his lips.

"The murder of our fallen comrade by these fascist thugs, with the probable collusion of the state,

exemplifies the threat posed to this Party and its need for internal security," the Party General Secretary ranted, like some detrimental robot from a pulp science fiction novel. "In these revolutionary times, the threat of an actual fascist or military coup is never far away."

Derek sat through the service like a penitent and even clenched his right fist and sang The International at the end. But beneath the surface, the hatred that now burned for Liam O'Leary (not to mention the Brothers Grimm at his side) was all but corroding his soul.

The stench of hypocrisy was overpowering, and Derek had to struggle not to be sick.

Besides, he'd done some digging since Americk was murdered, and it made for grim reading even as it woke the Party robot from his slumber.

In particular, between the beating he'd received from members of his own party in his own flat and his murder in docklands two weeks later, that were like bookends to the violent closing act of his life. Americk had testified to an internal inquiry by Lambeth Council into child sex abuse at the South Vale Care Home in West Norwood.

And what had the Brother Grimm whispered, like a character out of Kafka, other than that Americk should keep his mouth shut about the "other business."

What other business?

What were they talking about, these strangers whom Derek had served like a loyal but stupid horse all these years?

Another part of the jigsaw might have emerged a couple of days later when Derek was turning over the engine of O'Leary's polished black BMW car outside of the Party headquarters in the cobbled Victorian cul-de-sac that was Beehive Place in Brixton.

The polished BMW was O'Leary's pride and joy.

In theory, this was O'Leary's getaway car if he ever had to head for the hills should the imminent fascist coup that he kept on about ever actually happen. Most of the time, O'Leary, who shared a council house in Morden with his devoutly Catholic wife and daughters, drove around in an old Triumph Toledo *that befitted his proletarian image.*

In reality, of course, the BMW was a testimony to his vanity, a craven image of a false idol, all paid for by Party subs and dirty, Libyan money, like the secret double life that was hidden from the rank and file.

Derek turned over the BMW's engine every day as if he were O'Leary's valet and flunkey, as well as his knuckle-dragging thug, beating up the Party faithful and keeping them in line.

Derek had revved the car, and then he saw O'Leary in the cobbled cul-de-sac, cursing and arguing with a girl in her early 20s whom Derek immediately recognised behind the tinted windscreen from where he lurked. Susan Higgins from the valleys: his own daughter's best friend and a fellow member of the Party Youth wing, just as Americk and Derek had been best friends before The Fall.

Susan and Tracey even shared a room together in the University Hall of Residence.

Derek depressed the accelerator so he could hear every word and syllable that the angry Susan was shouting.

"Of course, I agree with abortion," Susan had yelled, with an edge of hysteria to the South Wales timbre of her voice. "It's not me who's locked in a priest-ridden marriage. But if we believe in choice, then my choice is to keep my child."

"You stupid little cow," O'Leary spat the words.

There was fear in his voice, and it made the rotund, multi-chinned bastard who was the Party General Secretary and self-styled leader of the proletariat even more grotesque than ever.

Derek's view of O'Leary was already jaded, but the idol truly had feet of clay now.

"If you were a real revolutionary, you'd put the Party first!" O'Leary concluded.

Susan shook her head in disbelief and disgust, and even through the windscreen, Derek could see the tears run down her cheeks like mercury on glass.

"Oh God!" she said. "What's the matter with you?"

She angrily walked away.

It was at that point that Derek decided that if he were to be cast in the role of Judas, then he would be Judas for a higher cause. Having already failed to protect his friend and allowing evil to flourish by doing nothing, he would have no qualms in betraying O'Leary whatever its consequences for the revolution — especially with what he now knew.

And so it is that Derek Judas Hepburn has decided to be, rather than not to be, to act rather than not to act and, having so decided, walks with far less hesitation than he might have thought towards the home of a reporter on the Number One Sun.

And as for the thirty pieces of silver, they have very little to do with it.

*

The phone had rung briefly and then abruptly stopped.

In the empty street outside, even the silence mocked her like some childhood Devil at her window at night. Like this very flat that seemed jinxed and even haunted at times — a place that was not her place, in a career that was not her career, in a life that was not her life.

The phone rang again, but as she went to grab the receiver, a figure emerged from the shadows cast by the street lights, headed with grim purpose towards the flat. The figure was male, tall and gangling, with longish black hair and dressed in jeans and a pea coat.

Meanwhile, the phone continued to ring like a demanding and persistent child.

Ring, ring!

Eventually, the answerphone kicked in, and it was a voice she recognised: the welsh accent was hungry with ambition for the beckoning land of gold and poison, running like blood down palace walls and part of Orla wanted to tell the owner of that voice not to bother and to stay where he was.

"Hello, Orla," the disembodied voice said, like a ghost in the machine. "This is Trevor O'Carroll. I might have a new lead on the Azazel killing in South Wales."

Orla ignored O'Carroll because her front doorbell was already ringing, meaning that Derek Hepburn was downstairs and waiting, like a vampire, to be asked in.

She pressed the buzzer and allowed him entry.

Clever Trevor O'Carroll would have to wait.

They would start the revolution without him.

Chapter Twelve

1979.

It is a grim day at New Scotland Yard, now that the turnip crunchers are coming, and in the fifth-floor offices of The Flying Squad, once regarded as The Met's Elite, the oppressive heat of an approaching thunderstorm is palpable across the ranks of empty desks and abandoned typewriters unusually silent for this time of day.

As for the detectives, all of whom are white and male, they huddle around the leading, chain-smoking figure of DCI Ridgeway, who in turn stares towards the Superintendent's Office and the heated conversation within.

The door is shut. Inside, the silhouette of DI Jack McCreevey speaks in an animated and emotional way, having just delivered his papers to the Superintendent's desk. It is a dumb shadow play that serves as an opening to the drama to come.

Ridgeway folds his arms in angry defiance, still drawing on the cigarette in his mouth, and a collective murmur of hostility passes through the group like a cabal of witches who are speaking in tongues. The overall impression, however, is that of the lynch mob they more precisely resemble.

Ridgeway unfolds his arms, removes his cigarette and exhales smoke.

"Goody two-shoes," he says as if it were a curse.

*

In the office, the Superintendent remains seated as McCreevey speaks. As well as McCreevey's resignation papers, there is a copy of a middle-market tabloid on the desk. The headline says it all:

You're Nicked! Top Cop Robert Mark Vows to Clean up Sweeney and Met.

The Superintendent exhales. He looks up at McCreevey, almost in accusation, and when he speaks, there is a hostile edge to his voice.

"I know that you've had your problems here, Jack, with some of your colleagues," the Superintendent says. "But you're a good copper, a good thief-taker. There's going to be a wind of change through this building, and we're going to need men like you in the future."

McCreevey swallows before he speaks. The glass of the Superintendent's office is opaque, but he can still feel the eyes of Ridgeway, and his cabal, boring into him like laser beams.

"It's not Countryman, *Guv!" McCreevey says. "My reasons for handing in my papers are personal."*

The Superintendent raises an eyebrow as if unconvinced.

"If you say so," the Superintendent says. "Personally, I blame the media. The rot started when the Sunday Times Insight Team *started slinging the muck at the Drug and Vice Squad back in 1969. Then the last bastard Labour government got in on the act — Royal Commissions and all that bollocks. To listen to these bleeding hearts, you'd think we were nothing more than a bunch of thief's ponces setting up half the armed robberies in London."*

There is a ghost of contempt in McCreevey's voice as he responds. Still. The Superintendent looks at him with hostility, and he can feel the wind of hate on his back.

"*I told you, Guv,*" he says. "*The reason I'm leaving has nothing to do with countryman. It's personal.*"

"*We kept the lid on the underworld, McCreevey; just remember that,*" the Superintendent says. "*Without us, there'd have been bleeding anarchy: Anarchy in the UK.*"

McCreevey is silent as an errant schoolboy brought before his headmaster. When the Superintendent stands up, his movements are awkward and uncomfortable, and when he offers his hand for McCreevey to shake, he reveals a Masonic ring of a type that McCreevey himself does not wear.

"*Good luck, McCreevey,*" the Superintendent says. "*Clear your desk and watch your back.*"

They shake hands with equal degrees of awkwardness, and then McCreevey turns to leave.

When he opens the door, it is to deathly silence and a collective gathering of hostile eyes like dirty crows that are waiting for carrion.

When he opens his desk, there is human excrement inside.

The cops titter.

"*Knew your desk was full of shit, McCreevey,*" Ridgeway says. "*But that's taking it a bit bleeding literal, know what I mean?*"

The Superintendent, from his office, stands and watches and does nothing.

McCreevey closes his drawer and walks up to Ridgeway, unafraid. He starts to stare him out.

Then begins the slow handclaps and the chanting: "Grass! Grass! Grass!"

Thirty pence is thrown at McCreevey's feet, and Ridgeway spits in his face. Only then does the Superintendent make his move.

101

*"For fuck's sake, you lot, knock it off!" he says.
"We've enough problems with A10 and the Commissioner sniffing around like flies round a cow's arsehole without you bunch of wankers making things worse."*

He then addresses McCreevey directly.

"OK, McCreevey, get out and don't ever fucking well come back!"

"Don't worry," McCreevey says as he wipes the spittle from his face. "I won't."

As McCreevey leaves, breathing a heavy sigh of relief, a group of senior uniform branch officers come marching towards him, headed in the opposite direction.

*

The team of turnip crunchers from Operation Countryman *enter the office almost the very moment after McCreevey has left.*

Ridgeway, already white-faced with anger, looks at the gang of immaculate uniforms with disbelief.

"All right, you lot," the leading officer says in what Ridgeway thinks is a Norfolk accent. "We're from Operation Countryman. You are all to stand away from your desks and leave the building immediately."

Norfolk? Like the singing fucking postman.

"Bastard sheep-shaggers," Ridgeway mutters under his breath.

He looks to the Flying Squad detective at his side.

"It's McCreevey," Ridgeway continues. "The cunt's stitched us up."

Suddenly, there is blue serge on his face.

"Please leave the building now," the sheep shagging officer says. "Or you'll be under arrest."

Ridgeway indicates for his team to join him outside. As they leave, another officer opens McCreevey's desk and sees the excrement inside.

"Shit!" the turnip cruncher says.

They go out into the corridor and down the stairwell, which is all starting to look a bit too alien to DCI Ridgeway, to put it mildly. In point of fact, it isn't just their careers that are on the line but the prospect of serious prison time. What with all the fit-ups and miscarriages of justice that are an epidemic in the UK – prison was no place to be a bent copper.

Once down the stairwell, Ridgeway turns to his men: to his gang.

"Right," he says. "We've got to get our hands on McCreevey and find out what the scumbag's told 'em."

The Superintendent stood at the top of the stairwell, calling out to Ridgeway.

"Just cool it, Ridgeway," he warns. "The Press and the Home Office are all over this one like a rash."

It's then that Ridgeway loses it.

"Fuck the Press and fuck the fucking Home Office!" he screams.

*

In the kitchen of her jinxed flat, Orla O'Regan was giving Derek Hepburn a hard time. She didn't want to, but the stakes on this story were high, as the murder of Croydon private detective Daniel Morgan by a cabal of bent cops in a pub car park in Sutton illustrated—that and the murder of Americk Fraser himself.

By his own account, Derek was a self-proclaimed Judas and one of O'Leary's thugs and had stood by while his best friend was beaten by the Brothers Grimm in his own flat. Orla had to be sure he was on the level before she proceeded to trust him.

Still, she smoked as she stared at him.

"The role of the SWP in relation to Carnival 2 and Brick Lane was despicable," she said. "They kept anti-fascists in Victoria Park while the National Front ran amok in Brick Lane. But then, where were Liam O'Leary and his merry crowd of paper sellers when it came to the crunch? The largest Trotskyist group in the UK and the RWL did nothing. No wonder the Asian Youth Movement don't trust the white left — political parties, who fucking needs 'em, eh? "

Derek looked up at Orla in a defensive way.

"O'Leary says," he began

Orla shut him down.

"O'Leary says that anti-fascist protests train the police in crowd control and also that the SWP used the ANL as a cynical recruitment conduit. Well, the second part is true, and they dumped it quickly enough after Swamp 82 and the riots. But let me present an alternative theory as to why O'Leary won't fight fascism."

Derek regarded Orla with suspicion.

"Both the National Front and RWL get money from Qaddafi's Libya," said Orla, thinking about the Hitler-Stalin Pact of 1939 as she did so. "As I understand it, there's an unspoken agreement between the leadership of both organisations to leave each other's members alone. Only the pond life of Milwall's F-Troop doesn't read Fiori, and nobody told them the rules. Americk had already been at Lewisham when *you* recruited him to the RWL. Then, when he was beaten up by fascists outside the *Den,* selling the *Sports Advance* to the punters, he defied O'Leary and got involved with the ANL once again."

Derek swallowed. He was taking a verbal beating here, and he hated it, but Orla wasn't done yet.

"For which Americk, your best friend, was expelled from the Party to which *you* recruited him," she continued. "Slandered and vilified as both a CIA and MI5 agent, no doubt, as is O'Leary's usual appeal to Party paranoia until Americk was rather conveniently murdered."

Now Derek was indignant.

"There was nothing convenient about Americk's murder," he said. "It was fucking horrible."

"It certainly was," Orla rolled her eyes as she stubbed out her cigarette butt. "According to the coroner's report, he was subject to various forms of torture that included cigarettes being stubbed out on his body. He was then handcuffed to a supermarket trolley, doused in lighter fuel and turned into a human torch before being propelled into the Thames like a fiery Angel cast to Hell."

"Fascist bastards," Derek responded hotly, but Orla could sense that the doubt was already there and had been for a while. Indeed, if it hadn't, then Derek wouldn't be here, would he?

"Fascists didn't murder your friend," Orla said while shaking her head. "The Police did. But only after he was fingered by members of your own piss pathetic organisation."

Despite the doubts that already gnawed at his entrails like hungry rats, Derek tried to laugh it off, but he wasn't a very good actor, despite his relentless referencing of Shakespeare.

"You what?" he said. "Why would any Party comrade do that?"

"Because Americk, who was a social worker employed by Lambeth council, was about to expose a paedophile ring linking a network of care homes in North Wales to a PR Firm in Pimlico and the Palace of Westminster itself."

Orla opened her neat box of assembled files and documents and started to produce them. They included a copy of the *Daily Advance* and *London Fightback,* the latter of which featured an interview with GLC leader Ken Livingstone. Conducting the interview was a well-known actor, prominent in the RWL, who was also on the editorial board of *London Fightback.* The typeface of both publications suggested that they had been produced on the same printing press.

"Your Party controls Lambeth council through a highly placed official close to the Council Chair," Orla said. "Through the Libyan financed *London Fightback,* you support the campaign to save the GLC the way that a rope supports a hanged man. But, like your esteemed leader Liam O'Leary, our friend at Lambeth Council has one important weakness in that he likes to screw young girls."

The image of O'Leary's argument with Susan Higgins was very clear in Derek's mind, and from the look on Orla O'Reagan's face, she knew it.

"What?" he said, as a stalling mechanism, knowing it was true.

But the real bombshell was yet to come.

"Oh, come on," Orla continued. "You must have suspected as much. Your Party refuses to fight fascism; beyond beating up Party dissidents like Americk and accusing them of being MI5 agents, what does the security directorate exist for beyond looking for young women for Liam O'Leary to screw?"

Derek shook his head as if to exorcise the words of Susan Higgins from his head, yet he'd been sitting at the wheel of O'Leary's BMW and heard the old bastard with his very own ears.

"O'Leary's in his 70s," Derek protested weakly.

"Hasn't stopped him screwing your own daughter, has it?" Orla taunted.

The bombshell had landed.

Derek got abruptly and violently to his feet.

"That's a fucking lie!" he bellowed, even though he knew in his heart of hearts that it wasn't.

"Sit down, Derek!" Orla shouted.

There followed an intense silence in which Derek and Orla seemed to stare each other out. But Orla could see from the tears that he was broken, that he believed her, and that he was completely under her control now.

Eventually and sullenly, Derek sat down. Orla lit another cigarette, and before she had the chance to exhale, the tough ex-miner had broken down in tears.

She gently put her hand on his.

"Believe me, Derek," she soothed. "He likes them a lot younger than your Tracey."

Chapter Thirteen

London Calling, 1979.

It had been a while since Roxanne Parry walked the street; for all that her cheap yet provocative attire and the seductive clicking of her heels suggest, she is no stranger to her surroundings nor else to the night. It wasn't exactly her chosen profession, of course, so much as the one that had chosen her after the routine abuse in the care home after which she was cast out like so much rubbish with no other place to go. As blowjobs and opening her legs were all she knew, it seemed the logical progression, albeit something of a downward spiral, and there were always booze and drugs to blot out the horror of it all.

Same as the care home, really, what with the whole fucking country being built on abuse.

Other girls are ranked, shivering yet fiercely protective of their turf, and shoot Roxanne a hostile glance as she struts past on her killer heels. Not that 1979 is exactly the safest moment in time to be a hooker, either. The Yorkshire Ripper is at large and on safari, after all, expanding his geographical hunting ground, and the cops certainly don't give a shit.

Dead Toms were just paperwork, a bit like her murdered brother Jack back in North Wales.

Just ask the victims of the Yorkshire Ripper up North.

Filthy bastards!

But maybe, hopefully, this one is different.

A car pulls up to the kerb beside her, and one of the occupants, in the passenger seat, winds down the window and calls to her.

"Looking for business, love?" he asks as the driver sneers unpleasantly.

It was always a bad idea with two Johns in the car.

"Fuck off!" she snaps and walks more quickly towards the warm sanctuary of a nearby pub.

Through the swing doors and she is in another world, or at least another era. The pub is crammed with punters under a heavy pall of cigarette smoke, and a pub rock band belts out rock standards of the last decade and before. Glam rock types seem to coexist with punks and what look like Mods and Rude Boys.

She finds the man that she is looking for in the snug, drinking real ale from a traditional jug.

"DI McCreevey?" she asks cautiously.

McCreevey indicates the seat facing him, and Roxanne obligingly takes it.

"It's plain Mr McCreevey now, Roxanne," the Detective says. "I handed in my papers this morning. And you're my first client. My PI agency hasn't even got an office yet, as you can see."

McCreevey makes a universal gesture towards the packed pub around them. Sam Spade and Philip Marlowe eat your heart out, he is thinking.

Roxanne furtively rummages in her bag and offers up a slender file of clues. These, on McCreevey's perusal, seem to consist mainly of newspaper clippings. Most refer to the alleged Road Traffic Accident in which Jack was killed, but there is also reference to a family from Liverpool who had disappeared on the same day.

"Jack the Giant Killer," Roxanne says. "That's what the other lads called him, on account he stuck up for

them. That's why the people running the care home hated him."

McCreevey smiles thinly as he turns the page, finding the photograph of an affluent looking black man (which he didn't expect!) next to Alan Llewellyn, the housemaster of Font-y-Llewellyn care home.

"Who's this charmer?" McCreevey asks.

"McLeod," Roxanne asks, astonished that McCreevey doesn't already know this. "None other than the top aid to Margaret Thatcher since Airey Neave was murdered earlier this year. He also runs a PR Firm in Dolphin Square, Pimlico, called East Gate or something. They're connected to the care home in some way, but I don't know how."

McCreevey looks up at her. His questioning is blunt and reminds her that he is a former job after all.

"And apart from your brother's letters and phone calls, have you any evidence that anything untoward is happening in this care home you talk about?" he asks.

Roxanne bites her lips and looks visibly apprehensive. As nobody in authority has ever believed her before, why should she expect things to be different now?

"Roxanne," McCreevey tries to sound reassuring. "I know you're hard up, so before I agree to take your hard-earned money, you need to convince me this wasn't simply a hit and run accident like the coroner and the police say."

*

A Ford Transit Van pulls up outside the pub with DCI Ridgeway at the wheel. In the van with him are two of the

Flying Squad detectives also suspended from duty that morning.

Ridgeway will give it Operation Fucking Countryman, and he'll give it Jack Fucking McCreevey, too.

"*He's taking his time,*" *one of the detectives whines slightly to Ridgeway's annoyance. "What's he doing in there besides getting pissed?*"

"*I suggest we go in and get him,*" *the second detective says.*

Not the brightest bulbs in the pack, as Ridgeway has already observed.

"*Just shut the fuck up!*" *he snaps. "Just shut the fuck up and do as I say.*"

*

McCreevey gives Roxanne a green pound note. Then he gets to his feet.

"*Get yourself a drink and take your time,*" *he says. "If what you say is true, then the less we're seen together, the better.*"

Roxanne looks up at him. She implores him with her eyes and her voice.

"*You will help me, Mr McCreevey, won't you?*" *she pleads.*

"*I'll go up and take a look around,*" *McCreevey says. "Make some preliminary inquiries. But I'm not making any promises, Roxanne.*"

Roxanne grabs his arm.

"*Promise,*" *she implores at the point of breaking down in tears.*

"*Alright, yes,*" *McCreevey says as if knowing that by doing so, he has actually cursed himself to oblivion.*

McCreevey leaves.

*

Just as his two accomplices are starting to really get on his tits, Ridgeway notices McCreevey leave the pub. He watches the former Detective Inspector light up a cigarette and then walk slowly towards the street where he lives.

"There he is, the bastard!" says Ridgeway as he starts the engine.

He puts on the headlamps and slowly starts to follow McCreevey down the road.

Suddenly, McCreevey seems to notice them and breaks into a run.

"Shit!" says Ridgeway and accelerates.

They come parallel with the running McCreevey and eventually swerve in front of him onto the pavement.

McCreevey turns to double back and immediately runs into two more powerfully built men in ski masks. They methodically punch him in the guts and balls and then throw him, choking, into the back of the van.

The men in ski masks climb on board, and Ridgeway drives off.

Lying on the floor of the van and badly blooded, McCreevey groans as if concussed.

Ridgeway screams at him.

"Fucking Countryman sheep shaggers come asking you questions, McCreevey; you keep quiet, you hear?"

He nods to his men, who give McCreevey a further beating.

Then they throw him out of the back of the speeding van.

*

McCreevy has staggered to the Pentecostal Church on the corner of the street where he lives. From the depths of this sanctuary, gospel hymns seem to welcome him to heaven.

Numb with pain, it is at this point that McCreevey keels over and passes out.

When his vision swims back into semi-focus, he sees a group of immaculately dressed black families and individuals gathered around him, looking down with concern.

One, an elderly Jamaican grandmother who is his neighbour, comes forward. She recognises McCreevey despite the swelling of his head, the puffed eyes and the blood that streams from his face.

"Oh God, Mr McCreevey," she says. "Oh God, we must call the Police.

Chapter Fourteen

Orla had lost track of just how long Derek had been in her kitchen nursing the same cold cup of coffee, but some of his initial scepticism had begun to return.

"If this Westminster paedophile network exists," he began.

Orla shook her head.

"Oh, it exists all right," she said. "And it played at least as important a role in bringing the present government to power as the military coup plot against Harold Wilson that your Party keeps banging on about."

Orla wasn't going to belabour that point as both she and Derek knew that the plot was real enough. But things hadn't stood still with CIA Director George HW Bush and his ultimatum to the last freely elected Prime Minister of Britain, either.

Now it was Derek's turn to shake his head.

"OK," Derek said. "So a bunch of rich pervs use their position of authority so they can bugger young kids. How's that connected with the Party?"

Orla could tell that Derek's suspicion was crumbling, but she was also beginning to get irritated with the Welshman. She produced another photograph that showed Margaret Thatcher together with the black PR guru Winston McLeod and the DJ Jimmy Saville, who had just been appointed by the Thatcher government to a key position at Stoke Manderville Hospital.

Winston McLeod, the first black member of the Monday Club: Winston McLeod, the first black Master of Hounds and a Royalist enthusiast in a civil war battle re-enactment society.

"No, Derek," Orla said, almost like a school teacher reprimanding a delinquent pupil. "This isn't about 'rich pervs' abusing a position of trust or systemic failure or any of that rubbish, although Margaret Thatcher certainly surrounds herself with paedophiles. The people who run this network have no more interest in buggering young kids, as you put it than you or I, but they *are* interested in using it to exercise power and control over people that do."

Orla then showed Derek a copy of MAGPIE, which was the cheaply produced magazine of the *Paedophile Information Exchange*.

"This publication, as an example," Orla said. "It isn't aimed at members of the Thatcher government but at their enemies, even though it was set up by a former civil servant based in Cairo, Egypt, who was a protected MI6 asset and certainly into young boys in Garden City. I can name you two prominent Liberal politicians who are subscribers, one of whom was drawn into a murder conspiracy by South African agents in Devon and the other of which is a notorious paedophile in Rochdale. Both were instrumental in the downfall, both of the Wilson and Callaghan governments."

Derek physically squirmed at what he was hearing.

"But their main target, increasingly, has been those deranged elements of the hard and Trotskyist Left who advocate the abolition of the age of consent," Orla said.

Derek now looked more miserable than ever. "I always had my doubts about that one," he said.

"Had your doubts?" Orla laughed, albeit with little mirth. "I should think so when your friend on Lambeth Council uses his position to get Labour MPs, who have no idea what they're supporting, endorsing the Campaign for Children's Rights because it opposes Corporal Punishment. Problem being that it's also a front for the Paedophile Information Exchange whose publication is even defended by elements of the National Council for Civil Liberties and NUJ."

Derek's hand was to his mouth as if he was about to vomit. He was beyond discomfiture and looked to Orla like a broken man. He was beginning to cry.

"Now the Deep State knows O'Leary has a taste for young girls," Orla continued. "Girls much younger than Tracey, and they'll use that, especially during the miners' strike. They'll use the fact that O'Leary screws young girls to screw your beloved labour movement and deliver the Iron Bitch the victory she craves."

Derek delivered a tearful outburst.

"Tracey was always a Daddy's girl," he cried. "She only joined the Party on account of me — this is all my fault!"

Judas wept.

Orla reached across the table. She touched his arm gently. Then she held his hand, feeling warm and feminine.

"No, it isn't," she said in a soothing way. "And you *will* get justice for Tracey. Only you can't reveal your hand, Derek. Not yet."

*

Derek returned to the East End pale and dejected and with the expression of an inexperienced and hungry ghost. The graffiti and posters were still there, of course, yet seemed strangely more alien to him than they did earlier on.

It was later now, and the homeless were gathering to sleep rough for the night. Here and there, braziers flickered as if in some post-apocalyptic vision and, like a character from a 1940 novel by Orwell, he imagined a dystopian future in which the homeless were in their thousands and Britain was like a third world country enslaved to the unbridled triumph of financial institutions.

The Beast, after all, was stirring, and its temples were being erected here, in Blake's East End, in Magick Albion, even as Derek sauntered to his lonely single flat.

They were all of them, Albion's Lost Children now, here in this grey, divided land.

And what had O'Leary and the RWL done other than to lubricate the rise of the Beast by offering sacrifices to Moloch, who was the very God of child sacrifice and war?

Derek entered the flat whose four walls and loneliness he could never stand. He saw his political posters and the complete works of Lenin ranked on a shelf above his bed. In what seemed a single action, he swept the books to the floor and tore the political posters to pieces.

He contemplated burning his Party membership card, but instead, in tears, he snatched up the photograph of his daughter Tracy.

Clutching it like a crucifix, he threw himself on the bed and cried himself to sleep.

Chapter Fifteen

Armageddon Time, 1979.

The Clash plays Armageddon Time, *on the car radio, as a bruised and battered Jack McCreevey tools his equally battered old Ford Corsair towards the Black Mountains and Wales.*

Croeso-y-Cymru, *the sign says.*

Welcome to Wales.

With two black eyes and a puffed-up face, McCreevey looks like Chi-Chi the Panda as he consumes his full fry breakfast in a truck stop café called The Lazy Trout. *Truckers regard his bruised features with both apprehension and bemusement, and a Mina Bird, in its cage, swears worse than a trooper in two different languages.*

This didn't happen in Dashiel Hammett and Raymond Chandler novels either.

Hours later and McCreevey is in Flintshire and parked at the gated entrance of the Bryn Llewellyn *care home, as if at the gates of a prison or concentration camp, at the end of the road without maps.*

Despite the brightly coloured billboard that alludes to a terribly dystopian future, the home itself, cast in Welsh stone, looks strangely sinister and foreboding, like something from a novel by William Hope Hodgeson or Edgar Alan Poe. To McCreevey, this House on the Borderland even looks to be haunted as if by an incongruous spirit and broken mind that is at war with itself.

McCreevey presses his foot down, gently, on the accelerator and proceeds up the gravel drive to the doors of the big house. There is a crunching sound that should be reassuring beneath his tyres. While McCreevey proceeds, as if into hostile territory, a small pale boy with the face of a bruised and fallen cherub stands watching him from the manicured grounds full of fear and suspicion. McCreevey smiles and winks at the boy as he gets out of the car and slams the door, but the response is as blank as the lost generation from which the boy is drawn.

Then McCreevey sees the housemaster staring at him through a leaded upstairs window, with an intense dark-eyed stare and nervously frayed lower lip, as if this night creature is Gwyndwyr, somehow turned out wrong, and yet still king of all he surveys.

Once again, in noir detective novels, Spade and Marlow never met anyone quite like this.

McCreevey holds onto that thought as he rings the doorbell and waits.

A surly prefect, like a trustee prison turnkey at the gates of Hell, bids him enter. The dark corridors smell unpleasantly of teenage testosterone and polish, and moments later, McCreevey is ushered into the housemaster's study. To McCreevey, its wood panels and a different smell, this time of ancient leather, serve as a shrine to Llewellyn's arrogance. The painted portrait on the wall reinforces this. Indeed, even the man's voice is as pompous as it is indignant. Llewellyn is standing by the window, looking across the kitchen garden to the woods, and with his back to the detective, drinking foul tea from a tiny china cup.

McCreevey hates people who do that, too.

"Mr McCreevey, what happened to Jack was a terrible accident," Llewellyn says. "But you can assure your client, whoever it may be, that there was nothing untoward about his death."

"Yes, but the boy was running away, wasn't he?"McCreevey ventures. "Alone, or so you suggest, on that bitter night with all that snow about."

The housemaster turns abruptly, with a rustling of his black gown, as if he really is a night creature from the imagination of Bram Stoker. His face, irritable at the best of times, seems drawn into a grimace. Or does he find the evidence of McCreevey's recent beating amusing?

"These are troubled young people, Mr McCreevey," Llewellyn says. "Their actions aren't always rational. We have had boys in our care run away before."

"Yes, I was coming to that," McCreevey continues. "Quite a few of them have tried to run away, actually. Why do you think that is, Mr Llewellyn?"

Now, Llewellyn becomes even more indignant.

"I find your line of questioning quite impudent, Mr McCreevey," he says. "May I remind you that you are no longer a policeman?"

McCreevey pulls a crumpled Missing poster from his pocket.

"Just one more question, as Columbo would say," he says. "The day Jack was knocked down and killed, this family went missing. You wouldn't know what happened to them by any chance?"

Llewellyn's grimace is now a mask of hatred, and his dark eyes burn like coals from the depths of Hades.

"How dare you?" he demands. "You come into this institution, where we offer care and love to these poor children and make these disgusting accusations. You interrogate me as if I were some criminal or thug you met in your previous life."

"Funnily enough, none of those were nonces, Mr Llewellyn, if you get my drift."

"Get out of my office, Mr McCreevey!" Llewellyn yells. "Before I call the real *police and have you arrested."*

"Oh, I'm going – for now," McCreevey says. "But I'll be back. You know something, Mr Llewellyn, in my experience in law enforcement, people only behave like you're behaving when they've something to hide. Tell the truth; I thought this case was a fool's errand until I met you. Now, I know different. I'll see myself out, as the cliché goes."

McCreevey mutters under his breath as he leaves.

"Evening all," he says.

Llewellyn calls after McCreevey as he leaves.

"I hear you're not a popular man with your former colleagues, Mr McCreevey," Llewellyn says.

McCreevey turns at the door.

"Is that a threat Mr Llewellyn?" he demands.

"Let's call it a promise, shall we?" Llewellyn smiles unpleasantly. "That if you don't desist from your present line of inquiry, my influential friends and I will start to make your life very unpleasant."

"I've been threatened by harder men than you," McCreevey sneers.

"But not so well connected," the housemaster responds with menace as McCreevey slams the door.

McCreevey leaves in angry silence, and the painted portrait eyes seem to follow him in hostile accusation down the panelled stairwell to the door.

Llewellyn is still staring at him through the lead-lined window when McCreevey reaches his car, starts up the engine and drives away.

McCreevey turns on the radio news as he drives from the gravel driveway onto the open road.

"The new government has reaffirmed its commitment to reigning in trade union power with new legislation promised in the New Year," *a reporter says in dreary monotone.* "At New Scotland Yard, continued speculation as to the likely outcome of Operation Countryman-"

All of a sudden, the young boy that McCreevey saw previously staggers into the road in front of his car like an inexperienced ghost. But there is nothing ethereal about the thud on the bonnet as McCreevey hits the brake. The next thing the detective knows, the young lad has scrambled around the bonnet to the side door and has climbed into the passenger seat as if taking cover from enemy fire.

"*Quick, we got to hurry,*" *the young boy blurts, barely coherent.* "*The giant's coming.*"

"*What?*" *McCreevey asks, confused.* "*What are you talking about, son?*"

The boy looks at him.

"*You're here about Jack and Stephen, right?*"

"*Jack* and *Stephen, you mean that two lads ran away that night?*" *McCreevey asks.*

What happened to the other one, McCreevey is wondering.

There is an awkward pause.

"*What's your name, son?*" *McCreevey asks.*

"*Andrew,*" *the boy says.* "*Jack wanted me to go with them, but I was too scared. Stephen said I was chicken.*"

Then, the boy starts to cry. He even punches the car dashboard.

"*I grassed them up,*" *he sobs.* "*I grassed them up like fucking Judas.*"

McCreevey puts his hand on the small boy's heaving shoulder.

"*Calm down, lad,*" *he says gently and at last.* "*Now tell me what happened the night that Jack and Stephen ran away.*"

*

In his study, Llewellyn broods as he stares through the leaded window, seemingly craving the night that is his true habitat. Under the dour sky, the image of a bleak and sombre countryside seems superimposed, in the glass, over his own, as if in Zen metaphor to his mood.

Eventually, Llewellyn reaches for the phone and punches out the appropriate number. Then he waits for the dialling tone and, on answer, follows protocol by not using his name.

"It's me," he says instead. "And we have a big problem."

*

Andrew recounts the night before Jack's death as articulately and precisely as he can as McCreevey drives.

Andrew reveals how he'd seen both Jack and Stephen bunk off from evensong and how he had followed them, wondering what they were up to. He added that he saw them break into the housemaster's study and prize open the desk like robbers of an ancient tomb.

Andrew then explains how Jack stole the photographs while Stephen stood guard and later urinated in the old bastard's office. But when McCreevey asks what was in the photographs, Andrew becomes strangely silent.

Andrew then recalls how they'd bumped into him as they ran towards the stairwell and an uncertain, dangerous freedom.

"Andrew," Jack had said. "Come with us, lad!"

Andrew had fearfully shaken his head.

"Come on," Stephen had said. *"Leave him; he's chicken."*

McCreevy heard how the two boys had then run into the night, towards the dark wood, and how they were then betrayed, like invisible men, by the anonymous covering of treacherous snow.

"You didn't think to follow?" McCreevey asks, confused.

"I was too scared," says Andrew, shaking his head. *"I was too scared of the giant."*

"And that's the last you saw of Jack," McCreevey persists. He tries to imagine the older, protective boy dragging Stephen across that Judas carpet of snow and into the woods as if the Devil himself were on their back.

Andrew blubbers and nods.

"Andrew," McCreevey persists. *"You say that two boys escaped that night, Jack and Stephen. Andrew, this Stephen, was he killed too?"*

"No," Andrew says, shaking his head. *"They brought him back to the care home the next day."*

"And is he still in the care home, this Stephen?"

"No," Andrew says, still shaking his head. *"They move the boys around. It's what they do."*

"You mean to a different care home?"

"Yes, I think so."

McCreevey puts his foot down on the accelerator.

"We've got to tell somebody about this right away," he says.

Suddenly, and as if on cue, Andrew panics. He grabs McCreevey's arm and causes the Ford Corsair to swerve as McCreevey drives.

"No, you don't understand," Andrew protests. *"He's too powerful: the giant. Fee Fi Fo Fum! Fee Fi Fo Fum!"*

125

McCreevey fights to control the car but fights more to understand what this frightened young boy is on about.

"You keep talking about the giant," McCreevey says. "I don't understand. Who is this giant? Is it Llewellyn?"

"No," Andrew says. "He's more powerful than that. He wears funny clothes at the top of the beanstalk. Jack was the giant killer, only Jack's dead."

"Andrew," McCreevey continues. "You're not making any sense."

"Oh, shit!" Andrew says, suddenly and in genuine panic. He is now white as the inexperienced ghost that he resembled earlier.

"It's him."

McCreevey looks forward to see a polished and official-looking Daimler that is headed towards them on the opposing side of the narrow country road. With its polished black livery, it somehow looks like a hearse.

Andrew dives to the floor just as McCreevey is forced to slow down, to let the bigger car pass. And there, at the wheel, is none other than Winston McLeod, absurdly dressed as a Cavalier officer, fresh from some historical battle re-enactment pageant.

He wears funny clothes at the top of the beanstalk.

Fee Fi Fo Fum!

The PR guru behind Thatcher's election victory stares straight at McCreevey.

"Right," McCreevey says as he increases speed. "I'm getting you out of here."

Andrew, agitated, claws at the unlocked door of the car.

"No, you can't stop them," he yells. "You don't understand."

The door opens, and Andrew bales from the moving car.

"Hey, wait!" McCreevey yells.

The Ford Corsair screeches to a halt just as Andrew, seemingly unscathed, scrambles to his feet. But as McCreevey gets out of the car, Andrew dives back into the woods.

The polished black Daimler is gone.

"Andrew, wait!" McCreevey calls out again.

But the feral urchin has gone, vanished into the undergrowth like one who is used to hiding from monsters.

McCreevy, standing in the road alone, runs his fingers through his hair in exasperation.

"Shit!" he says in complete exasperation.

Chapter Sixteen

1979.

No droning news report or soundtrack by The Clash *as a morose McCreevey drives his Ford Corsair towards the rural police station set in bleak moorland.*

Posters concerning Colorado beetle and an unlikely break-out or rabies indicate not much of a local crime wave, but then again, what did Sherlock Holmes say about rural communities?

To McCreevey's surprise, the Duty Inspector agrees to see him.

"Yes, there was a second boy," the Duty Inspector confirms, arms folded, with a slightly confrontational air. "Most upset he was to see young Jack knocked down and killed in that way – and all over a bit of Devilment, if you see what I mean?"

"No," said McCreevey. "I'm afraid I don't."

"Bunking off from the care home in that way," the Duty Inspector replied.

"Bunking off?" McCreevey responds, incredulous. "The boy was trying to escape! And you took him back there?"

"These boys come from broken homes, Mr McCreevey," says the Duty Inspector angrily. "Now, Mr Llewellyn, see, he looks after them. Now we all know how troubled lads like that can make up tall stories."

"Oh, so he did make a complaint, then," McCreevey says.

"Mr McCreevey, may I remind you that you are no longer a policeman," the Duty Inspector glowers.

"And you certainly don't have any jurisdiction in these here parts."

"I could go to a higher authority."

The Duty Inspector sneers.

"You could," he says.

There is an awkward pause.

"Mr McCreevey," the Duty Inspector continues at last. *"May I be extremely blunt and say that your reputation has preceded you somewhat? It seems that you're none too popular with your former colleagues."*

"Oh yeah," McCreevey says. *"And what's that supposed to mean?"*

"It means that you're a trouble maker, Mr McCreevey, pure and simple," the Duty Inspector continues. *"Same as these muckraking journalists and trade unions holding the country to ransom. Now, if you want to go grassing up your ex mates in the Flying Squad, then that's London business. But up here, we look after our own."*

"Right," says McCreevey as he gets to his feet. *"Unless they're orphaned kids being buggered and abused by the rich and powerful in some care home, right?"*

The Duty Inspector glowers at him with a face like thunder, and McCreevey seriously wonders what other colours he can do.

"Don't bother," he says. *"I'll see myself out."*

The Duty Inspector calls after him, the same way that Lewellyn had, or like any other oracle or seer to be ignored on a hero's rite of passage to his doom.

"Do yourself a favour, Mr McCreevey," the Duty Inspector says. *"Go back to London. Go back to London and fucking well stay there."*

*

Roxanne totters on killer heels in the blare of traffic somewhere near Kings Cross.

This is the new turf, apparently, now that Soho has been taken over by old queens looking for rent.

Something about the Ford Granada that pulls up in the kerb is troubling Roxy, and not just because there are two blokes in the car.

The car slows to a walking pace, keeping up with her tottering gait, and the window winds down. The next thing she knows, the Henry in the driving seat is waving a Police Warrant Card.

Roxanne looks at the two cops with genuine fear. In her world, which the police themselves refer to as "the rubbish", you avoided the filth to make sure they avoided you.

"We want a word with you, sweetheart," the detective with the card is saying.

"I ain't done nothing wrong," Roxanne protests and is shocked by the razor's edge of fear in her own voice.

"Then you've nothing to worry about, have you love," the cop replies as the Granada swings over, with a screech of tyres, and blocks her path.

Now both of the Old Bill are out of their car and, suddenly, Roxanne is very, very scared.

"Look! What do you want?" she almost pleads. "A bloody freebie same as all you coppers?"

"We hear you've been a naughty girl, Roxy, a very naughty girl!" the copper closest to her says as he reaches in his coat pocket.

"Look!" cries Roxanne, absolutely terrified.

"And you know what happens to naughty girls, Roxy," he says as he pulls out brass knuckles from his pocket. "They meet with a naughty boy!"

Roxanne's eyes bulge in horror at the sight of the brass knuckles, but before she can scream, the metal strikes her hard and bloody in the face.

The cop who struck her looks around him as Roxanne flops to the ground like a rag doll. For a second, the other cop seems to flinch and hesitate.

"Don't just stand there catching flies!" the cop with the bloodied brass knuckles orders. "Open the fucking boot!"

Roxanne is small but surprisingly heavy and flops in their arms, like a Marionette whose strings have been cut, as they bundle her, bloodied and unconscious, like so much rubbish, into the boot.

The boot is slammed shut with shocking finality, and they drive away.

Chapter Seventeen

No longer in Civil War attire, Winston McLeod sits in his exclusive London club with his new playmate and guest. Earlier that day, McLeod had met with Llewellyn, the housemaster in North Wales, to discuss the "McCreevey problem." Now it is DCI Ridgeway of the Flying Squad who sits awkwardly opposite as McLeod orders the meal.

The waiter eventually leaves.

"Nice place," Ridgeway says like the fish out of water that he is.

"Refreshingly expensive," says McLeod as he regards the corrupt police detective with disdain. "Keeps out the riff-raff, you see?"

The product of a private education, McLeod's cultivated accent reveals not the merest trace of his Windrush origins.

"You wanted to talk about McCreevey," Ridgeway says. "The turbulent priest, as you call him?"

Clearly, Ridgeway has never heard of TS Eliot, McLeod observes.

"Yes, he's becoming quite a bloody nuisance," McLeod continues. "We first thought, what with him being a private investigator, we could get him a plum job at MacAlpine's or someplace, working with the Economic League. You know, compiling dossiers on trade union troublemakers in UCATT and such like – the Red Robbos and Des Warren's of this world – providing he drops this Roxanne Parry case, that is."

"He wouldn't do it," Ridgeway says as he shakes his head. "Tell the truth; I think he's turned Red. Since

Grunwicks, probably – certainly since that Blair Peach bollocks in Southall. Red, nigger loving, cop-hating, and now he's working for a fucking hooker!"

McLeod stares at Ridgeway.

"And what about you, Chief Inspector Ridgeway?" he asks. "Is there any chance of you turning Red?"

It is almost a dumb question, given that most coppers join the job to escape being working class, much like the villains they pursue and all too often do business with.

Bad business!

Ridgeway shakes his head.

"No bleeding chance," he grins. "The Police Federation supported Maggie Thatcher's election campaign for a reason. This government is all that stands between this country and communism."

"Exactly, the same as Chile," McLeod nods in approval. "So here's the deal. Your men get rid of McCreevey, and his tart by whatever means, and our contacts in the Home Office make sure that all the Operation Countryman files pertaining to your team go missing."

"The Home Secretary," Ridgeway starts.

"The Home Secretary gives his full sanction and is part of this," McLeod assures him as he reaches into his case for a file. "Now, once you've dealt with McCreevey, we may have use of your services again, and some of it might be a bit unpleasant. So here's a sweetener."

Ridgeway looks at the file with eyes agog. He whistles.

"You have the underworld contacts," McLeod says. "Let's say that after the Moro and Roberto Calvi business, we owe a large sum of money to certain Italian

*patrons, but once they are paid off, the rest is yours and
your connections."*

*"Heathrow airport," Ridgeway says. "This will
be the biggest bullion robbery in history!"*

*"Think of it as your retirement plan, Ridgeway,"
McLeod says smugly. "Only invest it wisely as armed
robbery is soon to become a thing of the past. Also, from
your personal point of view, I suggest a transfer out of
London, maybe a return to Divisional CID. And
remember, you and your team are now on permanent
retainer to us."*

*"Providing we kill McCreevey and Parry,"
Ridgeway asks.*

McLeod smiles unpleasantly.

*"Like I said, rid me of this turbulent priest, and
the keys to the kingdom are yours."*

*

*Increasingly anxious, McCreevey is now talking to the
third prostitute in a row.*

"Do any of you girls know Roxy?" he pleads.

*"Why, love?" the hooker responds. "There's
nothing she can do that I can't."*

*"Look, I need to find Roxy," McCreevey persists.
He is starting to get angry, and the hooker sees this.*

"Why?" she taunts. "Are you her new pimp?"

McCreevey is both angry and exasperated now.

"Look, forget it," he says and angrily walks away.

*A second prostitute walks up to the girl as
McCreevey storms off. He hears her before he turns the
corner, out of earshot.*

*"' Ere, he don't look like a pimp," the second girl
says. "He looks more like a copper."*

"Same fucking thing," the first girl says.

No sooner has McCreevey turned the corner, down Caledonian Road, than two car headlamps come on behind him. On full beam, they resemble the menacing eyes of some metal machine beast. The roar of an engine follows, like the bellow of a Minotaur, and then the Ford Granada accelerates and screeches to a halt in front of McCreevey.

This time the whole of Ridgeway's posse gets out, led by the man himself. There is an unpleasantly triumphalist grin on Ridgeway's face as he flashes his warrant card.

"You're under arrest, McCreevey," he gloats,

"On what charge," McCreevey demands.

An already bloodied knuckle duster strikes McCreevey unconscious, and he goes down.

"With being a cunt," Ridgeway says.

*

In a yellow rubbish skip, somewhere in North East London, Roxanne Parry lies dead, surrounded by the rotting garbage and rats. To all outward appearance, the Yorkshire Ripper has extended his safari south, and this will be the line of investigation pursued by the Metropolitan Police until the incident is kicked into the long grass and forgotten.

A dirty crow stands sentinel and croaks as if it were indeed poised to convey her revenant soul to the underworld.

The fluttering crime scene tape will come later.

And the litany of murders won't end there.

After McCreevey's disappearance and the collapse of Operation Countryman, *the biggest bullion robbery in British history at Heathrow Airport will lead to the murder of a police detective by one of Ridgeway's logged and most trusted informants in the South London underworld. He will be exonerated of the crime. There will then follow the abduction and murder of an eight-year-old Asian Boy on the day of the Royal Wedding in 1981 and later found squalidly buried in marshland on a farm near the Hampshire-West Sussex border. Ridgeway and his team will not be responsible for the murder but will cover it up at the behest of their new masters and betters, who have completely bought their souls.*

The Lambeth Police, case hardened by the riots of 1982 and the Scarman Report and Police and Criminal Evidence Act that follows, will be in on the act by now, linked to corrupt social workers at the South Vale Care Home in West Norwood, operating much as in accordance with Llewellyn's template in North Wales. There will even be a torture chamber for creating snuff videos in a Lambeth nick. This will, in turn, lead to the murder of a South London private detective working for The Sun and to the subsequent undermining of a BBC Crimewatch investigation into the detective's death.

And then, as Ridgeway and his team count the months to their lucrative retirement on the Costa del Crook, one of the Crown's killers linked to this conspiracy will completely leave the reservation during the miners' strike and start killing O'Leary's tarts. And this killer, Azazel, cast from heaven into the infernal pit, is in possession of very dangerous information that, should it come out, could bring down the corrupt edifice of government and cause the very revolution that a self-serving Liam O'Leary simply rants about.

Chapter Eighteen

House of Fun, 1979.

An evil cackling fills McCreevey's ears, like those of demons or harpies, as he is dragged down the filthy recesses of a Victorian police station towards the foul reeking cells. The corridor is dark, and the tiles provide the appearance of a public toilet as McCreevey is dragged to jeers of his former fellow officers down the vortex, and S bends to his dire fate into the ninth circle of Dante's Hell, where Judas labours under the weight of his own hanged corpse forever.

In the cell itself, Ridgeway chain-smokes as he paces like a caged animal, while one of his confederates fumbles with a Toshiba cassette recorder and another holds a plastic bag.

McCreevey is forced to sit on a stool under a naked bulb and handcuffed accordingly.

The colour and texture of the pale yellow light are that of human urine.

Absurdly, McCreevey sees a rank of mechanical flowers lined against the wall.

Eventually, through the pall of nicotine smoke like sulphur, Ridgeway addresses him.

"You know what this is, McCreevey," he asks. "Never mind Orwell's Room 101 this is the torture room at Lambeth Nick, where we brought the jungle bunnies after the riots. This is the snuff room, mate: the House of Fun. This is the worst place in the world."

McCreevey nods to the subordinate with the Toshiba cassette recorder, who stands next to a rank of mechanical flowers. The subordinate depresses the recorder's start *button, and the carnival music starts immediately.*

Madness: The House of Fun!

The mechanical flowers dance along to the tune. And as they do so, the detective with the plastic bag places it roughly over McCreevey's head. McCreevey is now starved of oxygen and breath, and with the plastic bag clouding over with condensation. He jerks both violently and spasmodically to the good time soundtrack as if in some pornographic joke.

"Listen, McCreevey, you fucking Judas," Ridgeway bellows. *"The only decent grass is the grass that grasses to us, right? And now you're going to tell us everything you know about that care home in North Wales, and if you've written* anything *down, I want to know where it fucking well is!"*

Welcome to the House of Fun!

Welcome to...

*

......The Lion's Den!

And in such a den as this, it has come to pass, following the serpent's kiss in the Garden of Gethsemane, that Judas has arrived at the banks of a latter-day Styx, in the circle of suicides and traitors.

In lieu of Virgil, or the ferryman, or the demons that devour souls, there are McCreevey's own demon tormentors in the back of the rattling Ford Transit Van as it passes the signs for the London Dockland Development Corporation *that proclaim all hope lost for those who enter here and for generations to come. Beyond the burning watchtowers and sarcophagi, and with the dark waters of the Thames as Styx beyond, the false temples to finance and social cleansing are already being erected, behind stout mesh fences and coils of barbed razor wire, here on the buried broken bones and shattered pillars of Magick Albion, down in the depths where The Beast is finally stirring here in Hell and in the infernal pit itself.*

All hail to the Iron Bitch that serves the Beast and its profane Goata, which is the dark book of market forces.

Za-za-na-Satan!

Brick walls wear graffiti, like cheap and jaded prison tattoos on rotting flesh, as of some long dead and entombed giant that proclaims Class War *and* Kill the Rich *and* Turn Back or Die! *It is the defiance of a vanquished tribe in the face of Empire, and McCreevey's demonic tormentors, sworn to protect and serve, know this as they protect and serve the apostates of the waking Beast.*

Za-za-na-Satan!

The Transit van swerves a corner with a screech of tyres and turns its full beam headlamps upon a huddled group of homeless, warming their numbed hands at a burning brazier. To the homeless, with their stoned and terrified faces frozen in the cold beams of light, those approaching headlamps are like the eyes of some mechanical beast from a James Bond movie about Doctor No. *Feral and outcast, these Lost Children of Albion scatter as the van bursts through their flaming brazier and chases them for sport.*

Za-za-na-Satan!

In this land without citizens, where there are only those with money and their prey, we are all of us Albion's Lost Children now.

Za-za-na-Satan!

Even Orwell did not predict a nightmare future such as this.

Za-za-na-Satan!

The Ford Transit van draws to a halt, three sixes in a row, and the feral scattered homeless like ladybird's children have all now gone.

The door of the van swings open like that of a metal tomb, and the killer cops, who are the gaggling servants of The Beast, drag McCreevey out. Ridgeway, as head of their coven, emerges more slowly and scans the dead ground and rubble for signs of hostile activity and more prey to be sacrificed to the Beast.

Behind a ruined wall, a human feral with matted dreadlocks cowers, too terrified to act or move, like a rabbit on a sacrificial road, in a post-apocalyptic future where machines have taken over the world.

The policemen laugh and jeer.

"Come on, McCreevey, you'll fucking-well love this one, son!"

All Hail to the Beast.

McCreevey is handcuffed to a supermarket trolley like a sacrifice and is doused with lighter fuel like profaned Holy Water in the Temple of the Damned.

"Here's some Holy Water, you Papist cunt! You're about to come home to a real fire, mate!"

McCreevey's head is swollen and bloated, and when Ridgeway appears, half in shadow, to the detective's blurred vision, he really does look like the Angel of Death.

"Look at you, McCreevey!" *Ridgeway proclaims as if he is O'Brien in Orwell's dystopian fable.* "You're pathetic. You side with the rubbish, the runaway kids from broken homes, the trade unions and the fucking coons. You're everything that's wrong with this country since 1945. Us, we're the Romans in Britain, mate. And we're the fucking future!"

Ridgeway ignites his lighter like a heavy metal fan.

"Maggie Thatcher!" *he toasts.*

"Maggie Thatcher!" *cry the Greek Chorus of Flying Squad officers in response.*

Ridgeway throws the lighter onto McCreevey's prone and shackled body and watches him erupt, screaming, into flame, like something from the closing scenes of The Wicker Man. *For an instant, bathed in the space cadet glow of the flames and with its honey-pork stink of petroleum, even the sadistic faces of the execution squad seem subdued as if in awe of the terrible future that this rite will usher into existence.*

Hail Thatcher – za-za-na Satan!

All Hail the Beast- za-za-na Satan!

Spirit of the First Astral Plane – Lord of the Flies Favour Me Now!

Zaz-zaz-na-Satan!

Ridgeway kicks the supermarket trolley, and its flaming, screaming human cargo towards the Thames like a fiery angel, cast from heaven into the infernal pit.

It reaches the edge of the dock and is then propelled further into the dark and salty waters that consume the fiery meteor in a cloud of steam, like Jonah into the Jaws of Leviathan.

Bubbles burst through the dark and sluggish waters.

Then fewer bubbles…

And then nothing!

Gone!

Ridgeway stares in silence for an instant as if in contemplation of the airport bullion robbery and how he will work with his number one grass within the South London Underworld to pull it off. At the same time, part of his fractured mind can't help but wonder what they have let themselves in for, through this rite of sacrifice, on behalf of McLeod and of Moloch's sacrifice of children.

And so it is in silence, rather than reverie, that the assembled coven of murderous cops returns to the Transit Van.

And then they are gone, like hungry ghosts into the banshee wails and sirens of the night.

*

Dusk in 1985.

The town was like a cemetery or morgue that was dominated by the steel wheel of the pit head and its all-seeing Masonic Eye.

And in the morgue itself, Terry Vaughan stood in mute attendance alongside the black woman WPC as Susan Higgins lay lifeless on the cold stone slab, her face shattered as by an Egyptian Meshtyw to unleash her revenant soul to the underworld.

An ice pick, the coroner confirmed, rather than a blunt instrument, but still in a parody of a sex act.

On the opposing side of the mortuary slab, Mrs Higgins continued to heave and sob as if her own red face was also a wound, producing bitter tears in place of blood, just as the wounded orifice of Susan's face had cried a river of blood as in a dirge for all humanity.

Who would do such a thing beyond an apostate or understudy of Satan himself?

At Mrs Higgins' side, her miner husband put his arm around his wife, but there was already a barrier of grief between them. It was as if they had been reduced to strangers by the death of their only daughter.

Terry swallowed uncomfortably. Even at the best of times, and this was hardly that, intrusion on grief was the worst part of the job.

"I had two minds whether to put you through this, Mrs Higgins," he said contritely.

"No," Mrs Higgins replied and shook her head. "We had to identify her together."

Still, the barrier was between the Higgins', like a conversation in a play by Harold Pinter.

Terry waited a few seconds more before nodding to the attendant in the white coat to cover the body once more. Soon she would be in one of those drawers in the wall, Terry thought, archived like some artefact rather than a human being.

The husband fumbled clumsily with his wife's hand and kissed her head, but it was to Terry that she now looked and stared with puffy red eyes, like a night creature from a cheap 1980s horror video.

Somehow, something about those hard eyes unsettled Terry as the woman stared into his own soul like an oracle of antiquity through diamond-hard tears.

"Mr Vaughan," she implored in a voice as cold as a medium in a séance. "You will find him, won't you — the man who murdered our Susan?"

Terry tried to look compassionate, if uncomfortable, but it felt like the ghost of Judas himself was trampling on Terry's grave.

"Mrs Higgins, I'll do everything in my power," he began.

She touched him, imploringly, with fat chubby hands like those of a child.

"Yes, but you'll promise," she persisted.

143

Terry swallowed hard and then nodded solemnly.

"Mrs Higgins," he said. "I promise I'll nail the bastard whatever it takes."

So there it was, the pledge, and the Devil would take his soul if he didn't deliver.

The black WPC looked at him, slightly concerned.

Mrs Higgins smiled bravely at his reassurance as her husband led her away, and in that instant, Terry wondered if they *knew* their daughter was pregnant and by whom.

As if reading Terry's mind, Mr Higgins turned and faced him.

"She wasn't a slapper, Mr Vaughan," he said. "She was a good girl, whatever they say."

A further chill passed through Terry as the couple left the room. As if by instinct, Terry produced the crumpled flier he had taken from Susan's room and looked at it.

Liam O'Leary, General Secretary of the Revolutionary Workers League, was to address a public meeting in this one-horse town shortly.

Terry looked at the PC.

"What the hell did he mean by that?" he asked.

*

In the Shropshire Cottage, near the frozen wave of rock that is the Black Mountains, Azazel performs his alchemy with photographic emulsions as the words of the black mass reverberates inside his head.

Zaz-zaz-na-Satan!

GOETIA: the Dark Book of Solomon, as recited by Crowley in the bowels of the Great Pyramid of Giza and chanted over days.

On Azazel's bookshelf, still, are the books on fascism and cabalistic and runic Magick, the true faith that lesser mortals call Devil worship or witchcraft.

And on the wall before him, like a mirror to his own fragmented soul, the picture of the nine, cast from Heaven into Hell.

In the tray of solution, the image in the photograph forms — it shows Detective Sergeant Terry Vaughan and his wife, as heavily pregnant as Sharon Tate, coming out of a supermarket, putting coins into the bucket of a miners' strike support group.

Communist bastards!

Azazel ponders this and the level of psychic energy to be unleashed by butchering a pregnant woman in this way. What it would do to Terry Vaughan and how formidable an opponent he may or may not become when the hunter became the hunted?

Time would tell.

PART THREE: THE BIBLE OF HELL

Chapter Nineteen

After they got one up on the filth the day before, what with that blazing TNT truck at the other pit head, Johnny Vaughan knew that there would be bad trouble this morning, like a bad day at black rock.

His Dad was a big Spencer Tracy fan, after all.

And as the bastard PSU cops gathered like an army of Black Death, with their bastard riot gear and bastard white collars, their ugly bastard faces, a part of Johnny already wondered where in fuck Zack the Hack was that bleak and cold morning, as they gathered to charge into the valley of the shadow of death?

You couldn't just light the fuse and walk away, after all.

Could you?

The first bus of the morning lumbered into sight, and it was an Astons of Worcester scab wagon as usual. Already, the cops were in position with their snatch squads at the ready, but the pickets, boosted by the previous day's victory, were up for a ruck and lurched forward, yelling war cries, like Owen's damned youth of the Somme.

"Scab! Scab! Scab!"

Johnny joined the chorus as he was sucked into the vortex of struggling and writhing bodies. Suddenly, and for some bizarre reason, his attention focused on a striking miner in a party policeman's helmet, who was bobbing forward towards the front of the crowd like a cork swept into a writhing vortex of violent humanity.

The chorus continued.

"Scab! Scab! Scab!"

Johnny joined in even as he was elbowed in the face and the raging sea of humanity became a storm.

By now, the pickets were banging on the metal walls of the Astons of Worcester scab wagon like angry Zulus in their Kraal.

The next that Johnny knew, he was slammed against the wall of that self-same bus, with a writhing mass of struggling humanity pressing like a wind of hate at his back. The bus continued to crawl forward, and the frightened scabs inside seemed to look down on Johnny in moral terror. Some of them he recognised from school, but they were class traitors, and scum, and his sworn enemy now. The cops, always up for some recreational violence and especially after the previous day, were also in the melee, swinging truncheons and fists, and a singularly ugly specimen of the species grabbed Johnny by the collar.

Luckily, Johnny was yanked back out of the copper's clutches, and a wave of fighting humanity closed the gap like the closing of the Red Sea. Beyond the violent flailing of arms and fists and truncheons, Johnny saw once again the striking miner in the party policeman's hat dragged by cops in *real* helmets, like tits on their heads, towards the police riot vans with their meshed up windscreens and "Paddy pushers" on the front.

The bloke in the party hat was being thrown into the back of the van for a kicking.

"Bastards!" Johnny screamed. "You fucking pig scum!"

The scab wagon was through the gate now.

In the back of the riot van, three cops with concealed serial numbers were industriously beating the guy in the party hat to a pulp.

Like the Party said, policing with consent was dead and British democracy with it.

The revolution was the only answer.

But for the guy in the back of the van, the Party was over.

*

All but broken and still in his clothes, Derek had clutched hold of Tracey's photograph all night, like a security blanket, surrounded by the detritus of where he had smashed up his own flat the night before. His expression was that of a frightened child, his mirror cracked as in a poem by Tennyson and the scattered books, and broken belongings in the room looked like the ransacked contents of a broken mind.

In one act of defiant blasphemy, he had struck the complete works of Lenin to the floor, followed by *The Transitional Program, The Revolution Betrayed, The Permanent Revolution* and *The Stalinist School of Falsification.* There had followed *The First Five Years of the Communist International* and *In Defence of Marxism,* all by Leon Davidyovitch Trotsky himself.

To Derek, these had been sacred texts, together with those of Marx and Engels, up until now. In their place, or so it seemed, was a gaping black hole of anger, as if he had torn away a veil of lies to find nothing beyond.

A poster for the Revolutionary Workers League, complete with a hammer and a number four, was torn to shreds, like the Fourth International itself in 1953.

Derek rapidly galvanized into action, launching from his lonely pit of a double bed and looking less like Judas now as he stripped off his clothes. He strode naked, and with purpose, to the bathroom and showered, almost ritually, allowing the water to open his pores, to wash away the foul crap that was in the London air, like a snake shedding its skin and revealing the glistening new stuff beneath.

Staring into another mirror in the bathroom, this one not broken, his self-doubt seemed to finally give rise to a whole new identity and purpose.

Fuck Liam O'Leary and his fucking Party!

And fuck keeping his mouth shut like Orla O'Regan had said as if he owed the *Sun* journalist anything at all.

Not when that vile geriatric was shoving his cheesy false prophet's cock inside of Derek's little girl.

Derek dressed and pulled on his uniform pea coat which still had the Leon Trotsky badge and that in support of the miners, only now they glinted like the star of some wild west Sheriff for whom Brixton had suddenly become Tombstone. Derek opened a drawer and pulled out both an iron bar and a set of brass knuckles, pocketing both like six guns, and headed for the door as if he were Doc Holiday on a one-way mission to the OK Corral.

Condemned man that he was, he would eat heartily enough in the greasy spoon café before having it out with O'Leary in the Party Centre.

To be or not to be—a Judas!

To act or not to act!

Derek's Hamlet had made his choice.

*

From Ridgeway's office, DS Dermot Brady of Special Branch watched Terry Vaughan arrive in his Ford Sierra. He waited until the young Welsh detective got out and continued to stare as he slammed and locked the door.

It was at that moment that Terry looked up and that his eyes met and locked on those of Brady, in the High Tower, the king of the castle, or so he believed. Neither man had met before; of course, with his background, Terry would never have been chosen for political work, but at that moment, a frisson of knowing portent passed between them.

And it was hostile – Brady could feel it. He and Vaughan were going to be sworn enemies, and make no mistake.

Terry walked towards the entrance of the police station.

"So that's your boy wonder," Brady said with contempt. "A wet behind the ears sheep shagger from the Valleys who's never led a major crime investigation in his life."

"Which makes him perfect for our needs," Ridgeway said.

"When do you think he'll start growing pubic hair?" Brady sneered.

"He's got a sprog on the way," Ridgeway informed him.

"Probably the milkman's," Brady retorted.

He turned and faced Ridgeway, almost accusing.

"You sure this is a good idea?" Brady asked.

"Absolutely," the DCI said. "Vaughan fucks up as a leading investigative officer and takes the rap when we fail to get a result. Meanwhile, we track down Azazel our way, the way you and I always have, then slot the fucker and recover those photos and any other incriminating shit he's got to hand."

Ridgeway sneered.

"I'll give him angel of fucking revelation," he said, but there was uncertainty in his voice for all of that. Last night he'd dreamed of killing McCreevey in docklands for the first time in years.

Brady indicated that they should join the Murder Investigation Team, which was gathering in the open-plan office on the second floor of the building, and Ridgeway followed. Although he greatly outranked Brady on the job, he didn't outrank him in the craft. More to the point, Brady was linked to the Home Office source that had buried the evidence of Operation Countryman that Ridgeway and his Flying Squad team were at it during the 1970s.

Brady opened the door just as Terry was briefing the black WPC, still in civilian clothes. Seeing a woman in the room, and a spade to boot, made Brady sneer in a sexually predatory fashion.

"What's she for?" Brady demanded of Ridgeway. "Making the tea or the office bike?"

"Another of Terry Vaughan's bright ideas," Ridgeway said. "Apparently, she was with him when he visited Susan Higgins' parents, and she's 'good with people,' whatever the fuck that means."

Brady laughed.

"Sounds like Hendon Bright Boy bullshit to me," he said. "You said he has a couple of A levels. Ask me he's giving her one."

"You know I doubt it," Ridgeway said. "Strangely, Vaughan's one of those blokes who's really into his missus."

An unpleasant expression formed on Brady's face.

"Is he now," he said. "I'll remember that."

Heavy cigarette smoke hung over the police incident room as the detectives, who were mostly white and male, assembled and organised themselves. There were crime scene photos pinned to a board and an overhead projector. Ridgeway studied Brady as Brady joined Terry at the front, and he saw Brady shoot the younger man a hostile glance. He himself followed up more slowly.

"All right, boys and girls," he said. "Your attention here at the Round Window, please."

The assembled team of detectives fell silent like kids at a school assembly. Indeed, to Ridgeway, that was exactly what they were.

154

Sheep shaggers and bits of fucking kids!

"Now, as you're aware," Ridgeway continued. "Thanks to Arthur Scargill and the Communist scum of the NUM holding the country to bleedin' ransom, we're a bit short-staffed at the moment."

A wave of laughter passed through the room, but Terry, the miner's son, didn't join in, Brady noticed, and neither did the black WPC. Brady lit a cigarette and exhaled truculently before continuing to stare in a hostile fashion at Terry.

Ridgeway slapped Terry on the shoulder.

"Which is why young Terry Vaughan, here, with his A levels and his Hendon Fast Track Bright Boy Bollocks, is to be your leading investigative officer. Now, I apologise in advance for this.... "

Laughter again spread through the room.

"And commensurate with this responsible role," Ridgeway continued. "Terry is also promoted to Acting Detective Inspector with immediate notice."

Now it was applause that filled the room, and Ridgeway grinned at Terry like an assassin. Eventually, the applause died down.

"Now, this investigation is Terry's shout," Ridgeway continued. "So I expect you all to do as he says and give him all the support he needs to catch this bastard! But before handing over to your new guvnor, here, I'd like to introduce you to Sergeant Dermott Brady from Special Branch."

Terry looked slightly taken aback as Brady was brought forward and once more clocked his hostile expression and demeanour.

"Sergeant Brady will be joining the investigation as Terry's co-pilot," Ridgeway said. "This is due to the likely political dimension of this murder. Now, the girl was a Trot and was an activist in support of the strike. She was also from a striking miners' family. But that doesn't mean we afford any less importance to this investigation. The last thing we need is the kind of bad press the Old Bill got during the Yorkshire Ripper caper, is that understood?"

There were murmurs of approval, but Terry looked slightly angry as Brady moved to the fore to address the group. He held up a copy of *The Sun*, with a lurid headline and Orla O'Regan's bi-line attached to it. The detectives continued to smoke as Brady lectured them.

"Azazel," Brady said, referring to the theory in Orla's article. "First of the nine angels cast out following Satan's insurrection in heaven. The press love all this bollocks, don't they? Better than the telly. No, I've never read Milton's *Paradise Lost*, and I know fuck all about religion, but I'll tell you something. I've seen this kind of imagery before."

The blinds drawn, Brady operated the overhead projector. Images from the anti-fascist magazine, *Searchlight* depicted paramilitaries surrounded by runic and occult symbols. All gave Nazi salutes.

"Since the 1960s, a succession of neo-Nazi paramilitary groups have used occult and Satanic references from *The White Wolves* in Leeds to *Column 88* only five or six years ago," Brady said.

A photograph now showed Colin Jackboot Jordan and fellow Nazi John Tyndale looking equally absurd in brown-shirted uniforms and short trousers.

"The latter began as the colour guard to this Muppet," Brady said. "This is Colin Jackboot Jordan, leader of the British Movement. Now, Jordan was nicked a few years back for stealing women's underwear from Marks and Spencer's."

There was more laughter from the assembled cops.

"Apparently..."

Brady waited for the laughter to die down.

"Apparently," he continued. "He's into all this occult shit, too, but actually, we at Branch think this Azazel tag is more of a *Name de Guerre*, if you get my drift? They've used it before when they've claimed responsibility for stuff."

Another image appeared on the projected screen.

"Such as the attempted bombing of the RWL headquarters in Brixton," Brady continued. "This cunt blew himself up, by the way, so we know our murderer isn't him."

There was more laughter. Brady clicked another slide.

Now, an image of Amerik Fraser appeared on the screen with his long dreads. There was a newspaper reference to his murder, too.

"The murder of Americk Fraser, a black social worker also in Lambeth," Brady said.

Next up was a Jewish cemetery desecration complete with aerosol swastikas.

"This Jewish Cemetery desecration in Cardiff which is getting nearer," Brady continued.

A further click produced the Ku Klux Klan article by Orla O'Regan in *The Sun*, complete with its photo-choreographed cross burning in the Rhondda Valley.

Brady was warming to his subject now.

"And just in case you think these people aren't in South Wales, take a look at that," he said. "Now, there's an outfit called the National Front Political Soldiers that's a bit more intellectual than the BM. They infiltrated the *Stop the City* protests against the London Docklands Development Corporation, and we think they've been turning up on the miners' picket lines causing trouble, as well."

The next slide showed a group of third position fascists selling *National Front News* near the Market House on stilts in Ross-on-Wye, Herefordshire. The *National Front News* headline said: *National Front Supports Welsh Bombers.*"

"They've units in Wales and have most recently seen action burning Welsh holiday homes in the name of *Meibion Glyndŵr,*" Brady continued. "Want my money? They're our culprits, what with all this Roberto Fiori shit about getting their hands dirty and going where the terror is. Luckily, we've a network of informants, including some BNP tossers who like a quiet life, and we'll be pulling in anyone with form to see what shakes out of their pockets."

Brady looked toward Terry in a smug and superior way.

"Anything to add, boss?" he asked.

Terry raised an eyebrow.

"Well," he said. "Thank you, Sergeant, for an informative Cook's Tour of the Far Right, but may I remind everybody that we explore *all* avenues of investigation in a major crime inquiry. For example, the girl was pregnant, and I doubt it was by a member of the group's Sergeant Brady just mentioned."

There was more laughter.

"We need to know who the father is because the parents sure as hell don't," Terry continued. "Also, if Sergeant Brady's fascist groups are responsible, *as they might well be,* why have they not claimed responsibility?"

"Do you have an alternative theory, boss?" a detective asked.

"Quite possibly," said Terry, drawing hostile glances from Brady and Ridgeway as he did so. "For a start, I think this occult iconography is too elaborate simply to be a *Name de Guerre.* My reading is that the bastard actually believes in this shit and that, consequently, he regards himself as a superior being in some way. He also regards himself as an artist, which some may say is the same thing. The girl was placed at the centre of what was clearly meant to be some kind of art installation, but the killer was disturbed."

Like Jack the Ripper in Mitre Square, Terry thought as he cast Brady a glance.

"Artists aren't team players, Sergeant Brady," Terry said. "And with all these references to *The Book of Enoch* and *Paradise Lost,* I don't see him mixing with bone heads, with their brains in their hair, or burning crosses in fancy dress for *The News of the Screws.*"

"Anything else," Ridgeway asked, and there was a sarcastic edge to his voice that Terry didn't much care for.

"Yes," said Terry, still thinking about Jack the Ripper. "The organised nature of the crime scene suggests that we're looking at a serial killer who will strike again."

There were gasps.

"So that's what we're looking for, is it?" Brady sneered. "Satan's Right Hand Man?"

"No," said Terry. "But we might be looking for someone who thinks he is. And we also need to remember something. Angels, good or bad, are messengers, and this bastard's trying to tell us something. Work out what it is, and mark my words, we'll have our man."

Terry slapped his hands together and exuded a level of competence and efficiency that neither Brady nor Ridgeway seemed to care much for.

"Right," Terry said. "You all know what you've got to do. Any news on the forensics?"

"Should have the reports in a couple of days, Skip," the black WPC said. "Err, sorry, Guv."

Terry nodded in a self-satisfied way as the rest of the Murder Investigation Team sprang into action.

Brady and Ridgeway looked at each other.

"Everyone else knows what they're doing?" Terry asked. "Splendid, that's what we need: teamwork. Police investigations are ninety per cent boring bloody procedure and ten per cent inspiration. Remember that."

Brady slapped him on the shoulder and whispered in his ear.

"At least if this Azazel keeps this up, we'll have a few less lefties to worry about," he said.

Terry looked after the Special Branch officer with disgust.

"Terry," Ridgeway called over and indicated his office with his eyes. "Can I have a word in your shell-like, in private?"

Terry followed his superior into his office.

Brady's stare followed him, full of hate until he closed the door.

Chapter Twenty

Ridgeway slapped a copy of the morning's *Sun* on his desk. Reading the tabloid upside down, Terry clocked an "exclusive" story by Orla O'Regan and a "local correspondent," whom he immediately realised was Clever Trevor. The article was accompanied by a reproduction of the picture in which Azazel and the rest of the nine angels were cast from heaven.

"Some good points out there, Terry," Ridgeway said. "Only they're very similar to what's argued in this article, if you get my drift?"

"I'm afraid I don't, guv?" Terry replied, looking genuinely puzzled.

Now it was Ridgeway's turn to look quizzical. He stabbed the article with his finger as if to make a point.

"Don't you?" Ridgeway asked. "Well, let me explain. The bi-line for this article is by Orla O'Regan and 'a local correspondent,' which is in house media jargon for a local reporter, here, on another rag, who's phoned the story in. Like your mate, Clever Trevor on the Rhondda Daily Bullshit, for example?"

"Firstly," said Terry. "Trevor's not my mate—far from it, in fact. And he *was* at the crime scene, having himself been sent a communiqué by Azazel. We *did* take a statement from him, here at the station, to that effect."

"Yes," said Ridgeway. "And you were seen at the crime scene talking to Clever Bloody Trevor for a long time. We have channels for communication with the press in this station, *Acting* Detective Inspector Vaughan, through the Press Officer, who happens to be Inspector Pratt. We don't cosy up to the press and exchange information."

"I didn't," Terry swallowed.

"Good," said Ridgeway. "Because if you did, you'd be off this case, and you could kiss goodbye to your current *acting* position becoming permanent."

"I know that, Guv," Terry said. "I actually told Trevor that if he wanted any information, he was to talk to Inspector Pratt."

"Good," Ridgeway nodded. "That's the way we want it. And make sure you work closely with Sergeant Brady. He might not be to your personal taste, Terry, but he's a good copper with a lot of experience. He nailed the Birmingham Six, for fuck's sake!"

"Yes, Guv," said Terry, with little enthusiasm.

Ridgeway nodded but continued to look stern and serious.

"Good," he said. "Then we understand each other. Now get to it."

Terry left, both dismissed and uncomfortable and feeling slightly as if he'd just had his arse spanked. Ridgeway stared after him as he did so.

*

Still wearing his de facto Sheriff's badge, Derek looked a lot less like Judas as he stared into the black void of the underground railway tunnel, now on the Northern Line to Brixton. The numbers of commuters had thinned out as he headed south of the river, and the carriage was all but empty as it rattled on subterranean points, down here where the Beast was stirring in the bowels of this ancient city.

As Derek stared in white fury, pale as his balled fists, even the sound of the train seemed to mock him as it approached its destination.

O'Leary fucked Tracey, O Leary fucked Tracey, O Leary fucked Tracey.

Plus Susan Higgins, who had been pregnant by the dirty old predatory demagogue and who was now conveniently dead.

Just like Americk.

Derek had spent the night chasing Orla O'Regan's words like mice in his head, and having torn away the veil of lies, like the layered skin of an onion, he knew now that they were true. In truth, he'd always known it, with that part of his brain that had always loathed and detested O'Leary, that was not in denial as to the self-serving nature of his cult and didn't think that two plus two equals five.

But Orla didn't own him any more than O'Leary did, not anymore, and in defiance of the *Sun* journalist, the Ronan Samurai had it out with his former master once and for all.

Because Derek, like Hamlet, would be: because Derek, like Hamlet, would act.

And as for O'Leary, he was going to pay dearly for fucking Derek's little girl.

*

If Hitler had his bunker in the Eagles Nest, then Liam O'Leary had the Party fortress in Beehive Place, at the end of a Brixton cul de sac between the "Front Line" of Electric Avenue and the Tube Station. Beehive Place itself was cobbled from Victorian times, and the cobbles looked like the scales of the Beast that slept but was now stirring beneath the city streets, and on those cobbles was parked O'Leary's polished black BMW, paid for with Libyan money and Party subs, the icon to his cult of personality and vanity, like a phoney Shintu God. As for the Party Headquarters itself, with its barred windows and weathered Victorian brick, its metal-reinforced door and barbed razor wire, it had already been a fortified edifice to O'Leary's paranoia before the inept bombing carried out by a member of Column 88 from Morden, Surrey. Now, that paranoia seemed justified, as it dripped from the unkempt walls, the bare boards of the wooden stairwell and the filthy toilet.

Outside, a CCTV camera monitored the approach to the steel-reinforced door with its all-seeing electronic eye.

Tom Upward, academic and party intellectual, felt this cold dark sway of paranoia as he sat in the stark and Spartan conference room where both Central Committee and Politburo meetings were held. A member of the Communist Party before World War II, who had served as a naval rating after university and went down on the HMS Hood, Tom remembered the atmosphere of paranoid denial that had permeated *that* Party's ranks shortly following his resignation in the aftermath of the Hungary Uprising in 1956. And more than anything else, he recalled EP Thompson's reservations that in signing up to O'Leary's particular version of Trotskyism, Tom had traded one totalitarian demagogue (in the form of Harry Pollitt) for another. Brendan Behan, likewise, had quickly denounced his fellow Irishman, O'Leary, as a gangster with a *Riffifi* Citroen, while Robin Blick would later compare the Revolutionary Workers League with a religious cult, such as that of Jim Jones in Guyana. And yet Tom remembered the charismatic O'Leary whom he had first met all those decades before, hand-picked by James P. Cannon himself, as Trotsky's successor, to sort out the crisis in the British section after the Fourth International tore itself apart in 1953. There were no intellectuals or theorists in Britain in those days, and O'Leary had welcomed belated defectors like Tom with open arms to do the theoretical work for which O'Leary later claimed credit.

Yet Tom also remembered, almost with affection, the tough and charismatic class fighter standing on an orange box, ranting at the East London Docks, organising Irish labourers during the MacAlpine's strike for union recognition in 1960 or attacking members of Moseley's Blackshirts with a dustbin lid. What was to become the biggest Trotskyist Party in Britain was then built, initially within the Labour Party's Labour League of Youth, by recruiting Mods and other youngsters through music events and even beauty contests, while the Brothers Grimm convinced O'Leary to defend and internalise, the grotesque excesses of Mao's Cultural Revolution in holding the Party rank and file in check. Things had got worse; Tom recalled when

O'Leary inexplicably pulled the League out of the Labour Party in 1974 and used evidence of the then military coup plot against Harold Wilson's government to establish his Security Directorate. With the League also withdrawn from the decisive struggle against fascism after Lewisham in 1977, however, it had become abundantly clear that the Brothers Grimm and the army of thugs over which they presided were less concerned with protecting the Party from external attack than with imposing a regime of terror on its internal ranks akin to Stalin's Great Purge of 1935.

With the Miner's Strike now a year old, this had gotten worse, with the *Daily Bullshit* newspaper, financed by Libyan money, relentlessly telling them that either a revolution or fascist coup was simply a blink away.

"I'm not listening to some miserable pettybourgeois!" O'Leary screamed down the phone line from an adjacent room. *"I've had it with this counter-revolutionary shit!"*

The phone was slammed into its cradle, forcing Tom to tremble and almost drop the copy of *Capital Volume II* by Karl Marx onto the floor.

There was movement in the next room, akin to that of sinister giants in a children's fable, and the next thing Tom knew, the Brothers Grimm were framed in the doorway, looking at him with menace.

Tom quickly hid his notebook, in which he was writing about the circulation of capital, and the likely impact of financial deregulation in the City of London, on the global economy now that the Beast had been summoned to life.

O'Leary shoved past them, ignoring everybody as he headed for the filthy toilet, with its piled copies of the *Daily Advance* stored in their rightful place. One thing the RWL didn't spend money on, Tom reflected, was the décor and hygiene of its headquarters, and he imagined the great man doing a line of speed in front of the rust speckled mirror as he almost certainly was.

The old man's goodies, as Zack the Hack called them.

"I do hope that's not the second volume of *Capital,*" one of the Grimm Brothers said, so alike and inclined to finish each other's sentences that Tom had long ceased to distinguish the one from the other. "Liam's laid strict instructions that certain texts can only be read when supervised in a Party setting. The Party is the memory of the class after all."

Tom tried to recall where, in Lenin's *What Is to Be Done,* it might have said that, and part of him wondered if democratic centralism was actually not one of the great man's better ideas after all. He then imagined O'Leary in the toilet downstairs, staring at his craven and divided image in a mirror of insanity, full of self-loathing like Jack Nicholson in a Stanley Kubrick movie, as the amphetamine bisulphate pumped through his bloodstream and roared in his ears.

"It's just an academic text," Tom apologised, a little too eagerly. "For a history module, I teach at the university."

"I don't know how you can stomach it, peddling Bourgeois Ideology in an institution like that", the Brother Grimm continued. "Not to mention Stalinist bastards like Ralph Milliband, your boss. Where possible, we get student comrades to abandon their studies and get a job where they can join a trade union. The theory and thinking are best left to the Party, right?"

"Of course, comrade," said Tom, both breezy and nervous.

It was then that O'Leary entered, further filling the room with the vile sourness of his being like some kind of Zen Hex. He didn't blink as he spoke.

"Sorry to drag you from your Ivory Tower," O'Leary said, in his hectoring Tipperary accent and with heavy sarcasm. "Only the revolution comes first as always."

The Brother Grimm, who had taunted Tom like a schoolyard bully, was staring at him now as if his dark eyes were laser beams penetrating Tom's daily mask to root out his doubt and fear. The image of a medieval Inquisitor or early modern Witch Finder General was complete. If the terror within the Party were a plague, then surely here were its hosts.

"We were just discussing that, weren't we, comrade?" the Witch Finder General said.

His brother sneered, continuing the line of conversation in stereo like a pair of cheap killers from a James Bond movie.

"There'll be fuck all time for thinking and reading when it comes to the revolution or the coup," the second Brother said. "One or other will come in months if not weeks, just as Liam's editorial in today's *Daily Advance* says."

Written with an eye to your financial benefactors in Tripoli, Tom thought, who actually believes this crap. Nobody in their right mind now thought that the miners could possibly win the strike, devastating as the consequences of their defeat would be, and there certainly wasn't going to be a revolution or need for the triumphant ruling class to back a coup.

"Which is why we need you to go back to Malta to pick up more money from the Libyans," O'Leary said. "We've cleared it with our friends in Tripoli."

Tom now looked confused, as well as worried, considering that he'd only recently returned from the island where Prime Minister Don Mintoff was a fervent supporter of the mad Colonel since closing his ports to NATO. Most of the hotels on the island, for an example, were Libyan owned, and Tom was a regular visitor given that customs were hardly likely to check a mild-looking academic in horn-rimmed glasses, scruffy clothes and a cloth cap for contraband shipments of contraband cash in the false bottom of his suitcase.

Each time Tom made this milk run, as he called it, he felt like a drug smuggler, and part of him even wondered if *that* were beyond the RWL's Security Directorate, either. What with finance being the sinews of struggle, as Lenin and later O'Leary said. Only Lenin had shut down the *Praktiki*, headed by Stalin when its criminal activities got out of hand, and there was a fat chance of that where O'Leary's hunger for cash was concerned. Youth members were told to steal from their parents for the revolution, of course, and here in Brixton, small-time drug dealers were beaten at gunpoint and robbed both of their money and drugs unless they paid "shop rent" to be left alone.

Just like the IRA.

"I've already been to Malta to collect money for the *Daily Advance*", Tom protested.

"Yes," said O'Leary. "But this is extra revenue for the *London Fightback*. We intend that our comrades in control of Lambeth Council be at the vanguard of the campaign to save the GLC. Besides, as Mike and Tony say, the revolution or coup is almost upon us."

"There'll be a slightly different arrangement this time," the Second Grimm Brother said. "Because of the particularly large amount of cash you'll be carrying, we're sending a member of the Security Directorate with you – to ride shotgun, so to speak."

"The Security Directorate," Tom echoed anxiously. "Who?"

"Zack Miller, the *Equity* rep," the first Brother Grimm said.

Tom swallowed and looked more miserable than ever. He truly detested the TV soap star and celebrity who wore his faux working-class credentials like a phoney flag. In fact, Tom knew that Zack came from a bourgeois background and had attended a private boarding school, and he actually reminded Tom of the bullying prefects from his own miserable youth.

Secretly, he referred to Zack the Hack as *Flashman.*

"*My cup runneth over,*" Tom muttered beneath his breath.

O'Leary looked at him, accusing.

"You have a problem with comrade Miller?" he demanded as he pointed a meaty finger in Tom's direction.

The O'Leary finger had long been an in house joke in the party's ranks and was a trait that had been adopted by all party cadres in their steely-eyed role as zealots and O'Leary clones.

"No, Comrade General Secretary," Tom said.

"Good," said O'Leary. "I'm glad to hear it. Comrade Miller sets a fine Bolshevik example for us all."

"It's just that I've always been trusted with the money in the past," Tom all but pleaded and was shocked at the whining servility in his own voice.

"Yes, well, these are revolutionary times," O'Leary said. "An excess of history, as comrade Trotsky would have said. During the October Revolution, the Tsarist *Ochrana* even had agents on the Bolshevik Party Central Committee. Nobody is above suspicion, comrade. You, as a historian, must appreciate that."

Tom reflected on his predicament and his fate with all the enthusiasm of a hanged man headed for the gallows.

Chapter Twenty-One

Derek grabbed a burger in the Wimpey Bar opposite Brixton tube station and then entered Beehive Place through a narrow tunnel of stained and weathered red brick as a Northern Line tube train thundered over his head on the way to Morden. It was three years after Swamp 82, the riots, and Lord Scarman's vain attempts to improve policing and community relations in this City, but the riot vans still cruised the streets like an army of occupation here in Lambeth, much as in his native North Wales. The cops seemed to eye Derek with suspicion, as did a knot of black youths hanging around near the tube station entrance.

The Front Line: Living on the Front Line.

Perhaps the riot season was closer than anyone thought.

Graffiti, in this self-proclaimed *New Azania*, same as in *Crisis 2000* comic, told him to *Turn Back or Die!*

Turning the corner that was no longer his corner into a cobbled Victorian cul de sac that was no longer his cul de sac, he felt as much like Wyatt Earp or Doc Holliday as any inexperienced ghost returning to the scene of O'Leary's nursery crime.

Confronting O'Leary's polished black BMW, like the Wild West gunslinger he had become, he almost caught a glimpse of his own ghostly persona sitting at the wheel of that trophy car like the loyal cadre and stranger he had once been. To Derek, now, the dark reflection on tinted glass was like a mirror reflection of his divided self. He produced the metal pipe from his pocket, as if this were indeed the OK Corral, and tooled it like a heavy Colt pistol

In his mind's eye, he saw Susan Higgins, his daughter's best friend, now dead and discarded like so much rubbish, argue with the self-styled leader of the world proletariat.

"Of course, I agree with abortion rights, but it's an issue of choice," Susan had said. *"And my choice is to keep my child."*

O'Leary's response had been predictably loathsome and vitriolic, but there was a razor's edge of fear in that hectoring Tipperary voice like that of the Detrimental Robot that O'Leary most resembled.

The O'Leary finger, like a naked weapon, was out.

"You pathetic little birch!" he had almost spat the words. *"If you were a real revolutionary, you would put the Party first!"*

The last time Derek saw Susan alive, he now realised she was striding away with anger on her face and diamond-hard bitter tears.

"For God's sake, what's the matter with you?" she had demanded.

177

Now Derek gripped the metal bar in white knuckle determination. His teeth bared, he muttered through hot and angry breath.

"Darkness at fucking noon!" he said.

Derek smashed the window of the BMW with his metal pipe. He then proceeded to smash all the other windows, in a loud shattering of glass, before starting on the headlamps, turning the polished car into a sightless monster. Derek then produced his switchblade and started on the tyres.

The all-seeing electronic eye was upon him, like a Dalek in a shopping mall, and there would be panicked movement inside the Party's fortress to paranoia, he knew.

O'Leary and his thugs would appear at any moment.

Because Derek, like Hamlet, would be!

Because Derek, like Hamlet, would act!

And having so acted, he knew his life and that of the Party would never be the same again.

*

O'Leary and the Brothers Grimm heard the commotion outside.

The shattering of glass that fell in shards, like a tableau around the deflowered car as False God — like Rimi's mirror image of shattered historical truth.

178

"What the fuck?" O'Leary demanded as he headed for the window.

Tom watched in disbelief and not a little fear as O'Leary stared out of the window then mildly wondered what other colours O'Leary's face could do. The Party HQ had been attacked by a fascist bomber once before, but somehow Tom didn't think this was what was happening now.

The academic felt a wave of relief as O'Leary, and his two goons headed towards the door.

One of the Brothers Grimm now pointed the O'Leary finger at Tom.

"Stay there!" he ordered and was gone.

Cautiously, Tom approached the window like a small child bearing witness to domestic violence. From his viewpoint, in his High Tower Eyrie, he saw Derek Hepburn, whom he recognised and had never particularly liked, industriously destroying O'Leary's car.

Hepburn was ripping away the windshield wipers as O'Leary and the Brothers closed in. The windscreen itself was cracked, and all the other windows were gaping wounds.

Tom could just about hear Derek Hepburn grunt, like a becoming-animal, as the three thugs closed in.

"Hepburn!" O'Leary screamed. "Have you lost your fucking mind?"

*

Derek, breathless and seating, swung round to face O'Leary and his two goons. His face was a mask of white fury, and still, he tooled the crowbar like a weapon.

"Nice ride, O'Leary," Derek said. "Was it Party subs paid for that heap of junk or more blood money from Libya?"

One of the Brothers Grimm made to step forward, and Derek pointed the crowbar in a threatening way.

"Stay there, you!" he warned.

The thug stopped dead in his tracks. Derek then turned his attention to O'Leary.

"You fucked my daughter, O'Leary," Derek said, like a character from a Jacobean tragedy. "And she isn't the only one. She's 19 years of age, you disgusting, smelly old cunt!"

Derek was yelling that loud now they could have heard him in Norwood or Bermondsey. Tom Upward, whom Derek now clocked at the upstairs window, certainly must have heard it all.

Then Derek lunged at O'Leary with the pipe.

"I'm going to fucking well kill you!" he declared.

At that point, Derek was intercepted by one of the Brothers Grimm. He tasted the man's foul breath as he was punched and kneed in the groin.

Through a wave of pain, he saw the crowbar fall and then clatter loudly on the cobbled scales of the stirring Beast.

From the upstairs window, like a man in the High Tower, Tom Upward watched the methodical beating that Derek now received.

Now the flick knife fell to the ground.

Derek, now heavily blooded, was shoved against the wall and punched in the guts. Derek's brass knuckles bounced on the ground. As O'Leary watched, revelling in the Spectacle, both of the brothers beat Derek to a pulp.

O'Leary licked his lips in enjoyment, then spoke.

"OK," he said. "That's enough!"

The two brothers obeyed like trained dogs. Derek was allowed to slide to the floor. Now, O'Leary pointed his characteristic finger at Derek as he ranted.

"MI5 infiltration," O'Leary almost spat the words, still in the persona of the Detrimental Robot from the science fiction yarn. "This is precisely what we're looking at here—a deliberate attempt by the state to undermine the revolution and the revolutionary party. This is precisely why we have to be vigilant!!

O'Leary leaned over Derek like a priest hearing the confessional of a dying man. When he whispered into Derek's ear, the bloodied former enforcer could taste the great fraud's foul stinking breath.

"I'll tell you something else about your daughter," O'Leary whispered. "She was a lousy shag!"

As O'Leary walked away, the two brothers moved to follow him.

One of them spoke to Derek as they did so.

"Hope your Party subs are up to date," he said. "We'll be around your yard to make sure."

From the upstairs window, like the man in the High Tower, Tom Upward stared at the scene in misery and disbelief.

Chapter Twenty-Two

October 1984.

Two years since the riots on Eddie Grant's Front Line

Two years since Operation Swamp82 and Scarman, and the number one Sun *affording yet another platform to Enoch Powell.*

Two years since Up Yours Galtieri *and the sinking of the Belgrano delivered the consolidation of Thatcher's soft coup, paid for in blood in the South Atlantic and with a near fascist orgy of patriotism at home.*

The birth of Iron Britannia and of a toxic relationship between the bitch herself and Rupert Murdoch, for whom Orla O'Regan still works, however precariously, in the Street of Shame.

Orla smokes in front of a copy of the paper for which she continues to slave in the alcove of a Brixton pub as Linton Kwese Johnson sings that Inglan is a Bitch *on the Wurlitzer jukebox. The record is Orla's selection, as are the two tins of Jamaican* Red Stripe *lager on the table in front of her and the soft pack of* Camel *cigarettes that she continues to smoke to the butt.*

Her date is late and hard eyes already study her with suspicion as she looks at her wristwatch.

On the front page in front of her, a photo montage compares Arthur Scargill to Adolf Hitler.

The headline reads: After the Battle for the Falklands, the Battle for Britain!

The doors of the pub swing open like something from the Wild West, and Americk Fraser steps nervously in. The black social worker recognises Orla and walks towards her to take a seat.

"I read your report," Orla says. "Pretty shocking, I have to say, the way that the Revolutionary Workers League treats its own comrades. But these are serious allegations you are making against the Council itself. How do I know this isn't just revenge against the RWL?"

Orla exhales and stares at Americk, hard, through a cloud of cigarette smoke like ectoplasm at a séance.

Americk pulls the ring on the tin of beer as if it were a grenade. Froth appears, and on the jukebox, as if by magic, Linton is replaced by The Specials *singing:* Doesn't Make it All Right.

"Miss O'Regan," Americk says. "The RWL Security Directorate didn't beat me up in my own yard and force my best friend to watch because I was at ANL Carnival 2 and Brick Lane. It's because I know what's going on in Lambeth, on the council's watch."

Orla offers Americk one of her soft pack Camels. *He accepts.*

"OK," she says. "So why would a revolutionary party that controls Lambeth Council and uses Libyan money to defend Ken Livingstone and the GLC cover up

a paedophile ring linking care homes in North Wales and Northern Ireland to a PR Firm in Pimlico and Westminster MPs. I mean, my God, Profumo was nothing compared to this. This isn't merely the kind of thing that brings down governments. In the present inflammatory situation, with the dock and rail workers coming out in support of the NUM and a very real prospect of a general strike, this is the kind of thing that causes the very revolution your crowd wants."

Orla sips her beer and stares at him.

"I'm listening, Americk," she says.

"Because their man at Lambeth Council, the Town Hall Lenin as your paper calls him, likes them young," Americk says. "The same as O'Leary himself. I mean, what do you think the RWL Security Directorate is for, apart from beating up Party Dissidents like me? It exists to procure young girls for Liam O'Leary to screw. O'Leary's man at Lambeth Town Hall has also been a guest at Elm House, Miss O'Regan. The Paedophile Information Exchange, you see, does not exist to feed the perversions of those around the Iron Bitch. They have Kincora in Northern Ireland and a network of care homes in North Wales for that. It exists to target their enemies."

Orla raises an eyebrow, and Americk can see that he has her attention now.

"And O'Leary?" she asks. "Has he ever been to Elm House?"

Americk shakes his head.

"I don't think so," he says. "O'Leary's sick but not that sick."

Americk leans forward.

"What I do know is this," he says. "Through Lambeth Council, which is close to Pimlico, and where the police torture cell and snuff studio is based, several Labour MPs have unwittingly signed up to the Campaign for Children's Rights. What they don't know, at least most of them, is that it's a front for the Paedophile Information Exchange. And this man's the key."

Americk passes Orla a photograph. It shows Thatcher and Dominic McLeod leaning out of the window the night of the 1979 general election and waving.

"Dominic McLeod," Americk says. "He was CEO of Eastgate PR in Dolphin Square, Pimlico, before the convenient death of Airey Neave in 1979. He's now Thatcher's Right Hand Man."

Orla looks up at him.

"That's one hell of an accusation, Amerik," she says.

"McLeod's been positively identified by one of the surviving boys now living in fear of his life in Hove near Brighton." *Americk continues.* "I've been in contact with this boy, and they know it. This is the real reason I was beaten, Miss O'Regan."

Orla looks stunned.

"You mention the convenient death of Airey Neave," Orla says.

"Neave was briefed about the Kincora Boys' Home in Northern Ireland before he was killed." *Americk continues.* "By an Army Information Officer later framed on manslaughter charges in Arundel, Sussex. The INLA claimed responsibility for the car bomb in Westminster itself, which was completely beyond their technical capabilities. McGlinchey's claim of responsibility to the BBC got the details completely wrong."

"And this eight-year-old Asian boy," Orla continues to test. "The one you say was murdered."

"Abducted by a known paedophile, now dead, the day of the Royal Wedding in 1981," Americk says. "Abused and murdered by Westminster MPs connected to Dolphin Square and Elm House. But the murder was covered up by officers of the Metropolitan Police at the behest of McLeod and the Home Secretary in person."

Orla's mind was racing. The Tory Conference was due to start the following week, and Orla herself was due to be there on October 12.

"This young boy in Brighton," she says. "Would he talk to me?"

"Stephen?" Americk asks. "He might, but he's pretty scared."

Orla nods. She looks again at the picture of Thatcher with McLeod.

"It's time we nailed these bastards," she says.

*

Brighton, October 1984.

Killers on the street and at large in the Grand Hotel.

A murderous cabal of a government was laying waste to the very nation, built on the bones of murdered

187

children, Orla tells herself as she watches the sea of hate roll in from the cursed Victorian pier.

The last time Orla was here was in 1980, or was it 1981, during the Right to Work March that inspired Paul Weller to write Eton Rifles. *Her vivid memory was of the cops lined on the pebble beach in front of the Grand Hotel to stop the marchers bricking in the windows during the Tory Party conference.*

"Give Us a Job!" *the leaflets had said, like something from a Jimmy McGovern drama on TV.* "Put Thatcher on the dole!"

Back then, despite the soft coup in 1979, nobody had thought this bastard government would last, Orla tells herself. But then the Falklands intervened, and the septic wound would no doubt infest the nation's psyche for generations, consolidating an evil regime founded on the abuse and murder of children now poised to abuse and murder the country as a whole.

The Beast is stirring. These are disturbing and violent times.

Orla's sombre mood does not improve as she walks from the iconic clock tower in Churchill Square down towards the Grand Hotel itself. Then, as the Victorian façade comes into view, she feels almost like a criminal, or ghost, returning to the scene of a crime.

"Maggie, Maggie, Maggie! Out! Out! Out!"

A small crowd of left-wing paper sellers, held back by the cops, are already calling for a General Strike *at the Hotel entrance as the creep-show of politicians arrives. Orla stares at the politicians with disdain and then heads towards a nearby public telephone booth that looks out to sea.*

Close to the booth, like something from a Troy Kennedy Martin drama, cryptic graffiti tells her that The Life of the Wolf is the Death of the Lamb.

Orla places her call.

"Hello? Is that Stephen?" she asks. "My name's Orla O'Regan; I'm a journalist. No please don't hang up. I'm a friend of Americk's...."

The voice at the end of the line sounds agitated and paranoid, and Orla realises he has every reason to be. She stares at the graffiti on the wall, worn like a dirty prison tattoo, and realises the truth in those words.

"Believe me, Stephen," Orla pleads as if trying to persuade herself. "The quicker this is in the public domain, the safer you'll be. Look, I'm stuck in the Tory Conference until early evening, but here's my pager number."

She imagines him writing it down in the hovel in which he and his friends are warehoused, like the forgotten victims of a nursery crime that they are. Next, looking up, she sees the press pack move as one, like hyenas on the veldt, when a polished and official black Daimler arrives at the entrance of the Hotel. The vehicle rides slowly on its shocks as if armour-plated, as indeed it is, and close protection officers in oversized jackets are already in position.

An all too familiar face emerges from the car, but it is the man who is with her who chills Orla to the bone. Derek McLeod, in all his wretched glory, waves at the reporters as he heads with the Iron Bitch towards the door, like the medieval kingmaker that he is.

Orla stares as she replaces the phone receiver in its cradle.

"Got you!" *she says.* "Got you, you pair of evil bastards!"

Margaret Thatcher and her paedophile in chief enter the doors of Brighton's Grand Hotel.

*

The pit head silent, like an all-seeing Masonic Eye, Terry clocked another group of activists from the Revolutionary Workers' League as he arrived at the town library in his Ford Sierra. They were fly-posting, which was technically illegal, for all that Terry had more pressing business to worry about, but he noticed the contents of the posters just the same. In fact, it was for the very same public meeting that had been organised to call for a General Strike, the leaflet for which Terry had found in Susan Higgins' drawer.

Was he going to attend?

You bet your life he was.

Terry got out of his car, locked it and walked into the library that he hadn't visited since college.

Inside it was quiet as a mausoleum as he moved to the English Literature section and lifted a copy of Milton's *Paradise Lost.* But what he really wanted to look up was the newspaper references to the extreme Right that Brady had been banging on about back at the Police Station.

The reference to Column 88 attacking the RWL headquarters in Brixton he got from the Nationals.

For the synagogue desecration in Cardiff, he checked out the *Western Daily Press*.

The Ku Klux Klan and cross burning in the Rhondda seemed to be an exclusive by Orla O'Regan in *The Sun*.

The regional paper from Cardiff also had a reference to fascist connections with the Welsh terrorist "wannabe" group, *Meibion Glyndŵr*. The same photograph that Brady had shown them had a group of National Front Political Soldiers at the Market House on stilts in the Herefordshire border town of Ross-on-Wye. Their copies of *National Front News* said: "National Front Supports Welsh Bombers."

Apparently, setting fire to holiday homes was what Roberto Fiori and Nick Griffin meant when they talked about "going where the terror was" and "the future" lying "with those prepared to get their hands dirty." It was pitiful bullshit. Terry stared at one individual dressed in a Palestinian *keffiyeh* and wondered who the fuck this idiot thought he was.

Nobody detested Nazis more than Terry, but something about all this just didn't square right with the murder they were investigating.

And why did Terry have a gnawing feeling in his gut that Brady knew this?

Terry had been making copious notes and became so engrossed that he'd lost all sense of time.

Checking his watch, he saw that he was late.

"Oh, Christ!" he said as he got to his feet in alarm.

Terry booked out the copy of Milton before he left and walked into the dusk. He was a little taken aback at how quickly the shadows had claimed the street and how quiet it was.

Heading into the suburbs, where his semi-detached house was, he felt like an alien marooned on some parallel Earth. These streets that were not his streets in a town that was not his town — a school he'd never attended in a valley he'd ever regarded as a prison, from which he'd never dreamt of escape.

On the hillside, silent and brooding, like an HG Wells Martian, the pit head regarded all with its big steel wheel and all-seeing Masonic Eye.

Eileen, heavily pregnant, peered through the window and saw him swing the Sierra onto the block paved drive. She was out of the door and locking up before he had a chance to get out of the car.

"Sorry I'm late, love," Terry said apologetically.

"He's your father," Eileen reminded him.

They journeyed to the hospital in awkward and uncomfortable silence through the dead streets of rhetoric and ghosts. Calls for a General Strike that were not their General Strike to save pits that were not their pits.

Eventually, Eileen spoke.

"If your position as Inspector was made permanent, would you be eligible for a transfer?" she asked.

Terry grinned.

"You really don't like it here, do you?" he asked.

"This town's dying, Terry, with or without the strike," Eileen frowned. "Plus, your child's going to be a copper's kid in a school full of miners' kids. Do you really want that?"

They were at the hospital now, and both Terry's mother and Brother Johnny were standing at the entrance. Johnny wore the pea coat that was almost the uniform of the Revolutionary Workers League and a Trotsky badge, as well as another in support of the strike. He smoked defiantly.

"There's Johnny and Mum," Terry said as if to change the subject.

They got out of the car.

Mum stepped forward to greet Eileen with a forced smile.

"Hello, love," Mum said. "How's the baby?"

Johnny stared Terry out in hostile defiance as he walked past towards the entrance.

"And how's the class traitor?" Johnny demanded.

"Give it a rest, Johnny," Terry said.

They went inside.

Chapter Twenty-Three

The lone figure watched the Miners' Club in angry silence as his cigarette smouldered to the butt.

Inside was light and laughter. The bastards were full of it, what with the episode with the TNT truck and that flash Smart Alec, Zack Miller, feeding them false information through the phone tap at Miners' Strike HQ.

The lone figure was Sergeant Dermott Brady, and he stared at the fuzzy warmth of the club with hatred.

A pub rock band was banging out 1970s classics, as out of style as the striking miners themselves, and Brady could just see the portrait of King Fucking Arthur on the wall.

The Police Riot Vans, when they pulled up, were almost silent, like a school of marauding great white sharks. They had riot mesh across their windscreens and Paddy pushers upfront. The PSU riot cops, when they disgorged, all had white shirts that denoted them as members of the London Metropolitan Police. Most were battle-hardened veterans of Swamp 81 in Brixton, Brady knew, and a few were more recent recruits, here for the overtime and the repression.

The Police Federation had supported Margaret Thatcher, in 1979, for a reason, and she'd paid them back handsomely for their loyalty in the class war. The Police overtime alone, for the strike, would have kept the pits going for years.

Brady clocked the knuckle dusters and the other unauthorised weapons.

The beery faced Sergeant nodded at Brady in approval.

Brady nodded back.

*

"You watch your tongue, Johnny Vaughan," Mum reprimanded like the fierce Matriarch that she had always been. "And show your older brother some respect. He's a detective and has nothing to do with the strike. He's trying to find the killer of that young girl."

Johnny sulked but did as he was told, the big hard revolutionary that he was. Truth be said, he was more shit scared of his own mother than he would ever be of riot cops or scabs.

Terry himself forced back a grimace as he looked at his father, prostrate on the functional hospital bed. Silicosis is an ugly disease, and for all of the grotesque artwork involved in Susan Higgin's waterlogged corpse, this was his own father lying here like so much skin and bone. Father's head was drawn and skull-like, his skin sallow, and there was the stink of urine and near-death all around him. The breathing equipment was stationed nearby. On the bed was a well-thumbed Zane Gray Western that he loved.

Seemingly close to death, father came around then, trying to hold court as he had always done. His voice was a wheezing rasp. God, Terry fucking well hated seeing his Dad like this.

"This Trotskyism's no good to anyone, Johnny," Father said. "An infantile disorder, that's what we used to call them—all those lies about Stalin and the Hungary Uprising."

Terry smiled ruefully, albeit reluctant to come to Johnny's aid. Like most members of the Communist Party, Terry's father had a capacity to live in denial, to agree that two plus two could equal five, and like most of them, he'd never read Marx or Lenin in his life. In that respect, at least Johnny's RWL seemed to have an edge.

"I don't know about that one, Dad," Terry said.

"You were always the bright one, Terry," Father wheezed. "Good at history. You've even got A levels. You could have gone to university. And then you threw it all away by becoming a copper. It broke my heart when you did that, your mother and me."

Now it was Terry's turn to look uncomfortable. Then, the next thing Terry knew, his father burst into a coughing fit.

Mum was upon him in an instant, deeply concerned.

"Oh God, love!" she cried. "Don't upset yourself! Nurse!"

The Nurse hurried in and started to administer oxygen.

Terry wished that the floor would open up and consume him whole.

*

The riot cops were lined up like soldiers, poised to go into battle. Brady delivered a pep talk like he was Custer at the Battle of the Little Bighorn.

"Right, you lot," Brady said. "These bastards made us look like idiots the other day; you and me both. Now it's payback time, OK? Just imagine you're back with the SPG in Brixton, doing the nig-nogs. Believe me, they might not wear tea cosies on their heads, but these Taff Miners look like coons to me."

There was laughter from the assembled PSU cops, and then the singing began, like a football chant from the terraces.

"We're gonna send the blacks back. We're gonna send the blacks back, la, la, la, la! La, la, la, la! We're

gonna shoot the reds dead. We're gonna shoot the reds dead, la, la, la, la! La, la, la, la!"

Fearful miner's faces appeared crammed at the window like those of bullied children, all of them all too aware of what was going to happen next.

*

Geoff, who'd been with Johnny Vaughan on the picket line only days before, looked on in mortal terror as the chanting thugs in blue serge banged their truncheons on their plastic riot shields.

"We're gonna send the blacks back; we're gonna send the blacks back, la, la, la, la! La, la, la, la! We're gonna shoot the reds dead; we're gonna shoot the reds dead, la, la, la, la! La, la, la, la!"

Geoff swallowed hard.

"Christ, all fucking mighty!" he said.

The cops were already advancing when they broke into a charge.

Attempts by a few miners at the door to hold them back proved useless as the blue army of death burst inside.

They smashed the glasses and all of the optics behind the bar using their truncheons.

They smashed the soft flesh of miners' faces and miners' skulls.

They tore the portrait of Arthur Scargill from the wall and trampled it into the glass shattered floor in a deranged frenzy.

And still, they chanted and sang like a Greek chorus of the mad.

"We're Maggie Thatcher's boot-boys; we're Maggie Thatcher's boot boys, la, la, la, la! La, la, la, la! We're Maggie Thatcher's boot boys; we're Maggie Thatcher's boot boys, la, la, la, la! La, la, la, la!"

Outside of the door, and the mayhem and the fresh blood scattered sacrificially on the wooden club floor, Dermot Brady smiled and gloated like the night creature that he was.

*

Eileen sat in the car alone as Terry argued with his brother outside.

Through the windscreen, sat with the car heater on, she watched the pair of them shout at each other at the hospital entrance.

"You saw Dad in there, the state he was in?" Johnny demanded, or was it accused? "He nearly died in that ward, and it would have been your fault! Sitting on the fence, Terry, you get splinters up your arse. You need to decide which side you're fucking well on, mate!"

"Oh, right," Terry responded as he shook his head. "I'll just hand in my papers and forfeit my mortgage, not to mention my career, to die in the ditches for a lost cause and King Arthur's barmy fucking army!"

Terry walked abruptly and suddenly towards his car.

"Fuck off and grow up, Johnny," he said.

Johnny called after him as Terry got into his car.

"That's right, Terry," Johnny yelled. "Turn your back on your own. You know where you are? You're in no man's land: a class fucking exile. You don't know where you fucking well belong!"

Terry started the engine and reversed away.

"Scab bastard!" Johnny yelled after him.

*

In the cold night air, under a madman's moon, Brady continued to revel in the carnage in the Miner's club.

The sound of breaking glass: the sound of breaking flesh.

The smashing of their club and of their bastard, Taff, Communist faces.

The pub rock band had run for cover, escaping through the toilet, leaving their equipment and amplifiers to be destroyed.

Run, rabbit, run!

That would teach them to take the fucking piss, Brady thought.

Suddenly, he had the sense of being watched.

Across the road, through distended shadows that consumed a dark alley, he felt certain that there were hostile, predatory eyes staring at him.

And was that movement?

"Who's there?" Brady barked and was shocked at the fear in his own voice. "Reveal yourself!" Like a small child hounded by demons and by tales of giants and monsters, who was fearful of the dark.

At his back, like a wind of hate, the destruction in the club continued, but he no longer noticed, as the dark and hollow recess of shadows lured him towards it.

Brady fumbled in his pocket for a torch. His fingers were trembling.

Brady panned the Welsh stone of the alley with his flashlight. Whoever had been lurking there was gone. But the graffiti on those slate grey walls was as fresh as blood on a wound.

There were cabalistic and runic symbols, like something from a heavy metal album cover.

There were words, too, like something from Mitre Square in Jack the Ripper's East End.

They said: *"I Give You the Bible of Hell Whether Mankind Wants it or not!"*

And it was signed: *Azazel.*
Brady stepped back in fear.

*

Terry drove home in angry silence through the haunted streets that screamed mute with rhetoric.

The streets that were no longer his streets: the fight that was no longer his fight.

At his side, he could feel the eyes of his pregnant wife boring into him.

"Now, do you see what I mean about leaving this bastard town?" she demanded.

Terry shook his head. White knuckles gripped the steering wheel.

"Please, love," he almost pleaded. "Don't you start!"

"Me start?" Eileen responded both defensive and belligerent. "It's not my bloody family wants to throw your whole future down the toilet. I mean, you said it yourself, Terry. I heard you."

Eileen shook her head. As Terry drove, he willed her and silently pleaded for her to be quiet, hating it when they argued and when there was this bad shit between them. He knew, as he always knew at times like this, that he was on a hiding to nothing.

"Bloody Johnny-cum-Leon-Trotsky thinks he's a fucking intellectual just because he hangs around with that Zack Miller," Eileen continued, like a woman on a mission. "But he still lives with his Mum and doesn't have any responsibilities. Like a kid in a playground who never grew up. Join up for war! Join up for the fucking revolution! Jesus!"

"Eileen..."

"Yes, well," she closed him down. "Thinking he's a fucking intellectual makes your Johnny dangerous, right? What was it my mother always said? A little knowledge is a dangerous thing? Looking at your father, I see where he gets it from."

That last statement cut to the quick, and now Terry was angry. He punched the dashboard and raised his voice.

"Look, he might not have been much of a father, but the old Stalinist bastard's dying, for fuck's sake", Terry yelled. "So cut him some slack, OK?"

Eileen stared at him.

"This is your town, Terry, not mine," she said. "Your streets, your life and your family!"

"Yeah, well, maybe I'm different from everyone else, eh?" Terry replied. "Like Johnny said: an exile in no man's land."

Eileen shook her head. Her tone softened as she turned away from him, fighting back the tears that were forming in her eyes.

"Not when you're with them, you're not," she said. "Not when you're with your family. When you're with them, you change. And then it's like you're not my Terry anymore."

Terry swung the car into the drive of their home. The headlamps swept their frosty arc across the front door.

Eileen was out of the car first. With a slamming of the car door, she was strutting, as much as was possible in her state, towards the entrance.

Terry got out after her.

"Eileen, wait for fuck's sake, woman!" he called as he slammed the door.

Terry hurried into the house, but by the time he got there, she was already halfway up the stairs.

"Eileen, wait!" he all but pleaded.

"I'm going to bed, Terry," she announced flatly.

"Well, if you hang on a bloody minute, I'll come with you," he said.

"No, Terry," she replied. "I'm bloody well suffocating. I need my space. Good night."

Terry's hurt turned to anger.

"Fine!" he said as he opened the door to the front room.

"Bloody woman!" he added as he slammed it shut.

*

With a rattling of metal wheels on points, the train from Cardiff rolled into the small station of the town. It was dark now, but the platform was bathed in cold, sodium light as Tracey Hepburn stepped down from the train onto the concrete platform.

There was the sound of a whistle and the slamming of train doors.

Still wearing her badge in support of the Miners' Strike and also wearing a face that was a mask of anger, Tracey left the station by the side entrance, past the bicycle racks and onto the empty street.

The darkness and shadows seemed to mock her like a childhood demon in the dark.

Posters in support of the strike adorned the street's infinity of mirrors—the mute rhetoric screamed at the night under a brooding sky. There was heavy cloud cover and a threat of rain as if even the moon was hiding its face from all the evils of this world.

The light from the street lamps was the colour and texture of human urine.

Tracey passed the posters without comment.

Back at the station, the train was pulling away like a spurned lover.

It was then that sudden movement spooked her, causing her to spin around. A mangy dog fox emerged from a dustbin, and an errant sheep bleated in an alleyway.

Tracey heaved a sigh of relief. In spite of her anger, she smiled.

Tracey continued walking.

As she did, a distended shadow separated from the physical presence of the dark, and it followed her.

*

Terry had poured himself a stiff Jameson whiskey after the spat with Eileen on the stairs.

Eileen wanted her space.

A woman's thing that: wanting her space.

Bloody woman!

Bloody wonderful woman!

Shit!

Leaving the front light on, and with the sour taste of the whiskey still burning in his mouth and throat, he went to the front door and out to his car. When he opened the boot and looked at its contents by torchlight, he almost felt like a grave robber in the land where the Pharaoh died.

Next to the copy of *Paradise Lost* were all the photocopies that he'd taken from the newspapers in the library. He'd also made copious longhand notes in a spidery scrawl.

Terry took all of it into the front room and spread it across the dining table.

He read the epic poem first and made even more notes as he let the images fill his mind.

He saw the mutinous angels cast from heaven and transformed from bearers of light into serpents of the infernal pit.

He learned their names, with Azazel as the captain of their damned souls.

Slowly, he was trying to get into the mind of the killer that he stalked.

And then somewhere, amidst the ranks of the puissant legions, and between the wheel of fire and the abyss, he realized how late it was.

Exhausted and with a head full of the stuff of nightmares, Terry rubbed his eyes. He left the tableau where it was as he got to his feet, turned off the light, and went upstairs to bed.

Terry entered the bedroom in silence so as not to disturb his Eileen. He undressed quietly, assuming she was asleep.

It was then that she spoke through streaming tears.

"Terry, is that you?" she asked.

"Yes," Terry replied, sitting on the bed.

Eileen sat up abruptly and embraced him.

"Oh God, Terry," she sobbed. "I'm so sorry."

Terry kissed her.

"I know, love," he said. "I know."

Terry climbed into bed with his wife.

*

It was getting close to midnight, and the myths were still in town—poster after poster along the silent street.

Victory to the miners: coal, not dole.

It was then that Tracey came upon a poster of the *Revolutionary Workers League*.

The poster announced a public meeting to be addressed by no less than Liam O'Leary himself and the Regional Secretary of the NUM.

Its title was: *The General Strike and the Revolutionary Party*.

It was the same poster that Terry had seen being posted when he entered the library that afternoon.

Tracey stopped and stared at the poster in anger and at the accursed name. Her breath formed ghostly ectoplasm as she reached into her jacket for a pen. She then scrawled the word *bastard* beneath the photograph of the great charlatan himself.

By the time the town clock was striking midnight, Tracey was using the pen like a knife, stabbing and defacing the loathsome picture of the Party General Secretary.

In the shadows, from which he was composed and lurking as beyond a dark veil, Azazel watched her with growing exhilaration and murderous intent.

A night creature in a pea coat, anonymous as any soldier of the damned, and in his hand an ice pick gripped like a penis with broken wings.

Susan Higgins would not be alone for long.

PART FOUR: THE WHEEL OF FIRE AND THE ABYSS

Chapter Twenty-Four

The first picket line scuffles of the morning had long begun when rays of sunlight drew Eileen Vaughan from her slumber. The punching and yelling marked another day as a few more scabs joined the ranks of the desperate in the Astons of Worcester scab wagon.

Terry was gone, Eileen noted, and his indentation was cold as a grave, somehow filling her heart with emptiness, loss, and an unfathomable sense of dread. Eileen was not a superstitious woman, but for some reason, even the crow at her window seemed like an omen, croaking its warning in some ancient language, like something from a poem by Edgar Allan Poe.

Through the window, across the valley of green and slate grey, the pit head still stood sentinel, seeing all that was laid before it, and Eileen shuddered, for all that she did not know why.

Moments later and she was vomiting: morning sickness, she told herself. And still, the disquiet struck to the core of her very being.

As she washed her mouth out and cleaned up, she heard the phone ring downstairs, persistent as a demanding child. It took her a while to get downstairs and silence it in its crib.

"Hello?" Eileen asked.

"Eileen, love," her absent husband sounded on the end of the line. She imagined the CID incident room as a hive of activity, like something on TV, with her crime-busting husband at the epicentre of it all.

"Eileen, I'm not going to be able to make it tonight," Terry continued, apologetic. "But I've booked a table at the restaurant tomorrow."

Some of the previous night's anger returned to Eileen. Her brow knitted into a frown.

"But Terry..."

"I'm sorry, love," he continued, disembodied, down the line. "Something's cropped up at work—something important."

Eileen tried to make light of it, but the bitterness sounded in her voice: it was their wedding anniversary, after all.

"Like I said, the other woman", she continued. It was her running joke reference to Terry being married to his job.

"That's the one," Terry continued. "Oh, and Eileen, look in the cupboard under the stairs. There's something I want you to see."

"But Terry..."

"I love you. Bye."

He hung up.

Still feeling slightly angry, Eileen hung up and then moved to the cupboard at the bottom of the stairs.

When she opened the door, she found a big parcel, tied in a bow with the words, *Come on, Eileen,* straight from the Dexy's Midnight Runners song. It was what Terry had sung to her when they were doing their A levels at college, and he had first asked her out, the rather posh girl who had seemed to look down her nose at him at first.

There was also a bunch of red roses and a card which said: *Happy Anniversary, Sweetheart, I love you xxxxx*

Eileen opened the box and smiled.

"Oh, Terry," she said, delighted. "Terry, you mad Romantic idiot."

*

In the open-plan office of Divisional CID, a smiling Terry Vaughan replaced the phone receiver in its cradle. The black woman WPC whom he now knew to be called Patricia, was smiling at him, too.

"Wedding anniversary, right?" she asked.

"Right," said Terry as he looked at the flyer for the Liam O'Leary meeting that was in front of him on the desk. "And here am I, standing her up for the revolution."

He pocketed the flyer and got to his feet.

"Patricia," he said. "Can you go through that paperwork for me that we talked about? I've got to pop out.

Terry put on his jacket and left.

As he did so, DCI Ridgeway and Sergeant Brady studied Terry from Ridgeway's office.

They weren't smiling.

*

The soundtrack on Terry's car cassette player was by Dexy's Midnight Runners as he drove towards the Rhondda National Park.

He passed a group of pickets huddled around a brazier at the pit head and kept on driving.

A couple of the guys he recognised from school.

Eventually, he found the country pub that he was looking for and immediately clocked Clever Trevor's second-hand banger of a car.

Terry remained seated while the Sierra's engine ticked away like an unexploded bomb and scanned the beer garden until he saw his prey.

Clever Trevor was sat with Mickey Draper, a local medium-sized drug dealer, at a wooden table, laughing and sharing a joint.

It was the same Mickey Draper who, with Clever Trevor, had fucked over Johnny's head with acid in the senior common room at school.

Terry watched as Trevor passed Draper a bunch of green one-pound notes and received a package in return. There were affirmative nods all around.

Trevor waved Draper goodbye as he drained his pint, and the drug dealer left. Terry watched as the reporter went back inside the pub and then got out of the car.

Inside, Duran Duran blasted *Hungry like the Wolf* from a jukebox, but Clever Trevor was nowhere in sight. Terry headed straight for the toilet.

As soon as he entered, he could hear the reporter snorting away in the end cubicle, feeding his need for speed.

Terry quietly checked each empty cubicle as he made it to where Trevor was.

More snorting from inside found Terry curling his lip in disgust; then, he kicked open the door with violent force.

Trevor looked up, startled, like something from a Mike Hodges movie, only with white powder smeared all over his face. His mouth was open like something from a Victorian fairground attraction.

Terry stared at Trevor, both angry and triumphant, as another punter walked in.

"Can't you see we're having a cottage," Terry bellowed. "Fuck off!"

The punter obligingly complied.

It was then that Clever Trevor made his move on Terry which was a bad move from the reporter's point of view. Terry grabbed Trevor's throat, crowding him into the cubicle, then shoved his head violently down the toilet.

Terry pulled the chain.

"That's for fucking up my brother's A levels with drugs," he said.

*

Back in the beer garden, Terry placed a pint of Hancocks in front of Clever Trevor. The reporter looked sullen but accepted the pint of bitter in any case.

"I could nick you for possession with intent to supply," Terry said.

"What?" Trevor responded, indignant. "It's for personal use, and you fucking know it. A fine and community service and not worth the paperwork, and you know that, too."

Terry looked at Trevor maliciously.

"It would get you the fucking sack if Motormouth, your wanker of an editor, found out," Terry said. "Plus, it would put paid to your ambitions of getting a job on *The Sun*."

Trevor looked up, startled.

"What?" he blurted. "What do you mean?"

Terry slapped a copy of the tabloid rag in front of him. The front-page lead about Azazel was accredited to Orla O'Regan and a "local correspondent."

"Like you said, Clever Fucking Trevor," Terry said. "This town's dying. The pits and the miners are finished, and we're all doing what we can to get out of Dodge."

Trevor was sullen, but he was smart enough to know the lousy hand he'd been delivered; win, lose or draw.

"What do you want, Terry?" he pleaded.

"I've been down the library doing a lot of reading," Terry said.

"That's a dangerous pastime," Trevor responded. "You never know where it might lead. Like I said, what do you want from me?"

"Two things," Terry said. "First of all, I want you to use your contacts on the street of shame to find out all you can about a Special Branch Sergeant called Dermott Brady."

Trevor was already shaking his head.

"He's a Brummie," Terry continued. "And he had something to do with the busting of the Birmingham Six. But now he's down here and on my case like a bad dose of herpes."

You must be having a laugh, Terry," Trevor said, incredulous. "They put flags up at the Home Office for that kind of shit!!"

Terry rolled his eyes.

"Very well, Terry O'Carroll, I'm arresting you for possession of amphetamine bisulphate with intent — "

Trevor held up his hands in surrender. Then, sweating profusely, he ran his trembling hand nervously through his hair.

"OK, OK, I'll do it, OK?" he trembled. "Jesus! Anything else you want for your pound of flesh?"

Terry stared at the nervous-looking reporter.

"As a matter of fact, there is," he said. "I also want you to introduce me to your new girlfriend, Orla O'Regan."

Trevor looked at Terry in disbelief.

Chapter Twenty-Five

The sound of a male voice choir eddied from the miners club in town as the sun set behind the mountains like a ship that was shot to stern.

It was a valiant death.

The choir was singing *The International*.

Posters adorned the entrance to the hall, and two paper sellers, punks who looked like students, were optimistically trying to sell copies of *Socialist Worker* to the indifferent gathering that was entering the hall.

The portraits of Marx, Lenin and Trotsky, would be inside, together with the hammer and sickle of the Fourth International. And Peter Chapman, the middle-aged representative of the South Wales NUM regional leadership, would be looking nervous as he spoke to the RWL officials in their blue denim and pea coats.

Azazel looked at the two young punks, miserably trying to sell their pieces of brightly coloured paper as if they were prey.

"*Socialist Worker!*" they proclaimed. "Support the miners."

In the hall, in front of the portraits of Marx, Lenin and Trotsky on the podium, Chapman would be taking up his seat as Chair of the meeting.

The *Daily Advance* journalists, in the front seats, would be taking the photographs for the next day's edition.

219

Meanwhile, at the entrance to the meeting, thugs from the RWL Security Directorate moved in on the two young punks. They shoved them aggressively.

"You lot can fuck off!" one of the RWL thugs said. "Unless you want your fucking heads kicked in! The last thing we need is your revisionist shit about state capitalism around here."

One of the *Socialist Worker* sellers, English and almost certainly middle class, spoke to his friend.

"Come on, Julian," he said.

Azazel suppressed a snigger as the two young punks left.

The RWL thugs laughed.

"Fucking Julian!" one of them said. "Like something out of the fucking *Young Ones.*"

"Fucking students, I fucking well hate 'em, me!" his confederate almost spat the words.

Azazel's heart quickened the moment that Tracey Hepburn approached, and the Fallen Angel felt the promise of an erection between his legs. He imagined his blood gorged cock stiffening like a lead weight with wings.

Tracey still looked angry, exactly as she had the previous night.

And then, Azazel saw Terry Vaughan arrive and more excitement charged through his veins.

The hunter who would soon be the hunted, the Fallen Angel told himself.

Terry walked up to Party Cadres holding plastic buckets that proclaimed: *Victory to the Miners.*

Being suspicious was Terry's job.

"That for the miners or the Party," Terry demanded, already knowing the answer.

He walked inside.

Azazel, unnoticed, followed — because Azazel was part of the body: because Azazel belonged.

*

Inside the Miners Hall, there were more paper sellers, this time for the *Daily Advance* and a bookstall. Terry sat next to the back of the hall.

On the podium, the chair reserved for Liam O'Leary remained vacant. Peter Chapman leaned forward and, with a popping of feedback, spoke into the microphone.

For some reason, Terry's attention was drawn to an angry-looking young woman who sat across the room.

"Alright, comrades," Chapman said. "It seems like Liam O'Leary, the man you've all come here for, is a bit late, probably on account of the police roadblocks."

There was laughter, and even Terry smiled, albeit thinly

"My name is Peter Chapman," the warm-up speaker continued. "And I'm a member of the South Wales Regional NUM."

It was then that O'Leary marched in, flanked by his entourage, which included the Brothers Grimm.

The crowd stood, almost as one, and applauded the great man.

221

Terry got to his feet more closely and scanned the adoring crowd.

On stage, O'Leary shook hands with Chapman and then gave a clenched fist salute.

Terry's attention was drawn to where the angry looking young woman wasn't applauding or smiling.

"Comrades," O'Leary said in his hectoring Tipperary accent. "The prospects for a General Strike were strong from the moment that the dock and rail workers refused to handle scab coal."

True, Terry told himself, *but that was a year ago, now.*

"As usual," O'Leary continued. "It was the tome servers running the TUC that held us back. As for the Labour Party, it's a rotting corpse!"

More cheers, and at that moment, Zack the Hack Miller walked in, followed by Terry's brother Johnny like a small child in awe of a surrogate older brother. Terry noticed, for the first time, that he even walked like Zack the Hack.

Wish I could be like Zack the Hack!
Pash-pah-pah-pah-pah-pah-pah-pah!

Meanwhile, O'Leary droned on, and Terry watched, in disbelief, as the cadres with their faded blue denim and faded faces clutched their eyes shut, heads in hands, as they tried to absorb what the mad old bastard and charlatan was saying.

Terry had never seen a religious cult in action but wagered it would be a lot like this.

"The scientific analysis of history," O'Leary said. "Made possible through our Party's unique understanding of Marxism and of Dialectical Materialism, proves that a General Strike is still possible but only if led by a revolutionary vanguard party. And there is only one revolutionary vanguard party, comrades, and that's the RWL, the British section of the International Committee of the Fourth International."

There was more cheering, as if on cue, and still, Terry stared at the angry-looking young woman across the room.

"We know that reformists don't have the answers," O'Leary said. "Our mass-circulation *Daily Advance* says and proves that every single day. You want a general strike; you want to defeat the Tories and for the miners to win, then build the Revolutionary Party. Build the Revolutionary Workers League!"

Yet more applause followed in this secular equivalent of a Billy Graham rally, and it was at this point that the angry-looking young woman got up and left.

Relieved to be leaving this particular nut house, Terry got up to follow her.

He bumped straight into his own brother as he did so.

Johnny Vaughan wasn't smiling.

*

Johnny and Terry were now arguing outside the miner's hall. The angry-looking young woman was gone, and what with Terry's cover being blown, there was no way he was going to find her.

Besides, he had a more pressing problem now.

Facing him with a face of fury, Johnny ranted and was even pointing his finger like Liam O'Leary.

"What the fuck you playing at, Terry?" Johnny demanded. "You joined Special Branch or what?"

"Bollocks, Johnny," Terry replied. "I'm trying to find a killer: the murderer of a young girl who just happens to be one of your Party comrades. I don't give a flying fuck who he votes for!"

Johnny was incredulous.

"What?" he demanded. "You think a Party comrade murdered Susan? You're fucking losing it, Terry!"

"Oh yeah," Terry laughed. "Have you taken a look at the damaged goods cracked actors in that particular nut-house? It's a religious cult, Johnny, like Billy Graham and Jim Fucking Jones. Oh, what a friend we have in Liam, all the way to the fucking bank."

Johnny seemed momentarily hesitant.

"You know, I had a look at your *Daily Advance* the other day, just for a laugh," Terry said. "I mean, I wouldn't use it as toilet paper, not the way the ink comes off in your hand, but you know what I *didn't* notice. Not one obituary for Susan Higgins or acknowledgement that she even existed. Why do you think that is, Johnny?"

Johnny looked uncomfortable. Terry turned and walked away.

"Anyway, I've had enough of this bullshit," Terry said. "I'm off home. It's my wedding anniversary, just in case you bothered to remember."

Johnny was furious. He called after his brother.

"You bastard!" he said. "How'd you know he doesn't work for the state? How'd you know he isn't a copper, Terry?"

That one stopped Terry in his tracks. He turned and looked at his brother in astonishment.

"Now, what makes you say that?" Terry demanded.

"Well, he's one step ahead of you, isn't he?" Johnny retorted. "Or is it just because you're not very good at your job?"

"Good night, Johnny," Terry sneered. "Enjoy your Church service."

Terry walked away.

Chapter Twenty-Six

In the Miner's Hall, O'Leary was screaming to the point of hysteria down the microphone.

"And the next time I go to the Middle East," he said. "It will be to talk about guns!"

There was a roar of approval from the crowd, but on the podium, Peter Chapman looked very worried indeed.

O'Leary ushered his congregation to be calm.

"Comrades!" he said. "Join me in the singing of *The International.*"

The male voice choir began again to sing, and this time, with clenched fists raised, the congregation joined in, either singing or miming the words.

When the rendition had ended, there was further applause.

O'Leary's performance was at an end.

*

With the meeting at an end, the miner's hall was emptying like a Pentecostal Church on a Sunday.

The Brothers Grimm flanked the Great Man himself as O'Leary swaggered towards the Triumph Toledo.

Almost immediately, they noticed that someone had scratched the paintwork.

"What the…" O'Leary began.

Tracey Hepburn stepped out of the shadows like an angry and pale-faced spectre at the feast.

"Well, if it isn't the Detrimental Robot," she sneered and taunted. "Don't think much of the car, Liam. Bit of a shed, in fact. Then again, if your congregation of sheep saw your BMW, they might wonder what they pay their subs for?"

"What the hell do you want?" O'Leary demanded.

"Me?" Tracey mocked. "I want to talk, Liam. The way I'm going to talk to the papers about you."

"What?" O'Leary blustered while turning a darker shade of red. "What are you talking about? Talking about what to the fucking papers?"

He was sweating and shaking, too.

"About you," Tracey said. "About me: about how you got Tracey pregnant before she was murdered. About all the other young girls, you've been screwing in the Party and beyond."

"I've no time for this petty-bourgeois crap!" O'Leary seethed.

Tracey lunged at him, enraged.

"Don't turn your back on me, you fucking charlatan!" she screeched.

One of the Brothers Grimm grabbed Tracey and threw her roughly and brutally to the ground. O'Leary hurriedly got into the Triumph Toledo and started the engine as the two brothers hurriedly clambered into the car.

It sped off with a screeching protest of tyres as if they were plastic gangsters staging a getaway, leaving parallel lines of hot rubber on the tarmac

Still on the ground, Tracey looked to where she'd kicked in the rear lights of the escaping car. Then, like fury from Hell, she ran after it.

"Come back here, you fucking bastard!" she screamed through tears of hurt and rage.

The car vanished out of sight.

Tracey sniffed.

Slowly and more quietly, another car pulled up, its headlamps forming disembodied orbs in the cold dead street that was cheerless as the abyss.

Tracey recognised the car, and its driver, immediately.

Through tears, she smiled at the familiar face.

"Thank God it's you," she said.

On the car cassette player, Jim Morrison sang *Riders of the Storm*.

Tracey gratefully got into the victim's seat beside the Lizard King.

The car drove off.

Killer on the road!

*

Dawn found another ritual confrontation at the local pit head, as the steel wheel of the pithead observed all through its sightless Masonic eye.

The Martians were coming.

Maggie, Maggie, Maggie! Out, out, out!

More arrests and more beatings were being meted out by white-shirted bastards in the backs of police vans.

In his hovel of a bedsit, Clever Trevor O'Carroll woke to the strains of Elvis Costello and

Watching the Detectives as he snorted his first line of speed to face the day.

Then he washed and combed, like something from a Kris Kristofferson song, and left his crappy, cheerless abode to face the day.

Through streets that were not his streets, facing posters and rhetoric that was not his rhetoric. A fight that was not his fight, here, under the cold gunmetal sky, in this grey, divided land.

Clever Trevor arrived early at the office, before either Motor-mouth or the Screech Owl, and rifled through the office mail to see if anything was addressed to him.

It was.

Still sniffing, like the speed freak that he was, he slumped behind his desk and his Imperial typewriter, with the spiked copies and his contact directory, and lit up a cigarette from his soft pack of *Marlboro*.

Clever Trevor exhaled slowly before opening the letter.

Then he sat bolt upright as if he'd received an electric shock.

"Jesus Fucking Christ!" he said.

Trevor pressed nine for an outside line and was onto the local police station asking for Acting Detective Inspector Terry Vaughan.

Shortly afterwards, he was driving towards the Rhondda National Park with his foot heavy on the pedal.

*

The police convoy snaked into the national park with blues and twos blaring.

Terry, at the wheel of his own Ford Sierra, looked grim.

Eventually, he saw the Celtic stone circle in the distance, with the burial mound beyond.

Clever Trevor's banger was parked up nearby, and the reporter himself, his leather tie awry, was nervously chain-smoking from his soft pack of American cigarettes.

He waved to the Ford Sierra as it approached.

Terry pulled up, together with the other police vehicles, and got out of his car. Already, the SOCO officers were suited up, like white scavenger birds, as the uniform cops set up the blue and white crime scene tape.

Terry accepted the letter that Clever Trevor offered him before looking to where the girl's body had been laid out like an offering on the sacrificial stone.

A crow with ugly black wings emitted a croak and flew away like something from a poem by Poe.

Terry saw that the young girl's face had been smashed in exactly like that of Susan Higgins down by the canal. Almost certainly, the murder weapon was an ice pick applied to the girl's face in a grotesque parody of a sex act, and that meant that it was the same killer, striking again in the name of his murderous art. Only this time, unlike at the canal, the bloody installation was complete, with the body laid out at the very epicentre of those mute standing stones, like the petrified spirits of Los, and with cabalistic or runic graffiti worn like a tattoo on each and every one of them.

One message, however, was in English.

It read: *Behold the Bible of Hell which the World Will Have whether it Wants it or Not!*

"Blake this time, instead of Milton," Trevor said.

Despite the brutal and horrific nature of the girl's injuries, with the ice pick rupturing her face like an evil penis bearing death instead of life, Terry recognised immediately the angry-looking girl from the Liam O'Leary rally the previous night. It was the same girl that Terry had left the Miners' Hall to talk to when he had bumped into Brother Johnny.

Would she still be alive if Terry had gotten to her in time?

Had his ridiculous altercation with Johnny contributed to this young girl's death?

What dark secret had she taken with her to this desolate and open grave?

And why did everything seem to come back to that bastard charlatan, Liam O'Leary?

Terry looked down at the letter that Clever Trevor had received that very morning and saw yet again the elaborate image of the nine angels cast from heaven, transformed from bearers of light into serpents of the infernal pit.

On the flip side, in the same spiky, gothic handwriting and with the same artistic flourish were the same words that had been daubed on the standing stone, like evil graffiti. Only this time, there was more.

"Behold the Bible of Hell which the world will have whether it wants it or not," Terry read out, like an

231

exercise in English Literature at school. *"They gave O'Leary head, but my Magick Hammer gave them life. The world must know of this pageant of corruption and its role in the Bitch's coronation. We are all Albion's Lost Children, now!"*

Terry looked to Trevor.

"What the fuck does that mean?" he demanded.

Trevor smoked and shook his head.

"Fuck knows," Clever Trevor said. "I've a third class degree in English Literature, not insanity."

Terry looked to where the SOCO team, in their white coveralls, were already gathering evidence like scavenging birds in search of carrion.

Samples were being taken from beneath the girl's fingernails.

"Tell me more about Blake," Terry said.

"William Blake wrote *The Bible of Hell*," Trevor replied, matter of fact. "He also talked about Albion's Lost Children and believed there was an ancient civilisation in Britain before the Romans."

"Go on," Terry coaxed, staring at him.

"He also talked a lot about murdered Druids and broken temples being buried deep in the Earth," Trevor continued, struggling as if in reference to some half-remembered bad acid trip. "Down with the rotting wood and bones, or something like that."

"Sounds fucking charming," Terry grunted.

"Poor bugger was bipolar and had to cut up cadavers when studying anatomy," Trevor continued by way of explanation. "He couldn't handle it, see?"

"I know how he felt," said Terry, raising an eyebrow. "Did he talk about Magick Hammers?"

Trevor shook his head as he continued to smoke.

"No," he said. "That's Peter Sutcliffe, or *The Beatles*, or Charles Manson. Whatever mad prophet takes your fancy in this grey divided land."

The girl's body was being moved now, finally, onto the gurney to be wheeled away.

"I know about Milton," Terry said. "Tell me more about Blake."

"The last of the religious poets," Trevor replied, almost warming to his subject. "He was influenced by a German Protestant mystic who thought that angels and demons occupied the same space but couldn't see each other, each fighting for the souls of men: between the Wheel of Fire and the Abyss."

Terry muttered something as the girl was taken past, the body on its way to the meat wagon and mortuary slab.

"What's wrong?" Trevor asked.

"Nothing," said Terry. "Apart from the fact that I know who that girl is. She was at that bloody meeting last night. The one addressed by Liam O'Leary."

Trevor looked shocked.

"Then maybe Azazel is a fascist after all," he ventured. "Maybe all this mystic bollocks is just smoke and mirrors."

"Don't you start, what with you and Dermot Brady," Terry snapped.

This seemed to trigger something in Clever Trevor's memory.

"Oh, right!" the reporter said. "I've got something on that. Rumour control reckons Brady

233

for a bit of a wrong 'un. The legend is that Brady beat a confession out of the Birmingham Six and used dodgy forensics from RADRE in Sevenoaks, Kent, to back the confessions up. He then transferred to London around about 1980, where he became big mates with your Guvnor, Ridgeway."

Terry looked at Ridgeway, startled.

"Ridgeway was Flying Squad, right?" he demanded. "What's that got to do with Special Branch?"

Trevor rolled his eyes.

"Search me, but they were thick as thieves, apparently," he said. "Members of the same Lodge—funny handshakes. The Mafia of the Mediocre. Usual bollocks for your mob."

Terry watched as the girl's body was loaded onto the ambulance like a slab of meat. The door closed with what seemed like a shocking finality.

Terry spoke, and this time even he was shocked by the bitterness in his own voice.

"There was something going on last night, something between this girl and that bastard, O'Leary", he continued almost as if thinking aloud. "Shit! I was going to ask her some questions, but then my bloody brother turned up with Zack the Hack. Fuck! That girl's probably dead because of me!"

"Easy, Sheriff," Trevor said. "You're a cunt, but not in that way."

Terry looked to where Ted, the pathologist, was speaking to the ambulance crew, giving instructions and also looking in Terry's direction. He would come over soon, and this particular conversation was not for public consumption.

"OK, change the subject," Terry snapped. "Have you managed to arrange a meeting with Orla O'Regan, yet?"

"No!" Trevor said. "I left a message on her answerphone, but she's not got back to me yet."

Terry walked towards Ted as if ignoring Trevor.

"Then chase her up and get a fucking move on," he said.

Trevor snorted his sarcasm, blown like stale cigarette smoke into the air.

"Anything you say, boss," he said.

Chapter Twenty-Seven

Brighton, 1984.

On a podium in the Grand Hotel, the Iron Bitch proclaims her message of hate to the congregation of the damned. And they are out in force, Orla O'Brady notes, listening to this message of apocalyptic evil, like extras from The Evil Dead *or some movie about the Zombie Apocalypse by George A. Romero.*

At her side, some journalist from The Daily Mail, *with the stink of whisky on his breath, is starting to snore.*

Orla derives a moment of sadistic pleasure from this paradox when her phone pager comes to life, stirring the legion of the damned that is nearest to her from their slumber.

"Excuse me," Orla says with mock sincerity and is grateful to leave the hall.

In the foyer, as Thatcher's voice drones on like some disembodied, malevolent spirit, speaking in tongues, Orla finds a payphone booth.

She places a call while nervously looking around her.

"Hello, Stephen?" she coaxes when she gets a reply.

The voice on the end of the line utters sheer panic into her ear.

"We're trapped!" Stephen yells. "The bastard's locked us in!"

There then comes a bout of heavy coughing, as if from toxic smoke.

"You've got to help us!" Stephen manages at last. "The bastard's locked us in!"

Orla looks both alarmed and confused.

"You've got to help us!" Stephen pleads. "The flat's on fire!"

Orla is looking horrified now.

"It was him," Stephen says. "Azazel!"

The moment the phone goes dead, Orla dials 999.

*

In Farm Road in Hove, the building is burning, like Babylon, and with more than anxiety.

A fire engine is already in attendance when Orla pulls up in her blue and white taxi, along with other emergency services vehicles. A funeral pyre burns, as in Thatcher's vision of Hell Fire, through the hollowed out windows, coiling evil black smoke into the night sky, as if from some concentration camp at the end of a century that has already dripped from head to toe in blood.

And the worst, as they say, is yet to come.

Orla emerges from the taxi to the sound of sirens, like banshees, and of the troubled Undead turning in their graves.

She looks to the burning building, like the vision of some terrible dystopian future that it is, and her pale face glows in its space cadet glow.

The heat from the fire hits her like a wall. It is like a wind of hate blasted directly into her blue eyes.

Orla sees a fireman and walks up to him.

"What happened?" she asks.

"Places are a fucking death trap, anyway," the fireman snaps. "Absentee landlords don't give a shit. That said, I wouldn't have thought they'd lock off the fire escape or super glued the fucking locks."

Orla looks and is genuinely shocked.

237

"Then it's attempted murder?" she coaxes.

As if on cue, a body is pulled from the building.

"Not so much of the attempted," the fireman says. "There's three corpses in the room where the fire started. I mean, it's early days, but I've seen enough house fires to know that some kind of accelerant must have been used to make the fire spread that quickly."

The other two corpses are brought out now, making it three sixes in a row.

It is then that the cop appears, at Orla's back, throwing in his two penneth.

"Bloody druggies, what does anyone expect," the cop says. "Used to be a nice neighbourhood, here – decent families. Now all the rubbish has moved in."

Orla is immediately hostile to the cop. According to rumour control, should the Sussex cops in neighbouring Eastbourne find a homeless black person on the street, they routinely take them into the countryside for a beating and leave them for dead.

"Bit judgemental, isn't it?" Orla snaps. "You've no idea who started this fire."

"Oh yes, we do," the policeman laughs, like some cheap Victorian seaside attraction. "Tried to top himself, afterwards, with a paracetamol overdose. They pumped his stomach, and he's in hospital under police guard and on life support now."

*

Sussex hospitals have a chequered history, Orla knows, as she enters the crumbling Victorian edifice that is a testimony to the Tories market-driven war on the NHS.

In neighbouring Eastbourne, a suspected paedophile clergyman called Hubert Brasier had been the close associate of a Doctor John Bodkin Adams, based at the local NHS hospital. Adams had been a prolific serial killer and, much like Jack the Ripper was probably due to be one of the authors of the 21st Century.

This hospital in Brighton, Orla notes, has a similar aura to that of Bodkin Adams and a similarly decaying Victorian grandeur. As she enters the building and heads through its narrow labyrinth of painted brick, the first thing she notices is the patients on their gurneys, left in the corridors like the victims of some war. Eyes look at Orla with little comprehension as she follows the yellow brick line to the intensive care unit, where she knows the alleged arsonist, Simon, is to be found.

Once again, the patients, on their gurneys, look at her imploringly, as if they are the damned youth of the Somme, and Orla realises that both Clement Attlee and Bevan and even Beveridge are a long time dead.

A solitary young policeman in uniform stands sentry to the room where this Simon is.

Orla hesitates and then keeps on walking. Pinching her nose to prompt the tears, she addresses him with a combination of false frailty and allure.

"Hello," Orla says. "My nephew's in there. Can I please go in and see him?"

"I'm sorry, Miss," the policeman replies, shaking his head. "No visitors."

Now Orla turns on the phoney tears and grief. She implores him with all the acting skills she can muster.

Her aunt, in South Tipperary, always said she belonged on the stage.

"Oh, God, please let me through," she pleads. "I'm his only relative."

The policeman still sounds hesitant, but the tone of his voice indicates that he is weakening.

"OK," he says with a note of uncertainty in his voice. "But you'll have to be quick."

"Thank you!" smiles Orla.

Entering the ward, she finds Simon lying on a functional bed. He is breathing through an oxygen mask while a telemetry screen displays his vital signs. Other than for his breathing and the sound of the electronic apparatus, the room is as silent as a morgue.

"Simon," Orla whispers. "Can you hear me?"

There is silence for all that Orla is certain she sees him flinch.

Orla bites her lip and pounds the bed with her hand.

"Simon!" she urges, with a hint of a threat in her whispered voice.

This time his eyes open wide, and he stares at her, moaning, in genuine moral terror.

"Simon, they say that you started the fire," Orla rasps. "That you confessed. Did you?"

Simon shakes his head and moans. Again, Orla bites her lip and makes a decision to remove his oxygen mask.

His croaking voice is thin as a reed, and Orla needs to lean into him like a priest hearing a final prayer of contrition.

"He made me take him to the flat where Stephen and the others from the care home were," Simon confesses as if these were his last rites. "But I didn't start the fire. He did."

"Who, Simon," Orla persists. "Who made you take him to the flat? Who started the fire?"

Simon trembles and struggles to formulate words, as if his last rites have now become a ritual of exorcism.

"Azazel," he manages to say.

240

Orla shakes her head in confused irritation. The conversation has assumed all the clarity of a séance.

"*Azazel?*" *she echoes.* "*I don't understand. Who is Azazel?*"

"*Stephen recognised him straight away, from the day that Jack was killed,*" *Simon says.* "*He killed the father, then he killed the mother and then the child.*"

Simon's eyes are agog now.

"*Father, Son and Holy Ghost: Satan, Antichrist and False Prophet and three sixes all in a row.*"

Orla continues to shake her head in irritation.

"*Simon!*" *she urges,*

"*Azazel is the messenger who rides the pale horse, and the horse is named death,*" *Simon says.*

"*Simon,*" *Orla persists, angry now.* "*You're not making any sense. Who is Azazel? Where does he come from?*"

"*From Hell,*" *Simon says.*

On the wall, a digital clock strikes 2:45 am.

And in a room in the Grand Hotel in Brighton, a bomb explodes.

Chapter Twenty-Eight

The Devil looks after his own.

Ever the insomniac, the Iron Bitch isn't even in her room when the bomb detonates, tearing into the ceiling below and punching out windows in an angry orange fist. There are alarms and screams in Brighton's Grand Hotel now.

A crash of radio static and the solitary cop, standing sentry outside of Simon's room, is lured away to matters more important on the seafront.

Dressed in hospital blues, like a Milwall fan, and with a hypodermic needle held at the ready, Azazel prepares to make his move.

*

Orla's pager goes off like a secondary device. She looks at it in alarm and then towards Simon.

"Don't worry, I'll be back," she soothes. "Nobody's going to hurt you, Simon."

She leaves the room.

Eventually, in the corridor, she finds a payphone and rings her editor.

"Where the fuck are you, Orla?" he growls. "The fucking IRA's just blown up the Grand Hotel. They were trying to kill the fucking Prime Minister. Never mind playing Miss Marple. Get back to the Hotel and find out who's been killed. Important people – not the fucking rubbish."

The editor hangs up angrily.

242

Orla again bites her lip and runs back towards Simon's ward.

*

Azazel waits until the Irish Fenian bitch is gone, and then he makes his move.

Calmly he walks towards the room where Simon is and opens the door.

Simon, on seeing Azazel before him, whimpers, but beyond this pitiful sound, he seems momentarily speechless. Before he can shout, his eyes agog with sheer moral terror, Azazel has his hand across the young man's mouth.

Azazel applies the lethal hypodermic and then watches as his vital signs die on the telemetry screen.

The flat-line announces Simon's death.

It is then that Azazel hears movement in the corridor and hides in the closet.

Through the crack in the door, he sees Orla O'Regan come back into the room.

*

When Orla arrives back in the ward, she finds Simon dead.

"Shit!" she says, as much in shock as anything else.

Furtively looking around her, she opens up the locker drawer near Simon's still warm corpse, vaguely feeling like a grave robber as she does so.

Firstly, she finds Simon's UB40 card, proving that he is unemployed, but also a Post Office Savings Book registered in the Isle of Man with £9000 in it.

And there is something else.

A shocking and disgusting photograph which she picks up and studies, somehow half-aware — as if by instinct — that she is being watched.

"Got you!" she says triumphantly, her heart still racing.

Again, there is the sound of voices in the corridor.

Orla pockets the photo, the UB40 and the bank book and then leaves.

In the closet, still clasping the lethal hypodermic, Azazel has been deprived of another victim.

*

Late at night, in her flat in Fulham, Orla O'Regan stared out of her window into the mocking void.

On the table behind her, as if on display, were her trophies of what had become her obsession as well as, potentially, the greatest story of her career.

There was Simon's UB40, his Post Office Savings Book and the obscene picture that Azazel had failed to reclaim. There was also a year old copy of *The Brighton Argos,* claiming that Simon had confessed to starting the house fire before he died.

Her phone shrilled like a demanding child, and she let it ring out, ignoring its demands from its crib.

The answerphone kicked in.

"Orla, this is Trevor O'Carroll from South Wales," a familiar voice said. "I've already filed a report on the latest murder. They found the body this morning, and it's definitely Azazel."

Orla looked again at the copy of *The Brighton Argus* and wondered how close she might have come to confront the killer that night.

"Orla, I've been talking to the lead police investigator, and he wants to talk to you," Clever Trevor said. "His name's Terry Vaughan, an old school chum of mine, in fact — seems he's got it in for your mates Brady and Ridgeway."

Orla snatched up the phone in a shot.

"Trevor, it's me," said Orla. "What's this about the lead investigator wanting to talk?"

She imagined him standing in a phone box somewhere in whatever town in the Rhondda Valley where he was based.

"He thinks Special Branch is trying to hijack the police investigation," Trevor said. "Steer it up a blind alley."

Orla continued to stare into the black and hollow void above the dead street, where once-grand Georgian houses were lit by cold sodium lights. Her expression bordered on the fanatical as she gripped the phone receiver to her ear and smoked.

"Does he now?" she said coldly.

"I'll warn you, Orla, he can be a fucking arsehole at times, but he's straight," Trevor said.

"Is he Craft?" Orla asked anxiously.

"A Mason, no!" came the reply.

"OK, set up a meeting but don't divulge the location over the phone," Orla said.

She heard the sound of the phone being hung up.

Orla smoked and stared out into the emptiness of the night.

*

Leaving the phone box, Clever Trevor O'Carroll was startled by the bleating of a stray sheep that was wandering in the road.

*

In GCHQ Cheltenham, the Kray computers had kicked in the moment that Clever Trevor O'Carroll mentioned Azazel. Within hours, an IBM laser printer had produced a transcript of the phone conversation.

The transcript was then dispatched, by a motorcycle rider, for the attention of Home Office Department H4 in Whitehall.

By sunrise, it was sitting on the appropriate desk.

Chapter Twenty-Nine

Brighton, 1984.

Decades after Graham Greene wrote his seminal novel, Brighton Rock *is still rotten to the core.*

As for the Grand Hotel, it has been carnage on the dance floor, all right, as the whole of the seaside town continues to reel from the impact of the previous night's events.

Norman Tebbitt dragged, grimacing from the wreckage and not even on his bike.

The Iron Bitch herself survives the assassination attempt as if by Satanic intervention.

Hurrying along the seafront, towards the Police Station, and still nowhere near the Grand Hotel, Orla can hear the chatter of the punters, inane as the sound of seagulls.

"Murdering Irish bastards, they should bring back hanging!"

At the station, she finds the policeman she spoke to near Farm Road the previous night completely uncooperative.

"Can you tell me anything about the boy?" Orla asks.

"He was a druggie," the policeman says. "Rubbish, same as them three he killed. Fucking layabouts on the dole, never done a day's work in their life. He topped himself, probably high on drugs, end of story."

"What?" Orla demands, incredulous. "You mean there's to be no investigation?"

The policeman is starting to get angry now, and Orla is wondering what other colours he can do.

"*Look, Miss,*" he says with barely concealed contempt. "*With all due respect, my home town's just been bombed by a bunch of Irish terrorists, trying to kill our Prime Minister, who's the only thing standing between this country and anarchy, and you're worried about four dead druggies?*"

Orla concedes it might be time to look in on the ruins of the Grand Hotel.

*

By the time Orla arrives at the scene of the assassination attempt, Derek McLeod has called an impromptu press conference.

At his back, the hotel shows a clear image of bomb damage, almost certainly Semtex, and there is blue and white crime scene tape fluttering like tawdry bunting at a seaside fete.

It is starting to rain.

Orla clocks the tame press pack and sees the usual mediocre faces, all of them lobby journalists who couldn't recognise an investigative news story if it dropped on them from the gunmetal sky. It was the British media all over, Orla tells herself, expressive of a corrupt and toxic relationship between political power and a Fourth Estate that is supposed to hold it to account.

Not in this Jaded Jerusalem.

Not in this grey, divided land.

McLeod is on top form, like the former PR guru that he is: the first black member of the Monday Club and the first black master of hounds.

"*And you can take my word that it will take more than a handful of murdering Irish terrorists to shake this administration in its resolve to make this country great again," he says.*

To Orla's disgust, there is actual applause.

The fat hack from The Daily Mail, *who was snoring next to her the previous evening, pipes up.*

"Mr McLeod," he says. "Do you believe there was any connection between this bomb attack and the miners' strike?"

McLeod shakes his head.

"It's too early to say," the PR guru says. "There are many rumours of IRA supporters and activists turning up on picket lines up and down the country and further rumours of Libyan funding. As you know, the Mad Colonel is the main financial backer of the Provisional IRA, and we believe there is a direct Libyan connection to last night's bomb attack in the form of Abu Nidal."

There are murmurs of agreement from the tame press pack, like the nodding dogs you sometimes saw in the back of cars, Orla thinks.

"Mick McGahey condemned the bombing," another news hack says.

McLeod smiles in an irritable and unpleasant way.

"Yes, but Arthur Scargill didn't, and he's the organ grinder, isn't he?" McLeod says. "Not the monkey!"

There is laughter.

Orla raises her hand.

"Mr McLeod?" she asks.

McLeod smiles falsely.

"Yes?"

"Mr McLeod, when all eyes were on the bombing of the Grand Hotel last night, there was a house fire in Hove in which three young men were killed," she says.

"Well, I'm sorry to hear about that, but I don't see...."

"They were survivors from a care home in North Wales," Orla says. The Font-y-Llewellyn. I believe you're familiar with it."

McLeod looks worried: armed Special Branch confers about Orla.

"I think you're mistaken, Miss O'Regan," McLeod says.

"Well, that's interesting," Orla continues. "I have it on very good authority that the Llewellyn network of care homes in North Wales is directly connected to the Eastgate PR Firm, Dolphin Square, Pimlico, of which you were CEO before Airey Neave's murder got you an appointment to Thatcher's Royal Court."

There are gasps from the press packs tame flock of Eunuchs now, and the armed Special Branch heavies are moving to physically remove Orla like the flunkies to corrupt power that they are.

As for McLeod, his attempts at false pleasantness have gone, and the mask has completely slipped, giving a glimpse of the monster that lurks beneath.

"Frankly, Miss O'Regan," he says. "I'm shocked that you think this the time or the place to make such absurd...."

"Mr McLeod, what have you got to say about the paedophile ring that operates in Westminster or the abduction and murder of a young Asian boy during the Royal Wedding in 19 – "

One of the Special Branch thugs grips Orla. She struggles, and there is an edge of hysteria to her voice as she protests.

"Get your fucking hands off of me!" she shrills.

Orla is dragged away to the laughter of the press pack.

"This, ladies and gentlemen of the press, is exactly what we are up against when it comes to the Left and those who mean this country harm," McLeod continues in a truculent tone. "They're finished, let me tell you. The Parrot is dead. It is an ex-Parrot!"

There are murmurs of agreement as Orla continues to be dragged away. The surly Special Branch cop is talking straight into her ear as she struggles against his grip.

"Fuck off, you Red Bitch, before we book you!" he says.

"Oh yeah, for what?" she responds.

"We'll think of something," the cop growls.

Orla is released at the perimeter of McLeod's gathering, and the Special Branch cop swaggers back. She is isolated and alone and badly shaken, yet, even from this distance, she can hear the other reporters talking about her.

"What the hell was that all about, lousy timing apart from anything else?" One of the reporters asks.

"Name's O'Regan," the fat bastard from The Daily Mail is saying. "Irish, isn't it?"

"I know one thing," another reporter says. "She'll get a rocket from her editor when she gets back to town."

And all the while, McLeod continued to drone, the same way that the Iron Bitch herself had done the previous night.

"From the Falklands to the picket lines of South Wales and Yorkshire, we will do what it takes to make this country great again."

Still visibly shaking, Orla wanders off like the guilty schoolgirl she is perceived to be, up the hill to the clock tower in Churchill Square and to the train station beyond.

Orla is in tears.

251

Azazel watches her as she goes.

*

At the pit head that dominated the town, a token presence of pickets had long settled into the night shift as Eileen Vaughan, heavily pregnant, headed towards the only Indian Restaurant in town.

Inside, Eileen was ushered to a pre-booked table and given a menu.

She eased into her seat and began to order.

There was a couple already eating, in the restaurant, with a young child. The child was fidgeting and reading a Marvel comic about *The Mighty Thor* and his Magic Hammer.

Eileen checked her watch and then studied the happiness of the small family group again.

Where the hell is Terry on this of all nights? She wondered. *He couldn't possibly have forgotten?*

Could he?

Eventually, she began to eat alone.

Across the street, in the shadows that were his natural habitat, Azazel watched her eat.

The killer wasn't laughing.

Chapter Thirty

Sitting alone in the train carriage out of Cardiff Central, Derek Hepburn had struggled like *Hamlet* to contain his grief.

Distraught and broken, he now stared through the window at the once familiar valleys of green and grey that were somehow alien and distant to him, now.

Feigning madness in order to stay sane?

To be or not to be: to act or not to act?

That, as the Crazy Danish Prince said, was the fucking question.

First had come the revelation that his little girl had been fucked by that evil bastard, Liam O'Leary, and that his cheesy, seventy-year-old cock had been inside of Derek's Tracey, claiming her as some kind of trophy. Now had come the still greater bombshell that she'd been murdered to boot and in a particularly horrible fashion.

It was the worst of all possible circumstances for a homecoming, all those years since he'd peeled away, and Derek considered the prospect with a feeling of near-total dread.

Poe would have understood his mood, what with the Red Death holding sway over all.

Suddenly, Derek became aware that the train was slowing down and barely recognised the pit head on the hill that still dominated the town. That and the man-made mountain of slag that was straight out of a novel by Dashiell Hammett,

Derek had worked down that pit once and hated every last second of it with the passion of a character from an Alan Sillitoe novel who dreamed of escape. He'd hated the dank and dark and the taste of coal dust in his throat: hated the feel of that self-same coal dust under his fingernails and deep in the pores of his skin.

That pit that was not his pit: this town that was not his town.

Ghost town — and he the ghost of Christmas Past that was returning to it.

Like a criminal to the scene of his crime

He was at the small train station now, just as his Tracey had been the night that she was murdered, and for a fleeting instant, he almost thought that he saw her ghost standing by the closed waiting room on the platform. But it was an illusion.

The train came to a halt, and Terry opened the heavy door, stepping onto the cold Victorian concrete.

There was a single taxi waiting in the small car park that served the station. All of the porters and other staff had gone home, leaving the station deserted like the *Mary Celeste* cast out to sea.

In a moment of irony, he passed the poster for the Liam O'Leary rally that his own daughter had defaced.

Biting back bitter tears, he recognised her handwriting immediately.

Moments later, he was being driven to the hospital mortuary to identify his dead daughter.

*

Terry and the black WPC, Patricia, were becoming regulars now at the hospital mortuary. This time, they were with Yvonne Hepburn, the mother of the dead girl lying on the mortuary slab.

Tears welled up in Yvonne's red face that was now a wound, bleeding tears instead of blood.

Terry looked on, grim and uncomfortable, as Yvonne continued to cry.

Patricia, who, as Terry had noted, was good with people, was offering comfort to Yvonne, a woman whom Terry knew by reputation at least. The truth was that in the past, he'd never particularly liked the mouthy and aggressive woman from Glasgow who dealt and muled drugs for Mickey Draper. Add to that that she was a charmless bitch with a mouth as foul as a stale ashtray. That said, nobody deserved to see their own daughter, and flesh and blood, like this, with her face smashed in by an ice pick, her once pretty features reduced to gore.

Eventually, Terry cleared his throat and addressed Yvonne Hepburn with all the tact he could muster.

"Mrs Hepburn, your daughter and Susan Higgins were flatmates at the university, yes, in the halls of residence?" he ventured.

Yvonne nodded in the affirmative, sniffing back tears.

"Yes, they were friends, *Party Comrades*," she said in that strong Glasgow accent that the Police Interview Room knew so well.

Terry noticed how Yvonne's tone hardened when she referred to the *Party*.

255

"Same as her useless bastard of a father," she added.

Terry proceeded with his questions.

"Your ex-husband's a Party member?" he continued, trying desperately not to make it sound like an interrogation.

Again, Yvonne sniffed and nodded.

"Member?" she retorted. "He's a full-time enforcer for that bastard, Liam O'Leary. It's Derek's fault that Tracey's dead.

Terry looked shocked. The reports of domestic disturbances at the Hepburn's council house suggested that they had hardly parted on the best of terms but was Yvonne Hepburn lucidly claiming that her ex-husband had murdered his own daughter?

"What do you mean?" Terry asked.

"Tracey was always a Daddy's girl," Yvonne said. "Most of these youngsters are into the Anti-Nazi League and join the *Socialist Workers Party*, but Tracey joined the RWL because her Daddy was a member."

Terry stared astonished at Yvonne Hepburn as she completely opened up to him.

"Miners' strike or no Miners' strike, Mr Vaughan, being in the RWL got my daughter killed."

"You said she was a Daddy's girl," Terry persisted, wondering if Susan Higgins had been a Daddy's girl, too.

Now Yvonne's bitterness came through in waves, even overpowering her grief.

"Daddy's are more fun, aren't they, especially when they're hardly around?" she said. "Mummy's the bitch who struggles to put bacon on the table and dishes out the discipline to hold the family together. With Daddy, it's all fun and games. When he's not off in the land of gold and poison, that is, beating people up for Liam O'Leary and the fucking revolution."

"Your ex-husband's not working?" Terry asked.

Yvonne shook her head.

"He was a miner, but he couldn't stick it, all that dirt and dust," she said. "He said that Gramsci was talking bollocks about the nobility of manual labour because he never had to do any."

Terry looked at Yvonne with a compassion he'd never felt for her before. That hostility, he reflected, was all about drugs and about what Draper and Clever Trevor O'Carroll had got his brother into at school — fucking with his head and A levels, so he had to go down the fucking pit instead of escaping to university.

The way that Terry had escaped by joining the job — after a fashion.

Now, he saw a struggling single mother who had certainly made bad choices, once abandoned by a husband who had never properly grown-up. He still didn't approve of drugs, of course, but when all was said and done, she'd probably got involved with Draper to feed and clothe young Tracey and keep her small family together as best she could.

"Our Derek was all up the workers, but he didn't like being one," Yvonne continued. "He was on the dole in London, though I suspect he was actually paid a salary by the RWL."

Terry felt pained to ask the next question, but he had to — it was his fucking job. And intrusion on grief was always the worst part of the fucking job. "Mrs Hepburn," he said. "Most people who are murdered are usually murdered by people they know. The fact that Susan and Tracey were friends increases the likelihood of that. Mrs Hepburn, have you any idea who might want these two young girls dead?

Yvonne started to cry again as she shook her head. Patricia once more moved to comfort her.

It was at that moment that Derek Hepburn entered like some inexperienced ghost or unwelcome spectre at a feast.

He looked to where his daughter lay dead on the mortuary slab, and all the pent up anger that was inside of him exploded like a bomb.

"O'Leary, you sick bastard!" Derek yelled.

To Terry's astonishment, Derek then sank to his knees in front of his dead daughter, as if in contrition, like some latter-day *King Lear*.

"Dear Jesus, look what the bastard did to my little girl," Derek continued.

How, how, how?

Terry and Patricia exchanged confused glances. Then, as Derek struggled to his feet, Yvonne shook free from Patricia and attacked her former husband, clawing his face.

"You useless bastard, where the fuck were you when she was alive?" she yelled.

It was then that Yvonne's violent rage broke down into floods of tears. She stopped hitting Derek, whose cheek was now bleeding, and cried in his arms instead.

Derek kissed her.

Patricia stepped forward, but Derek signalled for her not to. He also indicated for the two cops to leave the mortuary.

Terry nodded to Patricia, and they complied.

Outside, in the corridor, he spoke to her.

"We'll leave them to it for now, but we'll need statements from them both in the morning," he said. "In particular, I want to know what the father meant about O'Leary back there. There's a connection to that old bastard, and I know it."

"Yes, Guv," Patricia said.

Then, all of a sudden, Terry looked like he'd remembered something.

Eileen would be waiting for him in the Indian Restaurant for their anniversary meal.

"Shit!" Terry said and ran out of the door. "I'll see you tomorrow, good night!"

Patricia looked after him, confused.

*

Azazel had been watching Eileen Vaughan in the restaurant for a while now. He felt a quiver of excitement and even an erection as his hand gripped the ice pick thrust deep inside his pocket.

Eventually, he saw her pay the bill and leave, clearly upset.

The couple with the small child had also gone.

As Eileen walked away alone down the street, Azazel separated from the shadows and followed her.

Past posters that were not her posters: past rhetoric that was not her rhetoric.

A town that was not her town and maybe a marriage that was not her marriage after all?

Azazel could feel her anger and fear from here.

But it was as nothing to what she'd feel when his ice pick, like a Magick penis, ruptured her pregnant belly and face.

Against the power and psychic energy that he would derive from this particular ritual kill, that of O'Leary's two young whores would be as nothing.

Besides, it was high time that Terry Vaughan, his so-called nemesis, knew what it was like to be hunted.

*

In his cold and draughty office in the Palace of Westminster, Derek McLeod was on the phone, listening to the ringing tone. He was irritable and in a foul mood. In front of him were the GCHQ transcripts of the phone conversation between that bloody Irish bitch, Orla O'Regan, and Clever Trevor O'Carroll of the sheep shagging Daily Bullshit, whatever he or that may be. Also on McLeod's desk was Orla O'Regan's file, fresh from MI5's F-Branch, complete with her photograph and an official motto that said *Regium Dorum: Defence of the Realm.*

"Come on, damn you!" McLeod snarled.

Eventually, in the police headquarters deep in the Rhondda Valley, Dermott Brady answered without ever identifying himself on the phone.

"Hello?" Brady asked.

"Hello, Brady," McLeod said. "This is the Ghost of Christmas Past."

McLeod imagined the fat Brummie thug, with his beery face and fists like hams, sitting up abruptly from where he was slumped in his chair.

"Jesus fuck!" he heard Brady say. "What do you want?"

McLeod sneered and responded in a patronising manner. There were many reasons why he actually detested Brady, with the fact that he was a product of the West Midlands working class being prominent among them. In McLeod's view, the world went to Hell after 1945 when the upstart proletariat no longer knew its place.

"Now, is that any way to speak to your benefactor?" McLeod asked. "I need your services, Detective Sergeant, but it may also be to our mutual advantage."

McLeod imagined the fat detective, who had beaten a confession from the Birmingham Six, lighting up a cigarette in his office.

"OK, shoot!" Brady said.

McLeod studied the GCHQ phone transcript that was in front of him.

"You'll be familiar with Acting Detective Inspector Terry Vaughan, the lead investigator into our renegade scout who's left the reservation?" McLeod said.

"Acquainted?" Brady sounded openly hostile. "Sherriff Terry's been a thorn in my side from day one. I've tried to control things here, but he's like a fucking terrier with a rabbit. Plus, I think

261

the bastard's turning Red, like the rest of his family, particularly including his Trot bastard of a brother."

"Red," McLeod echoed. "Like Jack McCreevey, you mean?"

This time, the fear was palpable in Brady's voice and made him even more ugly than usual.

"Now listen, McLeod," he snarled.

McLeod responded with menace.

"No, you listen, Brady, and remember who pays your fucking wages, you and Ridgeway," McLeod said. "Vaughan's set up a clandestine meeting with this journalist, Orla O'Regan, a trouble-making bitch we've been watching for some time. I need to know what's said at that meeting. After that, we'll decide an appropriate course of action."

"Course of action," Brady echoed, still clearly worried.

"Whatever it takes," McLeod snapped. "You've done it before, and if need be, you'll do it again. Good night!"

McLeod hung up.

*

Terry drove his Ford Sierra at speed through the empty streets of a town that was already dead.

At the wheel, Terry was in an anxious state. He hated being in Eileen's bad books at the best of times or if there was any conflict or barrier between them. But now, there was something else gnawing at his policeman's gut as if he knew that something was seriously wrong, with an impending sense of dread.

The Red Death held sway over all.

Even before Terry arrived at the restaurant, Terry could see that there were no customers inside.

Eileen was gone.

Terry parked up and went inside. Perhaps she was in the toilet or had told the staff where she was going.

Terry felt a knot in his stomach as if his entrails were being consumed by a sack of hungry rats.

*

Azazel was closing on Eileen Vaughan now. Already, his ice pick, like his naked weapon, was out.

And more than the thought of the kill itself, what excited Azazel the most was what this would do to Acting Detective Inspector Terry Vaughan.

His nemesis turned into prey.

How would Terry feel when he knew that he had lost the two most important things in his life that were laid out on that very same mortuary slab?

Above all, how would he feel when he knew that he was the hunted one now?

PART FIVE: THE LOST CHILDREN OF ALBION

Chapter Thirty-One

Night had made these streets its own as Azazel closed in on his prey.

Like the Yorkshire Ripper before him, he realised how the urge got stronger with each and every kill, giving him the erection that he'd been thus far denied in temporal and mortal life since his fall from heaven into the infernal pit.

The words of GOETIA, which was the Dark Book of Solomon, were recited, now, inside his head, by the dark angels that he alone could see beyond the veil. It was the same way that Crowley had seen them, in his vision in the Great Pyramid of Giza, after days of wandering in the desert wastes that were forsaken, like he, by God.

Here, between the Wheel of Fire and the Abyss.

In Azazel's pocket, the ice pick was like an evil penis, bearing death instead of life, yet preserving his victims forever as installation art.

Eileen Vaughan would make an interesting addition, he thought.

Excitement once more caused his heart to quicken, pumping the blood through these mortal veins, and then he heard the car engine behind him.

Two headlamps bore into the night, approaching like the eyes of some metal machine beast.

Azazel ducked into the side alley just in time to see Terry Vaughan hurtle past in a Ford Sierra, horn blaring to get his wife's attention.

"For Christ's sake, love," Azazel heard Terry shout through the open window of his car. "Why didn't you wait?"

Even from his concealed location, Azazel could see that Eileen was both furious and tearful.

"An hour, Terry, you were an hour late, and on our wedding anniversary too, you thoughtless bastard!" she cried.

"Look," Terry pleaded. "You can call me all the bastards you want at home, OK? I'll take it on the chin. I fucking well deserve it! But I won't have you walking the streets, not with a serial killer on the loose."

"Serial killer," Eileen asked in confusion through her tears. "What are you talking about?"

"There's another girl been murdered," said Terry. "That's why I'm late, woman! Now get in the bloody car!"

Eileen stood there stunned and Azazel, still in the shadows, clasped his *magick* ice pick in white knuckles. Terry slammed the dashboard of his car in anger.

"Look, to hell with all this politically correct feminist bollocks!" he yelled. "I'm your fucking husband, I fucking well love you, and I'm ordering you to get into this fucking vehicle!"

From his concealed location, Azazel watched Eileen get into the car.

"I still hate you," Eileen said as Terry started the engine, but she cuddled into him protectively just the same.

"Yeah, yeah, fucking right," Terry said as he drove away.

*

"Are you any closer to finding him?" Eileen asked.

They were awake in bed, having returned home more than an hour before. Terry, for one, couldn't sleep on account of the mice running somersaults in his head.

"I'm no longer sure I even think it's a 'him,'" Terry said.

Eileen looked confused.

"What," she asked. "You think it might be a woman?"

"No," said Terry. "I mean, I think there may be more than one of them. Like the original Jack the Ripper was probably a group of people stalking a group of women who knew each other. Real serial killers, like Sutcliffe, select their victims at random and then become more erratic the more the urge to kill grows. You know, like a sex thing. Both Susan and Tracey knew each other. They were close. And there's something going on with that bastard, O'Leary, I know it."

Eileen, while clearly scared and chilled at what Terry was saying, also seemed to be enthralled by her husband's acumen.

"You don't think he's mad then?" she asked.

"I think he's evil," said Terry. "But I think he's probably as sane as you and me. Well, you anyway. I also think he's sending some kind of message and that whatever's driving him to kill these young girls is rooted in his past. I'll find out more when I talk to this Orla O'Regan, tomorrow."

Eileen touched him lovingly.

"You're pretty bloody good at this detective lark, aren't you," she smiled. "My Terry, I'm so proud."

"You don't hate me, then?" he smiled.

Eileen embraced and kissed him.

"Of course not," she said.

"OK, now listen," Terry continued. "Our anniversary meal is going to have to wait. But I'm also concerned that he's watching the police, and that includes me. I'm going to make sure a WPC stays with you at all times, after dark, when I'm not here."

Eileen was about to protest. Terry shut her down.

"This is a fucking order, OK," he said. "I don't want you going out of an evening on your own until this bastard's caught. Now, let's try and get some sleep, yeah?"

Terry turned out the light.

*

Opposite Terry and Eileen's semi-detached house, a monster lurked among the shadows from which he was formed.

He had been cheated of his quarry tonight, but there was still time, Azazel knew.

And it was on the side of the fallen angels, not of the cops who were trying to catch him.

*

Dawn brought another ritual confrontation on the picket line as Terry drove to work.

Coal not Dole: Victory to the Miners!

Maggie, Maggie, Maggie! Out, out, out!

As Terry drove to work, Brady met with Ridgeway in the Chief Inspector's office. Ridgeway had already been briefed about the previous night's conversation with McLeod, and a GCHQ transcript of Clever Trevor's phone conversation with Orla O'Regan was now on Ridgeway's desk.

Brady was at the office window. He indicated the file as he spoke.

"What's that they say about giving 'em enough rope?" he asked.

"Not a word to Terry about this," Ridgeway growled. "If we reveal our hand too soon, he won't meet with the bitch. I want to know what she knows and what the fuck she's up to."

"We'll be digging two graves then," Brady sneered.

Ridgeway looked up at Brady in a severe way. His tone was angry.

"Just take it one stage at a time, will yer," he said with a trace of threat. "I'm still your Guvnor, Brady, Craft or no Craft, so just remember that, OK?"

"Here he is, the Boy Wonder himself!" said Brady, peering through the Venetian blinds.

Terry had just pulled up in the car park.

Minutes later, he was talking to Patricia, the black WPC, in the open-plan office. The crime room itself was a hive of activity as was to have been expected under the circumstances.

Ridgeway studied Terry for a moment, having concealed the GCHQ transcript and Orla

Brady's MI5 file. He went over to the office door and called out.

"Terry!" he said. "A word in your shell like."

Terry came over and saw at once that Brady was already in the office, smoking. Terry nodded at the Special Branch Sergeant in false courtesy.

On Ridgeway's desk, now, *The Sun* carried a front-page lead on the second Azazel killing. Ridgeway nodded to the bi-line by Orla Brady and a local correspondent. Motor-mouth must really be thick if he didn't know that Clever Trevor was moonlighting, Terry thought.

Terry closed the office door behind him.

"So then there were two," Ridgeway said. "Looks like you were right about this being a serial killer, Terry."

"Except that the two girls knew each other," Terry said with a heavy sigh. "That might or might not put a dent in the serial killer theory."

Brady and Ridgeway looked at each other.

"Anyway, I've arranged for a briefing in the crime incident room in half an hour," Terry said. "And as DCI Ridgeway is aware, I've also organised a press statement this afternoon for the local and national media: an appeal to the public, so to speak. We've also got BBC's *Crimewatch* coming, too."

Brady raised an eyebrow.

"Well, if we're on *Crimewatch*, we're celebrities, right?" He said sarcastically. "How photogenic are you, Terry? A bit camera shy, me."

Terry snorted.

"Now, you say that these girls knew each other, and they were both political, right?" Ridgeway said. "Both reds under the bed, as it were.

Which I think brings us back to Sergeant Brady's point about a likely political connection involving the fascist Right. That's why I've taken the liberty of giving him the go-ahead on a possible lead."

"With respect, Guv, I'm the lead investigator," Terry said. "I'd have liked to have been consulted first."

Ridgeway seemed irritated.

"It's not a pissing contest, Terry; it's called teamwork," he said angrily. "As you know, Sergeant Brady worked the Hilda Murrell case in Shropshire, interviewed some of the usual suspects on the Far Right but had to let them go due to lack of evidence."

"So?" Terry asked.

"So it seems that some new forensic evidence has cropped up in regard to *that* murder which might connect it to ours," Ridgeway said.

"I'm having RADRE, in Sevenoaks, compare the new forensic evidence on Murrell with ours pertaining to Susan Higgins," Brady said. "And, of course, with your permission as lead investigator, Terry, with anything we find on Tracey Hepburn as well. This one wasn't in the water, Terry. Our lad might have got careless."

Terry's brow knitted into a frown.

"They're good, Terry, the dog's bollocks," Ridgeway said. "Sergeant Ridgeway tells me they helped get a result on the Birmingham Six, but it appears they also helped secure a conviction on Judith Ward and a whole raft of terrorism-related cases as well."

Terry tried not to sound sceptical.

"Well," he said. "As they say at Hendon, I'm all for pursuing every line of inquiry on this one, but the MO *is* completely different Guv. For one thing, and discounting the age factor, there's no evidence whatsoever that either of these girls was sexually abused by their killer."

Brady stared at Terry intently.

"There *was* evidence of Satanic Ritual in relation to Hilda Murrell, Terry," Brady said. "Besides, we don't know if this *is* the work of a serial killer in the pathological sense. You said it yourself that the girls knew each other and were both politically active. My money's still on a political motive and that all this hocus-pocus about Azazel and the Nine Fallen Angels is simply a clever ruse to throw us off the scent."

"Very well," Terry nodded. "Bring it up at the briefing in twenty minutes. Now, if there's nothing else, I'd like to go and prepare."

Ridgeway gestured for Terry to leave, but, as he did so, the DCI called after him.

"We need a result on this one, Terry," Ridgeway said. "We don't want it dragging out like the Yorkshire Ripper, with us looking like cunts chasing some phantom, like *Wierside Jack.*"

"At least there's some good news," Brady grinned falsely.

Terry turned.

"What?" he asked. "Don't tell me you've won the football pools, Brady."

"Better than that," Brady grinned. "Zack the Hack Miller's fucked off to Valletta, Malta, for a Holiday in the Sun. At least *he's* out of our hair for a few days."

"Yeah," said Terry. "But what's he up to?"

Chapter Thirty-Two

The soundtrack was by the *Sex Pistols* as the battered old Peugeot taxi rattled through the narrow curving streets of Valetta.

In the back seat, next to a nervous-looking Tom Upward, Zack the Hack Miller looked like he thought he was Don Johnson on *Miami Vice*. As the taxi rattled past two attractive looking women in summer dresses, walking in the opposite direction, Zack looked back and licked his lips in a predatory fashion.

"Very nice!" he said. "What do you think, Tom, one for you and one for me? You can seduce 'em with one of your history lectures from the university."

Tom looked miserable. Zack thought Tom's Che Guevara beret made him look ridiculous.

"It's all right, Tom," Zack sneered. "I know you don't like me very much, but that's all right. *Flashman*, isn't that what you call me?"

Now, Tom had gone from miserable to furtive. He hated meeting the Libyans at the best of times, but now he really did wish he'd come to Malta on his own.

"Yeah, I know," Zack continued. "I know everything about everyone in this whole organisation, and you know why? Because Liam O'Leary thinks I do perfumed farts, mate, and that my shit doesn't stink. That's why. Next to the

Brothers Grimm, I'm the top honcho in the Security Directorate and never forget it."

Zack sang a bad rendition of Gary Glitter's: *You wanna be in My Gang.*

"A regular Felix Dzerzhinsky, right?" Tom smiled falsely.

"Who?"

"He was head of Lenin's political police, the Cheka, or would Beria be more your style?" Tom said.

Zack stopped smiling.

"That's not nice, Tom," Zack said. "They sent Beria to the firing squad in 1953."

Maybe it was the shock of seeing what happened to Derek Hepburn a few days back and why. But Tom had developed some uncharacteristic backbone and was certainly enjoying Zack's discomfiture. Zack preferred it when Tom reminded him of a swot to be bullied at his own minor private school.

"The thing is, Zack, I don't pretend to be something I'm not," Tom said. "I admit that I came from a privileged background before I joined the Communist Party at Oxford and then O'Leary's outfit in 1956. That said, I remained a rating in the Navy during the war when the likes of James Klugmann were working for Churchill and Stalin in SOE. In fact, I spent half the war teaching the other blokes to read."

"I forgot about your wartime record, Tom— your medal for going down on the HMS Hood." Zack sneered.

Tom snorted. His strange and newfound defiance was unsettling Zack now.

"I'm a historian, Zack, not an actor," Tom said. "I don't pretend to be working class or cultivate a fake accent that I picked up in Salford on the set of *Coronation Street*."

Tom mimicked Zack's phoney working-class accent causing the Party enforcer to flash him an angry glance.

"Eh, up, comrade Marx, chuck! You've no time to be reading Blue Books int' British library. You've got to be out selling copies of *Daily Advance*. And mind you abide by the Party line because that's what Marxism is all about, lad. No time for books. And don't try thinking for yerself until you've attended a bullshit lecture on dialectical materialism at Red House int' Derbyshire."

They'd arrived at their destination, by now, at one of the more prestigious hotels owned by the Libyans on the island. Zack stared at Tom as the taxi drew to a halt.

"That's Revisionism, comrade," Zack said. "I'll be reporting this conversation to Liam when we get back to London."

*

Fleet Street, October 1984.

The open-plan office of The Sun *still looks like a sweatshop as Orla enters, to the relentless tapping of heavy typewriter keys. A heavy pall of cigarette smoke gathers like storm clouds over the toiling scribes, one of whom is collapsed, blind drunk, at his desk, with a bottle of whiskey in hand.*

The editor, a bully in shirt sleeves, is in his office with a flame-haired young woman whom Orla does not

275

recognise. The moment he sees Orla, he yells across at her, filling her heart with dread.

"*Orla!*" *he shouts.* "*Orla Fucking O'Regan!*"

The newsroom continues to rattle and hum. The editor, full of menace, slams down a metal ruler, and the open-plan office becomes silent. He stares at Orla with something approaching hatred, and there is spittle on his foul lip.

"*Orla, get your fucking arse in here, now!*" *he bellows.*

All eyes are on Orla. The news hacks watch her in fearful silence as she heads towards the office.

The door slams shut behind her.

In the office are wall-to-wall page three tits out for the boys.

The editor slaps a copy of the previous day's paper in front of Orla. It has the grimacing picture of Norman Tebbitt being dragged from the ruins of The Grand Hotel in Brighton.

"*You know I've had occasion to slap journalists in the past,*" *the editor says.* "*And don't think I'd hold back on account of your being a woman.*"

"*I'm sure you're an equal opportunity employer,*" *Orla says with defiant sarcasm.*

"*Orla O'Regan,*" *the editor sneers.* "*That's an Irish name, isn't it?*"

"*I don't see the relevance of that, but you know it is,*" *she says.*

"*The relevance is that you didn't show much sensitivity when your Mick Chums tried to murder our Prime Minister in Brighton,*" *the editor glowers.*

"*Sensitivity being our mission statement here in this venerable institution,*" *Orla says.*

The redhead whom she doesn't recognise stares at her with loathing.

"Don't try to be fucking smart, Orla," says the editor in a threatening way.

"Who's Boudicca?" Orla asks, indicating the redhead.

"Rebecca's my new secretary, only I've had her working down at the Daily Mirror *on Maxwell's rag,"* the editor explains. *"Hanging around in the ladies bogs, listening to the chit chat of the journalists, nicking their stories, know what I mean?"*

"So that's what we're reduced to when we're not doing the tits and the bingo," Orla says.

Rebecca, the redhead, continues to stare at Orla hatefully.

"Let me tell you what we do at this paper, sweetheart," the editor says. *"We destroy the lives of people we don't like, we keep Maggie in power at all costs, we choose every successive government in the UK forever, and we keep the scum of the working class on its knees. And with our loyal support, the current government is rolling back all this socialist bollocks that's been introduced since the Second World War."*

Orla fights to hold back her disgust. The editor's monologue assumes the form of a fanatical rant.

"And there's no way on earth that King Arthur's barmy army, Red Ken Livingstone, some disgruntled coon of a social worker in Lambeth or a bunch of drugged-up fairies in Brighton telling pork pies are going to fuck that up!" he bellows.

"You've been following me during my investigation?" Orla responds indignantly.

"We've a team of private investigators working for this paper, darling, all ex Scotland Yard," the editor says. *"And that's not to mention the team of ex SAS neck breakers on our payroll."*

277

Orla stares at the editor with as much loathing as disbelief.

"You know your trouble, Orla," the editor says. "It's that you didn't learn your trade as part of our paper's big happy family. All that NCTJ crap you learned about journalism ethics? Here, we like to train our people in house in our way of doing things – like Rebecca here posing as a cleaner down at The Mirror. She'll go far this one," the editor chuckles with unconcealed admiration.

"What?" Orla demands. "You're threatening to replace me with her?"

The editor points at her.

"You want to survive the move to Wapping, Orla; you'd best start toeing the line," he says and then slaps two files down in front of her. "Fortunately, those private detectives I mentioned have got you a couple of juicy stories to help you forget this care home bollocks: one, to prove to us that you really are opposed to terrorism and one to appease your lefty conscience."

Orla flips open the first file to see a middle-aged man, as well as a crime scene photograph in a rural setting.

"SNP politician and full time lush who just happened to top himself with his own revolver near Loch Ness," the editor continues. "It seems he was linked to terrorism in the form of the Scottish National Liberation Army. Apparently, said Scottish National Liberation Army is run by some tosspot called Busby based in Dublin, and that's their PO Box Number."

Orla looks up from the file. She stares at the editor.

"They're bad people, Orla," the editor says. "They were planning a Risin attack in Birmingham, likely Abu Nidal connection, which means Libya, and we're the only paper with the story. In the wake of the Brighton bombing, and with the government promising *further counter-terrorism legislation, that is what I call a scoop."*

"Sure," says Orla. "And the fact that our Scottish MP campaigned against US nuclear submarine bases in Scotland has nothing to do with it."

"Those bases are there for our protection," the editor threatens. "You know what's going down in Afghanistan and Nicaragua. Or do you really want the Ivans rolling up the Mall with snow on their boots?"

"Pity you can't connect the Soviets to the miners' strike as well," Orla says sarcastically.

"But we can, Orla, all through the Mad Colonel in Tripoli", the editor smiles unpleasantly.

Orla opens the second file and finds a picture of men in Ku Klux Klan hoods burning a cross in the Welsh Valleys.

"What's this one?" Orla asks.

"Ku Klux Klan in South Wales should be right up your street," the editor says. "There's been some Jewish cemetery desecrations in Cardiff as well."

"Ku Klux Klan in South Wales," Orla pouts. "Pose for the cameras, did they?"

The editor resumes his threatening mode.

"Write the stories, Orla, then take some leave," the editor says. "And stay away from Americk Fraser if you still want a job when you get back."

Orla leaves the editor's lair, feeling uncomfortable.

As she does, she sees the drunken journalist shoved into the "sin bin" next to the open-plan office.

Rebecca, the redhead, studies Orla balefully as she leaves.

*

279

In the conference room of the big hotel, Tom Upward nervously counted a large amount of cash as if he were part of some drug deal in a movie like *The French Connection*. As for the gangsters, their role was assumed by Zack and by the Libyan intelligence officers travelling on false documentation from Libyan Arab Airways. All wore expensive Armani suits and, being Senussi Bedouins, bore more than a superficial resemblance to the Mad Colonel himself.

On the wall, a picture of Qaddafi hung next to that of Maltese premier Dom Mintoff.

Big Brother is watching you, Tom Upward thought.

Zack fawned over the suited thugs like the secret police wannabe that he was. Ton Upward cringed as he saw the cracked actor perform the role of the school bully's best friend.

"Rest assured, comrades," Zack said. "This additional money will be well spent as the miners' strike is merely the beginning. The revolution in Britain is just months away."

Still counting the money, Tom looked up in angry disbelief.

"You say that this Peter Chapman wants to talk to the Colonel directly and to address the Peoples' Revolutionary Council in Tripoli?" one of the Libyan goons said.

Tom's angry disbelief now turned to visible alarm.

"Yes," said Trevor. "Comrade Chapman sits on the Regional NUM in South Wales, and I had a meeting with him, very recently, in the Rhondda Valley. He thinks it's time for the Colonel, and the

Revolutionary People of Libya, to start supporting the Miners' Union by financing it directly. With the revolution in Britain being so close, that is."

The Libyan goon smiled unpleasantly.

"That will be for the Colonel to decide," he said. "However, this Peter Chapman is welcome in our country. As guest of honour in addressing the Revolutionary Council, he will stay in the Colonel's tent."

Zack nodded.

"He'll appreciate that comrade," he smiled. "Thank you."

Zack turned to Tom dismissively as if the university lecturer were his flunky.

"Have you counted that money yet, you being an educated man?" he asked.

"I learned to count at school, Zack, not university," Tom said. "The money's all here."

"Splendid stuff!" said Zack.

He shook hands with the Libyan goon.

"Always a pleasure, comrade, and I look forward to visiting your country in the very near future," Zack said. "To see for myself what it's like to be actually building socialism."

The case of money locked, Zack ushered Tom to the door and into the foyer.

The academic almost gasped with horror as he recognised the group of younger men sitting there, waiting for their own appointment with the Libyan goons, like a queue in a dentist's surgery.

The younger men, all British, leered at the academic unpleasantly and in a threatening way, clearly aware of who — or at least *what* — he was.

Tom began to speak.

"What the — "

"Be quiet and keep walking," Zack snapped his order.

"But they're — "

"Shut up, Tom!"

The young men followed them with leering, hostile eyes. Their names, as Tom was aware, were Nick Griffin, Patrick Harrington and Derek Holland. The skinheads who were clearly their minders Tom didn't recognise.

Outside, Tom turned on Zack just as the taxi arrived.

"What's going on, Zack?" Tom demanded. "That was a delegation from the National Front's Political Soldier faction sitting in the lobby."

"So what," Zack continued to sneer.

"So I fought a war against Hitler and fascism, not to mention Railton Road in '47 and Notting Hill in 1958!" Tom said.

All of a sudden, Liam O'Leary's refusal to support anti-fascist mobilizations since Lewisham in 1977 assumed a very different perspective.

"You fought a war for the British Empire, Tom, and don't you forget it," Zack said.

"Jesus," said Tom. "This whole thing fucking well stinks, and what's this crap about there being a revolution in months; and Peter Chapman being a guest of Qaddafi?"

Zack indicated the taxi.

"Get in the car, Tom," he ordered. "You're carrying an awful lot of illegal cash."

Tom complied angrily. He sat in the back of the taxi, sulking, as Zack joined him.

"Tom, I'll do a deal with you," Zack said. "You don't mention this Peter Chapman deal to the old man, and I won't mention your disloyalty to the Party earlier on."

"What?"

"It's 40 years since James P. Cannon placed Liam in charge of British Trotskyism," Zack said. "Tell the truth; the old bugger's losing it, turning senile. There's going to be some changes, Tom, and I want you to be part of it, OK?"

Zack winked at Tom.

Tom looked uncomfortable as the taxi drove off.

Chapter Thirty-Three

In his cottage at the gateway to Hell, Azazel watched the BBC *Crimewatch* pageant on TV.

He toyed with an automatic as he did so — the same automatic he'd used to kill the Walker family, on the sacrificial road, in 1979.

On-screen, Terry Vaughan, DCI Ridgeway and Inspector Pratt of the West Glamorgan Constabulary sat on a platform for the media cameras. In the small audience in the hall were the tearful parents of Susan Higgins and Yvonne Hepburn.

Derek Hepburn was significantly absent, Azazel thought.

Terry was speaking.

"What we know is that someone out there knows who this man is and is either protecting him, like the Yorkshire Ripper's wife or nurturing suspicions," Terry said. "And we ask those people to come forward, in confidence, and talk to us before he strikes again."

Azazel stared at the cop who was hunting him, revealed in low resolution and rasta-lined colour. Already, the voices of his fellow angels spoke in tongues in his head.

"As for the killer, I've got a message, and that's that I'm coming for you, me and my team," Terry said. "You can run, my friend, but you can't hide!"

Azazel gripped his pistol and shot the TV like he was Elvis.

*

It was a lot of years since Ridgeway had been on a stakeout, the Flying Squad so long ago it felt like it had happened to somebody else. Now, outside his own station, his own manor, factory and turf, he sat next to the camera-shy Sergeant Dermott Brady of Special Branch and waited for Terry Vaughan to appear.

"Well, there's ace reporter Roger Cook," Brady said at last, as Terry appeared at the entrance.

To their surprise, Terry walked straight past his own car.

"He's left the station on foot," Ridgeway protested. "Why's he left his car?"

"Fuck knows," said Brady. "Just follow him at a distance and make sure the bastard doesn't see you."

Ridgeway complied, following Terry at a distance.

Terry walked.

Suddenly, a battered old car approached at speed. It was an ancient A35 van seemingly held together by rust. It overtook Ridgeway's car and screeched to a halt beside Terry.

There was a brief altercation, and a suspicious-looking Terry got in the car.

Ridgeway looked astonished as the car sped off.

"What the — "

"Curiouser and curiouser said Alice," Brady piped up. "Just follow the bastards. With any luck, they'll lead us right down the rabbit hole."

Ridgeway complied.

*

The moment the banger had screeched to a halt next to Terry, Derek Hepburn had popped his head out.

"Get inside, Detective," Derek said.

"What—"

"Just get in, will yer," Derek snapped. "For fuck's sake, Orla O'Regan sent me!"

Terry looked suspicious as he complied.

The old vehicle drove away.

Derek gripped the wheel of the van with white knuckles, looking desperate and close to the edge. Some people said you got a better view from there, but somehow, Terry doubted it. To Terry, he looked like a man on the razor's slit of absolute breakdown, like Hamlet, Lear or any tragic hero from Shakespeare that you cared to mention.

But he was still a suspect in his own daughter's murder, Terry told himself.

"I noted that you weren't at the press conference, Derek," Terry said. "Your ex-wife could have done with some support."

The awkward pause simply reinforced Terry's suspicion.

"You sure you're up to this?" he asked after a while.

"I'm Desperate Dan, Sheriff," Derek said. "Finding my little girl's killer's all that's keeping me sane. I'll have my nervous breakdown later."

"Well," Terry rolled his eyes. "What with you being in the Security Directorate of the RWL and me an instrument of the bourgeois state."

"I was in the RWL before I found out that O'Leary was screwing my Tracey: Tracey and Susan Higgins!" Derek said.

"What?" Terry was incredulous. "Come on! O'Leary's knocking 80, man!"

"It's a religious cult, Detective Inspector," Derek snapped. "And sex is power, and this is what religious cults do. What do you think the Security Directorate is for when it's not beating up Party dissidents and demanding money with menaces? I mean, it's sure as fuck not for fighting fascism, is it?"

Derek sounded both angry and bitter.

"Ask your brother's new playmate if you don't believe me," he said after a while.

"Zack the Hack," Terry responded. "What about him?"

"He's O'Leary's personal pimp," Derek said. "How'd you think he's got the old bastard's ear? I mean, it's hardly for his keen grasp of Marxist theory, is it?"

Terry stared at Derek, stunned.

"Zack pimped Susan *and* my Tracey for Liam O'Leary," Derek continued. "Only Susan fell pregnant, and my Tracey found out about it. And now they're both dead. Think about it, Detective Inspector Vaughan."

They were heading out of town now: the magical mystery tour indeed.

Still, Derek looked desperate as he drove.

A ghost: like the high plains drifter?

"You think O'Leary had the girls killed," Terry asked.

Derek shook his head.

"O'Leary's a cunt, but I don't believe he's a murderer," Derek said. "Besides, *they* don't want him removed as RWL leader just yet. Not when they can use him to stuff the NUM."

"*They* – "

"F-Branch: MI5!"

"Oh, right," Terry laughed. "Here we go, here we go!"

"Yes, Terry," Derek responded angrily. "Here we fucking go! Orla's done quite a bit of digging on Zack the fucking Hack and, believe me; his left-wing credentials are as bogus as that working-class accent of his he picked up on the set of *Coronation Street.*"

"That applies to half the leadership of British Trotskyism, barring Liam O'Leary," Terry said. "He just surrounds himself with guilt-ridden bourgeois academics and actors to do his theoretical work for him."

"Yes," Derek nodded in affirmation. "But as well as coming from a well-heeled background in Yorkshire, did you know that Zack flunked officer training at Sandhurst or that, despite his privileged upbringing, he developed a taste for football hooliganism at a very young age. That and right-wing politics, Sheriff, *extreme* right-wing politics."

"What are you suggesting?" Terry demanded.

"That Zack the Hack was already in the National Front and then the British Movement when he was recruited as an informant to the Police National Football Intelligence Unit during Operation Red Card. After he grassed up half his mates, he was kicked upstairs to be handled by Special Branch, just as the Column 88 paramilitary group emerged from the BM."

Terry stared at Derek.

"Brady said that the name of Azazel was identified with Column 88," Terry said.

"Which grew out of Colin Jackboot Jordan's Colour Guard," Derek said with a nod. "And Brady should know on account that he was Zack's handler at SO15. Specifically, Column 88 tried to blow up the RWL headquarters in Brixton, at which point O'Leary formed his Security Directorate."

Derek was looking in his rearview mirror now. He noticed that a pair of headlamps had been following them from town.

"By which time Zack's been to drama school and joins the Party via Equity," Derek continued. "And here he is now in pole position on account of O'Leary's cheesy and perverted cock."

Derek nodded at the rearview mirror.

"Speak of the wolf, and his tail appears," he said.

They pulled up at a red light, and the car behind, with the headlamps, did likewise. Despite the hour, there was traffic coming the other way.

Derek looked at the red light, then at the traffic. He then accelerated with a screech of tyres.

There was a blaring of car horns.

The car that was following them hit another vehicle coming the other way.

Terry was horrified.

"What the—"

Incredibly, they didn't hit another car. Derek hit the pedal, and they tore up the road like a meteorite, leaving lines of blue rubber on the sacrificial road.

"Are you fucking crazy or what?" Terry demanded.

"Like Hamlet, you mean: to act or not to act?" Derek laughed. "Just remember I'm security trained, Detective Inspector."

*

Still shaken from the collision, Ridgeway punched the dashboard.

"Shit!" he said.

The driver of the other car had just gotten out of his vehicle. He slammed his car door and angrily strode towards Brady and Ridgeway.

Brady lowered his window and showed the driver his police ID.

"We're Old Bill, so fuck off," he told the driver, who nervously complied.

At Brady's side, Ridgeway reached for the car radio. Brady, incredulous, grabbed his wrist.

"What are you doing?" he demanded.

"Putting out an all-points on that boneshaker," Ridgeway replied.

"Are you fucking crazy?" Brady demanded.

Chapter Thirty-Four

The band gigging for the miners were called *New Model Army,* from Yorkshire, and they were fucking good.

They were a product of the One-in-12 club in Bradford and playing a track called *1984* when Derek and Terry arrived.

Terry noted that some of the band's followers actually wore wooden clogs.

A girl with long blonde dreadlocks looking midway between a punk and a hippie was collecting at the door.

The plastic bucket indicated that it was in support of the miners' strike.

"Will you make a contribution, lads?" she asked.

Derek, who was clearly skint, looked to Terry.

"It's OK, Terry," he said. "It's for the miners, not the RWL."

Terry put £5 in the bucket.

Derek led him through to a room at the back.

In the office, Orla O'Regan sat smoking behind a desk. There were posters, in support of the miners' strike, behind her.

As Derek led Terry inside, the detective had a vague sense of being in enemy territory.

Orla smoked.

"Orla, this is Detective Inspector Terry Vaughan, an old school friend of mine," Derek said. "You probably saw him on BBC *Crimewatch* earlier.

Orla smiled as she got to her feet. She shook Terry's hand.

"Pleased to meet you, Detective Inspector," she said.

"It's *Acting* Detective Inspector, and I reckon I'll be back directing traffic if I don't catch this killer on the loose," Terry replied.

They sat down, facing each other around the table.

"Well, Derek's given me some interesting leads about Zack the Hack, but I'm still a bit confused," Terry said. "I mean, for one thing, Miss O'Regan, where do you fit into all this? I mean, you're hardly a comrade or a member of the RWL."

"You still don't know the half of it, Acting Detective Inspector," Orla said.

Applause sounded from next door.

"Six years ago, two young boys escaped from a care home in Flintshire, North Wales, where they had been systematically abused," Orla said. "The killer was the man now known to you as Azazel, a member of Colin Jackboot Jordan's colour guard and of Column 88. He was hired to track down the two boys and recover some incriminating photographs, as a result of which young Jack Parry was killed. As well as Jack, Azazel murdered an English family of holidaymakers, but it was all covered up by the local police, as was the abuse at the care home itself."

"Hang on," Terry asked, vexed. "Why would they do that?"

"Because the care home and others like it were part of a network supplying paedophiles in the House of Commons itself," Orla said. "The key to this network was Eastgate PR operating out of Dolphin Square in Pimlico."

Orla pushed a photograph of Dominic McLeod towards Terry.

"The CEO of Eastgate was this man, Dominic McLeod, who specialised in cash for access at the time," Orla said. "After Airey Neave was murdered, also we believe by Azazel, McLeod became Margaret Thatcher's principle aid."

"Shit!" Terry said, both astonished and shocked. He looked up at Orla.

"OK," he said. "But how does this tie in with Liam O'Leary abusing young girls?"

"After the military coup plot that destabilized Harold Wilson's government, the Westminster Paedophile ring played a major role in the current government's rise and consolidation of complete power, especially after the Falklands conflict," Orla said.

"How, I'm not with you?" Terry demanded.

Orla passed Terry a copy of MAGPIE, the publication of the Paedophile Information Exchange.

"The boys at the home were used to service politicians and others close to Thatcher," the reporter continued. "But this publication with similar origins in the Deep Establishment was mostly aimed at the Tories' opponents. I can name two prominent Liberal MPs who were paedophiles who played a major role in bringing down Callaghan's coalition government."

"It gets worse!" Derek piped up.

"During the 1970s, a number of Trotskyist organisations stupidly started to argue for the abolition of the age of sexual consent," Orla said. "Talk about a home goal."

Terry laughed mirthlessly. He shook his head.

"Actually, the Deep State probably exaggerated how many paedophiles there were on the Left," Orla continued. "But they hit the jackpot with O'Leary because he *really* had a weakness for young flesh. So, too, did his sleeper in Lambeth Council, where the paedophile network also operated through the South Vale Care Home in West Norwood."

"This is the punch line, Terry," Derek said.

"Through Lambeth Council, they got Labour MPs to support the Campaign for Children's Rights because it opposed the use of corporate punishment in schools," Orla continued. "Those MPs largely didn't know that this was a front for the Paedophile Information Exchange. They also got elements of the NUJ to support the publication of MAGPIE."

Terry looked at the wretched publication in front of him. He shook his head miserably.

"Good grief," he said, simply then looked up at Orla. "What's your source on this?"

"Americk Fraser," said Orla, causing Derek to look sheepish.

Terry's brow knitted in a frown.

"The black social worker in Lambeth murdered by fascists?" he asked.

Orla shook her head.

"Americk wasn't murdered by fascists, Terry," she said. "It was Americk who put me onto

Stephen, the boy who witnessed Azazel's killing of Jack Parry and the English Family and who could identify the killer. But he and two other care home survivors were murdered in a house fire in Brighton the same night the IRA bombed the Grand Hotel."

Terry stared at Orla.

"So what happened then?" he asked.

"After I confronted McLeod about the Westminster Paedophile Ring at Brighton, I was placed on a tight leash by my editor," Orla said. "I also knew I was being watched, at the very least, by the private detectives working for the paper. Americk made the mistake of phoning me at my office and arranging to meet me on the Isle of Dogs. Ironically, he chose a docklands site belonging to the London Docklands Corporation where Thatcher's new temples to Mammon were about to be built."

Terry rolled his eyes.

"On the bones of murdered Druids and Albion's lost children, no doubt," he said. "It's OK, Orla; I've been reading a lot of Blake since this caper began. In between Milton and the *Book of Enoch*, that is."

"I did my best to shake off any tails with the result that I was probably late," Orla continued.

She stubbed out her cigarette.

"You can probably guess the rest," Orla said.

*

London Calling, 1984.

Orla has been working on the probably bogus Ku Klux Klan story from South Wales when the phone rings in her office.

The caller is Americk, completely agitated, asking to meet her at a clandestine location in the Isle of Dogs.

Already the office pariah, she looks furtively at her colleagues in Murdoch's Ministry of Fear, none of whom she now trusts.

Confident that the editor is otherwise occupied, she slips out.

Paranoid eyes, crammed with suspicion, follow her as she leaves and heads for Charing Cross tube.

The rattler will take her to the East End, where the Beast is stirring, and the Temples to its wretched glory are being constructed on the bones of murdered Druids and empty docks and homes.

In the 1950s, you'd have seen the ships coming in from streets where children played.

Now the ships have gone the way of the dinosaurs, and the dark and sluggish Thames is eerily silent as Orla approaches the empty and haunted docks.

Billboards on stout mesh fences announce that this is the property of the London Docklands Development Corporation. *Coils of barbed razor wire have been erected against the native population, against whose interests and needs these new and wretched temples are to be built. However, some of the natives are still defiant.* Class War *proclaims a piece of graffiti with an anarchist symbol, followed by:* Kill the rich." *More graffiti tells Orla to* Turn Back or Die.

It is then that Orla hears movement and angry male voices.

Like Alice, chasing the white rabbit, she crouches as she advances and dares to look around a corner of grimy and weathered industrial brick.

She sees Americk bloodied and struggling, handcuffed to a supermarket trolley.

She sees a man she will later know as DCI Ridgeway, Flying Squad, preside over a grotesque ritual in which Americk is doused in lighter fuel.

"Here's some Holy Water," Ridgeway chuckles. "Fucking bless you, my Jungle Bunny son!"

Ridgeway then delivers a toast.

"To Maggie Thatcher," he says.

"To Maggie Thatcher," the other cops reply.

They set fire to Americk, who screams. His flaming body, chained to the supermarket trolley, is projected into the dark and sluggish waters of Conrad's interminable highway.

"Oh my God," Orla blurts out in horror.

As if in response, someone lights a cigarette as if he thinks he is Orson Welles in a movie by Carroll Reed. In the flickering light, she sees the florid, beery face of a man she will later know as DS Dermott Brady, Special Branch.

Americk, in flames, screams as the trolley rattles towards the water's edge,

Orla turns and runs.

Ridgeway and his posse of killer cops see her and take off in hot pursuit.

"For fuck's sake, after the bitch," Ridgeway roars.

Her heart beating and pounding like a madwoman in her head, Orla somehow escapes and evades the gang of murderous predators. From her concealed location, she sees the killer cops hunt high and low for her like she was the Scarlet Pimpernel.

"The little cow gave us the fucking slip," Ridgeway bellows.

"Come on," Brady replies. "We got to get out of Dodge, now."

In the yellow rubbish skip, where she is covered in dusty cardboard, Orla hides among the stinking trash and detritus of a building site. She fights the urge to cough or be sick.

It is then that she hears the rustling of something close to her face.

Two beady eyes stare at her in the dark like something from a novel by James Herbert.

In Margaret Thatcher's Airstrip One *in 1984: of all the horrors, a rat.*

*

Terry stared at Orla, and it was clear that all his doubt had gone.

"You say that both Brady and Ridgeway were there?" he asked.

Orla nodded.

"Ridgeway had done it before to the private detective hired by Jack Parry's sister, Roxy," she said. "She was passed off as a victim of the Yorkshire Ripper. Brady joined the team later, long after he fitted up the Birmingham Six. Around the time that this eight-year-old Asian boy was abducted and murdered by the Westminster paedophile ring, the day of the Royal Wedding in 1981, in fact."

"And Azazel, who the fuck is he," Terry coaxed.

"Can't you guess?" Orla asked.

"So you think he's Zack the Hack," said Terry.

Orla raised an eyebrow.

"Don't you?" she asked.

298

Chapter Thirty-Five

When Terry made CID, he'd told himself he'd never bring his work home, that Eileen would be shielded from the crap that he had to deal with every day.

That was when he still believed in the police and in institutions of the state.

Now, in bed, she was his only confidante, as he whispered as if in Holy Confessional.

Eileen touched his arm with concern.

"Terry, you're scared," she said softly. "I've never seen you scared before, love."

"I think I've opened up a door to a dark and very frightening world," he said. "What was it Blake said about the gulf between the wheel of fire and the abyss? About doors between things that are known and not known?"

Eileen shook her head.

"What are you talking about, Terry?" she demanded.

"I'm saying that maybe some doors shouldn't be opened," he said.

*

Talk about dead woman's shoes.

First day at the Number One *Sun* and Clever Trevor O'Carroll was already easing himself into the seat behind what was formerly Orla O'Regan's desk.

In Fleet Street, the street of shame, built on the site of London's public gallows and of the buried Fleet River, pumping bodies and evil as from a cursed lay-line into the cold, tidal waters of the Thames.

On the desk, there is a picture of Orla, smiling and picking up a Press Association award.

Talk about Judas and the thirty pieces of silver, Trevor thinks.

Pricked by conscience, he places Orla's photograph face down and then goes to the toilet to do a line of cocaine.

*

Once more from their eyrie, in Ridgeway's office, he and Brady watched Terry arrive for work.

Ridgeway waited until Terry was at the coffee machine before making his move.

"Terry, my office, now!" he barked.

Terry complied, and this time, it was Brady who slammed the door behind him.

Two murderers, Terry told himself.

Ridgeway slapped the morning edition of *The Sun* in front of him. Terry was shocked to see an article with Clever Trevor O'Carroll's bi-line.

"You want to cough up, Terry, about your dealings with the press?" Ridgeway asked.

Terry swallowed.

"You were at the press conference yesterday; we—"

"I'm not talking about that, you smart-arsed Welsh cunt!" Ridgeway said. "I'm talking about your private communion and confessional with Saint Orla O'Regan of fucking Fleet Street."

"Built on the site of London's public gallows, apparently," Brady said.

Terry started to talk, thinking on his feet.

"Guv –"

"Shut it, Terry!" Ridgeway bellowed. "The only reason you're not suspended is that I need to keep you on a tight leash and my beady and all-seeing Masonic eye on you and what you're about. But you're in hot water, my son. You might want your Federation Rep present when we have a real talk about your future, insofar as you've got one."

Terry started to protest.

"In the meantime, you're no longer the leading investigator, and Acting Inspector Brady wants you in *his* briefing in the incident room in ten minutes."

Brady did nothing to conceal his look of triumph.

"Guv," said Terry.

"Are you still here, Sergeant?" Ridgeway sneered.

*

Terry moved back into the open-plan office as the preparation for the briefing began. The black WPC, Patricia, was once more in uniform and looked towards Terry nervously as he came in.

Terry shook his head.

Brady took the lead and started speaking in front of an overhead projector.

"Right, you lot, lend me your ears before we saddle up the posse, that is," Brady said. "Recently, I got a top team at RARDE in Sevenoaks to compare the forensics on Hilda Murrell's murder with that of Susan Higgins and guess what? We got a match. It's something new called DNA profiling, apparently."

Brady turned on the overhead projector. Once again, it showed a group of fascists who were members of the National Front's political soldiers, selling the *National Front News* in front of the market-house on stilts in Ross on Wye.

The *NF News* headline said: *National Front Supports Welsh Bombers.*

If Tom Upward had been in the room, he'd have immediately recognised two of the skinheads from the foyer in the Libyan owned hotel in Malta. But it was the young man in the Palestinian *keffiyeh* that Brady pointed to.

"Andrew Evans," said Brady. "I then put what we had through the Police National Computer at Scotland Yard and came up with Andrew Evans' name. He's part of a National Front political soldier Unit that operates locally under the guise of *Meibion Glyndŵr.*"

Terry raised his hand.

"As well as burning down holiday homes, they've been turning up on miners' picket lines pretending to be lefties," Brady continued. "What is it, Terry, and no, you can't go to the fucking toilet."

"Hilda Murrell's been in the ground for over a year, and Susan Higgins was immersed in water for a prolonged period," Terry said. "How reliable is this evidence?"

"Fuck me, Terry, you're a sore loser," Brady said. "Do you want in on this bust, or do you want to stay back in the sin bin and sulk."

There was a pregnant silence as Terry's colleagues, who were no longer his colleagues, stared at him.

Brady slapped his fat hands together — those same fat hands that had beaten a confession out of the Birmingham Six and helped to murder Americk Fraser in docklands.

Terry and Patricia once more exchanged worried glances.

"OK, saddle up the Palominos and don't forget to wait for armed backup," Brady continued. "These bastards are all about getting their hands dirty and going where the terror is, so we've no idea what to expect in Evans' gaffe."

The detectives filed out of the room.

Brady looked to where Terry and Patricia were.

"You two coming or what," Brady demanded.

Terry and Patricia miserably complied.

Brady gave a thumbs-up sign and winked at Ridgeway before he left.

Ridgeway stared hatefully after all of them.

*

Andrew Evans lived in a council house on a sink estate on the edge of town. The unkempt garden looked like a rubbish tip, and there was a large Welsh flag in the window.

In his front room, that more correctly resembled a crypt, Andrew Evans smoked a joint and tried to exorcise the demons in his head.

Jack and Stephen running from the care home, urging Andrew to join them across the treacherous snow. Andrew being too scared and playing Judas to their flight!

Andrew bolting from McCreevey's moving car the moment he noticed that black cunt, McLeod!

Only where are my thirty pieces of silver, he asked himself.

On Andrew's wall, as a testament to his newfound faith, were posters of British and European third position fascism, some of them taken from Fiori's missive on *The Political Soldier.*

Although Andrew was barely literate, there was a copy of William Pearse's novel, *The Turner Diaries,* on top of a copy of *National Front News,* next to an overstuffed ashtray.

The turntable played *Death in June,* by Sol Invictus, for all that *Skrewdriver* was secretly more to Andrew's taste. After Joe Pearce nailed his colours to the mast, taste in music had become as important as rhetoric in the ranks of Britain's fragmented fascist Right.

A poster on the wall proclaimed the latest Party slogan: *Tear down the Cities.*

It was part of Darre's proclamation as to the return to feudalism and the new nobility of blood and soil.

A year ago, Stephen had died in a house fire in Brighton, and Andrew knew that he'd been topped. He also *knew* that the *Illuminati* and New

World Order run by the World Zionist Conspiracy were responsible.

Andrew smoked his joint and cried like a child.

*

Outside the house, the Police Armed Response Units signalled each other using their hands.

They were armed with Heckler and Koch HP-5 sub-machine guns and MP-50 recoilless carbines.

Perhaps, Terry thought, in the new and ever Jaded Jerusalem that was being forged by the Thatcher administration, all cops would look like soldiers one day.

Terry clocked Brady tooling his own Smith and Wesson 38 like he was Doc Holiday at the OK Corral.

The armed cops smashed down the door with an enforcer and advanced in military formation, skirmishing in pairs.

Armed police! Armed police!

Brady followed the armed response cops, and Terry came in behind.

The stink of cannabis hit Terry like a wall as he entered the building, and he thought of Johnny and Clever Trevor O'Carroll in the senior common room at school.

In the front room, Andrew Evans sobbed as he was pressed to the floor and handcuffed. He was dressed only in his underpants and looked like he needed a shower. The smell of cheesy feet mixed with that of the dope.

"Surprise, surprise," Brady said. "It's the Zionist Occupation Government come to take you away, you piece of murdering crap."

Brady kicked Evans hard in the side.

"You are under arrest for being a horrible piece of shit," Brady said. "You have the right to remain silent, but anything you say will be taken down in evidence."

Brady turned to a cop wearing plastic gloves.

"Tear this disgusting hole apart," he said. "I want everything bagged up in evidence."

Brady left the room and shoved into Terry as he did so. The black WPC, Patricia, was with him.

"Nothing to do, Terry, or are you two waiting for a bus?" Brady snapped.

"You seem to have the matter in hand," Terry sneered.

Brady leaned toward Terry in a threatening way.

"It's a lead, Terry and probably a result," he said. "And it's a fuck sight more than you came up with, Inspector Fucking Clueso!"

Andrew Evans was frog marched to a police van, still dressed only in his underpants.

The neighbours stared at him, agog. Part of Terry imagined them dropping milk bottles like something out of *Get Carter*.

Andrew's head was slammed against the door frame deliberately as he was bundled inside.

Inside a filthy downstairs toiler, Brady found another uniform WPC kneeling by the bowl. There was a pile of pornographic magazines together with a *Political Soldier* pamphlet by Fiori and a copy of Alecstair Crowley's *Magick in Theory and Practice.*

"Knock! Knock!" Brady said and indicated the tome by Crowley.

"In the bog," he added. "Probably the best place for it."

It was then that the WPC found something. She looked up at him.

"Guv, these wankmags include kiddie porn," she said.

Brady nodded. His lips curled in disgust.

"Fucking disgusting," he said. "But at least we can formally charge him with something. Good work, constable."

"Guv," another wooden top called from the corridor.

Brady stepped out of the toiler and gasped.

The device that the uniform cop was holding, with a digital timer, was very clearly a bomb of some description, and it was eating away the digits towards zero.

In Northern Ireland and elsewhere, the National Front Political Soldiers had infiltrated the Animal Liberation Front after all.

"Fuck me," said Brady, matter of fact. "That's a bomb, and it's started working. Christ! Stand still, son and don't move. Everyone else out and call the bomb squad!"

The cops started to evacuate the hovel. Patricia was looking around, concerned about where Terry might be.

Terry himself stood at the top of the stairs, watching Brady instruct the uniform with the bomb.

"OK, our kid, now hand that bomb to me, carefully!" Brady said.

The uniform cop complied. His hands trembled, and Terry swore he could smell the sweat from where he stood.

"Good lad, now on your bike," Brady said. "You heard, and that's an order."

After the cop left, Brady put the bomb to one side. He then went inexplicably back into the room that had just been cleared.

The timer on the bomb continued to eat the seconds to zero.

Brady, inside the room, had removed a drawer and was looking for an envelope taped to the underside. It was as if he knew exactly what he was looking for, Terry thought.

Brady hummed and sang as he studied the envelope's contents, which comprised a bundle of Polaroid photographs that Terry couldn't see.

"*Nice and sleazy, nice and sleazy, nicely, nicely, nicely does it all the time.*"

Brady pocketed the photos and walked straight into Terry in the doorway to the room.

"What are you up to, Brady?" Terry demanded.

There followed a struggle and altercation.

The counter on the bomb hit zero.

The suspect device exploded at Terry's back, punching out the downstairs windows of the council house as it did so.

*

Patricia saw and heard the blast as it punched out glass across the council house lawn. The very ground itself shook, in the small cul de sac, as if they were witnessing a minor earthquake.

"Oh, God," she screamed. "Terry's still in there!"

Patricia tried to rush forward, but a detective stopped her.

"It's too dangerous," the detective said.

Evil smoke pumped and coiled from the punched out windows, and she could see the fires beyond, in the hallway, like the fires of Hell.

*

In the front room, Brady and Terry lay unconscious as the flames roared all around them.

A living entity, the fire had already clambered the walls and ceilings like a malevolent, hateful child.

And all the while, a hundred giggling demons welcomed them both to Hell.

PART SIX: THE POLITICAL SOLDIER

Chapter Thirty-Six

Docklands, 1979.

The docks are empty now, but for the ghost ships, doomed like the dinosaurs before them.

Here in the East End, the Beast stirs and prepares to consume its victims.

Around a flickering brazier, a group of the homeless huddle, like Albion's lost children as in a dystopian vision of the nation's terrible future.

Prominent in their feral ranks, a young man with matted dreadlocks tries to cook by the open fire.

Two headlamps reveal themselves, like the eyes of some metal machine beast, and the homeless scatter like rabbits from a gun.

There is a roar from the machine beast's engine.

The vehicle, which is a Ford Granada, comes to a halt, and a cabal of cops emerge, led by Ridgeway, and holding the sagging body of Jack McCreevey between them.

All of the cops are Flying Squad: the so-called elite of the Yard.

The young man with the matted dreadlocks peers fearfully from where he hides. He sees Ridgeway's murderous cabal drag McCreevey, bloodied like some sacrificial offering, towards a supermarket trolley, to which the private detective is cuffed.

The brazier crackles unattended.

"Oh, Brave New World and all the creatures that are in it," Ridgeway says.

As if in ritual, McCreevey is doused in lighter fuel.

"How about some Holy Water, McCreevey?"
Ridgeway asks. "Bless me, father, because I have fucking
sinned."

Then comes the toast.

"Maggie Thatcher!" Ridgeway declares.

The young man with the matted dreadlocks
watches them leave.

In the dark, cold waters, McCreevey feels his
lungs fill with water and the popping in his ears. It won't
be long, he knows, until he drowns.

Almost unconscious, he half thinks he sees a
young man in shabby clothes swimming towards him.

Moments later, having broken the handcuffs free
from the supermarket trolley, the young man brings
McCreevey to the surface.

Jack McCreevey is alive!

*

A vortex of flame engulfed the council house as
Terry stirred.

At his side, Dermot Brady was still
unconscious.

They had moments to get out; Terry knew
before they were overcome by smoke.

He cursed as he raised Brady's dead weight
using a fireman's lift.

Terry coughed.

"Come on, Brady, you corrupt bastard",
Terry said. "We're checking out!"

With the heat searing his face, Terry
staggered towards the door, carrying the sagging
form of Brady as from a flaming mouth of rage.

*

Patricia and the other cops looked physically relieved as Terry emerged from the burning entrance. At Terry's back, evil coils of snaking smoke continued to coil from the shattered windows of the house and upwards towards the dirty grey sky.

Neighbours cheered.

In the Police van and in handcuffs, Andrew Evans looked on miserably, still dressed only in his underpants. From where he sat, bleeding from a head wound, he saw a fire engine and Army Bomb Disposal Van arrive almost simultaneously. Already, uniformed cops were clearing the occupants of the cul de sac and adjacent street on account of the natural gas supply.

Terry dumped Brady on the ground amidst a fit of coughing.

"*Attention! Attention! It is imperative that all civilians disperse and evacuate the estate!*"

Patricia touched Terry's arm. At his feet, Brady was coughing, too, as he stirred to consciousness.

"Are you OK, Guv?" Patricia asked.

Terry nodded towards the Brummie detective lying fat and prostrate on the ground.

"You should give up smoking, Brady," Terry said.

*

In the council house that he shared with his wife and

daughters in Morden, South London, Liam O'Leary, self-appointed leader of the world's proletariat, stirred.

Reaching for his glasses, the first thing that came into focus was a huge crucifix at the end of the bed. For years he had thought it was there to mock him or, more likely, to exorcise his malign presence from the household.

"Backward Papist bitch!" O'Leary said as he got to his feet.

Downstairs seemed somehow worse than the usual inquisition though the room dripped with Catholic iconography, as usual, hanging off of the priest-ridden walls. His two daughters were watching the banality of morning television as O'Leary entered the room and considered their father with baleful contempt.

There were no Daddy's girls here, he thought to himself.

His wife was in the kitchen, cooking breakfast. She cast him a hateful glance.

O'Leary sat at the breakfast table and muttered. His wife practically threw his breakfast in front of him.

Once again, he saw the hateful stares of his daughters, like mute loathing in stereo. O'Leary slammed the table with his fist.

"What the fuck's wrong with everybody," O'Leary demanded.

As if in answer, his wife slapped a copy of the *Sun* in front of him. O'Leary shook his head as he started to eat.

"You ignorant priest-ridden bitch," he said. "I told you never to bring bourgeois newspapers into this house. We get all the information we need from the *Daily Advance.*"

"Read it, Liam," his wife said. "Read it and explain yourself."

The front-page exclusive, by Trevor O'Carroll, revealed that at the time she was murdered, Susan Higgins was pregnant with Liam O'Leary's child.

O'Leary looked up at his daughters. They stared back at him hatefully.

"Well, this is just typical of the MI5 propaganda that we've seen since the beginning of the strike," he said.

His wife shook her head.

"You might get away with that one with your idiot supporters, Liam, but this is me you're talking to," she said. "And I know you. I know you can't keep your dick in your pants, you dirty, disgusting old bastard, and I know you like them young, Liam...*Too Fucking Young!*"

O'Leary threw down his knife and fork. Still, his daughters stared at him hatefully.

"I've no time for this shit," O'Leary said. "I've a revolution to run."

He got abruptly to his feet, leaving his breakfast uneaten. His wife, in a fit of rage, picked up the breakfast and threw it at his head.

"Bastard!" she screamed.

It narrowly missed him and shattered against the wall.

"Fucking bitch!" he screamed.

O'Leary leapt across the room. He punched his wife in her flaccid arm.

The daughters looked on in mute horror, then collectively moved to protect their mother.

O'Leary's wife was pleading to him now through angry tears. To O'Leary, she looked completely sexless, like something that was used up and fit for the bin.

"Why do you hate me so much?" his wife demanded through painful sobs. "Why do you hate me when I gave you two beautiful daughters?"

She burst into tears. The two daughters were standing, now, still protective of their mother, and still, they stared at O'Leary with pure hatred.

"To be sure, there are no Daddy's girls here," said O'Leary bitterly.

He slammed the door as he left.

Chapter Thirty-Seven

With blues and twos blaring, the Police van hurtled towards the police station.

Flanked by uniform cops, Andrew Evans sat in handcuffs, looking scared.

On the bench opposite sat Dermot Brady, Acting Detective Inspector, with Sergeant Terry Vaughan at his side. This, suffice to say, was the same Terry Vaughan who had just saved Brady's miserable life.

Brady stared at Andrew.

"You're fucked, Evans. Do you know that — royally fucked!" Brady said. "Possession of kiddy porn *and* explosives *and* conspiracy to commit explosions under the Prevention of Terrorism Act, but what I really fancy you for is the murder of those two girls!"

Andrew looked up, frightened.

"Yeah, that's right," said Brady. "You shit blue lights and bricks, mate. I like a tidy clean up rate, me. I like a result."

Terry looked worried.

"I didn't kill no girls," Andrew whined, like the bar coded victim of abuse since childhood that he was. "I'll cough for the holiday homes, but I didn't kill anybody, right?"

"That's what they all say?" Brady sneered.

"Look, I'll give you the SP on the bombs," Andrew said. "They were part of a batch made by Animal Rights activists in Northern Ireland that we

317

got our hands-on. The explosives are co-op mix, homemade crap using moth balls, hydrochloric acid and hydrogen peroxide. But the digital timers are dead sophisticated — "

Brady was in his face, angry and irritated. He seemed determined to shut Andrew down.

"Just shut it, right?" Brady said. "Me and my mate here nearly got killed today because of you. You and your terrorist wannabe chums who want to play Guy Fawkes with holiday homes and toxicology labs and whatever else takes your fancy!"

Andrew stared at Brady. Despite the moral terror in those eyes, there was also a ghost of defiance.

"You forget, Brady, that I know you," Andrew said. "That I knew you before the Hila Murrell caper that you also tried to pin on me."

"You what?" said Brady.

"I've known you since — "

Brady took a lunge at him.

"You fucking slag," Brady screamed.

The next thing Terry knew, Brady was remorselessly beating the suspect.

"You're going to cough for those murders, you spasticated piece of crap!" Brady yelled. "You're going to cough the way that the Birmingham Six coughed and the same fucking way. And fuck the fucking Police and Criminal Fucking Evidence Act!"

As Brady referred to PACE, each letter of the recent legislation was punctuated by pounding his ham-like fists into Andrew's face.

Terry dragged Brady off.

"Oi! Oi! Oi!" Terry yelled. "Just fucking cool it, OK?"

Brady stared at Terry hatefully. He sat down and wiped the sweat from his face with his sleeve.

"Told you, Terry," he said. "You're a bad fucking loser."

*

It was a high-end restaurant in London's West End, and striking and struggling miners would have been horrified to see Peter Chapman of the NUM Regional Executive in South Wales eating there.

They also would have been horrified to see him reading *The Sun*.

"O'Leary's finished, and after the performance, I saw the other day good fucking riddance," he said. "Mind you; King Arthur will be pissed off. The *Daily Advance* is one of the few national platforms he's still got on his side."

Sitting opposite, at the same table, Zack Miller presided over the remnants of an expensive meal. He sipped a glass of wine and spoke.

"Don't worry," Zack said. "In a few days, we won't need O'Leary anymore. Plus, any muck associated with the RWL will automatically stick to the NUM."

Chapman stared at Zack.

"The important thing now is to establish a direct financial connection between the NUM and Qaddafi," Zack continued. "That way, the miners and the bloody revolution are done for!"

"What should I tell King Arthur?" Chapman laughed mirthlessly. "About my going to Libya, I mean? I can hardly tell him it's a fucking holiday."

"You know the Jackanory bollocks we agreed to," Zack said. "You're going to persuade the Mad Colonel not to sell oil to the UK during the strike. Arthur will buy that. Probably get you a first-class ticket with Libyan Arab Airways, seeing as we'll all be travelling first class under socialism."

Zack laughed as Chapman got to his feet.

"I got to go," Chapman said. "There's a delegation of striking miners coming up from Kent."

"Have fun. Rather you than me, mate," said Zack.

Chapman indicated the remnants of the expensive meal.

"I assume this is on F-Branch," Chapman said.

"*Regium Dorum,* mate, defence of the fucking realm," said Zack, with a wink.

Zack sipped his wine and watched Chapman leave. Zack then clicked his fingers at a waiter.

"Dog and bone, old boy," he said.

Zack was presented with a stylish retro telephone. When the waiter had gone, he made his call.

He recognised Dominic McLeod's voice immediately.

"Punctual as ever, Zack," McLeod said. "I assume everything's going according to plan."

"Absolutely smooth as a nut," Zack beamed. "Our broken and turned Stalinist has-been is just about to have his last supper with King Arthur

Scargill and kiss the cheek of his former Christ in the Garden of Gethsemane."

Zack shifted forward and assumed the tone of conspiracy.

"Thing is, with the going rate of inflation, he'll want more than thirty pieces of silver, which brings me to the Holy Grail," Zack said.

"If by the Holy Grail, you mean the al Yamamah Arms deal, then the Prince will be flying in from Saudi Arabia very shortly," McLeod replied.

There was a pause.

"You do realise, Zack, that this is the biggest arms sale in British history," McLeod continued. "But the Prince is a man of exotic taste. Deliver on this, and you'll have earned your percentage Mr Miller."

The biggest arms deal in history, Zack thought. It would be lubricated by the same paedophile network that had delivered the Iron Bitch to power, and it would deliver the financial deregulations and rise of the hedge funds to come.

"I assume the North Wales merchandise doesn't appeal to our mutual friend?" Zack asked.

"No," said McLeod. "Despite attending a British Public School and being a member of the Bullington Club at Oxford, the delights of Dolphin Square and Elm House are not for him. However, he's most impressed by the exploits of our renegade scout who's gone off the reservation down your neck of the woods. What a naughty boy he is. The Prince told me that he's never killed anyone before. He wonders what it would be like to exercise that degree of power over another human being. But I'm afraid the Police Station in Lambeth might be off-limits for a while."

"Don't worry," Zack grinned as he flicked over a photograph. "I've another House of Fun sorted out: another Romper Room, as they say in Northern Ireland and another snuff star for our latest blockbuster. With Azazel on safari, one more won't notice."

The photograph that Zack was looking at showed a young RWL activist. In the photograph, with a clenched fist, she was protesting and raising money for the miners' strike.

"Then, the Sandman can take out Azazel himself, and all of Albion's lost and naughty children can go to sleep," Zack said.

"Yes, it's a shame about the Desolate One, considering all the spring cleaning he's done for us in the past, from Lord Lucan to Airey Neave, in fact," McLeod said. "But as you say, he's left the reservation and, what with these cryptic clues he keeps leaving at the crime scenes, who knows what he might say if he were ever caught. Sanction with extreme prejudice, Zack, and bury the bastard's heart at Wounded Knee."

Chapter Thirty-Eight

Sundown found Andrew Evans reciting his Hail Marys in his police cell. This caused Dermot Brady to grin and chuckle as he burst in upon him.

Brady menaced Andrew, moving as quickly as twenty stones of lard possibly could. Brady's tone was flippant and mocking, but the words were from an actual black mass.

"*Lord of the Flies, Favour Me Now,*" he said. "*Prince of Darkness Favour Me Now!*"

Andrew stopped praying. He stared at Brady in moral terror as if he had been physically struck.

"Would have thought that was more your style, Azazel, you being Satan's Right Hand Man since the fall from heaven, so to speak? " Brady taunted. "'*Fiery the Angels Fell. Thunder Rolled Against Their shore.*' There transformed from bearers of light into serpents of the infernal pit or some bollocks like that."

"There's only one Devil's Disciple round here, and I'm fucking well looking at him," Andrew whined.

"Is that right?" taunted Brady.

Brady threw the younger man against the wall and started to beat him remorselessly. His foul nicotine breath was in Andrew's face and lungs now.

"You're going to cough for those murders, son," Brady yelled. "I've got a nice confession typed out for you already. Guards!"

Two uniformed cops appeared at the door.

"Take the next contestant here to interview room one," said Brady. "There's something he wants to get off his chest."

The uniformed cops grabbed Andrew.

"No!" Andrew blubbered. "Please!"

Andrew was dragged away.

Brady looked after him hatefully.

*

The Central Committee had been gathered at the fortress in Beehive Place, Brixton, on account of the article in that morning's *Sun*.

They were a mixture of trade unionists, actors, academics and youth organisers, most but not all of whom were men. They were of all colours, but in the main, they were ageing, too.

Since their failure to engage with Anti-Fascist politics after Lewisham in 1977, the RWL had had trouble recruiting youngsters.

And there were other reasons for that, as Clever Trevor O'Carroll of *The Sun* had revealed that morning.

From his office, next to one of the Brothers Grimm, O'Leary watched the Central Committee arrive in clusters. He already wondered what some of them had already been discussing in the Wimpey Bar opposite Brixton tube station.

"Now I know how Julius Caeser felt," O'Leary said.

"Don't worry, Liam," said the brother, who'd been at his side since the McAlpines' Strike in 1960. "You'll be home in time for *Dallas.*"

O'Leary smiled thinly. It was a longstanding joke in the Party's inner circles that *Dallas* was his favourite program and *The Godfather* his favourite movie.

"What was it you said, Tony, during China's Cultural Revolution?" O'Leary asked. "About all revolutions displaying excesses because they are, in essence, excesses of history."

"You said we were wrong to support the Cultural Revolution," Brother Tony said. "That Mao was worse than Stalin. But actually, the quote comes from Leon Trotsky himself."

"Yes," said O'Leary, his tone bordering on self-doubt. "But I wonder what he had in mind?"

Flanked by both the brothers, O'Leary walked into the room where the Central Committee assembled, in what almost looked like a classroom.

Tom Upward was in conference, he noted, with a lecturer from Sheffield University and another from Middlesex Polytechnic.

O'Leary opened the meeting and, in a roundabout way, came to the public charges against him. To make his point, he raised an offending copy of *The Sun.*

"Which brings us to the lies and slanders in the bourgeois media, against me personally," Liam O'Leary said. "These are precisely consistent with those against Comrade Arthur Scargill and the NUM, which originated with MI5's F-Branch and which surfaced in the *Daily Mirror* and on the Roger Cook Report."

Tom Upward looked up with open hatred.

"Besides, we all know that the history and politics of the RWL were not made in the bedroom, and neither will be that of the revolution that is close to hand," O'Leary continued.

There was laughter from some quarters of the room, but Tom Upward didn't laugh, and neither did the two academics with him. The Brothers Grimm scoured the room like children of the Cambodian Killing Fields, looking for signs of thoughtcrime and dissent.

"What we must build for now is a general strike," said O'Leary. "We — "

"May I say something there, Comrade General Secretary," Tom Upward interrupted.

All eyes were on Tom. Some shared the hatred of the Brothers Grimm, while others, hatchet-faced and miserable, simply willed him to be quiet.

"Without a doubt, a General Strike was a realistic prospect a year ago when the dock and rail unions refused to handle scab coal," Tom said. "And the *Daily Advance* was absolutely correct to condemn both the TUC and Labour Party leadership for failing to support the miners and call for such a strike. But as a Trotskyist organisation, what *transitional demands* did we attack to such a call for a general strike?"

Tom paused, measuring the stony silence in the room.

"Beyond, that is, the usual tired mantra that reformists don't have any answers and the usual call for the building of a revolutionary party because Labour is a stinking corpse," Tom said.

There were gasps at his blasphemy. O'Leary himself was seething with hatred, and Tom had to fight to be heard over the muttering in the room.

"Where was the call for a Workers Government?" Tom asked. "And besides, the moment is passed. Calling for a general strike now is a fucking pipe dream that will never happen. The only way — the only way — that the miners and wider labour movement won't be defeated now, allowing the Thatcher government to inflict a terrible future on subsequent generations, is if we build connections between the miners and the struggle to save the Metropolitan Councils, particularly the GLC."

Tom held up a copy of *Die Spiegal* to make his point.

"In an interview to this German magazine, Thatcher herself has candidly admitted that she can't fight two battles simultaneously, against the miners and the metropolitan councils and win," Tom said. "Now, the RWL is active in both these campaigns. So why have we never raised a slogan to unite and combine these struggles? It might not lead to revolution, but it would rid us of this bastard government and save our children and future generations from the decade on decade of misery that unregulated free-market capitalism would inflict."

Tom laughed.

"I mean," Tom asked as he pointed to O'Leary with a finger of his own. "What is all this Libyan money for beyond building a self-serving religious cult whose leader likes to abuse and shag young women?"

There were now more roars and gasps, and O'Leary's attack dogs, in the form of the Brothers Grimm, moved in for the kill. Tom was thrown against the wall, punched and kicked and then dragged to the stairwell. That he was about to be thrown over the side seemed obvious when the academic from Sheffield came up behind the Brothers Grimm. He started to drag the brothers off, and slowly, other members of the Central Committee joined him.

"Fucking leave him alone!" the academic from Sheffield bellowed.

The one from Middlesex Polytechnic helped Tom sort himself out.

"Come on, Tom," he said, "We're leaving this fucking mad house!"

About a third of the Central Committee followed Tom and his two friends out of the building. O'Leary screamed at them in a bullying yet impotent way.

"Come back!" he yelled. "Come back, do you hear me, you bunch of disgusting petty-bourgeois. You're all MI5 agents! You're all in the payoff, the CIA! You're all expelled, and I hope you're up to date with your subs!"

The Party was over all right.

Chapter Thirty-Nine

Brady and Terry faced Andrew in the interview room, and in accordance with the recently passed Police and Criminal Evidence Act, there was a cassette tape recorder operating in the room.

"Look, I don't even understand all this Mumbo Jumbo," Andrew moaned. "Azazel and the nine fucking angels. I can hardly read and write, can I?"

"Thought the Political Soldiers were the intellectual end of things?" Brady sneered. "Darre? Fiori? All that shit that Griffin, Harrington and Holland are into?"

Andrew lashed him a nervous glance.

"I was following Joe Pearce, wasn't I?" he moaned.

"Yeah, free Joe Pearce!" Brady mocked. "I tell you, if Joe Pearce is free, I'll have half a dozen of the fuckers!"

Brady looked up at the terrified halfwit.

"Now, two dead girls," he said. "Come clean and get if off your chest, son."

It was then that Terry intervened.

"What did you mean when you said you knew who Acting Inspector Brady was, Andrew?" he asked.

Brady flashed Terry an angry glance.

"We've met before, haven't we, Andrew, the Hilda Murrell murder" Brady sneered. "And I still fancy you for that one, too, mate."

"What?" Andrew protested. "Even though I can't drive or disable a phone? Anyway, I wasn't talking about that. You know what I meant."

Brady leaned across the tape machine. He checked his watch.

"This interview's terminated at 20:48 hours," he said and turned the tape machine off.

Andrew looked terrified.

"Now we'll have a proper chat, the old fashioned way," Brady said,

Terry, alarmed, piped up.

"Acting Inspector Brady, under the 1984 — "

"Fuck the fucking Police and Criminal Evidence Act," Brady exploded in rage. "We didn't need PACE and all that Lord Scarman shit when I got a result out of the Birmingham Six, and I don't need it now."

Andrew was still terrified but also strangely defiant as if he knew he no longer had anything to lose.

"This is how you were before when you were a prefect in the fucking care home," Andrew yelled.

Brady, enraged, knocked Andrew sprawling to the floor. Next, Brady produced his police issue, Smith and Wesson 38.

"You slag!" bellowed Brady to Andrew, like he was lower than the shit on his shoes.

"Brady!" Terry warned.

The uniformed cop in the room was like a statue, hearing, seeing and speaking no evil. Brady, his naked weapon out, walked across to Andrew's prone form and started kicking him repeatedly.

"You know what I'm doing, you cocksucker?" Brady asked and then kicked him again. "I'm singing in the fucking rain!"

"I'm warning you, Brady, that's enough!" Terry yelled.

Brady pointed his gun straight at Terry. His face was a mask of fury.

"Shut it, Terry!" Brady yelled. "You're just a country copper from the fucking Valleys who doesn't know the price of fish.

Brady kicked Andrew again. Spittle formed in his mouth as he ranted.

"How green was my fucking Terry!" yelled Brady.

Brady put the gun barrel to Andrew's head.

"Listen, son," Brady said. "I've got your confession to two murders all nice and typed up upstairs, and mark my words that either your signature or your fucking brains will be all over it before the pub shuts."

"Outside, Brady, now," Terry yelled.

Brady stared at Terry as Terry went to the door. Brady dragged Andrew to his feet and rammed him against the wall. He punched Andrew in the guts and sent him down again.

"You keep an eye on this spastic until I get back, right?" Brady ordered the uniform cop and left.

Andrew was coughing up blood as Brady went through the door.

In the corridor, Brady confronted an angry-looking Terry.

"So this is what happened to the Birmingham Six, is it?" Terry demanded.

"You want to remember what team you're batting for, *boyo*," Brady said.

"Really, Terry taunted. "So what did he mean by you being a prefect in a care home? Wouldn't have been in Flintshire by any chance? That lad's about the same age as three young men killed in a house fire in Brighton last year. Nasty fire — might have been caused by a co-op mix incendiary with a digital timer if anyone had bothered to look."

"Bollocks, you sad Welsh fuck!" Brady said, indignant. "So I'm an orphan who grew up in a care home in Taff land, so what? At least I did what I had to do to get out of that crap hole, same as you did, Terry — turning your back on your own precious mining community that's dying on its feet by joining the job. We all have our price, pal."

Terry looked enraged. Brady pointed towards the cell.

"That piece of crap's got victim written all over him and always did have, what with the life of the wolf being the death of the lamb," Brady said. "The losers on the fucking picket lines and dole queues and sleeping rough on the streets. Twenty years from now, thank God and especially thanks to Maggie, they won't even be citizens. In fact, they'll be nothing but fucking prey!"

Terry physically lunged at Terry. The two men fought. It was then that Patricia appeared in her WPC's uniform.

"Terry, Terry," she yelled. "It's your father!"

Patricia seemed genuinely shocked to see Terry about to punch a fellow officer in the face.

"It's the hospital, Terry," Patricia said. "I'm sorry, but your dad's dead."

Terry released Brady and abruptly left. Brady, red-faced, rubbed his throat and bellowed after him.

"You're fucking dead, Vaughan. Do you hear me?" he yelled. "Dead — same as your Communist bastard of a father!"

*

The streets of Morden were silent when Liam O'Leary, defrocked former leader of the world proletariat, pulled up his Triumph Toledo outside the council house where he lived.

Fucking place!

Angrily, O'Leary entered the front room of his home and turned in the light. With just as much anger, he confronted a picture of Jesus that had mocked him all these years and the rest of the Catholic iconography that was dripping off the walls. He then saw a collection of his wife's prayer cards and began to tear them up. Then, like a feral animal, he smashed up the Jesus picture and attacked the cross.

It was then that his wife entered the room. She looked horrified.

"Liam!" she yelled. "Have you lost your mind?"

O'Leary roared. He attacked his wife, and she screamed in terror as he attacked her.

"Shut up, you stupid sexless cow", he yelled. "Do you want the fucking neighbours to hear?"

Chapter Forty

When Terry arrived at the hospital, he found his wife, Eileen, consoling his mother, who was in tears. His mother looked up at him.

"Oh, Terry," Mum said.

Terry stepped forward to embrace his mother just as Johnny emerged from the ward.

"Terry," said Johnny. "Dad's in here!"

Terry went to join his brother. He took Johnny by the arm. Inside, he found his father lying dead in bed, with the oxygen equipment standing useless in the corner.

Silicosis: a miner's disease and the butt end of jokes by cunts like Dermott Brady.

Terry looked grim and sorrowful but was staying strong and calm for his family the way he'd always had to. Johnny was in tears. He lunged forward, attacking his father's corpse on the bed.

"Fucking pack it in, Dad!" Johnny yelled. "A joke's a fucking joke, but that's enough! Come on, wake up! Wake up, you old Stalinist bastard!"

Johnny broke down uncontrollably into tears. Terry stepped forward to comfort him. He embraced his kid brother, who had never been safe to be let out alone on the street. And as he did so, it occurred to him that none of Johnny's new playmates, in his great fucking revolutionary Party, had bothered to be with Johnny when his father died.

*

An angry mob had gathered outside the Police Station, and sniffing blood, the provocateurs were back in town. Indeed, if Tom Upton had been in the Rhondda, he'd have immediately recognised the two skinheads from the hotel foyer in Valletta who were also in the photograph, with Andrew Evans, in Ross on Wye.

There were placards among the angry crowd: *Justice for our Girls!*

In the station, Patricia had gone in search of coffee from the machine, as the police canteen was long shut. She heard the chanting crowd before she saw it through the window.

The crowd was like a feral animal and in an angry mood.

"Shit!" Patricia said and ran off.

In the interview room, she found Brady standing over Andrew, who was slumped unconscious at the desk. There was blood in his mouth and a signed confession in front of him. He looked dead.

Patricia started to speak.

"Inspector Brady, there's — "

The statement trailed off as she saw the state that Andrew was in. Her mouth was open in shock.

"Better get an ambulance for this one," Brady said negligently.

*

The ambulance, when it arrived, had to negotiate the crowd. As it inch-wormed towards the entrance, with uniforms holding back the punters, the two fascist provocateurs nodded at each other.

As Andrew was brought out on a stretcher, someone shouted from the ranks of what was fast transforming itself into an angry and feral mob. For over a year, this community had suffered, largely at the hands of the police, transformed from guardians of the peace into storm troopers of a hated occupational government. The struggle had been, and remained, one of life and death, and now the miners were losing, and a grim future beckoned under the long distended shadow of the Beast. Then, some sick bastard had started preying on their own daughters, their own flesh and blood, and on activists who supported the strike, with the same apparent contempt and indifference from the authorities that they had already shown towards the victims of the Yorkshire Ripper.

"That's the bastard!" someone cried from the churning sea of human rage. "That's the bastard that killed Susan and Tracey!"

The two fascist provocateurs, their faces concealed by Palestinian *keffiyeh,* nodded at each other. Both wore pea coats and Leon Trotsky badges to misidentify themselves as members of the RWL and of Liam O'Leary's dying and dwindling posse.

The crowd surged forward, as if in some kind of pitch invasion, as Andrew was carried on a stretcher into the ambulance. Grim-faced local cops, now no longer reinforced by the white-shirted PSUs, forced the wave of human fury back with all the seeming helplessness of a King Canute.

The ambulance moved, with the sound of its siren and blue light flashing, crawling into the human sea of anger and rage.

Fists pounded on the metal hull of the ambulance.

The crowd's fury focused on the ambulance; the two provocateurs moved with stealth towards the police station itself. Molotov cocktails were produced as if by magic, and paraffin rags stuffed into milk bottles full of petrol, water and detergent were lit as if in ceremony.

When the bombs were thrown against the wall of the police station, bursting into flame like exploding suns, the crowd roared in approval. For an instant, the sea of angry faces, stuffed with red eyes, was illuminated in the chrome and orange space cadet glow.

The ambulance broke loose from the clutch of the crowd and sped away.

Now, the target of the crowd's fury was the cops themselves, and they beat a tactical retreat into their bunker of a police station as if it were Fort Apache.

*

The blues and twos continued to blare and blast as the ambulance hurtled down the dead and empty street.

The mute rhetoric from the posters still rang defiantly, yet now they were also weathered and looking strangely lost as if the history of the strike itself was already beginning to fade.

337

In the ambulance, his vital signs flat-lined, Andrew lay silent on his gurney and stared at the vehicle's roof with sightless yet accusing eyes.

The paramedics looked at each other and shook their heads.

The siren was turned off.

At the edge of town, shrouded in darkness and with distended shadows that claimed the cursed Earth as its own, another girl lay dead in a ditch.

Once again, the madman's moon looked down on all that was evil in the world.

Dermot Brady had beaten a false confession out of the wrong man, backed up by defective forensic evidence, exactly as he did it with the Birmingham Six.

And now that suspect was dead while the killer was still at large.

*

In the Fleet Street offices of *The Sun,* built on the site of London's public gallows, new boy Clever Trevor O'Carroll had been burning the midnight oil. As he headed from the silent, open-plan office, past the sin bin and to the toilet, he could almost feel the sick and malignant energies that passed through the poisoned lay-line and buried, subterranean river beneath his feet.

Back on the streets of a dead town in the Rhondda that was no longer his dead town, with its dead streets that were no longer *his* dead streets and its ever-shrinking picket lines, the myths were still at large beneath the pit head's wheels of steel, and it's all-seeing Masonic Eye.

Trevor went into the toilet, alone, and did a line of coke before looking at the stranger in the mirror before him—his divided self and the *other* Trevor O'Carroll he had become. His name would be mud now, he realised, with Orla O'Regan, with Terry Fucking Vaughan and with all the guys in the band.

Fuck 'em!

Trevor couldn't have given a shit if he never saw that fucking town again as long as he lived, yet for all that, he couldn't quite fathom the emptiness in his soul. Vaguely, albeit for a fleeting instant, he wondered if this was how Judas indeed felt when he gave Jesus Christ the serpent's kiss in the Garden of Gethsemane

Trevor went back into the office and to the vacant throne once occupied by Saint Orla O'Regan, the award-winning investigative journalist that she was.

Slumped in the seat, like the usurping pretender that he was, he read the next morning's edition and the story from the valleys that carried his own bi-line, like a final parting shot.

The photograph showed the cop shop where Terry Vaughan worked being petrol bombed.

The headline read: *Striking Miners Petrol Bomb Police: IRA Activists among Scargill's Welsh Thugs.*

Trevor tossed the paper behind his spiked stack of back copies and savoured the receding rush from the line of cocaine.

He suddenly spotted Orla O'Regan's picture still staring at him.

Angrily, Clever Trevor threw Orla's picture into the bin.

Chapter Forty-One

As the sun rose above the pit head, with its wheel of steel, the discovery of the third victim had quickly become a crime scene cordoned off with fluttering blue and white tape.

Ted and his SOCO team, in white coveralls, were already gathering evidence to a crashing soundtrack of police radio static as Ridgeway arrived, from the firebombed police station, to where Dermot Brady was now master of ceremonies.

Terry wasn't there.

Sitting with WPC Patricia what's-her-face was a shaken pensioner who had discovered the corpse while walking her dog.

Brady looked at Ridgeway furtively as Ridgeway got out of his car. He was in for a top-level bollocking, he knew, as Ridgeway took him to one side.

"You dropped a bollock last night topping Andrew Evans in custody," Ridgeway said. "This isn't the 1970s, Brady. The last thing we need is CIB sniffing round like flies in a cow's arsehole."

"Recovered those *Font-y-Llewellyn* photos, didn't I?" Brady responded defensively. "Plus, if there was any other evidence in that disgusting kip of his, the bomb took care of it."

"All very well, but next question," said Brady. "What about Andrew Evans? How do you explain to a coroner that you beat the cunt to death?"

"The dodgy forensics from RADRE links him to the Hilda Murrell murder, but there's no mention of Azazel," Brady said. "We put out an all-points; Evans legged it and was killed in an RTA."

"RTA," Ridgeway echoed. "You've got some fucking front, Brady!"

"Already sorted, the wonders of the craft, old son", Brady winked. "Not a secret society but a society of secrets."

Brady went to wander off, but Ridgeway grabbed his arm. Brady's lack of caution was beginning to piss Ridgeway off, especially as his cock was on the chopping block as well.

"You're forgetting something," Ridgeway sneered with a ghost of menace. "Evans had access to a PO Box Office account connected to *Celtic Warrior Services* or some bollocks like that and operating in the name of *Thormynd Times*. You need to clear out anything that's in there and fucking close it, right?"

"Whatever you say, boss," Brady grinned.

Ridgeway released his grip, and his subordinate walked away.

*

When Derek Hepburn got back from the train station to the council house that Johnny Vaughan shared with his mother, he found the young man sitting in quiet desolation on the old sofa, watching *shite* on morning TV.

In silence, Derek went to the kitchen and made two strong cups of tea. He'd also spoken to

342

Terry that morning, whose status was somewhere between compassionate leave and suspension and who'd omitted to check in with Ridgeway and his superiors before leaving the Rhondda Valley reservation on a mission of his own.

"Here you are, lad," Derek said as he handed over the steaming mug. "Get that down your neck. Believe me; I know what grief is."

Johnny accepted the steaming cup of tea with what Derek noted to be a trembling in his hand.

"Dad's been dying of silicosis for years," Johnny said. "I can't imagine what it's like for you, mate."

"Like I said to your brother the other night, I'll have my nervous breakdown later; after we've caught the bastard who murdered Susan and my Tracey," Derek said.

Johnny looked around him and was a bit surprised to see a copy of *The Sun* with Clever Trevor O'Carroll's bi-line, describing the petrol bomb attack on the police station the previous night. The Vaughan household was usually a Murdoch-free zone.

"What, no *Daily Advance* this morning?" Johnny asked.

"Nope," Derek shook his head. "Something's going down in London, mate. That young comrade from the Post Office was down at the train station this morning for the Red Star parcel, and it didn't arrive. Nobody's answering the phone at the centre, either. Ask me the Party's over, mate, and good fucking riddance."

Johnny flinched. He looked up at Derek with what was still a ghost of accusation.

"Just think about it, Johnny," Derek said. "Who's been round from the local branch to offer you condolences on our father's death? Same as my Tracey, who was a fucking comrade, but we all know about that one, don't we?"

Johnny nodded and sipped his tea.

"Well, you were right about Zack the Hack, but I reckon you could have found something better to buy than the *Currant Fucking Bun,*" he said.

Derek nodded at the paper.

"I bought the *Daily Bullshit* for a reason," he said. "Look at it, man."

Johnny picked up the paper. For the first time, he saw the front-page article and Clever Trevor's bi-line.

"Fucking Trevor turned out to be a right Judas," Johnny said,

"Never mind that; look inside," Derek replied.

Johnny opened the paper to find a picture of Andrew Evans. Once again, the bi-line was by Clever Trevor O'Carroll. The headline said: *Hilda Murrell Suspect in Hit and Run Death in Wales."*

"The lad was a fascist and no less to humanity," Derek said. "But he was also a victim of that care home in Flintshire, and according to your brother, he was beaten to death in the police station by Acting Inspector Dermot Brady last night."

Johnny looked up, shocked.

"Fucking hell!" he said.

"There's more," Derek continued. "According to that Young Comrade I saw at the station this morning, Andrew Evans had regular access to a PO Box down at the Post Office. I'm going there to check it out now before the filth gets around to it. You stay here with your mother."

Derek got up to leave. Johnny called after him.

"Speaking of the filth, where is Terry?" Johnny asked.

"Colwyn Bay, and don't ask me what he's doing because I haven't a Scoobie," Derek said, "Let's just say I'm no stranger to trying to outrun your grief."

Derek left.

*

The soundtrack was "Eton Rifles," by *The Jam*, as Terry drove north towards the Celtic Sea coast. Somehow, the desolation of the countryside and sparse grass on the hills reminded him of a TV film he'd once seen involving a nuclear attack on Sheffield. Seeing his own home town from a distance, as if he were an alien, he thought about apocalypses and holocausts and about machines taking over the world.

Twisting along the mountain roads, through this wasteland without maps, he spotted a bus pulled over in a lay-by. In a casual cutaway of history, PSU cops were roughly dragging flying pickets from the vehicle, many by their hair, and beating them to a pulp with batons and knuckle dusters. At that precise moment in time, Terry thought he hated the police force of which he was still almost a member as much as the community from which he was derived and understood the class hatred both of his brother and late father completely.

Terry gritted his teeth.

Maggie Thatcher's boot boys: absolutely fucking right!

And yet, what of the alternative, he asked himself. On the *Right to Work March* to the Tory Conference in Brighton that had inspired Paul Weller's song, an official of the Socialist Workers Party fucked a different girl each night in his tent, which was just a shot away from what Liam O'Leary was about.

Small wonder that Thatcher was winning, the evil bitch, Terry thought. Especially given that the Left was such a corrupt shower of shit.

The cops were putting in the windows of the bus as Terry drove away, revelling in their recreational repression and in all the decades of thuggery to come.

That one wasn't covered by the Police and Criminal Evidence Act, Terry knew, as he carried on driving into no man's land and an uncertain future.

*

From his office, Ridgeway could still see the scorch marks from the previous night's petrol bomb attack looking like the branded image of a cloven hoof.

Uniformed cops were still clearing up the detritus from the previous night's riot.

Ridgeway replaced his phone receiver in its cradle and looked to Brady, who was also, as usual, in his office.

"No sign of Terry Vaughan; he's like the Scarlet Fucking Pimpernel," Ridgeway said.

"His father pegged it last night," Brady sneered. "The bastard's probably crying in his beer someplace."

"Brady, I know you're an orphan but let me tell you something about losing somebody close," Ridgeway said. "You keep busy to stop from falling apart, and Vaughan's idea of keeping busy is making trouble for us. Have you sorted that PO Box yet?"

"I was —"

"Well then, get a fucking move on," Ridgeway yelled at him. "Get down there for fuck's sake before Vaughan does."

*

Down at the Post Office, Derek entered by the side loading bay where the red post office vans were lined up. He looked around him furtively and then entered the sorting office area by walking up a concrete ramp. He was relieved to see that the young comrade he'd met at the train station that morning was on duty at the PO Box office.

"All right, lad?" Derek asked.

"Hello, Comrade," the young fellah replied. "Still no news from London?"

"Not a sausage, mate?" Derek shook his head grimly. "Not looking good, is it?"

The young comrade looked worried.

"You think the coup's started?" he asked.

"Well, I don't think there's tanks in Westminster," Derek said. "Not the way that O'Leary sees it. Only there's more than one way of skinning a democracy.

Outside the Post Office, a Police Van had pulled up, complete with meshed up windscreen and Paddy pushers up the front. The town was on high alert since the riot and petrol bomb attack at the police station the previous night, and when Brady got out of the van, he was flanked by thuggish looked PSUs with white shirts.

The cops, like a blue serge army of death, nodded at each other and then marched with purpose towards the sorting office.

Inside, Deputy Derek had convinced the young comrade to hand over the contents of the PO Box. He handed Derek a small package plus a handwritten note.

"Here you are, Comrade," the youngster said.

"Nice one," said Derek. "If there's a coup, these bastards will be part of it."

Derek was already leaving as Brady and his posse of goons turned the corner. Derek looked away and kept on walking. Brady, clearly, didn't recognise him as Derek had not been at the photo opportunity for BBC's *Crimewatch* after his daughter's murder.

Derek shoved into the bastard, anyway.

"Sorry, pal," said Brady negligently.

Derek kept on walking.

*

It was High Noon when Terry arrived at his location, at a slate mine and café that overlooked Colwyn Bay. It was out of season, too, and there was only one other car parked outside the gift shop as the Ford Sierra pulled to a halt on the tarmac.

His engine ticked like an unexploded bomb, and the waves lapped slick on the sandy shore below.

Terry got out of the car and walked to where a sign said the café was *closed.*

He opened the door and entered the gloom in any case.

The TV was on in the empty café, and the miners' strike seemed to be reaching its endgame on the TV. Once again, Terry saw the recreational and routine repression dished out by his colleagues in the blue serge army of death. The miners sounded defiant, but it was the defiance of the defeated, Terry knew, like Wilfred Owen's damned youth of the Somme.

"We're not going back! We're not going back!"

Orla sat with a disabled man in a wheelchair, watching the repression and stirring of the Beast on TV. The man's hands were gnarled, and he looked horribly disfigured, as if by fire.

Terry nodded at him with respect.

"DI McCreevey," he said. "You pulled off quite a disappearing act six years ago, Guv."

PART SEVEN: THE PYROTECHNIC SERAPHIM

Chapter Forty-Two

It had been close to midnight when Zack the Hack returned to the Rhondda, like a thief of souls to the scene of his nursery crime. The ghosts and myths were in abundance, as petrol bombs exploded in rage against the concrete walls of the police station and another loose end lay dead in a paramedic ambulance whose siren had just been switched off.

That Johnny Vaughan's father had also died, Zack didn't know, as the MI5 officer tooled his flash Triumph Stag through those dead streets that the shadows had claimed as their own.

On the car cassette system, the soundtrack was by the Beatles.

Helter Skelter!

Charles Manson's theme tune, Zack told himself.

Bryoni was waiting for him at the corner of the street, the way he'd asked her to, but she wasn't alone. She had a friend with her of similar age, and that was a problem. Zack told himself he would have to improvise.

Zack honked his horn and drew the car to a halt, winding down his window.

"O'Leary's finished," he told her. "He's been expelled from the Party, and we're building a case against him."

"Do my mum and dad need to find out?" Bryoni asked, worried.

"Not if we do this right," said Zack as he got out of the car.

A second man, Sad Eric, emerged from the shadows as Zack got the two girls' attention. He struck the second girl hard with a hammer, crushing her skull and killing her. Bryoni, splattered with warm blood, was still in shock when Zack rendered her unconscious with a taser.

It was all over in seconds.

"What are you gawping at?" Zack barked. "Get that other bitch into the alley and make it look like the real thing."

Sad Eric, who was also a product of the care home system in Flintshire, did as he was told.

Zack jacked his boot and picked up Bryoni's limp body like she was a rag doll. He dumped her in the back of the Triumph Stag and slammed the boot door shut.

Sad Eric emerged from the alleyway where the other girl's body had been dumped like so much rubbish.

"Move it!" Zack snapped, and Sad Eric complied.

From a concealed location, the real Azazel watched them in angry silence as the two imposters drove off.

*

The plastic surgeons had done their best, but McCreevey's badly burned face was still a grotesque mask. To Terry, it looked as if he had literally been to Hell and returned like some inexperienced revenant, somewhere between life and death.

"Everyone thinks I'm dead, Acting Inspector Vaughan, and that's the way I'd like to keep it," McCreevey said in a croak of a voice. "The surveillance culture in Britain isn't that developed yet, that you can't create a new identity for yourself — National Insurance and so forth."

McCreevey indicated the scenes of picket line violence and of the Battle of Orgreave on TV.

"The miners are about to be stuffed, Detective Inspector and God help this country when they are," McCreevey said.

Terry sat down next to Orla.

"No disrespect, Sir, but you look like you've been to Hell and back," he said.

"Indeed I have," McCreevey replied. "And all thanks to your guvnor, DCI Ridgeway."

Terry looked at Orla.

"It's exactly what happened to Americk, exactly!" she said.

"Ridgeway headed up the Police Death Squad that turned me into a human fireball the year of the Iron Bitch's coronation," McCreevey continued. "But believe me, it was only the beginning of his Pact with the Devil."

McCreevey developed a coughing fit. Orla took up the story.

"Jack McCreevey had already retired from the Flying Squad as a result of corruption before Operation Countryman started," she said. "He was also the private detective hired by Roxanne Perry, the sister of the boy who took the incriminating photographs from the care home and was murdered."

"Jack the Giant Killer," said McCreevey.

"The other boy was killed in the arson attack that I witnessed in Brighton last year," Orla said.

"Using a co-op mix bomb with a digital timer made by Animal Rights activists," Terry suggested. "A third boy, Andrew Evans, was murdered in police custody last night."

McCreevey indicated that he knew the name. It was the boy he'd spoken to in the car in Flintshire who'd baled when he saw Dominic McLeod.

"He was beaten to death by Acting DI Dermott Brady," Terry continued. "The murder was then passed off as a hit and run, at least according to Orla's successor at *The Sun*, Judas O'Carroll."

"Andrew ratted the other two boys out," McCreevey said, nodding. "I tried to save him, but he returned to the fold. He'd have belonged to Llewellyn and McLeod after that."

"What about Ridgeway?" Terry asked.

"Ridgeway?" asked McCreevey. "Ridgeway and his corrupt cabal of Flying Squad officers operated as thief's ponces and were organising most of the armed robberies in London by the late 1970s. But the days of armed robbery were coming to an end, and organised crime was turning corporate through drugs and vice. The idea of staunch villains keeping a lid on the underworld was always bullshit, in any case, and a justification for corruption, but there would be no moral boundaries in Margaret Thatcher's Brave New World."

"Go on," said Terry.

"Ridgeway and his gang were under investigation by Operation Countryman, but powerful forces had the ear of the Home Secretary, who was compromised in any case," McCreevey said. "If Ridgeway and his cabal rid them of their turbulent priest, meaning me, they promised to sink Operation Countryman and make the charges against the Flying Squad go away."

McCreevey pushed a photograph towards Terry.

"McLeod was central to the whole conspiracy," McCreevey said. "He pimped out the boys from the care homes through his PR firm in Pimlico. Then he became Margaret Thatcher's chief aid on the convenient death of Airey Neave."

Terry looked at the photograph. It showed McLeod with the BBC DJ, Jimmy Saville, at Stoke Manderville hospital.

"The deal that McLeod made with Ridgeway was to have Roxanne and me killed," McCreevey said. "Roxanne's death was passed off as another casualty of the Yorkshire Ripper. The cops didn't give a shit about dead prostitutes in those days and probably still don't. But I was a cop. Once Ridgeway killed me, he'd belong to Llewellyn and McLeod for good."

Terry looked and felt disgusted like he was dirty. Orla was staring at both him and McCreevey.

"Fortunately, I was saved by one of the rubbish, as the police still call them, a good Samaritan," McCreevey said. "I even lived rough myself when I was discharged from hospital until I could get my hands on a false identity."

"What about Brady and Zack?" Terry asked.

"Zack, I don't know," McCreevey said. "Brady had links to the Home Office, being Branch. He helped Ridgeway bury that young Asian boy who was abducted the day of the Royal Wedding and murdered by Tory MPs in Dolphin Square. They were offered a stake in the Brinks Matt robbery for that one—their retirement plan. And they murdered another private detective in a pub car park in Croydon to cover their tracks."

Terry shook his head.

"I knew Ridgeway was bent, but this takes the fucking biscuit," he said.

McCreevey slapped a file in front of Terry.

"My life's work," McCreevey said. "It's a copy, but do with it as you wish."

*

Call it the House on the Borderland: call it the House of Fun.

Near derelict, the farmhouse stood on unkempt and desolate moorland, under the shadow of heavy crags, like a hollow skull that had emerged through erosion in the sparse earth. It was a hollow fossil of a place, but lately, its door had been reinforced, and someone had scrawled it a name and painted a skull and crossbones above the door.

Pandy Kincora, it was called.

The House of Fun: the House of Pain.

Down the muddy track that led to the farmyard, there was a stout farm gate and coils of barbed razor wire. The place was an old firing range, after all, and the sign from the Ministry of Defence still ordered: *Keep Out!*

In the caged cell upstairs in the House of Fun, Bryoni yelled and screamed to deaf ears, and nothing but the ghosts who inhabited the sacrificial moors. Beyond the bars, where she was incarcerated like a circus animal, were overtly Nazi posters courtesy of the National Socialist Alliance in the US and Ku Klux Klan hoods hanging up like Halloween fancy dress.

There were automatic weapons in a cabinet, too.

Bryoni vented her fury, then pleaded, then vented her fury again.

"Help!" she yelled. "Let me out of here, you fucking bastards!"

Chapter Forty-Eight

Dominic McLeod had good reason to look pleased with himself as the official Daimler, black and polished, pulled away from Heathrow and headed westward toward the M4.

At his side, immaculately dressed in a silk suit, the Saudi Royal Prince studied McLeod as the Prime Minister's aid looked at a file.

"Excellent," said McLeod. "You know the Prime Minister's son has a personal stake in this?"

The Prince gestured with his hand.

"And what of my gift?" he asked.

"You'll like her," McLeod smiled unpleasantly. "She's Welsh and feisty!"

*

Back at the House of Fun, Sad Eric had returned. He was also doing what he did best and had been doing for the network for years by filming Bryoni in her cage.

Snuff, they called it — the latest side-line in the network's trade in young flesh.

Still, The Beatles pounded *Helter Skelter* in the background.

"Why don't you let me go, you sad bastard!" Bryoni yelled. "From the look of you, you're a fucking victim yourself!"

*

Terry had returned to his mother's house in the Rhondda and was inside, talking to his brother and Derek. There was a map spread across the kitchen table and files as if they were planning a military operation.

"Right," said Terry. "Mother's staying with Eileen, and I've got my trusty WPC Patricia staying over to keep an eye on them. So it's down to business, right?"

Terry indicated the package that Derek had liberated from the Post Office box. It contained all, or at least a considerable number, of the photographs that Jack and Stephen had stolen from the care home in 1979.

"Those photos are enough to turn any right-minded person's stomach, but they confirm everything McCreevey says in his file," Terry said. "And they're a smoking gun."

"How so?" asked Johnny.

"It means we've got Llewellyn and McLeod bang to rights and can prove that this whole sordid paedophile business goes right to the top," Terry replied. "Now, what else was in that lucky dip down at the Post Office?"

"Nothing, but I did get the originating address," Derek said.

Derek pointed at the map. A position was indicated in red biro.

"It's a disused farmhouse on property owned by the Ministry of Defence, an old firing range", Derek continued. "At first, I thought it was fake. But then I turned up a photograph at the library. Look at this."

Derek presented the photograph alongside Orla O'Regan's article in which the Ku Klux Klan burned their fiery crosses in the Welsh countryside.

"It's a match, the same location, Terry, and it's all coming together," said Derek. "There's just one piece missing."

"What's that?" Terry asked.

Derek stood erect.

"Zack the Hack," Derek said with determination. "You think he's Azazel and that he murdered my little girl, and that's why I'm here. We need to find that fucker."

"Well, I know where he'll be this evening," Johnny piped up.

Derek and Terry turned to face him.

"You what?" Terry asked.

"That posh hotel near the train station," said Johnny. "He's meeting Peter Chapman of the NUM Regional Executive before Peter goes to Libya. Peter's going to try and persuade Qaddafi, on King Arthur's behalf, to impose an oil embargo on Britain in support of the strike."

*

Dusk found Peter Chapman's Jaguar parked next to Zack's Triumph Stag in the hotel car park. Whatever hardship the striking miners were experiencing, neither man was part of it. Indeed, in the back bar, they were already on their second bottle of champagne.

"Help yourself, Peter, and enjoy," said Zack, his phoney working-class accent now banished. "It's dry in the Mad Colonel's Kingdom."

Chapman slapped a file on the table.

"Here you are, a complete dossier on Trotskyist infiltration of the NUM, compiled by the Communist Party of which I'm a member," said Chapman. "Tell the truth, that's how I started working for you bastards at MI5. The Trots are a fucking menace. Like that maniac O'Leary, supporting the IRA and screwing all those young girls. This will help bring him down and Arthur and the NUM with him."

"*The Trots, the Trots, we've got to get rid of the Trots,*" Zack grinned. "Only a stake in the biggest arms deal in British history helps to appease the conscience, doesn't it, Peter?"

Chapman looked miserable. Zack leaned forward.

"Very well, Agent Chapman, let's go through your mission in Libya," Zack said.

*

Terry walked with purpose towards the hotel.

It would be playing a wild card, confronting Zack with the evidence in front of the Union official, but these were extraordinary times.

A sudden click distracted him as he approached the hotel entrance.

The barrel of a Smith and Wesson 38S Revolver stared at him like a sightless eye.

*

"Now, pay attention, 007," Zack lectured his asset. "You're Qaddafi's guest of honour, right? So you're staying in the Mad Bastard's tent and will be expected to address one of the Peoples' Revolutionary Committees the way that O'Leary used to do it when he was singing for the RWL's last supper. The only difference this time is that a British television news crew will be present to record the event, so plenty of revolutionary rhetoric is required."

Chapman stared at him.

"What do you suggest?" Chapman snorted.

"The main thing is that you emphasise, to the British media in Libya, that you are there to procure direct funding to the National Union of Miners on account of the CIA and MI5 attacks on the RWL. You pledge your support for Liam O'Leary and emphasise that the allegations of sexual misconduct against him are a pack of lies."

"Anything else," Chapman asked.

"Well, you could express support for the Brighton IRA bombing," Zack grinned. "With any luck, we could get half these Trot groups banned under the Prevention of Terrorism Act."

*

At the entrance to the same hotel, Terry Vaughan was staring down the barrel of a gun.

Holding the weapon, rock steady as a pool cue, Brady stared at his nemesis with hatred.

362

"That's the second time you've pointed a gun at me in two days," said Terry. "What's the fucking matter with you, Brady?"

"It's you that's the problem, Terry," Brady replied. "You're out of control. You know that Ridgeway's put you on suspension, and now the grief over your father's death has tipped you over the edge a bit like that dead MP up in Scotland. But one way or another, your career's over, mate."

"You murdered Andrew Evans in Police Custody," Terry said.

"What, a fascist piece of shit?" Brady laughed. "Thought you and your family of reds were on the other side, mate?"

"He was cannon fodder and a victim of abuse at a care home where you were a prefect," Terry said. "And that made him a threat to you personally."

"What?" Brady mocked. "How do you work that one out, Columbo?"

"Well, there's that Asian lad murdered by Tory MPs the day of the Royal Wedding—the one that you and Ridgeway covered up by fucking with the missing person's investigation," Terry continued.

"This is bollocks," Brady looked shocked. "I'm taking you into protective custody. You're a menace to yourself."

"What?" Terry laughed. "Like you and Ridgeway took Jack McCreevey into protective custody or Americk Fraser? Bet you enjoyed that one, Brady; you not liking black people very much. Only it's strictly business for your masters and betters in the corridors of power, isn't it?"

"Shut it, Terry!" Brady snapped.

He was clearly starting to lose it.

"Americk knew too much, didn't he?" Terry taunted. "About the care home paedophile ring linked to Dolphin Square, to Elm House and Westminster, all with your chum McLeod sitting like a big fat spider in the middle of the web."

Brady's finger moved to the trigger guard.

"I'm warning you, son," Brady said.

"And let's not forget the Paedophile Information Exchange and how it was used to lure a corrupt, self-serving scumbag like O'Leary into your grubby and murderous conspiracy against the working class," Terry continued.

"I said—"

Terry grabbed Brady's wrist. He forced the pistol away as it discharged and then kneed Brady in the groin. He then rammed Brady against the wall and repeatedly head-butted the bastard till Brady dropped the gun. Then, Terry grabbed Brady by the balls and head-butted him again.

Brady responded by punching Terry in the guts. Terry staggered back, winded. Brady's face was streaming blood now and contorted into a mask of glistening hate, making him appear like a feral demon.

"You Welsh sheep shagging cunt!" Brady bellowed.

Terry lunged back into Brady, and they fought, with much gouging and biting, as if they were both back at school. Brady tried to thrust his finger into one of Terry's eyes.

Terry drove his fist into Brady's guts. He punched him hard in the head and then threw him to the floor. Terry stood over Brady, bloody and defiant and then picked up the gun. He pointed the weapon at Brady's head, and then he spat.

"No fun is it when the rabbit's got the gun," Terry said.

Terry kicked Brady in the guts.

"Tell you what," Terry said. "Fuck all this PACE and Scarman bollocks!"

Terry kicked Brady in the head again and again.

"Let's have a good old fashioned 1970s interrogation," Terry bellowed. "We can call it *Singing in the Rain,* can't we? You know, like in *Clockwork Fucking Orange?"*

Terry crouched and put a gun to Brady's head.

"But I tell you something; I'm taking you in," Terry said. "I'm going to type you a confession, and either your signature or your fucking brains will be on that document before the pubs shut."

There was a Police Car siren and a flashing blue light. Brady and Terry were caught in the full beam of an approaching police car like moths in the light of a flame. Terry shielded his eyes from the slow, dazzling glare.

It was Terry who now had a gun to a fellow officer's head.

"Shit!" he said.

Terry ran across the car park. The police car set off in hot pursuit but had to negotiate parked cars outside the hotel.

Terry ducked down an alley that was closed to traffic and heard the police car screech to a halt at his back.

Emerging into a deserted street, Terry ducked sideways.

An old van screeched to a halt beside him.

Terry stopped running when he saw a white-faced Derek at the wheel.

"Get in!" Derek ordered.

Terry complied and found his brother also in the van.

"And get down!" Derek said.

Derek drove off slowly, letting the police car thunder past him in the opposite direction. Terry, lying on the floor in the back, was getting suspicious.

"How did you know?" Terry asked.

"We had a tip-off, mate," Johnny replied.

"What?" Terry asked.

"We don't know who, but it fits in with everything that we know," Johnny said.

"There's been a development, Terry," Derek said as he headed out of town. "Another girl's been taken; only we know where she is, right?"

"Now wait a cotton-picking minute; what's this about a fucking tip-off?" Terry demanded.

Derek was close to losing it. He punched the dashboard.

"Look, Terry, we're going to save this fucking girl, OK?" Derek yelled. "The way we didn't save my Tracey!"

The Van drove into the valley.

Chapter Forty-Nine

Sat in the front room of Terry's Mum's council house, Eileen and Mum were watching the news on TV. There was a picture of a young girl called Bryony Jones on the screen, and the item made for grim viewing.

Patricia, the black WPC, joined them.

A news reporter was speaking.

"The fear now is that Bryony Jones might become the fourth victim of the serial killer known as Azazel—already considered by police to be the most prolific murderer of his kind since the Yorkshire Ripper."

A chill passed through Eileen as she wondered where in the name of Hell her husband might be.

*

Terry was no longer lying on the floor of the van as it headed towards the farmhouse on MOD property.

"OK, apart from Brady's shooting iron, which now has five up the spout, what weapons do we have?" Terry asked.

"What?" was Johnny's panicked response.

"Well, if we're going to the gunfight at the OK Corral, we might just need to be tooled up," Terry said.

"I raided the armoury of the local RWL Security Directorate," Derek said. "We've got switchblades and some CS grenades we picked up in France, knuckle dusters, iron bars, a pickaxe handle and a shotgun."

"And I've got a maroon flare," said Johnny.

Terry laughed and nodded.

"And Johnny's got a combine harvester," he said with heavy sarcasm. "Is that it?"

Johnny was indignant.

"We're the RWL, Terry, not the Baader Fucking Meinhoff gang," he snapped.

"Yes, well, right now, that's a fucking pity," Terry said.

It was then that Terry spotted the CB radio under Derek's dashboard. He nodded towards it.

"That CB," said Terry.

"What of it?" Derek asked.

"I need you to muster up every striking miner you know," Terry said.

The van sped on through the night towards the sacrificial farm.

*

The ringing of the doorbell brought Patricia to the door of the Vaughan household. Through the spy hole, she could see that it was Acting DI Dermott Brady and that he was clearly injured.

At the best of times, Brady looked like a bloated corpse. Right now, his head was swollen like a balloon, and two black eyes gave him a passing resemblance to Chi-Chi the Panda on a bad day.

"My God!" said Patricia as she opened the door. "Guv, what happened?"

"Not good," Brady said as he entered the semi-detached house. "I'll explain later."

Brady looked to where Eileen and Terry's mother were. Both women looked horrified and worried.

"Eileen, you got to come with me, love," Brady said.

"But—"

"It's Terry," said Brady. "He's in hospital. I'm afraid he's in a bad way."

The shock showed itself on Eileen's face. Then she composed herself and nodded. She grabbed her things and walked toward him.

Brady addressed Patricia.

"You look after Terry's Mum, OK?" he said.

*

At the farmhouse on the borderland, Terry and his team had parked up and were now using stout wire cutters to tear a hole in the perimeter fence. There was a full madman's moon, and the cold light made the approach to the farm look strangely desolate.

Derek, Johnny and Terry advanced by stealth. Derek had the pump-action shotgun, Terry the revolver and Johnny an iron bar. As they approached, they could see the light from an upstairs window of the farmhouse, looking like a solitary eye.

Johnny raised his hand, and they all stopped.

"Hang on," he whispered. "What's that?"

"What?" Terry demanded. "What is it?"

"Fucking music!" said Johnny.

From the direction of the farmhouse, they could hear Duran Duran singing *Hungry Like the Wolf.*

The three looked at each other and then proceeded further towards the farmhouse, crouching as they ran.

Moments later, all were flattened against the porous stone wall of the building on either side of the door.

Still, the sound of the music pounded from inside.

There was shouting, too—a young girl's voice yelling obscenities at somebody, in a voice that was both terrified and yet defiant.

At least Bryony was still alive.

Terry nodded to Derek, who had the pump-action shotgun.

Derek shot the lock away.

Then Terry kicked open the door, and they crossed the threshold from the wasteland into Hell.

*

Overlooking the Severn Estuary, not far from Bristol, the official Daimler bearing McLeod and the Crown Prince passed into Wales.

In the back seat, McLeod looked at the Crown Prince and smiled.

"Not long now, Your Royal Highness," he said.

Croeso i Gymru, the sign said: "Welcome to Wales."

And there was a red dragon on the sign while beneath, the dark waters of the Severn and the Goddess Sabrina silently pumped into the sea.

*

In the upstairs snuff studio of the romper room, Duran Duran was pounding from a large ghetto blaster cassette player, drowning out the screams and threats from the caged Bryony. Framed in the lens of Sad Eric's handheld VHS home movie camera, the young girl cursed and swore and looked to the snuff cameraman like Regan in *The Exorcist* or *Little Red Riding Hood* turned out wrong.

As for Sad Eric himself, he was an old hand at this game and a regular, particularly at the torture chamber in the South London Police Station Cells. That was where they made the snuff videos, with the care home kids, whether from North Wales or from South Vale in Lambeth and where he'd filmed the killing of a young Asian boy by MPs on the day of the Royal Wedding in 1981.

The films were made for financial reasons but also for blackmail, even as academics proclaimed that snuff movies were urban myths.

And today's contestant and killer would be a Saudi Royal Prince, no less, who would be celebrating the al Yamamah arms deal with his very own virgin kill.

Eric was thinking about this and all the terror he had caught on frightened young faces when he heard the shots and commotion downstairs.

Still, with his camera rolling, he headed for the landing.

A youngish looking bloke was standing at the bottom of the stairs holding a Smith and Wesson Revolver with two hands. On seeing Eric, the youngish looking bloke shot him fatally in the stomach, causing pain to seer from his ruptured gut like a thousand bee stings.

Pumping blood and dimly aware that this was a fatal shot, Sad Eric fell to the ground.

His camera was still running and was now filming Eric himself through the slow and agonising process of his own death.

The man with the gun and two others thundered up the stairs and past him. They included an older and desperate looking man with a pump-action shotgun.

And as Eric's slow and inevitable death continued to be filmed, on his terminal landing, he noticed how the incendiary device wired to the door had been triggered by the forced entry of the door.

A crude co-op mix bomb but with a highly sophisticated digital timer made by animal rights activists in Belfast.

Eric was dying, all right, and the fiery jaws of Hell would be opening up soon enough.

Chapter Fifty

Duran Duran continued to pound from the big ghetto blaster on the table as the three of them entered the romper room. In what, under other circumstances, might have been humorous, a rank of mechanical flowers were dancing along to the strains of the song.

The first thing they noticed was Bryony, alive, in her cage.

"It's OK, love; we're the cavalry," Johnny said.

Derek smashed the cassette player with the butt of his shotgun, producing silence. He picked up some keys and began, with fumbling and trembling fingers, to open up the cage.

Derek embraced the sobbing Bryony and kissed her.

It was then that Terry heard a vehicle pull up with a crunch of tyres.

"Christ, your mates were quick!" Terry said as Johnny went to the window.

As soon as he did, the colour drained from Johnny's face.

"Shit!" he said.

Outside, a group of armed fascists were disgorging from a four-wheel-drive vehicle that looked like something from an African Toyota War. They were the same fascists who had been in the photo opportunity, with Andrew Evans, in front of the Market House on stilts in Ross-on-Wye, selling

National Front News and proclaiming support for Welsh bombers. They had also worn Ku Klux Klan fancy dress for a similar photo opportunity, to serve the story fed to Orla O'Regan on the Number One *Sun*.

More recently, they had leered at Tom Upton in a hotel foyer in Valetta in Malta and participated in a petrol bomb attack on the Police Station where Terry worked.

"Fascists!" said Johnny. "They're armed, and they're not here to deliver the mail.

As the first fascist, armed with an automatic weapon, strode towards the gaping farmhouse door, his confederate started to empty the contents of a large can of petrol on the ground, as if spilling blood in a sacrificial rite. Clearly, he intended to encircle the whole farmhouse in a ring of fire.

The first fascist entered the front door, and it was at that point that Johnny pushed past his two accomplices, producing the maroon flare.

Standing at the top of the stairs, he fired point-blank at the advancing fascist, who was transformed into a screaming, human torch.

"Combine fucking harvester, eh?" Johnny yelled.

The burning fascist continued to emit a blood-curdling scream as he staggered back into the yard. The other fascists now looked on in horror as their comrade staggered, screamed and died.

In the process, however, the burning corpse of the fascist also ignited the ring of petrol, which surrounded the farmhouse, while also killing the second fascist whose plastic container of fuel exploded in his hand.

The ring of fire around the farmhouse roared like the gaping jaws of Hell.

"Fuck holiday homes!" a third fascist yelled. "Come home to a real fire, lefties!"

He gave a flat handed Nazi salute.

In the farmhouse, Terry smashed open the glass front of the cabinet containing the building's small but lethal armoury. He helped himself to a Mac 10 submachine gun and started to load a magazine.

Derek, with his shotgun, continued to comfort Bryony.

"What?" Johnny asked. "We gonna shoot our way out?"

Terry handed Johnny the revolver.

"You got any better ideas, Butch?" he asked. "Come on!"

Terry led the group down the stairs as if he were some latter-day Pied Piper.

It was then that the digital timer on the co-op mix bomb hit zero, causing the entrance of the farmhouse to explode and turning it into a hogshead of flame.

Like a death trap bedsit fire in Hove, Terry thought, as a hateful wave of searing heat hit his face like an invisible hand.

There was a quivering heat haze to accompany the roar of the fire, and suddenly, all three of them were crouching.

"Shit!" he said as he realised they were now trapped inside by a wall of flame.

It was then that Derek grabbed his shoulder.

"Terry," he said. "I've got an idea."

*

Outside the farmhouse that was destined to become a living funeral pyre, the surviving Nazis were bathed in the quivering orange as in a space cadet glow.

Eventually, as if at their very own Nuremberg Rally, they raised their flat hands in salute.

"*Seig Heil! Seig Heil!*"

It was as if a *Skrewdriver* gig had met with the Night of Broken Glass, they thought, and revelled in the thought of ritual holocausts to come.

*

Perversely, at a point when death was laughing, sadistically, in their faces, Derek had remembered playing cowboys and Indians at a farmhouse, much like this one, when he was a kid.

It was what gave him the idea.

"Terry, these places always have cellars," he said as he indicated the wooden bannister.

It, too, would be in flames soon enough.

"Man overboard?" Derek asked.

Terry, already coughing on the heavy toxic cloud of smoke, nodded. Next, having clocked where the door to the cellar was, he led them over the side into the flaming vortex of the hall.

The heat was almost unbearable now.

Terry raised the Ingram Mac 10 and shot the lock of the cellar door to matchwood using the machine gun.

"Come on!" he said and led them into the cellar's dark void. He now resembled the Pied Piper slightly less than Ahab.

The building was opaque with smoke now, and Derek held Bryony close as they descended the cellar's stone steps into a circle of Dante's Hell.

To be or not to be? To act or not to act?

Derek held Bryony closer like she was the most precious thing in the world.

He'd have that nervous breakdown he kept talking about later.

Chapter Fifty-One

There was darkness at the edge of town as Brady drove his Ford Granada.

Out of the town, that was not his town. Away from the pit head that was not his pit head. Out into the sparse Welsh countryside where the house on the borderland was to be found, along with unmarked and unquiet graves on the lonely and sacrificial moor.

As Brady drove, Eileen, at his side, looked at him with growing suspicion. Raised by her parents to respect the police and authority, she had nonetheless heard bad things about this man from her very own husband.

"Terry was shot, you say?" she tested. "How? How did it happen?"

Brady smiled unpleasantly.

"Don't worry about your Terry; he's a tough bugger," Brady said. "Smart, too. Smarter than we reckoned! Jumped up sheep shagger of a Detective Sergeant from the sticks, still wet behind the ears and fresh out of Hendon!"

Brady shook his head in grudging admiration.

Eileen saw the bi-lingual sign for the hospital as they sailed past.

Still, they were headed out of town.

"We figured he'd Dick around clueless and take all the shit from the media while Ridgeway and me tracked down Azazel for ourselves," Brady continued.

A shock of realisation dawned on Eileen's face.

"You and Ridgeway?" she asked. "You've known who Azazel was all along, and you've fucking well protected the bastard!"

Brady shook his head.

"No, we're going to kill the fuck, but it has to be done our way," he said. "The way we've always sorted out problems, in house, so to speak."

Brady was staring at her, now, fanatically.

"Azazel knows too much," Brady said, matter of fact. "He's done too many fucking favours for the people who really run this country, and never mind the Iron Bitch in Number 10."

Eileen looked at him, appalled.

"Who'd you think topped Lord Lucan?" Brady asked. "When Lucan kept shooting his mouth off about the military coup plot that got rid of Harold Wilson, or Airey Neave when Nieve was briefed by some trouble maker from Northern Ireland about all the care homes?"

Eileen's look of horror turned to disbelief and then disgust.

"All the care homes?" she echoed.

"There's a network, and not just in North Wales," Brady said. "That's why Azazel had to kill young Jack Parry in Flintshire and those other three losers in that house fire in Brighton. A regular pyrotechnic seraph when he puts his mind to it is our Azazel."

"We're not going to the hospital, are we?" Eileen said. "Where's Terry? What have you done with him?"

Brady smiled unpleasantly.

The Ford Granada drove on into the night.

*

The farmhouse was ablaze, now, and the fire a living revenant, or poltergeist, which hungrily consumed all in its searing wake. In its fiery jaws, it consumed all the fascist regalia that was put up for show, including the Halloween Ku Klux Klan robes worn as fancy dress for Orla O'Regan's article in the Number One *Sun*.

Yet the fire's hunger remained, and now it had turned its attention to the dying and suffering prostrate form of Sad Eric himself.

Still, the blood pumped from his gut wound, like a ruined mouth that cried painful betrayal, only now he was half screaming, half choking, against the searing heat and toxic smoke as well.

On the floor, the camera continued to record the last painful moments of Sad Eric's life, and when his body, still alive, caught fire, the camera caught this, too. It was to be Sad Eric's final snuff video and his masterpiece — an epitaph, like a character from a JG Ballard who was addicted to car crashes and eventually died in one.

When Eric burned and screamed and was dispatched in flames to Hell, the camera caught this, too, before it too was eaten by the all-consuming fire.

Indeed, the fire would continue to consume until it ate itself, with nothing left to burn, leaving only the promise and vision of the holocaust to come.

This Eric would not film — because Sad Eric was Dead!

Bye, bye, Eric.

Bye, bye.

*

The smoke from the house fire was now settling like malignant ectoplasm in the cellar, where the four of them coughed, spluttered and suffered, and somehow found their way to the cellar's external entrance in the backyard.

The door was locked, of course.

They always are.

"Fuck!" said Terry.

*

A convoy of vehicles burst through the gates of the Ministry of Defence facility on the sacrificial moor.

Inside the vehicles was the posse of striking miners that Johnny had radioed earlier.

As in an old-time western, the Cavalry had finally arrived.

The fascists looked at the advancing vehicles in disbelief.

*

Eileen could see the fire in the distance as they approached the farmhouse on the borderland, where the victims of nursery crimes were buried in unmarked graves on the sacrificial moor.

"There's a fire up ahead," Eileen said. "What's going on?"

"Search me?" Brady retorted bitterly and with menace towards his pregnant hostage. "How the fuck do I know what goes on in the House of Fun? I'm the monkey, me, not the organ grinder, same as when I was back in that care home in Flintshire."

Eileen turned to look at him sharply. Brady sneered.

"I bet your Terry misses his dad," Brady continued. "I never knew mine. I had to drag myself up in a care home here in Taff Land and do what I had to do to survive."

"You were abused?" Eileen ventured.

"Fuck that, sweetheart; there's killers and victims in this world," Brady laughed. "Me, I was a prefect, a bit like the whips in Lindsay Anderson's *If.* Me, I held down the other kids while they were buggered up the arse."

Brady's tone had turned to bitterness and an approximation of self-loathing.

"Perfect training for the job!" he continued. "Trouble is, once you do something like that for those fuckers they own you for life."

Eileen grabbed the door handle and opened the door. Pregnant or not, she was going to try and jump out of the speeding vehicle.

"You sick fuck!" Eileen yelled.

The Ford Granada hurtled and swerved with the door flapping open like a flightless metal bird in a state of total distress.

Brady punched Eileen hard in the face. He then produced a Beretta Automatic and pointed it straight at Eileen's head.

"Shut the fucking door, Everhard!" Brady said.

Eileen miserably complied.

"That's better," Brady said. "You want to see your hubby again or what?"

Eileen shot him a defiant but fearful look.

"Nice gun this," said Brady. "Police upgrade — tooling up for the class war to come. And it all started, same as this government, in a care home in North Wales. Believe me, when people look back, they'll know that buggers like Llewellyn and McLeod created the twenty-first century."

The Ford Granada sped towards the fire as if on the road to Hell.

Chapter Fifty-Two

When the posse of striking miners arrived, they found the farmhouse a blazing inferno, surrounded by a handful of surviving fascists.

With horns blazing and full beam headlights, Dan and Geoff were in the leading vehicle as they drove headlong towards their first victim.

They were friends of Johnny's from the picket line, who used to talk politics after the shoving and yelling of the morning was done.

They were the same friends who had considered Zack the Hack with abject suspicion.

Now, they drove headlong towards a fascist skinhead, who had been in Valetta, and was now caught in the slow dazzle of their full beam. The bastard was struck headlong by the vehicle, bowled over the hood and roof and was killed.

Dan pulled up his heavily dented vehicle, and they disgorged.

The surviving fascists now faced the posse of miners' vehicles that were crunching to a halt.

The miners, when they disgorged, all had pickaxe handles and baseball bats.

There were roars like battle cries, and a pitched battle ensued.

And then another bloody vision of the dystopia that was to come was played out against the burning tableau.

*

The cellar was now even more opaque with the thickening pall of toxic smoke.

Terry coughed and spluttered as he tried to form words.

"Stand back!" he croaked.

A staccato burst from the machine pistol briefly lit up the cellar, and then Terry thrust open the entrance into the yard.

Two surviving fascists saw Terry and the others emerge through the quivering heat haze as if space and time were being warped at the edge of a black hole.

Both the fascists were armed.

As Derek and Johnny helped Bryony out of the cellar, a bullet ricocheted nearby.

Terry turned and saw the two fascists, like shadowy marionettes, through the wall of flame. He returned fire with the Ingram MAC 10 and shot one of the two fascists dead.

The other fascist, still armed, turned and fled.

Terry shot him in the back and killed him, too.

*

In the Vaughan household, the phone shrilled like a demanding child.

Patricia answered.

"Hello?" she said

On the other end of the line, it sounded as if the Devil himself was speaking in tongues.

"Who is this?" Pamela demanded.

Within minutes of Azazels' phone call to Pamela from a public box, a convoy of vehicles had left the Police Station with blues and twos blaring.

They included a Police Armed Response Unit.

*

Still cast as the Pied Piper or as Virgil, Terry had found a trough of filthy and rusty water at the back of the burning farmhouse, in front of the circular wall of flame. Like some deranged John the Baptist, he doused each of his team in the profaned liquid and then shoved them through the wall of fire as if expelling them from Hades.

At the front of the house, the striking miners continued to do pitched battles with the fascists.

Finally, Terry doused himself with water and passed through the fiery veil, like he was Dante, or Orpheus, escaping from Hell. But this time, Terry's coat caught fire as he leapt through the wall of flame.

Now it was Terry who looked like the fiery angel, cast from heaven, transformed from an angel of light into a serpent of the infernal pit.

Screaming, Terry discarded the burning coat like they were fiery angels' wings.

The others helped him put out the flame.

Now, covered in sweat, Terry noticed some rope and grabbed it, together with the machine gun, and strode to the front of the burning house.

He contemplated the pitched battle for seconds before firing into the ground.

386

The fighting stopped, like Christmas in the trenches in World War One.

The damned youth of the Somme, as Wilfred Owen would have said.

"Right, comrades, nice work," Terry called out. "Well done! Now I need you to tie these fascist cunts up."

Terry threw the rope on the gun and trained his gun on the surviving fascists who were huddled into a kneeling group.

Terry watched as the miners tied them up.

"We need them alive and talkative," he continued. "To tell the world who put them up to it."

He kicked a fascist in the spleen, causing him to cry in pain.

"Like Brady and Ridgeway, isn't that right?" Terry demanded.

There was the click of an automatic pistol, and Terry looked up to see Brady staring at him with the beady eyes of a rat. Brady was also holding a Berretta automatic to Eileen's head, and Eileen looked terrified.

Terry fought to conceal the alarm on his own face.

"You're pissing in a barrel, Terry," Brady said. "I mean, who's going to believe you — you and your communist posse, here? Terry's Irregulars! The judges and the politicians — they're all part of it, mate, if you haven't cottoned that part yet!"

Brady ordered the surviving fascists.

"Get up, lads," he said.

"What do you want, Brady?" Terry snarled.

"Me?" Brady asked. "I want protection. I'll even let your missus go and tell you and Orla O'Regan a fucking story, but I want protection."

"OK," said Terry, like he was humouring a madman. "We'll organise Police Protection only first you let Eileen go, OK?"

"Fuck sake, Terry!" Brady exploded. "I want protection from the fucking Police!"

Terry stared at him.

"You still don't get it, do you, Sheriff, just how useless your fucking badge is?" Brady taunted. "You're like the Milky Bar Fucking Kid! Now me, I know how the world's wired up, and I'm offering you a shot at the title."

A red dot bounced between Brady and Eileen like Tinkerbell.

"I'll tell you here, in front of witnesses, who Azazel is," Brady said. "And it ain't Zack the fucking Hack. Its — "

The bullet from a Police MP50 recoilless carbine caused the back of Brady's head to explode like a blood gorged melon. His bloodied brains and offal, the colour and texture of a dinosaur's snot, were splattered hot and salty all over Eileen.

Terry's wife shrieked hysterically as Dermott Brady fell to the floor, dead.

Terry ran forward to embrace his Eileen.

At the perimeter fence of the hitherto MOD firing range, Ridgeway and Zack Miller stood side by side, next to the Police sharpshooter who had taken Brady out.

The Police Armed Response Units moved forward as Terry hugged and kissed his wife.

Eventually, Ridgeway walked up to him.

"Topman, Inspector Vaughan and a job well done," Ridgeway said. "Brady signed a confession before he abducted Eileen."

Ridgeway looked to where Brady lay dead.

"He was Azazel, all right," Ridgeway said.

Terry still had hold of Eileen.

Derek still held Bryony as tight as a crucifix.

Terry closed his eyes. He began to speak.

"Now look—"

"We'll save the debrief till later, shall we?" Ridgeway smiled falsely. "OK, lads, take all these men into custody. We'll sort out the cowboys from the Indians back at Fort Apache."

Both fascists and miners were cuffed by the Armed Cops and led away.

Geoff led a defiant chant as they did so.

"The workers, united, will never be defeated. The workers, united, will never be defeated!"

Eileen reached for her swollen stomach.

"Terry, I'm having contractions," she said.

Ridgeway nodded to Terry.

"Police escort," Ridgeway said. "Get your wife to hospital, quick!"

As Terry led Eileen to a Police car, Zack called over to him.

"Watching you, Terry!" he said.

Terry pointed at Zack as he joined his wife in the Police car.

"Yeah, and I'm watching you, too!" he said.

*

The polished Daimler drew up close to the entrance of the burning farmhouse.

Inside, the Saudi Prince looked at the scene in disbelief.

"Oh, Dear," McLeod sighed. "I think we'll give this one a miss, don't you?"

The Daimler engine started up.

Before it could pull out, a Police convoy thundered past, taking Eileen Vaughan to the hospital.

Chapter Fifty-Three

Dawn broke over the funeral pyre and what remained of the farmhouse on the sacrificial moor.

In the hospital, where Terry anxiously awaited news of his wife, the shafts of sunlight were coming through the windows and Venetian blinds like water into a sinking boat.

Terry barely noticed the news on the nearby TV.

Not picket line violence, this time, but the Battle of the Beanfield, as Thatcher's net of repression extended together with the criminalisation of all dissent.

Criminals today, terrorists tomorrow. Welcome to the future.

Eventually, the images of Police thuggery were replaced by that of Peter Chapman.

Terry barely heard the droning monologue of the newscaster.

"Meanwhile, evidence that the year-long miners' strike might be coming to an end as formal links between the NUM and the Qaddafi regime in Libya are exposed. The regime, whose agents murdered WPC Yvonne Fletcher last year, have links to European terrorism that include Abu Nidal and the Provisional IRA."

Now, Chapman's image was replaced by that of Dominic McLeod.

This time, the news item grabbed Terry's attention.

"Another blow to the government with the death of Dominic McLeod, one of Mrs Thatcher's top aides and a former CEO of a leading PR Firm in Pimlico. Mr McLeod was visiting a friend, a Mr Llewellyn, at his retirement residence in Hampshire when a fire broke out in the house."

Terry stared at the still image on the screen. It showed McLeod with Thatcher and the DJ Jimmy Saville at Stoke Manderville hospital.

"Evidence suggests that the fire might have been started deliberately and involved a type of device identified with Animal Rights groups. Mr Llewellyn was a master of hounds –"

"Detective Inspector Vaughan," a voice distracted him from his daydream.

Turning, he saw a pretty nurse whose job would be privatised out of existence if the current government got its way.

"Detective Inspector Vaughan," the nurse smiled. "Mother and baby are fine!"

*

Terry was in Ridgeway's office, staring at his superior, whom he knew to be a corrupt killer.

All of a sudden, everything in Terry's life was surreal, in this town that was no longer his town and whose rhetoric had never been his rhetoric but now his very value system seemed turned inside out, like emptied pockets whose contents had been scattered on the floor, like those of ransacked and broken mind.

Terry had joined the job to escape his wretched working-class lot in a town and community that was already dying, even before the strike. But he had also joined the Police to make a difference, like Gary Cooper in *High Noon,* and now he found his core value system, including his belief in the law, shaken to the very core of his being. Shedding skin, like any serpent of the pit, it was as if Terry were now the revolutionary, while his brother found all his past idols to have feet of clay.

Across the desk, Ridgeway grinned at him like a Cheshire Cat.

"You'd better scrub up, son, if you're going to Buck House," Ridgeway said. "Queens Police Medal and all that bollocks. Plus, your promotion to Inspector's to be made permanent, pending your transfer to your wife's home town of Newport."

Ridgeway fairly beamed like he was a phoney Father Christmas in a shopping mall.

"Never really cared for the Valleys, did she?" Ridgeway beamed. "Can't say I blame her. It's not a place I'd like to bring up a sprog, not now at any rate. I mean, it's great PR, the son of a miner, like you, catching a serial killer and being a hero and the Chief Constable's full of bollocks about building bridges now that the strike's over. But you and I know it's crap. The Mining Community fucking well hates us, and they always will."

Terry cleared his throat.

"I don't understand, guv," he said. "I thought I was on suspension."

"I don't know what you're talking about, son — suspension for what?" Ridgeway laughed. "You're on leave to be with your wife and baby daughter until you take up your new position in the CID in Newport."

Terry looked bitter and confused.

"You're one of us, now, son," Ridgeway said. "We look after our own."

There was an awkward pause before Terry resumed talking.

"The thing is, even f Brady was Azazel – "

"No ifs, Terry," Ridgeway closed him down. "It's bad enough we found a rotten apple in the barrel. Weeding out bent coppers and dinosaurs is what the Police and Criminal Evidence Act is all about. It's all over, Terry. Everything else is just bookkeeping."

"If Brady was Azazel, he must have had an accomplice," Terry said.

Ridgeway's expression started to harden.

"The case is closed, Terry," he said severely. "Do I make myself clear? It is no longer an active investigation, and you are no longer based at this station."

"But Guv," Terry started to protest.

Ridgeway was starting to get angry, now,

"We don't want CIB sniffing around, do we?" he taunted. "I mean, you did kill four blokes out there in the Badlands, and your brother and all his striking miner mates were released without charge. Now, thanks to yours truly, all that evidence is safely hidden away under lock and key."

"But – "

Ridgeway pounded his desk in anger.

"For fuck's sake, Terry!" he exploded. "I've got a wife and kids, too!"

Suddenly, Terry was silent. Ridgeway calmed down, too.

"Now, do your wife and sprog a favour," Ridgeway soothed. "Get the fuck out of Tombstone and never come back."

Terry swallowed.

"Yes, Guv," he said.

Ridgeway stared after him as he left.

*

Terry was met in the Police Station reception by Susan Higgins' parents. The father still looked every bit as broken as on the BBC *Crimewatch* appeal; it seemed ten thousand centuries before. The mother greeted Terry with a Joan of Arc smile and took his hand.

"Thank you, Detective Inspector," she said through sniffs. "Thank you for nailing my little girl's killer as you promised."

Terry smiled at her weakly but with genuine kindness.

He felt like Judas as he left his old Police Station for good.

Outside, the streets were empty and awash with deprivation. The political rhetoric was still there but fading, like the posters that were beginning to peel and disintegrate, flapping in the wind like decaying flesh. Everywhere, he saw the hallmarks of a defeated population, as if the working class had gone to war and lost and faced a terrible dystopian future as a consequence.

The Iron Bitch, in Number 10, had read and understood her Machiavelli and knew the importance of committing all her atrocities at once.

She also knew, as did Machiavelli, that in order to subjugate a population, one had first to disconnect it from its history and erase its identity as a community. Worse, it was as if history itself was now being obliterated, to be replaced by some horrible dystopian present forever framed by the media as a spectacle.

"We control history at all its levels," so had said O'Brien in Orwell's *1984,* but the real-life 1985 suggested a future far worse even than Orwell had envisaged while dying of tuberculosis after the Second World War.

Terry got into his Ford Sierra and headed for the graveyard.

*

Boot hill.

At the town's graveyard, Terry found Derek Hepburn standing sentry, alone, at his daughter's grave. Johnny and Orla O'Regan were nearby, watching him, and silently acknowledged Terry as the Detective Inspector approached.

"Any news," Terry asked, in a subdued tone, as if reticent to intrude on Derek's grief. Perhaps their *Hamlet,* or *Lear,* could now have that nervous breakdown that he kept promising himself, with all the cathartic purging that such a metamorphosis involved.

Or perhaps, Terry thought, there might still be business to be done.

Orla looked at Terry.

"We may have a lead," she ventured.

Terry nodded in satisfaction.

They would need to tread carefully, but this was his posse now.

About The Author

Former crime journalist Roger Cottrell is a former member of the Workers Revolutionary Party Central Committee who experienced the miners' strike in South Wales first hand. He studied for an MA in movie script writing at Dun Laoghaire Institute of Art and Design Technology and a PhD in English Literature (on British Crime Fiction) at Queen's University Belfast.

For the last 12 years he has worked in the British and Irish University sector while writing screenplays, TV long form drama scripts and now novels. In particular, he is the creator and writer of Blood Rites, a six episode urban thriller set in contemporary Dublin, which is being made by Telegael Productions supported by Screen Ireland. Jaded Jerusalem, which is part of a trilogy, already exists as a six episode TV series script.

About The Publisher

L.R. Price Publications is dedicated to publishing books by undiscovered, talented authors.

We use a mixture of traditional and modern publishing methods to bring our authors' words to the wider world.

We print, publish, distribute and market books in a variety of formats, including paper and hardback, electronic books, e-books, digital audiobooks and online.

If you are an author interested in getting your book published; or a book retailer interested in selling our books, please contact us.

www.lrpricepublications.com

L.R. Price Publications Ltd,
27 Old Gloucester Street,
London, WC1N 3AX
(0203) 051 9572
publishing@lrprice.com

Printed in Great Britain
by Amazon